Beautifully Scarred

P. RAYNE

About Beautifully Scarred

Lilah

Growing up, all we had was each other.

Jimmy's always been the one who protected me—at any cost. I was content to let him clean up my messes. And when he kept his promise to get us out of our hometown and living the lives we always dreamed of, I was happy to pretend everything would be okay... for a while.

While Jimmy was able to leave the past behind, mine felt like a tattoo I could never scrub clean.

Jimmy thinks he can fix me—he tries, and tries, and tries.

Sometimes love isn't enough to heal all the wounds from the past. Sometimes even your savior thinks you're not worth saving.

And he'd be right... until everything changed.

Jimmy

I've loved Lilah for as long as I can remember.

And for as long as I can remember, she's pushed down the traumas of her past until they became poison running through her veins, infecting everything she touched.

Watching the woman you love destroy herself piece by piece is the slowest, most painful form of torture I know.

Giving her up may be the only way to save her. But how do I just walk away from the one person I love most in this life?

BEAUTIFULLY SCARRED

Dedication

For everyone one of us who's made mistakes along the way. Live, learn, do better.

"Another day won is better than another day one."

Part One

JIMMY

Newspapers slam down in front of me, one after the other, sending loud thumping sounds throughout the silent conference room.

My elbows rest on the boardroom table, fingers threaded through my dark hair, eyes squeezed shut so I don't have to read what's printed. A quick internet search of my name this morning told me all I need to know.

"HOLLYWOOD'S GOLDEN BOY IN BAR BRAWL!"
"THE REGULATOR DOES BAD!"
"THIS IS OUR NEXT SUPERHERO BOX OFFICE STAR?"

"What the fuck were you thinking?" Bernie glares at me from the end of the long mahogany table, leaving the papers in front of me like a grenade with the pin pulled.

I blow out a sigh and glance at him. His white polo shirt stretches over his protruding belly and his slacks are creased at his groin. It's obvious my actor-behaving-badly stunt pulled him away from his early morning tee time.

He's the head of the movie studio. People probably call him for permission to take a shit. So when one of his up-and-coming stars has a run-in that makes the press, he's the first to get the call.

His beet-red face and the slightly crazy, enraged look in his eye makes me wonder if I'll recover from this fuck-up. Maybe the grenade with the pin out is my career, not the papers.

"The other guy swung first. What the hell was I supposed to do?" I argue.

My agent, Keane, clears his throat next to me. It's a warning not to poke the bear, but it's too late for that.

They couldn't squeeze any more bodies in this room if they tried. My agent, my publicist, the studio's PR reps, the director of my next film, and Bernie. The only one missing is my manager, and that's only because she's fixing someone else's screw-up. Time is crucial. We have to figure out our plan of attack about the mess I created.

"What's the media's take on what happened?" Bernie directs his question to his PR goons.

The middle-aged woman with a few streaks of grey in her hair speaks first. "Most aren't sure what to think. A couple of the blogs have picked up on the fact that Lilah Robbie was there and are speculating that the fight probably had something to do with her."

Everyone in the room looks at me for confirmation. I sit silently, not wanting the reaction that'll come if I agree with the woman across from me.

"Why don't you tell us exactly what happened, and we can figure out a way to spin it in your favor?" Kyra says in a reassuring tone. At least my own PR rep is on my side.

"It's pretty simple. A group of us went out last night and some guy was bothering Lilah."

Groans and sighs commence around the table, but I continue anyway.

"He didn't much care for when I asked him to leave her alone and threw a punch at me." I lean back in my seat with my arms folded over my chest.

Everyone waits for Bernie's response. Of course they do. His word is like a messiah's in Tinsel Town.

"Let me guess," he says, leaning in, palms flat on the table and spearing me with his gaze. "What you mean is that Lilah was high as a kite or shit-faced drunk, shaking that tight ass of hers on the dance floor, and some guy came on to her. You decided to act like her daddy and intervene."

God, I hate this guy. He's such a dick. But he's a dick who holds the power to end my career with one phone call.

"Should I have just watched while some douchebag took advantage of her?" I ask, trying unsuccessfully to keep the bite from my tone.

"What you should do is stay the fuck away from her! She's going to drag you down with her." Bernie loses the last of his composure, and all eyes fall to the table.

I chew the inside of my cheek and fist my hands to control my temper. I can't help my impulse to protect Lilah. It's an automatic response whenever someone tries to take advantage of her. The need is practically ingrained in my DNA.

"Look, I'll issue an apology, and by tomorrow, the press will be on to someone else's mistake," I say.

"I have a better idea," the other PR person for the studio says. We've met before. I think his name is Jake or something. "Why don't we issue a statement saying that James saw someone taking advantage of a drunk patron in the bar and intervened on her behalf? That way we're painting him as the hero rather than an instigator."

There're a few rumblings around the table while they confer.

"What if the press asks if the patron in question was Lilah?" Keane asks.

"We redirect. Say we want to maintain the individual's privacy, that it doesn't matter what the woman's name was because she represents all the women in this country who have to put up with unwanted attention from the other sex." Jake's an intelligent guy. Why does he work for Bernie?

"That might work," the female PR rep for the studio says.

We all turn our heads in Bernie's direction. His chest is heaving, and he looks as if he's trying to rein in his temper.

"Fine," he says. "Let James's PR people release the statement."

I hate when they talk about me as though I'm not in the room, but I realized a long time ago that all I am to them is a fucking means to an end, the end being profit in their pockets.

"Any more shit like this and I don't care whether you've known her since you were sucking on your mom's tit. You're gonna cut all ties if you want to stay on this movie." Bernie points at me as if I'm a child.

Staying silent goes against everything in me, because I will never cut her out, but I have no choice, so I nod. Lilah will always be in my life. She's my best friend and I love her, but it's more than that. We're... well, we're complicated.

"I'm serious, James," Bernie drones on. "This reboot is a big deal. I can't have The Regulator in the headlines for being on the wrong side of the law."

I push back from the table and stand. "It won't happen again."

Without another word, I leave the room. I'm pissed off and I don't even know at whom. Myself for getting in the fight in the first place? Lilah for once again putting herself into a situation I needed to get her out of? Bernie for trying to dictate how I live my life? Who knows. But right now, I'm pissed off at the world and need to get the hell out of here before I say something and spur one of Bernie's legendary tantrums.

I exit the building and the Los Angeles sunshine beats down on my head. I squint until my eyes adjust.

As soon as I'm in my car, I dial Lilah's number. She doesn't pick up, so I dial it again then fire off a text, asking where she's at. When I don't get an answer, I toss my phone on the leather passenger seat, trying my best to ignore the steady and constant worry that pricks at the back of my neck like a tattoo needle.

The responsible thing to do would be to go home and sleep. I was up late last night, and tomorrow is my first costume fitting for the movie that starts shooting next month. I shouldn't chance the paps clicking a photo with Lilah and me.

Leaving the parking lot, instead of turning left to head to my place, I turn right.

Screw Bernie. Screw his reps. Screw my people.

Lilah comes first.

LILAH

"**C**'mere, girl!"

Daddy's voice boomed throughout the decrepit shack we called home. I slid under my bed until my back pressed against the makeshift wall.

When I didn't answer, his footsteps echoed through the living room, my heart thumping in my throat the nearer he drew. He stopped and I held my breath, hoping he'd change his mind and not come looking for me. Maybe he'd think I was still out playing with Jimmy.

But a minute later, he stomped closer to my room and stepped inside. It didn't take long before the scent of whiskey was all I smelled. Today must have been sampling day.

He and Jimmy's dad made moonshine in the deep woods and sold it secretly to people. Every time they went to check on their stills, they came home drunk. I tried to stay away from home those nights, knowing what they meant for me, but Jimmy had to help his aunt, who lives farther up the mountain, with some new pigs. So tonight, I was alone.

"I dun know where you are, girl, but I'm not goan be happy when I find yah."

Daddy was slurring, and I squeezed my eyes shut. Eight is old enough to know that being unable to see his muddy boots on the floor didn't mean he wouldn't be able to see me if he bent over and looked under the bed.

This felt like the worst part. The anticipation of what was coming. You'd think the during would be worse, but to me, it was always the before.

He walked slowly to stand in front of the bed. He knew I was there. We had so few things in our place that there really weren't many places to hide. My only hope had been that he was drunk enough that he'd forget about me and pass out.

No such luck tonight...

"Now I got'cha."

When I opened my eyes, I saw that he'd lowered himself to his knees, his scruffy beard and glossy eyes set on me.

"When I call you, girl, you answer." He gripped my wrist, yanking me out from under the bed.

I fly up into a seated position on the couch, covered in sweat, my strained breaths heaving in my chest. The sick panic that always encompasses me after one of those dreams seeps into my stomach and turns it over, bile rising into my throat.

I bend over, throwing up all over the floor, and resist the urge to scratch at myself, the fear of being trapped in my own skin more than I can bear.

Wrapping my arms around my knees, I rock back and forth.

It was just a dream. Just a dream. You're not back there. Never again.

KNOCK!

KNOCK!

I look around to figure out where I am. My heart calms when I recognize Derek's apartment.

KNOCK!

KNOCK!

I know better than to answer Derek's door—there's no telling who's behind it. I might be self-destructive, but I don't have a death wish. Not today anyway.

Derek emerges from his bedroom, wearing only his boxers, his plethora of tattoos on full display over his thin frame. "What the fuck, man?" Running his hand through his dark hair, he peeks through the peephole and scowls back at me. "It's your goddamn boyfriend."

"He's not my boyfriend," I mumble.

It's true. Although there isn't a definite answer to what Jimmy and I are to each other. We exist on an ever-changing cycle of break up and make up, yet somehow that doesn't define our relationship. What we are to each other is far more complex and far more than one descriptor could ever encompass.

I stand from the couch and walk toward the door, fighting to stay upright. Shit, Jimmy's going to be pissed I'm still drunk. Derek swings open the door and turns to head back to his room.

"What the hell are you doing here?" Jimmy stomps across the room, reaching me before I topple over.

The sound of his shoes on the hard floor reminds me of my dream. I flinch.

Hurt flashes in his beautiful, soft brown eyes. "Why do you insist on hanging out with this douchebag?"

"Don't start with me," I say instead of the truth. *He always has what I need.*

He grips my elbow. "C'mon. We're getting out of here."

I don't argue. There's no point. Jimmy won't leave until he knows I'm okay and we both know if he leaves me here, I won't be okay.

He leads me out the door and down the hallway that reeks of a mixture of food odors and cooked meth. We head down the graffiti-spray-painted stairs and out the door.

"I'm taking you back to my place." Jimmy flings open his door and deposits me into his fancy Audi.

"I'm so—"

He raises his hand to stop my apology. I'm not even sure what exactly I'm apologizing for, but the words come naturally when he finds me at Derek's. Rounding the front of his car, he clenches and unclenches his fists. He's really angry this time. I can usually scale Jimmy's anger toward me, and this one is above a ten.

Jimmy slides into the driver's seat, turns the key over, and drives away from this shitty neighborhood in one fluid motion. I curl up in the passenger seat, the tinted windows blocking the blinding California sun high in the sky. My head dips, and I fight to keep my eyes open. As in many areas of my life, I lose the battle.

Chapter Three

LILAH

A stream of light falls over my eyes, stirring me awake. The smell of Jimmy and the softness of his sheets says I'm snuggled underneath his covers. A familiar feeling—half hungover, half edgy from the drugs wearing off—accosts me. His curtains are closed, but it must be late evening from the intensity of the orange sun that gleams through the crack of his drapes.

I lie there for a moment, unable to garner the energy to move, trying to recall how I got here. I was out with Jimmy and some of his friends. We were at the club, partying together. Then everything's foggy. The rest of the night is black, but he did drag me out of Derek's this morning.

Something must've gone down last night if I made my way to Derek's after the club.

I climb out of the bed at the pace of a ninety-seven-year-old great-grandmother instead of a twenty-seven-year-old model. In the en suite, I start the shower. While the water turns as hot

I can stand it, I head to the sink and brush my teeth with the toothbrush Jimmy lovingly left out for me.

The only thing certain is I need to get my shit together before I see Jimmy and find out what I did. I push the shame and guilt to the back of my mind and zone out while the spray hits the back of my skull. At first it feels like a thousand tiny jackhammers peppering my brain, but after a few minutes, the heat seeps into my neck and my shoulders relax. I enjoy the feel of hot water running over my skin, rinsing me of whatever I did.

Once I've towel-dried my hair and wrapped one of his plush bath towels around my naked body, it's time for me to face the music. Reluctantly, I leave the bedroom, in search of the person who means the most to me in the world, even if I don't treat him like it.

Jimmy's in his den, sitting at his desk, his eyes focused on his computer screen. He doesn't look up when I enter, but from the way the muscles in his jaw tighten, he knows I'm here.

"What happened last night?" I ask in a low voice, tiptoeing to the leather chair that sits adjacent to his desk.

He ignores me for a minute. Punishing me for misbehaving—again. A punishment I likely deserve. But sometimes I don't think he understands what lives inside me on a daily basis.

He pushes his chair away from the desk and swivels in my direction. He's dressed in a grey V-neck T-shirt, and his five o'clock shadow perfectly matches his dark brown hair that's a little mussed. His legs are spread wide in a pair of well-worn jeans. Jeans we picked out together shortly after we arrived in Los Angeles and he'd made his first real money acting. Does he think of that day every time he slips his feet into the soft denim, the same way as I do?

After shopping, we went for a drive to check out the Hollywood sign and we had sex in the bed of his beat-up Chevy truck. After he came, he said to me, "This is it, Lilah. This is the beginning of a new life for both of us."

It wasn't his words that made the day so memorable to me. He's long promised me our lives were going to change—before and after that day. But that was the first time I truly believed him. It wasn't hope that sprouted inside me when he said it that day—it was faith. And those are two very different things.

I blink a couple times and return to the present. "What happened?" I ask again.

His eyes seep with a mixture of anger, bewilderment, and affection in the way only Jimmy can pull off. The reason he's the hottest up-and-coming actor. "See for yourself."

He clicks the keys on his laptop and turns the screen in my direction. I slide to the edge of the chair and read as he slides the screen on his MacBook, each one with headlines of the fight he got into last night, questioning whether the two of us are off or on. Worst of all, calling out his golden boy status.

I don't need to ask for the details of exactly what happened. I can fill in the blanks for myself. I drank too much, among other things, and someone hit on me. I liked the attention and led the guy on. Jimmy got pissed and said something. Punches were thrown. Same story, different day.

"I'm sorry. I really am." You'd think after the number of times I've said those words to him, they'd lose their meaning, but his shoulders relax a bit, suggesting maybe he does understand what lives inside me on a daily basis.

When Jimmy's mad at me, it's like a thousand-pound weight I have to carry around my neck, but it's still not enough for me to stop using.

"The guy was out of line. That's not your fault."

Typical. He's always making excuses for me.

"Even so." I rise from the chair and step closer to him until I'm standing between his legs. "I feel terrible." I drop to my knees, staring up at him with my best pitiful eyes.

He looks down at me with half-lidded eyes. When Jimmy looks at me like this—like I'm the only woman in the world. Like he can barely keep his hands off me. Like he feels the need to claim me—I feel in control... I feel almost whole.

His tongue slips out, and he wets his bottom lip.

"Let me make it up to you." I slide my hand up his thigh, and the hard muscle beneath the denim flexes under my touch.

I reach his rigid length and squeeze his cock. I lick my lips, eager for the taste of him. Jimmy groans, and I move my hands to release him. I unbutton his jeans, and I'm about to pull the zipper down when his hands clamp down on my wrists.

"No. You can't always fix it this way."

I still and dart my gaze up to meet his. His stern face says he's serious.

"Why not? You never had a problem before."

He releases my wrists, and I pull my hands back. "I know, and that's the problem." He buttons his jeans back up.

I stand, embarrassment flushing through my body. "Funny, the last time you came down my throat, it wasn't a problem for you."

He springs up from the chair. "Don't do that." As he looks out the window, his fingers weave through his thick hair.

I lean against the wall, wishing I could disappear. "Do what?"

"Act like I'm one of those men you let use you." His eyes are steady on me as he closes the distance between us. I step backward, my back flush to the wall, but he grips my shoulders as though he thinks I'll run. "It's time to get your shit together. Enough of the constant partying and the drugs and the alcohol."

Another conversation that makes me hate myself. Perfect.

"Don't start," I say with annoyance, trying to wiggle free, but he steps forward, locking me to the wall.

His hand slides down my arm and wraps around mine. "Something bad is going to happen to you if you don't get control of yourself. What if I hadn't been there last night?"

"Then I guess I would have gotten laid."

His nostrils flair and he releases my hands before crossing his muscular arms over his chest and narrowing his eyes. "Would you have preferred that I just left you there and let him do whatever he wanted with you?"

"What do you care, James?" I purposely call him by his working name to annoy him. In public, I have to refer to him that way, but in private, he hates when I use it. Jimmy and James are two completely different people.

He steps forward, letting his hands drop to his sides and leaving no room between us. "You know I care."

I ignore my pleading body that wants to fall into his arms of safety and tell him how much I care too. "Only if I'm Miss Perfect and become exactly what you want me to be." I slide along the wall until I have space to clear the room and Jimmy.

"That's not true and you know it. Wanting you to lay off the drugs doesn't mean I want you to be perfect."

"Well, good thing. Because I've never been perfect, nor will I ever be. You know that better than anyone." I spin around to escape the room and his judgmental eyes, but he's quick, coming up behind me and pulling my back into his chest.

"Exactly," he says, his breath fanning across my neck and causing my nipples to pebble. His hard length presses into my lower back. "I know everything about you. Which is why I don't want to see you go down a road you can't turn back from."

We stand in silence for a minute. The only sound in the room is our breathing as it picks up pace and we begin the final leg of our sick cycle. Get along, fight, fuck, apologize. Rinse and repeat a thousand times over. Sometimes we start at the beginning and go full circle in the course of a day. Other times, there're weeks in between.

His hand wraps around my throat and slides down the valley of my breasts, slipping between my legs. I'm already wet. Of course I am. His finger coasts over my nub, and I bite my bottom lip from the pleasure only he can spark. Instantly I long for the oblivion he delivers. I let my head fall against his shoulder and give in to his demands.

He places a chaste kiss on my ear and whispers, "Just say you'll at least think about it."

His spell is broken.

I rip myself from his arms and turn around to spear him with my most lethal look. "I've already had one father, and that was more than enough. I don't need someone else telling me how to live."

I spin around and run out of the room. He lets me leave, as I knew he would when I compared him to a man both of us believe was the devil.

Chapter Four

LILAH

Two weeks and not a word from Jimmy. I've sent text after unanswered text, but I tell myself it's for the best. That's the truth—it's the best... for him. One of these days, I'll be strong enough to leave him alone for good. Let him move on with his successful career and live a happy life without the detriment of me.

But right now, the thought of not having Jimmy is too soul-crushing. I'm well aware how selfish I'm being.

I can't stand the silence from him any longer. Jimmy's where-abouts tonight are heavily rumored. The studio finally announced today that he's signed on to star in the reboot of their superhero series, *The Regulator*. So he'll be at the Regent to celebrate this milestone in his career.

What better way to get his attention than to wear my skintight, mid-thigh-length red dress with a V down to my belly button? Add a pair of gold stilettos and if that doesn't spur him to talk to me, I'm positive my nipples poking through the fabric will.

Jimmy's my only close friend because I don't do girlfriends—or boyfriends for that matter. Mostly because opening yourself up to someone makes you too vulnerable, especially in this town, and I've had enough pain to last a lifetime. But I have a few model friends who like to party, so I give them a call.

By the time Trina, Courtney, and I arrive at the Regent, I've mustered the courage to talk to Jimmy. The alcohol coursing through my system has quieted the logical part of my brain. Alcohol and drugs work the best at making me forget how worthless I am, how I came from nothing and will always be nothing. They numb me against reliving all the awful things my father did to me.

"I'm heading to the bar," Trina says, not waiting for Courtney or me to answer.

Courtney catches the eye of some guy dressed in a nice suit, no tie, and the top couple buttons of his dress shirt undone.

"I'll catch up with you guys in a bit," she says, smiling and stepping in his direction, hips swaying.

"Guess I'm on my own."

Good thing I'm used to that.

I decide to check for Jimmy. I should grab another drink too, so I'll have the nerve to approach him and try to make things right between us. I walk around the outskirts of the dance floor toward the VIP area. After all, he's celebrating and deserves to sit in the VIP section.

"Hey, beautiful," a guy says, his finger brushing down my arm. "Want to dance?"

"No." I continue toward the VIP section, ignoring the unwanted touch.

He back steps, staying in line with me as I walk forward. "You don't wear an outfit like that unless you want attention." His eyes focus on my nipples.

"I don't want attention from you." I turn on my heel, sliding between a throng of drunk girls rushing to the dance floor.

The creep doesn't follow.

I lean against a huge white column so Jimmy won't spot me. I need to figure out what to say to persuade him to forgive me after I viciously compared him to my piece-of-shit dad.

My eyes scan along a white leather couch, landing on Jimmy beside his friend Tripp. *Fucking Tripp.* That prick hates me and is constantly driving a wedge between Jimmy and me.

The two of them sip their drinks, deep in conversation. Jimmy nods in agreement with whatever Tripp's saying and shifts his attention to peruse the dance floor. Tripp's probably telling Jimmy to stay strong and not return my texts. Maybe the guy should look in the mirror once in a while. He's not so perfect either.

I step to the side to hide behind one of the large columns set in a semi-circle around the outside of the dance floor. After I've counted to sixty, I chance another peek at him.

I stumble back and grab the column for support.

Two women are seated on the couch, one beside Tripp and one beside Jimmy. Tripp is stroking the blonde's thigh while sweet talking her with his usual flirtatious smile. Jimmy laughs at whatever the lame brunette sitting next to him says. Worse, his reaction is genuine. It isn't James's laugh; it's Jimmy's, where the small wrinkles by his eyes appear. As if that isn't gut-wrenching enough, she puts her hand on his knee, leaning

"I'm Dan."

"Oh, right. I'm Lilah." I pretend to feign interest in him, but it's hard when the rest of the coke sits on the counter.

"You did that modeling campaign for LV, didn't you?"

I nod.

"What do you want to do now?" Dan skims his hand over my breast, thumbing the nipple. It's clear he wants me.

I want his coke.

"Let's do another bump and then decide," I flirt in a way that promises him whatever he wants after I do another line.

He grins and nods toward the white powder—ladies first and all that. What a gentleman. I lean over with the rolled bill in my hand and snort another line, exhaling in relief as my face grows number and the familiar burst of energy that accompanies my high finally kicks in.

He takes the bill from my fingers before I offer and finishes off the coke.

"Ah, fuck, that's good," he says, letting the bill fall in the remnants of the powder. As soon as he straightens, his gaze dips and he twirls me around, pressing me against the full-length mirror on the one free wall in the room, my back to his front. "Don't you just love this feeling?" He uses his other hand to pull my dress up over my ass and gather it at my waist.

"Mmm-hmm," I say as he slips his hand between my thighs.

"Don't you love fucking when you're high?" he growls into my ear.

When I don't respond, he slips my thong aside and pushes one finger into me, then another. My head falls back onto his shoulder. He mistakes the action as acquiescence when in reality, I need to move. The pent-up energy and anger inside me are itching to be expelled.

"Let's take this party onto the dance floor," I suggest. Doing so will allow me to take care of both my anger and my energy issues.

"You sure?" he asks, punctuating his question with a pelvic thrust that drives his fingers farther into me.

"Yeah, I need a drink. We can get back to this later," I say.

To my surprise, he slips his fingers from me and steps back. I realign my dress so that my ass isn't hanging out and double-check myself in the mirror.

Dan unlocks the door and lets me walk out first. A security guard is making his way down the hall to do a check. He gives us a knowing look but doesn't say anything.

I hit the bar as soon as we're back in the main part of the club and order a shot and a double martini. Dan partakes in a shot with me but opts for a whiskey sour. Once we've slugged back our drinks, I drag him onto the dance floor, careful to situate us so that we're within view of Jimmy and Tripp, but not so close that it looks as though I've positioned us there on purpose. If he wants to play, I'll show him I can too.

The bass of the music thrums through my body, adding to the tingling sensation assaulting my limbs. I feel powerful and full of energy, as though nothing can bring me down.

Dan presses against my back, his hard-on completely obvious as it pokes me in the ass. My grinding against him is affecting him, and I feel his warm breath on my ear. He wraps one arm around my waist as we continue to dance, and I spare a glance in Jimmy's direction.

He's still enthralled by the slutty brunette. He and Tripp are laughing and carrying on as if they're the only two women in this club.

I lean back into Dan, swinging my arm up behind me so it's around the back of his neck. Dan's hand runs up and down my body, stopping just underneath my breasts. I close my eyes, lost in the sensations assaulting my body. Everything around me fades into darkness, and I ride the euphoric high as a willing passenger.

When I finally open my eyes again, I glance at the VIP area and see that Jimmy is gone. Tripp and the two women are there, so he must have gone to the bathroom.

Dan grinds into me from behind as he turns us in a circle, moving with the deep bass in the music. We turn in the opposite direction of the VIP area, and that's when I spot him.

Jimmy stands on the edge of the dance floor with his hands fisted, laser-focused eyes mixed with rage and betrayal.

Guilt floods me, but I push it aside. He's the one who wouldn't speak with me. He's the one who came here with someone else. He's the one who hurt me.

I grind a little harder into Dan as Jimmy watches. Disappointment flashes across his face before he shakes his head and walks around the perimeter of the dance floor, back to his booth.

The all-too-familiar look on his face cuts me to the core. Rips my heart into pieces of useless flesh.

There's nothing I can't stand more than when Jimmy is disappointed in me. His anger I can handle. But that look he gave me burns like acid on my skin and kills my high.

"Let's head back to the bar," I yell at Dan before stalking off in that direction.

I order two shots and another double martini while Dan makes a trip to the bathroom. I want to go with him to see if I can score another bump off him, but I'm not in the mood to fuck him and that's what he wants. So I settle for the haze alcohol can bring me. I can still feel the cocaine in my bloodstream, but it's wearing off and I'll need to find more soon.

By the time Dan returns, I'm done drinking and raring to go. We head back out onto the dance floor, bouncing along to the beat as EDM blasts through the speakers of the club. I spare a glance at Jimmy, who tries to act as though he's not watching me, but his eyes keep shifting between the dance floor and his new girl.

It's the one thing I can always count on—Jimmy will never stop being my bodyguard. He should just admit it now.

JIMMY

"**F**uck her, man. She's always fucking with your head," Tripp yells into my ear.

On the other side of me is Brooke, some wannabe actress that Tripp's trying to hook me up with. Really, I just agreed to be his wingman tonight since he's hooked on her friend, Robin. Not that he needs a wingman. Tripp is Tripp Savage, lead singer of one of the biggest rock bands in the world—Savage Revolt. He can get pussy with the crook of his finger.

"You don't get it man," I say in return and sip my drink, eyeing the dance floor.

"You're always saying that. But maybe you're the one who doesn't get it."

I shrug. He has a point. It's not as if I don't know that I'm blind when it comes to Lilah. But no one understands what we've been through. We've always come out on top and I'm certain we will again, once I can get her to clean up her act.

All night I've been trying to keep myself from watching the douchebag she's dancing with do his best to fuck her on the dance floor, but it's impossible. My gaze will always naturally move to Lilah when she's around.

It's a product of our fucked-up childhoods, where I was the only one she could count on. Always double-checking she's okay. But she's an adult now and needs to take care of herself. Truth is, she can't, and I have no idea how to fix her.

"You should be celebrating tonight. Living it up! You're the talk of the town, and as long as you don't fuck up this movie, you'll keep being that." Tripp sucks back the rest of his drink and slams the glass on the table.

He's right. My picture deal was announced today, and I should be on top of the world. I'm already considered a success in this town, but this movie is going to make me an A-list star with the likes of George or Brad or Chris—hell, any of the Chrises.

Instead, I'm fixated on the way that sack of shit on the dance floor is all over Lilah. It's like déjà fucking vu from a few weeks ago at the club. I can't afford any more bad publicity, but rage is building in my chest just watching this shit. Sitting idly to the side goes against every instinct I have when it comes to Lilah.

"C'mon, man, have another shot," Tripp yells over the music.

Beside me, Brooke rubs her hand up my thigh, signaling that she's more than willing to be a notch on my bedpost. But that's the thing with this town. It's filled with women like Brooke, who want to try to hitch a ride on your star as it's headed up into the stratosphere.

I accept the shot glass from Tripp. I have no idea what the hell is in it, but I'll take any distraction I can right now. After clinking my glass with his, I toss back the liquid and enjoy the burning sensation sliding down my throat.

Tripp slaps me on the back. "That's my man."

I smile at him as best I can because I know he means well. I met him by fluke when I first moved to town, and we hit it off even though he was already mega famous, and I was just starting out.

I make small talk with Brooke for the next hour, ignoring her insistence that we should leave. I like getting laid as much as the next guy, but I'm not into it tonight. I'm trying not to be too obvious about keeping an eye on Lilah, but Brooke sees me glance in that direction a couple of times and follows my gaze.

"Do you want to dance?" she asks.

The blond douchebag Lilah's been hanging off of all night leads her off the dance floor toward the restrooms, and I decide to use the opportunity to my advantage.

"Maybe in a bit. I need to hit the head." I stand and exit the VIP area.

Tripp's calling after me, but I ignore him, knowing I need to be quick to stay on Lilah's tail. As I turn down the hallway that leads to the restrooms, I spot Lilah and her flavor of the night make a right at the end of the hall. When I make it there, I see that most of the doors are closed, signaling that they're occupied.

Deciding to start at the beginning, I knock on the first door. When a woman who isn't Lilah answers, I move on to the next and the next until I reach the one at the end of the hall.

I knock, and no one answers. I knock again.

"Piss off, it's occupied," a male voice shouts through the door.

"Lilah, are you in there?" I yell back.

"Go away," she yells and laughs.

Visions of the two of them fooling around assault my brain and I can't stop myself from jiggling the handle to see if the door is locked. It isn't, so I open the door.

Lilah is bent over the counter with a rolled-up dollar bill pressed into her nostril while the guy paws at her ass. When she straightens, she looks at me with a smirk, her pupils so dilated I almost can't see the blue in her eyes anymore.

"What the fuck, Jimmy?"

The guy spins around to look at me, and he's just as messed up as Lilah. "I thought I told you to piss off?" He steps up to me, puffing out his chest.

"Lilah and I have some things to discuss. Take a hike." My hands are fists at my sides, clenched so hard they hurt, but I can't afford any type of scene people whip out their cell phones for, so I decide to try the civil route.

"Not happening. We were just about to get down to the good stuff," he says with a cocky grin. It takes everything I have not to wipe that look off his face.

"Yeah, we can talk later." She sidles up to the guy and runs her hand down his chest until it hits his belt buckle and stops there.

"She'll meet you out in the bar, buddy. Just give me five minutes," I say.

He looks as though he wants to tell me to fuck off again, but he surprises me when he turns to her. "It's up to you."

Maybe I've already gained some clout in this town.

She seems to give it some thought before propping herself up on her tiptoes and whispering something in his ear. Whatever it is, he likes it, because he smiles and rearranges his junk.

"I'm gonna hold you to that," he says before squeezing her ass and sliding by me to get out the door.

I waste no time in slamming the door shut and flicking the lock.

"What are you doing?" Lilah crosses her arms, her hip cocked out to the side.

"Better question is what the fuck are you doing?" I motion to the powder and the dollar bill that's still rolled up and lying on the counter.

"Don't start," she says and tries to make her way by me.

I put my arm out, pressing my hand against the wall and blocking her way. "I'm sorry I didn't return your calls or your texts."

She says nothing.

"But what you said... comparing me to your father..." I let the words hang there because she fucking knew what that would do to me.

She glances at me, and her entire demeanor changes. Hurt and loneliness and regret play across her features before she moves into me, wrapping her arms around my waist and resting her head on my chest. "I'm sorry. I shouldn't have said that."

I knew she'd be sorry as soon as the words left her mouth, but that didn't mean they didn't inflict the pain they were intended to.

I cup her head. "I know. I'm sorry too. I don't want to fight with you."

"Me either. You're the only real friend I have," she says.

I pull back a bit and tilt her head up by her chin. Tears rest in the corners of her eyes, and God, it cuts me to see her like this. All I ever imagine when I see her so strung out is the nightmares she's running from. The nights I couldn't be there for her. What did he do to her to make her turn into this person?

"It's only because I care. You know that, right?"

She nods, biting her bottom lip. Lilah knows what it does to me when she does that. It's long been my undoing when she presses her teeth into her plump bottom lip. There's something so sexual and yet so innocent about it.

Our gazes lock for a minute, and the tension in the small room builds to the point that it feels as oppressive as the summer humidity in the deep south.

The weeks away from one another have left my body in a state of want that only she can ever quench. I shouldn't allow her to seduce me, but my resolve breaks as the sultry, teasing look deepens in her eyes.

I'm not sure which of us moves first, but we crash together in a searing kiss. Her mouth opens for mine, and our tongues meet like the first spark on a nest of kindling. My hands roam her body, coasting over the thin fabric, and when I momentarily picture the guy who was in here earlier and the way he had his hands all over her, I grip her ass and squeeze. She's mine even though I've never claimed her. I swallow her moan, wanting everything she'll give me. I'm greedy for every last piece of her.

Her hand comes between us, and she grips my hard length through my pants, squeezing and rubbing it through the fabric until I'm on the brink of exploding. No woman can do for me what Lilah can. She has the singlehanded ability to make me lose sight of the past, the present, and the future. It's always just us.

She drops to her knees without any preamble and makes quick work of my belt buckle and the zipper on my pants. Before I can blink, she has me in her hand and is pumping my rigid length.

"Fuck, Lilah." I squeeze my eyes shut and let my head fall back. I dig my hands into her silky hair, wanting her lips wrapped around me.

She moans when she first wraps her mouth around the head and swirls her tongue. I straighten my head and look down at her bobbing on the end of my cock, then I look to the side at the full-length mirror to get a better visual of the two of us together.

I notice her purse strewn open on the counter and a little baggie of coke she must have bought off the guy. Through the mirror, I see a girl who is half coherent, sucking my cock. Her hair isn't silky; it's sweaty. Her mascara-smeared eyes stare up at me, and I want to bend over her to throw up in the toilet.

What the fuck am I doing?

I hoist her up under the armpits. I don't screw around with Lilah when she's messed up. In my mind for those brief moments, it was my Lilah, but this isn't her.

She stands there for a second, looking shell-shocked while I do up my zipper and refasten my pants. "Jesus. Again?"

"You're fucked up right now."

"It's not taking advantage of me if I want it." She steps up to me and attempts to loosen my belt, but I push her hands away. Her eyes narrow. "Fine. I'll go find Dan and see if he feels like having any fun."

She tries to step by me, but I grip her shoulders and force her back. "The only place you're going is home."

"Pfft. As if."

She tries to pass me once more, and again I force her away from the door.

"Why don't you get back to your little date and leave me be?" she sneers.

"You know why." I cup her face. I want to scream in her face that she's better than this shit. What will it take for her to stop using?

She must notice something in my eyes because she falls back on her heels, her eyes casting to the ground. She's ashamed. Still high as a fucking kite, but she knows I know what she did.

"Stay here, okay? We're going to leave out the back door, so no one sees us, but I'm gonna need Tripp's help. Give me a few minutes and we'll leave together, all right?"

She stares at me for a minute and eventually nods.

"Who did you come here with tonight?" I ask.

"Trina and Courtney."

Figures. Some of her cokehead model friends.

"Okay, listen. Stay. Here." My voice comes out more authoritative than I mean for it to.

"I get it. All. Right?"

I stare at her for a beat before I stretch my hand out, my fingers closed in a fist with my pinkie finger extended. "Pinkie swear?"

She doesn't move before she lets out a long sigh and hooks her little finger with mine. "Pinkie swear."

"That's my girl." I kiss her forehead before leaving the room, being sure to shut the door behind me.

The pinkie swear is something we started when we were young and living in a small community on the side of a mountain in the Appalachians. Every time I left her, she made me pinkie swear that I'd return when I said I would. She was afraid that if I didn't come back, she'd be left alone with her father. It is our most sacred promise. I usually don't pull it out unless it's something big, but something in my gut tells me that letting her out of my sight tonight will mean bad news. Lilah has never once lied to me or broken a promise when a pinkie swear is involved.

The music thumps through my chest as I step into the main room of the club and toward the VIP area.

"Where the fuck have you been?" Tripp yells when he spots me. His face falls when he sees my expression.

"Can I talk to you for a minute?" I ask him then lean toward Brooke. "I'm really sorry, but something has come up and I have to jet. It was nice meeting you."

"You're leaving *now*?" she says as if she can't believe I'm not sticking around to claim my prize.

"Yeah, sorry." And with that, I turn and walk to where Tripp is waiting for me at the end of the VIP area.

He knocks back some of the drink in his hand then looks at me with a dull expression. "Let me guess. This has to do with *her*."

I push my hand through my hair. "Listen, I'm not in the mood to deal with your shit right now. Will you help me out or not?"

His jaw muscles clench a few times. "What do you need?"

"Thanks, man." I clamp his shoulder. "I want to take Lilah out through the back. Since the paps saw us come in together, I'm thinking that if you leave out the front, they'll assume I'm not far behind. Then Lilah and I can make our getaway."

"You're seriously cockblocking me, man?"

"I know it's a lot to ask. Take the girls with you if you want. I don't give a shit."

He pokes my chest. "You owe me."

"I'd say we're even, seeing as I had to play wingman tonight and listen to Brooke go on and on about how she shouldn't have lost out on Mandy Moore's role on *This Is Us*."

He grins, and right there, I know he's not that pissed at me. "Why do you think I set myself up with Robin and not her?"

"Asshole."

Tripp tosses back the remnants of his drink and sets the glass on the tray of a server leaving the VIP area. "When do you want me out of here?"

I pull my phone from my pocket and check the time. "Five minutes?"

"All right. Sure thing. But know I'm doing it under protest."

"Noted. And thanks."

He nods and heads back to the table. I watch as he leans down to tell the women what's up. They look pissed, and I feel bad as I head back down the hall to get Lilah. The one thing Lilah doesn't get is that her fuck-ups don't only ruin her life.

I text the car service I use and tell them to meet me behind the club in a couple of minutes.

I enter the bathroom I left her in. The white powder around her nose and above her lip says Lilah's done another bump out of the baggie in her purse. I don't bother acknowledging it. There's no point when she's this fucked up.

"You ready?" I ask.

"You tell me. Seems you're the one calling the shots tonight."

I glance at my phone. Tripp should be leaving now.

"Let's roll. The car will meet us out back," I say.

She grabs her purse off the counter and brushes by me to exit the bathroom.

I lead her by her hand to the back door, where we sneak into the waiting car and drive off without incident.

At least one thing goes as planned tonight.

Chapter Six

LILAH

I wake up alone in Jimmy's bed once again. I look under the covers and see that I'm still in my underwear, but I'm wearing one of his T-shirts.

Regret drowns me as it usually does the morning after. Questions assault me about what I did, who I offended, and how pissed Jimmy is now.

I stagger to the toilet, fall down on the seat, and lay my pounding head in my hands. After relieving myself, I slowly open my eyes in the mirror.

Christ. I look like I belong on a street corner.

I use Jimmy's face wash to remove all the smeared makeup and use his comb to brush out my long hair. There sits the toothbrush, my toothbrush, that he leaves out for me after nights like last night. When I feel almost human again, I figure it's time to leave the bedroom in search of a glass of water and to face the music for my behavior last night.

I head straight to an empty kitchen. Opening the fridge, I find a supply of expensive glass bottles of water. Since when did he get so high and elite to not drink out of the tap? A bottle's resting on my lips when I spot him out on the patio that overlooks the ocean. His back is to me and he's on the phone, so I finish my drink while studying him to see how bad last night was.

When he bought this place on the beach, I told him how funny it was that he'd swapped a mountainside for an ocean. Our lives here are worlds away from back home.

He finishes up his phone call and rests his hands on the glass guards, gazing out over the rolling waves falling to shore.

Sometimes I forget he's not the poor boy with knobby knees and jeans hanging to mid-calf who sneaked into my bedroom at night. His muscles are defined now. He's shirtless, wearing only a pair of low-slung athletic shorts. Jimmy was always good-looking, even when he was the poor boy living on the side of a mountain a thousand miles away from here. But now he's set to become one of Hollywood's bona fide heartthrobs, and as happy as I am for him, I have mixed feelings about it.

Jimmy's a dreamer. Always has been. Although I'm not, I can't deny his dreams became reality. He's worked hard to fulfill all the dreams we used to talk about. I'm not sure he ever doubted them, but Jimmy never shows me weakness. Sometimes I wish he would.

And here he is, on the pinnacle of getting everything he's always wanted. Only one thing stands to ruin it for him, and as hard as it is to admit, that's me.

He turns and sees me through the glass that runs the length of the open floor plan. Our eyes lock, and we stare at one another. His disappointment and my apology. The cycle of our relationship—or at least the last few years of it, since I got into modeling and was introduced to coke.

I'm drained, physically and emotionally, and I don't have one ounce of energy left to expend rehashing our fight. If only Jimmy could pretend it didn't happen, as I'm apt to do with most things, but Jimmy doesn't roll that way.

After a minute, he steps toward the sliding doors and comes inside. I used to know what he was thinking from just looking at him, but now, since the drugs, it's harder.

"Hey," I say when he joins me in the kitchen.

"How are you feeling?" He reaches in the fridge and grabs his own fancy water bottle. He unscrews the top and downs a quarter of it in one gulp.

I shrug. "Been better. Been worse."

He nods and presses his lips together. "I got a call from Elaine when she couldn't reach you this morning. I guess you missed your call time on set." There's no judgment in his tone, just the disappointed eyes.

Panic hits me swift and sure, spreading out from my gut as if someone punched me. "Shit!" I scramble to set down the bottle and race to the bedroom to change.

"Hey." He grips my forearm, and I still. "It's too late. The client fired you."

My arms drop and his do too. "Seriously?"

"I guess this isn't the first time they've had a problem with you."

Again with the monotone voice, but I know he's judging me. Telling me what a loser I am that I'm missing opportunities to fulfill our dreams. Why doesn't he just put a "look at me" sign above his head? He's not a fucking angel either.

"Go have a shower and clean yourself up. I want to take you somewhere."

I shake my head. "I want to go home."

"You're not going to go get fucking high. Get dressed."

He knows me way too well. I stand in front of him, hands on my hips. "I'm not going to. I just want to go home."

"I'll take you there after a stop. Go get dressed." He drinks more of his water, leaning back on the counter, eyebrows raised as he waits for me to do what he's asking.

"I am not wearing that dress from last night anywhere. I'll look like I belong on the corner of Hollywood and Vine."

The corner of his mouth tips up. His reaction gives me hope that I haven't fucked up too badly this time.

"I'm pretty sure you have some clothes in the dresser in my guest room. Maria always washes clothes you leave here."

Maria. I do love her. Too bad she's not here today. I could use one of her miraculous hangover concoction drinks.

"Where are we going?"

He grips my shoulder and turns me to face the hallway. "Go. You'll find out soon enough."

I do as he says, knowing Jimmy's not going to tell me no matter how much I try to get it out of him.

AN HOUR LATER, I've showered, downed another bottle of water, and eaten a grapefruit at Jimmy's insistence that I have to get *something* in my stomach before we go. How very responsible of him.

Halfway into our trip, I figure out he's taking me to the pier. Roughly an hour later, we're in Santa Monica. My heart strums gently, because it's one of the first places we visited when we arrived in LA from rural Virginia.

Jimmy's silent on the ride down. I try to make some small talk, but he doesn't seem into having a conversation, so I lean my head back on the headrest and take a quick nap. Guilt still drowns me, so I'm happy Jimmy doesn't lecture me the whole ride down.

The first time we came here, we flung open the doors of his Chevy truck and barreled down the pier. Today, Jimmy won't get out until his ball cap and aviator glasses disguise him.

"Here." He hands me my own cap.

I'm nowhere near as well-known as Jimmy is, but if I happen to catch someone's eye, it's possible they'll look for Jimmy, since we're always in the tabloids together, and that's trouble. Being surrounded by hundreds of fan girls trying to grab a scrap of Jimmy is borderline dangerous. Once we had to have the cops called so that we could leave a store.

"How do I look?" he says and looks at me and grins.

"I'd never pick you out of a crowd." I smile back, finding the calmness of Jimmy and me enjoying a day together.

He waggles his eyebrows and opens the door. It's my first glimpse of the guy I adore since I saw him this morning.

I join him outside. After he sets the alarm on his car and pockets his keys, he takes my hand and entwines his fingers with mine. The feel of his palm against mine calms the ever-present anxiety in my chest, and I breathe a little easier.

We weave through the parking lot, and we don't need to speak because we know where we're going. Our footsteps lead us to the other side of the pier. We stop and remove our sandals to walk barefoot in the sand. The warm sand wiggles between my toes, and the breeze blows my freshly washed hair as it wafts from the ocean. We walk away from the crowd near the pier until we find a more secluded spot.

The both of us sit on the sand and face the ocean, watching in amazement as the waves fall to shore. Memories of our first time and many since play out in my mind. How spectacular the ocean felt the first time we came here.

Jimmy stretches out his legs and holds himself up with his arms behind his back. "Do you remember how we used to talk about this all the time?" His voice sounds wistful, almost as if those days we were barely surviving were the good ol' days.

"I do."

My stomach hollow and gnawing from hunger. My heart pounding every time I heard the muffler of my dad's truck. My eyes unable to close at night because the minute they did, I was awoken.

I spot a small stick in the sand, probably left behind by someone's dog. I dig it up and trace lines in the sand in front of me.

"Did you ever think we'd really make it here? It felt like a desperate dream from a pair of kids who didn't know any better, but somehow we made it." Jimmy's eyes never stray from the beautiful ocean, the sun beaming down on our necks.

I'm quiet for a minute, dragging my stick absentmindedly through the sand. "We both know if it weren't for you, we wouldn't be here."

I leave out the fact that maybe he should have left me behind. The words don't have to be spoken for me to feel the weight of them bearing down on us.

Jimmy takes my hand and squeezes it while he looks at the waves. "You know I'd do anything for you."

I squeeze his hand back as tears burn my eyes. "You've proven that more times than you should have to."

He drops my hand and turns in the sand to face me. "Lilah, I'm worried about you."

I drop the stick and shift to face him. "You don't need to worry about me anymore. We're free of that place. Look around." I gesture to our surroundings. "We're in paradise now. Like you said, our dreams came true." I fail to mention they were Jimmy's dreams. Sometimes I think I just came along for the ride.

"True, but sometimes I think you're still living in the past. You're still that scared little girl—"

"Stop." I raise my hand. "You know I can't talk about him."

"Maybe that's part of the problem. You haven't faced the demons. I know I wasn't there, that what you endured—"

"Christ." I stand, wiping the sand off my ass, and head toward the road. There has to be a bus stop around here somewhere.

Jimmy's on my heels. "Stop." He touches my arm to stop me.

A couple of girls' eyes stay on him as they walk by. I can't be the reason he gets recognized.

I lower my voice. "You make it sound like I'm on death's doorstep. Give me a break. I'm young and I'm having fun. It's not a big deal."

The girls are farther down, but one keeps looking back.

"You were fired this morning. You finally have everything you wanted and you're throwing it all away." Cue his judgmental tone. He's trying to disguise it, but I'm not stupid.

He doesn't understand why I can't be like him. Forget where we came from or what we experienced for the majority of our lives. The itch surfaces again. The need to remove myself from this situation beats on me like a drum, but I owe Jimmy so much, and I force myself to sit back down next to him.

"I'll totally stop, okay?"

He leans into me and cups my cheek, brushing his thumb lightly across my skin. "Maybe you should talk to someone?"

That's not going to happen. I'd rather stay clean than tell someone what my father did to me.

He never holds out his pinkie, because we're on the same page. We've had this conversation before. He tells me to slow down. I say I'll stop. Deep down we both know it won't happen. If we pinkie swear, that would put our friendship to the test.

I nod, staring into his brown eyes. I desperately want to quit the drugs, but even I know I won't. Once the anxiety inside me returns, I'll find the lure of nothingness too hard to resist.

He presses his lips to mine in a chaste kiss. I close my eyes and enjoy the sensation, wrapping my arms around his neck. When his tongue glides across the seam of my lips, I open for him and I'm met with his familiar taste. He moans when our tongues meet, and we languidly kiss while the sun warms our skin and the ocean air blows around us.

This should be enough to bring me happiness. There's no threat of my dad coming for me. Jimmy's right; if I got my act together, I'd have a growing modeling career. Which makes the fact that all I can think of right now is where to score my next bag of coke sick and fucked up.

* * *

WE SPEND the rest of the day strolling the pier, going on a few rides, and playing some of the stupid games rigged so that you can't win until you've dropped a few Benjamins. As night falls, we notice a few people giving us double-takes, their focus lingering a little too long. We're out of time. If we don't leave now, we risk being recognized, then we'll have a mob—or worse, the paparazzi—surrounding us and we'll never be able to leave.

"I had fun today, thank you," I say as Jimmy leads his car onto the onramp of the freeway.

"You're welcome. I thought we could both use the reminder of how far we've come." He glances at me and smiles. He's happy. I love seeing Jimmy happy.

It's no wonder he's a movie star. Even if he wasn't ridiculously beautiful, charisma oozes out of his pores. If James Crawford is in a room, it's difficult, if not near impossible, not to be drawn to him.

I return his smile and lean my head against the window.

Sometime later, I wake up in Jimmy's arms as he carries me into his house.

"I fell asleep?" I yawn, shaking off the lingering tiredness from the night before.

"Yeah. You're always so peaceful when you're sleeping."

That amazing true smile of his warms me, and I wish I could be who he wants me to be. "You can put me down now. I can walk."

"Let me?" He asks so nicely there's no way I can argue.

I relax my head into his chest while he brings us inside and deposits me on his couch.

"Are you hungry?" The way he's looking at me, I can tell that he has things other than food on his mind.

I shake my head, smiling, and bite my bottom lip to test my theory. His nostrils flare and his Adam's apple bobs. Thought so. Even so, I've been humiliated the last few times I initiated anything with him, so he'll have to be the one to bridge the gap between us this time.

"Are you hungry?" I tilt my head, giving him the same look I do the camera when a photographer asks for sexy with a side of innocence.

Jimmy drops to his knees in front of the couch and threads a hand through my hair. "Yeah, I am."

My stomach flips.

"I just want you. The same thing I've wanted since we were kids."

He kisses me softly, but as always, it's like someone fired the starting shot at the races and we're free to release all the wild emotions that run through us. His tongue thrusts into my mouth as if he's doing with his tongue what he wishes he were doing with his cock. I wrap my arms around him and dig my fingernails into his soft cotton T-shirt.

Why can't this make me forget? Jimmy's love and adoration for me shows as his hands explore my body as if he's feeling my curves and contours for the first time. My nipples peak, wanting and needing more, when his thumbs brush over them. I trail my hands down his chest and press against the large bulge of his erection. He pivots his hips forward silently and groans into my mouth.

This is where we are one. We've always been able to come together when we're so starved for affection from the other, we can barely see straight. For the past few years, we've been fighting more than we've been happy, so I'm thankful I'll remember this come morning.

He pulls away and looks at me.

"What are you doing?" I ask, afraid he's going to reject me for the third time this week.

Without warning, he bends at the waist and tips his shoulder down. Before I know it, I'm hanging upside down over his shoulder.

"Jimmy!" I laugh and squirm on his shoulder as the hardwood floor passes by my field of vision through my hair.

"Complaints?" He smacks me lightly on the ass. My panties grow damp with the sensation of his hand coming down on me.

When we reach his room, he drops me in the middle of the bed and wastes no time crawling over me. Through a series of heated kisses and tangled limbs, our clothes come free, stranded wherever we fling them. He sprinkles kisses on my forehead, my nose, and my mouth as he's suspended over me, hands on either side of my head. Jimmy's arm muscles are taut with the effort and his six-pack begs to be licked. We're not touching, but like an addiction, his body calls to me.

"We still good for bareback?" he asks.

The wariness in his eyes almost has me saying no. Does he not trust me to tell him?

Neither of us has ever been with anyone else without using protection. It's something special we only share with one another. I may play fast and loose with my body and my life in general, but that's one way I would never betray Jimmy.

"Of course. Just had my Depo shot," I say with a smile and pull him down to me, wrapping my legs around his waist.

His smile before he kisses me is a mixture of relief and pride. Still, he needs that affirmation from me and that hurts. His hard length presses between us as our tongues meet. Unable to stand the wait any longer, I position him between my legs. He takes the hint and settles himself so that he's lined up with my entrance.

He says my name softly, and I lock gazes with him. Only then does he push inside me, and the rush of Jimmy claiming me propels like a rocket through my body. He brushes the hair off my face, and the intensity between us builds until I smash my lips to his.

He thrusts in and out of me, and I tighten my legs around his waist as he grinds against me in a circular motion once he's fully inside me. My heart hammers and my breathing shallows when he rolls us over, positioning me on top. I splay my hands on his chest and ride him while he plays with my nipples.

"I love watching you above me," he says. "You're so beautiful."

My forehead creases and I close my eyes so I don't have to see him watch me. I move over him at a steady pace as the tension in my body coils tighter and tighter. I'm already on edge when Jimmy's hand travels from my breast to between my legs. His thumb rubs my clit, and I'm unable to stop the tidal wave that crashes into me.

"Oh God, Jimmy." I gasp as I contract around him and struggle to breathe. I jerk against him a few times, my fingernails digging into his chest, and I ride out my orgasm until I'm wrung out with nothing left to give, collapsing on top of him.

He doesn't let me stay that way long before he lifts me off of him and positions me so that I'm on my knees. Threading a hand through my hair, he says, "You have no idea what it does to me when you scream my name when you come."

He thrusts into me from behind. There's nothing sweet or tender about this, and the tension builds again.

"You're going to come again and milk my cock when I finish inside you."

I shake my head, my sweat-soaked hair sticking to my face. "No, I can't," I pant even though my body is already preparing the anticipation of another orgasm.

He drags himself in and out of me, hitting just the right spot that makes my body buzz and tingle, giving me the sensation of floating away. "Yes, you can, and I want my name on your lips when you do."

His chest is pressed to my back now, and he curls himself over me to reach around. Sweat slicks us as he covers my body, his hot breath on my ear. His fingers coast down my side before landing on my clit again. Sometimes I forget he knows my body and what I need.

Seconds later, I combust, and his name leaves my mouth on a hoarse cry that sounds like something between adulation and a curse.

He stills before he thrusts a couple of uncoordinated pumps, emptying himself inside me.

I drop down to the mattress, sweating and panting, trying to catch my breath. Jimmy rolls off to the side and onto his back, his arms raised over his head, his chest rising and falling as he draws in air. I admire him for a moment—the extraordinary man who gives me so much of himself and looks at me as though I'm the love of his life. My body is physically sated, but my mind is full of turmoil. Guilt fills me, and I roll over to face away from Jimmy. The bed shifts, and his finger glides up and down my spine as my thoughts drift to our first time together.

"Please, Jimmy?"

"I already told you to forget it."

We were in my bedroom. I was fifteen and young, but my dad had already made sure I knew all about sex.

The reason I was asking my best friend was because I wanted to know what it felt like to actually welcome someone of my own choosing into my body.

"Why not?" I crossed my arms, and his eyes dipped to my chest.

"Because you're just a kid." He lifted himself off the mattress to leave, but I pushed him back down and stood my ground.

"You're only two years older than me," I argued.

Jimmy wasn't a virgin. He didn't talk with me much about that stuff, but when I started at the high school this year, I could tell that a few girls looked at him as though they knew *him.*

"Don't you want to?" I asked, and even I could hear the hurt in my voice.

His face fell, and he took my hand and pulled me down to sit in front of him on the mattress. "Believe me, that's not the problem." He let my hand go and pushed his own through his dark hair while he blew out a breath.

We'd made out and done some heavy petting, but always with our clothes on.

"Then why won't you?" Much to my humiliation, I felt tears gathering in my eyes. I prided myself on being tough and able to handle anything. My vulnerability made me feel weak, and I hated myself for it.

"I don't know how to explain it… I would feel like I was taking advantage of you. You're only fifteen." His dark eyes begged me to understand.

I shook my head. He didn't understand. I pulled up the tattered ends of my tank top, leaving me wearing only my bra as I sat in front of him.

His jaw slackened, and he swallowed audibly. Both his nose and his eyes flared as his eyes soaked me in.

That was the first time I realized that I could use my sexuality against people to get what I wanted. It was a lesson I never forgot.

It was summer, and the long days were thick with humidity. Crickets chirped in the background, mixed with Jimmy's labored breathing.

I leaned into him, threading one hand through his hair and pressing my chest to his bare one. "Please, Jimmy. I want to know what it feels like to be with you."

Jimmy's face softened because he understood what I meant was, "not him." Slowly, he wrapped his arm around me. "Are you sure? Really sure?" His finger tucked a strand of my hair behind my ear.

I nodded, excitement threading through my belly.

"Once we do this, things will be different with us."

The way he said it made it sound like a promise, and at the time, all I wanted was for things in my life to be different, so I nodded again and bit my bottom lip.

He groaned deep in his throat.

"Please do this for me," I whispered. "Please let me know what it feels like to be with someone I want to be with."

"I'd do anything for you. You know that." He leaned in and kissed me. It was hard and fast and fierce, and I never wanted it to end.

From that day on, we were even more inseparable than we had been. Lost in a bubble of lust and love. For the first time, I thought of my future, a future only with Jimmy.

"What are you thinking about?" Jimmy's voice draws me from my memories. He places a chaste kiss on my bare shoulder.

"Just remembering," I murmur, leaving my back to him.

"Good or bad?" His fingertips strum along my spine.

"Hard to say."

He doesn't respond for a long time, leaving us in silence. My self-hatred grows thicker as his yearning for more information grows impatient.

"I wish you could see yourself the way I do." He nudges my shoulder, urging me to roll over onto my back.

"Don't start with that again," I say.

"It's true."

My head shakes before he finishes saying the words. "Stop."

"You know how I feel about you."

I sit up and turn away from him, my legs dangling over the side of the bed.

"Why won't you give us a chance? A *real* chance?" There's irritation in his tone. Jimmy's not going to let me leave until we tread down this familiar path.

"We've talked about this." I stand up and head toward the bathroom.

He catches my hand as I pass him. "You care about me. I know you do."

"I love you, you know that. But I wouldn't make a good girl-friend, and you know that too."

I can't tell him what I know as truth. I'd ruin any love between us. Jimmy is the most important person in my life. I risk a lot of things with my body and life, but Jimmy isn't one of them. I'd rather live with a taste of him every now and then than not have him in my life at all.

"You have some issues you need to work on—"

"Like the bathroom right now," I say.

He sighs and drops my hand. I race to the bathroom and shut the door, squeezing my eyes closed and wishing I could be someone else. Someone good enough for him. Someone he'd be proud to have on his arm. Someone who wouldn't ruin his future and shatter his dreams.

After convincing myself not to cave to the temptation of classifying what Jimmy and I are to one another, I finish up and open the door. Jimmy's sitting up in bed, the sheets open for me to slide back in so we can pick up the conversation where we left off. Before I get the chance to join him, a voice rings out down the hall.

"James, where you at?"

I've never been happier to hear Tripp's voice in my life. He's a welcome distraction.

"Give me a minute!" Jimmy yells. He sighs as he drags himself out of bed and pulls on his boxers.

He stops before leaving the room, pausing at the door. His gentle smile and tilt of his head say the topic isn't closed. Silently asking me to think about it. Jimmy has never accepted the word no. If he did, we wouldn't be standing in his Malibu beach house right now.

JIMMY

"Hey, man, what are you up to?" Tripp looks back from rifling through my fridge, already making himself at home. Normally my house is his house, but today, I'm irritated by his impromptu visit.

"Nothing. What are you doing here?"

He closes the fridge and pops the top off a beer before tossing the lid on the counter. "Can't a guy stop in to see his best friend?"

I raise my brows.

"Okay, okay. I wanted to see how you made out last night after we went our separate ways." His words are a reminder of the favor he did me.

"Thanks again for helping me out."

He shrugs, sipping his beer. "What are friends for? You missed out though, let me tell you."

I chuckle and walk over to the cabinet that holds my glassware. "Oh, yeah?"

"I took them both home, and let's just say they work well as a team." He waggles his eyebrows.

I laugh. "Maybe I was the one doing you a favor then?"

Tripp's attention darts behind me, then his eyes narrow at me. Lilah must have made her entrance.

"Didn't realize you had company," he says dryly, setting his beer on the counter.

"Nice to see you too."

I circle around to Lilah. She's fully clothed with her bag in her hand. She's taking advantage of Tripp's interruption to make her getaway, as I knew she would. Anything to avoid a *real* discussion.

"I've gotta go," she says, directing her words to me.

"By all means, don't let me chase you out," Tripp says with a sneer.

She glances at him. "Like I give two shits about anything having to do with you." Lilah looks back at me. "I'll call you tomorrow."

I step forward with my hand outstretched, wanting to lead her to the door—to be able to touch her again.

But she busies her hands with her bag. "Stay out of trouble." She turns and practically bolts out of the room.

A few seconds later, I hear the front door open and close.

"Nothing's changed there, I see," Tripp says before taking another swig of his beer.

Shaking my head, I walk over to the fridge and grab myself a beer. "I wish you two could get along." I twist off the cap and toss it on the counter near Tripp's.

Tripp narrows his eyes at me. "Are you serious? Out of the two of us, I'm not the one who needs to get my shit together. The only reason I have a problem with her is because she drags you down."

Needing fresh air, I make my way over to the sliding doors that lead out back.

When Tripp stands beside me at the edge of my patio, over-looking the water, I say, "You have no idea what her childhood was like."

"Maybe not, but that doesn't mean it's okay for her to pull you down with her."

There's no easy way to make him understand. Not without betraying Lilah's confidence. And not without exposing myself.

I swallow a swig of my beer. "She's a part of my life, so either you accept her or not."

"Whatever, man." Tripp shakes his head, and we're both silent for a minute. "So, you all set for filming to start in a couple of weeks?"

"Should be. We have a table read this week, and I have my final fitting for the costume." I lean my back to the glass rail, staring at my house. Even now, I can't believe it's mine.

"You don't sound like a guy on the verge of having his career blow up."

He's right, of course. My lingering worry about Lilah dulls even the shiniest moments in my life these days.

The one thing nice about hanging out with Tripp is, I can be excited about this film and the fact I landed this role. It's not that Lilah isn't happy for me, she is, but lately when we're together, all we do is talk about her latest antic.

"I've just got a lot going on, that's all." I tip back my beer.

"You mean Lilah has a lot going on."

"Christ, is it impossible for you to let her go?"

Tripp is a good friend, but Lilah is a permanent fixture in my life. If he can't accept that, *he'll* be the one to go.

He raises his hands in a placating gesture. "I'll keep my mouth shut then."

"Good."

* * *

A WEEK LATER, I pull up to the gate that protects my new director's mansion from the real world and press the button. This isn't my first time in Calabasas—I've been to a few parties out this way over the past few years—but this is the first time I've been to Scott Franco's house.

From what my agent tells me, he likes to have the cast and some of the crew over before shooting begins to help establish comradery before filming. He has a reputation for being a fair director who doesn't deal well with drama on his sets. As horrible as it is, I'm not sure I can invite Lilah to the set. I can't blow this.

"Can I help you?" a voice says.

"Yes, I'm James Crawford. I'm here for the party."

"Yes, Mr. Crawford, we're expecting you. Come on through."

A loud buzz sounds, and slowly, the metal gates open with a groan. I drive down the winding driveway to a two-story Mediterranean-style mansion that's well over ten thousand square feet. I park behind a Rolls Royce and pull my keys from the ignition. Even after a decade, I'm still in awe of the wealth people have in this town. Never in my wildest dreams growing up did I think I'd see the inside of a place like this. For most of my life, all I thought about was survival. Both mine and Lilah's.

I step out of the car and pocket my keys to head up toward the house. Scott stands in the open doorway, a huge smile on his face.

"You found me," Scott says and pulls me in for a bro hug.

"A satellite could find this place." I gesture to the enormity of the property.

He chuckles. "True enough. Honestly, I'd be happy with a small place down in Malibu, but the missus needs something to show off to her friends." He smiles, and I don't know him well enough to know if it's a joke or not.

He leads me inside, and after a twenty-minute tour of the main floor, he leaves me with his wife in a bustling kitchen. Scott's wife, Melody, is about his age—in her mid-fifties—but is one of the most sincere, down-to-earth people I've met in this town.

"Do you think you're ready for what this film is going to do with your life?" Melody leads me onto a massive covered patio that stretches the length of the house.

"Everyone keeps saying stuff like that, but I think I can handle it."

A bunch of A-listers and crew are already farther out, lingering around the pool, drinks in hand. I follow Melody to the far end of the patio, past a table that fits twelve people on each side, to the makeshift bar.

"Success has a way of changing people." She looks thoughtful for a moment. "But I hope, as you said, that you can handle it." She smiles before she gestures to the bottles of booze. "Now, what will you have?"

"Just a beer is fine. I have to drive home later."

The bartender reaches in the cooler and pulls me out a cold bottle of Stella.

"Thank you," I say, accepting the open bottle.

Scott joins us again while I'm taking a swig of my beer. "Why don't you go mingle while we check on a few things with the chef?"

I nod. "Will do, and thanks again for having me over. And for the opportunity to play the part of The Regulator."

He clasps my shoulder. "You're the right guy for the part. I have no doubt about that."

I smile before taking a short cut across the lawn to reach the people gathered near the pool. Recognizing a couple of producers I've worked with before, I join their small group and chat with them for a while. It didn't take me long after arriving in Hollywood to figure out that relationships are what make you what you'll be in this town. It truly is "who you know" in the entertainment industry.

I mingle and make small talk until there's a soft tap on my shoulder. I spin around to see a cute brunette who's about a foot shorter than me. We met briefly during her casting tryout for my love interest, Destiny.

"I wanted to introduce myself," she says, her hand outstretched. "I'm Adelaide."

I place my hand in hers. "James."

"Nice to officially meet you." She timidly smiles.

"Same."

We stand in silence for a beat until she giggles, and I chuckle from the awkwardness, dissipating the tension.

"So what do you think of all this?" She gestures around to the mass of people.

I shrug. "Any excuse for a party, I guess, right?"

She smiles and nods.

"Seriously though, I think it's a thousand times better than working on a set rife with tension."

She grins and her eyes sparkle. "Have you worked with Harris Boivin?"

My eyes widen. "Ha! You too?"

She nods. "That guy is such an asshole."

"Total creep. I was never so happy for a film to wrap than on his movie *Dissonance*."

"When he directed me in *The Culling*, he made one of the production assistants cry and break down on set. She never came back."

"That's awful."

"He's a total dick. I'll be more than happy if I never have to work with him again," she says, bringing her glass of white wine to her lips.

"Unfortunately, this business is full of people just like him and we don't always get to choose if we want the part." I down another swig of my beer.

"That's the truth."

Scott approaches and wraps an arm around both of our necks. "Glad to see my two stars getting along so well."

"Yeah, we were just chatting about some mutual friends." I wink at Adelaide, and her cheeks flush the lightest pink.

"Awesome. We're just about to eat, so why don't you guys come join us on the patio?"

"We'll be right there," I say as Scott heads off to corral another group for dinner.

"I'm really looking forward to working with you," Adelaide says. There's a hint of something in her words, but it isn't like the usual way the leeches in this town say it.

"Me too." And it's the truth. She seems easy-going, and she's nice to talk to.

Adelaide and I chat as we make our way across the lawn to the patio. She's single, and this is her first big role. It turns out she's from Kentucky and grew up in the sticks too.

I've been so stressed out, worrying about Lilah while having the weight of my first big-budget movie riding on my shoul-ders. Adelaide's easy conversation makes me forget those facts for a moment, and it's a welcome surprise.

Chapter Eight

LILAH

I drag my ass off the elevator of my condo at a slug's pace. Last night was... well, I don't remember much about last night, truth be told. I headed over to a friend of a friend's place to party—some up-and-coming photographer, I think. The drinks were flowing, as were the lines of powder. I must've mixed too much because the night goes black halfway through the party.

I stumble down the hallway toward my apartment at the very end. My key is already in the lock when I notice a red piece of paper taped to the door.

What the hell? My mind, still half dead from the abuse I subjected my brain to in the past twenty-four hours, can't put all the letters together to form a word. I blink a few times.

EVICTION NOTICE

What. The. Fuck.

I rip the letter off my door and spin on my heels, storming down the hall to the elevators. The ride down to the main floor lasts forever. I stomp directly to Mr. Owens's office, and without a knock, I enter, nearly ripping the door off the hinges.

"What the hell do you think you're doing?" I scream, holding up the red paper.

The little shithead superintendent is seated at his desk, not surprised by my reaction, judging by the smug look on his face. He leans back in his chair. "I think the notice is pretty self-explanatory."

"This is bullshit, Chris."

"Actually, it's not. You're three months behind on your rent."

"Says who?" I step forward, my bag dropping to the floor beside me.

"Says me and my accounting software. I've left you voice messages, slipped notices under your door, reminded you when I see you coming in." He crosses his pudgy little arms above his strained stomach.

He's wrong. He told me once and I paid him.

Didn't I?

"Whatever. I'm not some loser who can't pay her rent."

"Whether you have the money or not doesn't matter. You're behind on your rent and I'm within my rights to send you packing." He uncrosses his arms, tilting the chair back down onto all fours. "The fact is, I'm tired of your shit. I have to chase you for your rent, deal with your neighbors complaining about your all-night parties... I know what goes on in your place. I wasn't born yesterday."

"Whatever you're thinking, that's not the case."

"I beg to differ." His eyes focus on a piece of paper on his desk, dismissing me.

"So that's it then? I'm just out on the street?"

"I'm sure you have friends to help you out," he mumbles and scribbles something on the piece of paper he finds so important.

"What about all my stuff?" I ask.

"I'm not a complete asshole. I'll give you a week to make arrangements. Hire movers, con your friends into helping you. I don't give a shit. But if it's still there this time next week, it's in the trash."

I stand in front of his desk, with his half-eaten cheeseburger next to him, stunned for a moment. I can't believe he's kicking me out. I can't believe I'm three months behind on my rent.

What can I do? What can I do?

Changing my expression to a sultry smile, I slowly sway my hips as I round the side of his desk and touch his collar. "There must be some kind of compromise. Something I can do for you to give me another chance."

His eyes widen and dip to my breasts for a second. He slides out his desk chair and I eye his open legs, looking for a spot to kneel in front of him.

"You need to leave." He points at the door.

"Come on, Chris." I place my hand on his knee and lower my body. "Please. I'll do anything."

He stares me in the eyes, his hand wrapped around my upper arm, stopping me. "Go."

I stand. "Fine. But you and I both know that you'll never get a better offer than this." I slide my hands down my body, straightening my dress.

I whisk my purse up off the floor and stomp out of his office, then I push open the heavy glass doors of the lobby with rage. I'm not in dire straits. I have some money in the bank, but not enough for first and last month plus the security deposit for a new place.

Stepping over cigarette butts, I sit on the concrete wall of the small garden in front of the building and open my purse to grab my phone. The small baggie of oxy pills I scored last night lies next to it. I glance around to be sure I'm alone and slide out a pill. Clasping it in my palm, I search the area once more before I toss the pill to the back of my throat and swallow.

I grab my phone. In about twenty minutes, all the hurting, jagged edges of my current predicament will blur, becoming less potent and less real.

After calling a couple of my model friends, none of whom pick up, I relent and call Jimmy. The fact that he's the last person I call when he'd be the first person to help says a lot about what I want, not what I need.

It's been a few days since I raced out of his house after he put pressure on me to open up about why I won't be with him in any real way.

He picks up on the second ring. "Hey."

"Hey, Jimmy."

The echo of his tires rumbling along the highway says he's driving.

"What's wrong?"

I thought I'd done a pretty good job of schooling my voice, but I shouldn't be surprised. I know when something is wrong with him too. "I was wondering if I can crash at your place for a few days."

"Of course. What's wrong with your place?"

I pause, wondering if I should make up a story about a rodent problem or extermination. He'll probably find out anyway. "I've been evicted."

He's quiet.

Should have gone with extermination. Something that isn't under my control.

"I'm just heading over to the studio to do a table read, but I'll be back this evening. Use your key." There's elation in his tone. Elation that I'll squash.

"Thanks," I croak over the lump in my throat.

"You'll be there when I get home, right?" He doesn't phrase the request like an order, knowing I would purposely not be there if he did.

"Yeah, okay."

Right there is the real reason I tried to find somewhere else to stay. Living with him means Jimmy will know all the ins and outs of my daily life, and he won't want me to be a permanent fixture in his future once he finds out.

* * *

At seven thirty, the front door of Jimmy's place opens and shuts. I've spent the day lounging around, dipping into his liquor cabinet and calming my frayed nerves with another dose of oxy. Right now, I'm floating on a cloud of contentment, where the shame and anxiety about the position I'm in are like the cloud itself—not tangible enough to really grab a hold of.

I mute the rerun of *The Bachelor* that I was watching and lock gazes with Jimmy when he enters the room.

"Hey, how'd the table read go?" I ask.

"Good." He tosses his keys on the coffee table and sits beside me.

He looks like my Jimmy today. A snug T-shirt shows off his broad shoulders. A pair of shorts and flip-flops. The only thing new is the concerned glint in his dark eyes. A new expression of his in the last few years.

"So, why were you evicted?"

Jimmy always cuts right to the heart of things. No need for small talk.

A sigh escapes me. "I was behind on my rent. That's usually why they evict you, isn't it?" I shouldn't snap. There's no reason to, especially when he's helping me out by giving me a place to stay. But he consistently acts so holier-than-thou now, which raises my hackles and makes me come out swinging.

"Do you need money?"

"I've got money."

"Why didn't you pay your rent then?"

I stand from the couch, unable to be near him. "I guess I lost track of when the rent was due, I don't know." I stumble over my feet but grip the edge of the couch, hopefully before Jimmy notices. Shit, I might have overdone it today.

"Well, didn't they give you notice or something, so you can make good on it?"

I shrug. "You know how it is. I must have lost track when I was working in Europe." I head to the kitchen, sensing his eyes following me. "I have a week to get my stuff before Chris throws it on the street."

"Chris is your landlord?" Jimmy asks.

I nod, opening the freezer. My hand shifts to the bottle of vodka. Maybe I can sneak a sip without him seeing.

"Move in with me?"

His words stun me. The freezer door shuts on its own and I spin back to see if he's joking. There's an earnest expression on his face. He's completely serious.

"I can't do that."

He stands, and his long legs eat up the distance between us in a few short strides. "It can be like when we first moved to LA."

Back when we arrived in California, we shared a small studio apartment until we were both making enough money to afford our own places. I think he wanted to continue living together, but I pressed the issue, using the excuse that I'd never been on my own and I needed to know I could do it.

I'd lied because I was sick of sneaking around behind his back. Having my own place meant I could come and go as I wished and do what I wanted without the guilt that I was doing something wrong.

"I'm a terrible roommate, you know that."

"You're not so bad." He strokes his thumb along my cheek, making me feel delicate and special in the way only he can.

My eyes drift closed as I enjoy his intimate and loving gesture.

"Please. Just stay for a little while. I'm worried about you." He tucks my hair behind my ears and kisses the tip of my nose.

I open my eyes and stare into the depths of his chocolate-colored ones. I wish I could be the person he wants me to be. Maybe I could be? If I'd try for anyone, it'd be him. "I don't know…"

The hopeful look on his face bolts over the walls I've built around my heart and hits its mark.

"Fine. I'll move in for a bit. But only until I find a decent place of my own."

The smile that transforms his face relieves the lingering doubt inside me. It's rare lately that I get granted a Jimmy smile, and I forgot how special they are.

"Thank you." He pulls me in for a hug,

I snuggle into his chest, purposely turning my face away from his so he doesn't smell the alcohol on my breath. "I should be the one thanking you."

His heartbeat is music. His smell is home. His warmth is safety.

"You know I'd do anything for you, Lilah."

His words spread joy throughout my veins, before the shame overtakes my elation.

"So what do you want to do with the rest of our night, roomie?" I ask with a smile, changing the subject.

His hands dip to my hips, and he hoists me onto the counter. "I don't know about you, but I'm starved. Since the extent of your cooking skills is opening the door and paying for takeout, why don't you sit here while I whip us something up?"

I slide down to a stool at the large island, my hands under my chin and a smile on my lips as I watch him pull vegetables and meat from the fridge. When he's finished cutting the vegetables, he pulls out some metal skewers for shish kabobs.

Sometimes I wonder how he's so well-adjusted when we both came from the same poverty-stricken upbringing and screwed-up childhoods where we suffered abuse of one kind or another. We were both there that fateful day more than a decade ago...

"You okay?" Jimmy gives me a strange look.

I force a smile. "Of course."

I push that memory away. That day revisits me enough in my dreams. I don't need to let it haunt my waking hours too.

Chapter Nine

JIMMY

After a long day on the set of *The Regulator,* I return home, wanting nothing more than a hot shower, a cold beer, and my bed.

Being the lead actor means I'm on set almost daily and working out between my scenes to keep in peak physical condition. Not that I'm complaining. My costars are easy to get along with—there're no big egos and everyone's really positive.

Blowing out a breath, I exit my car as pounding music greets me from inside my house. God knows what's going on inside. I love Lilah, but if she's having a party, we're gonna have to talk. My call time tomorrow is five in the morning, and since this is a physical role, damn if I'll be entertaining any time soon.

I open the door, shocked my place isn't crawling with leeches, a.k.a. Lilah's friends. After dropping my keys on the front table, I walk farther inside the house. Discarded beer bottles and glasses litter the coffee and end tables. I glance at the kitchen from the living room and find half-drunk bottles of booze that weren't there when I left.

She's probably passed out already.

I'm about to head for the bedrooms when movement on the patio catches my eye.

Lilah pulls herself out of the pool, wearing a skimpy bikini—the black one from the shoot she did in Laguna Beach for a swimwear designer. Just as it did when I saw that ad, my blood heats as she stands with droplets of water running down her lithe body.

She's the most beautiful creature I've ever seen, back on the mountainside and in Los Angeles. Lilah is the perfect mix of innocence and debauchery. Her entire being is a juxtaposition in and of itself.

She doesn't notice me as she wrings the water out of her long blonde hair before sitting on a nearby lounger.

I quietly slide the patio doors open and wait to speak until I'm standing behind her. "Deep in thought?"

She startles and looks over her shoulder with a sad smile. "Something like that. How was your day?"

"Good." I walk around the lounger and sit on the one next to her. "Scott seemed happy with the dailies."

"That's great." She returns her gaze to the sky above us, rather than the dark ocean reflecting the moonlight past the deck. Her demeanor screams she's used tonight—alcohol maybe, but probably drugs. She thinks I'm stupid.

We sit in silence for a few minutes, which is fine by me. I'm happy to shut my eyes.

"Do you remember how many stars we used to be able to see back on the mountain?" she asks in a quiet voice.

That she's bringing up our childhood, a topic she's quick to change most days, shocks me from answering right away. She turns her head in my direction, looking for my response.

"We used to think we could see every star there ever was," I answer.

"Remember that book about the constellations that the library had? And you pretended that you lost it, so you wouldn't have to return it, because I loved it so much?"

I link our hands together, squeezing. "I couldn't bear to give it back. You loved finding the constellations and hearing the stories behind them. I wasn't going to return it until we found them all."

She squeezes my hand back and gazes at the stars above us. Neither of us mentions the fact that my dad was one steel-toed-boot kick away from hospitalizing me after he received notice of the fine because I'd "lost" the book.

Minutes pass in silence before her voice pulls me from the edge of sleep.

"Do you think a person can ever really change who they are?" she asks.

I turn my head toward her. "Of course I do. Everything is a choice. Someone can be whoever they want to be..."

"But then are they just pretending to be something they're not? Making choices that don't come naturally to them? Maybe at a certain point, we just are who we are." She looks my way.

She's gorgeous in moonlight. Always has been.

"That's not how I see it." I shake my head. "Look at us. We're no longer a pair of poor, half starving kids hiding from our parents. We're adults with goals. We've already changed who we are."

A sad smile tilts her lips. "You had the dreams. I was just along for the ride."

"That's not true." Irritation colors my voice. We both had the dream to come to Los Angeles. To free ourselves from that shitty place with no future. If she'd believe in herself, she'd be the "it" model.

Lilah huffs a sigh. "Do you ever think about that night?"

My irritation turns to anger. Why does she have to bring that up? We agreed to never talk about it. She's so insistent tonight on poking at the carcass of our past to see what undesirable things might fall out.

"We're not discussing it." I push a hand through my hair and meet her gaze. "We agreed."

"I know." She stares at her hands in her lap for a minute before she raises herself off the chair.

"Where are you going?" I ask, disappointed that what was a relaxing night has soured.

"To get a drink," she says over her shoulder, and she steps inside the house.

How stupid of me to ask a question when I already knew the answer.

Chapter Ten

LILAH

The sunshine heats my skin, and the alcohol I've drunk weighs me down on a sun lounger on the patio. Life is pretty good today.

My cell phone rings. I look at the table and feel at my sides. No phone. I groan, staring into Jimmy's house, through the open floor plan, and spot it on the kitchen island. I left it there when I went in for a refill. Shit. The kitchen is, like, a mile away. Getting up is too much effort, so I let the damn thing ring. To hell with it.

It starts up again a few minutes later. I release a frustrated breath and slowly peel myself off the slats of teak wood before trudging to the sliding doors. Entering the house, I pull my sunglasses off my face and toss them on the coffee table. My agent's name flashes on the screen. I debate not picking up, but I might as well get the call over with, especially since I'm already up.

"Hey, Mina."

"You sound rough," she says in her mousy voice.

"Yeah, thanks. What's up?" I plop down on the couch and stretch my legs out on Jimmy's coffee table.

"I got a call from the House of Carlisle. They're considering making you their face next year, so they want to set up a meeting."

I run her words over in my head a few times to make sure I heard her correctly. Her voice holds no inflection, so it can't mean what I think it does. The House of Carlisle is a high-end fashion house that normally works solely with runway models. Since my five-seven stature is too short for runway, I'm surprised they want me.

"Are you sure?" I ask.

Mina chuckles. "Yes, I'm sure. Though I'll be honest, I'm as surprised as you."

"Why aren't they using one of their usual girls?"

"They're trying to attract a different sort of customer. They're going to have their regular line as always, but they want to move into the millennial market with a high-priced line that's still somewhat affordable to a high-end shopper. Investment pieces, so to speak."

"Wow. I don't know what to say."

"Say you'll cut the partying and get your head on straight so you can land this campaign." One minute monotone, another happy, and now snarky. She's bipolar. Maybe she should take a pill and calm the fuck out.

I tuck my knees up to my chest and wrap my free arm around my legs. "I'm staying with Jimmy right now."

Mina responds with a sardonic laugh. "You and I both know that as hard as he tries, he cannot keep you in line."

She's aggravating me, so I might as well keep this conversation to logistics. "When's the meeting?"

"In a few days. I'll email you the details. Lilah, I'm serious. Stay off the booze and whatever else you've been using. They're interested, but your reputation precedes you and it's a hurdle we need to overcome if you're going to land this campaign. I have twenty clients who would kill for this opportunity."

"I know, I know. I won't disappoint you."

"Make sure you don't." The line dies.

I should slip her an oxy next time we have lunch. She'll thank me.

Anxiety squeezes my chest as Mina's news sinks in. So much responsibility if I land the job. I should be dancing around the room and calling Jimmy. He'll be so happy, happier than me probably, to hear I have this big of a shot. It's his dream. I chew on my fingernails, tension building in my body. Once I calm my nerves, I'll be ecstatic.

I head to the spare bedroom and lift the corner of the mattress to grab my stash.

I grab my weed and rolling papers, head back to the living room, and roll myself a joint. One inhale and my body sinks into the couch as I exhale the puff of smoke. My eyes slowly shut, and the panic attack subsides.

* * *

Hours later, I'm woken by the door shutting.

"Where's the party?" Jimmy walks past the island, lifting the half-empty vodka bottle and waving it.

He probably draws lines to know how much I've drunk daily.

Shit. So far since staying with Jimmy, I've done a good job of getting rid of any evidence of what I do while he's on set.

"I had one drink after dinner," I lie.

He doesn't need to know a joint was my dinner.

He surprisingly doesn't respond and sits next to me on the couch. His new fresh-and-earthy smell mixed with soap tells me he showered in his trailer.

"How was filming today?" I ask.

"Good. It's a great crew, so we get through everything pretty quickly. We were scheduled to film tomorrow, but it's an outdoor shoot on the beach. Since it's supposed to rain, they're pushing it a day."

"The curse of outdoor shoots," I say. "Remember that time I had a shoot over in Morocco and the sand storm came through?"

He chuckles and squeezes my knee. "How could I forget? You looked like something from a horror movie in the picture you sent me. All covered in sand with a bandana over your face."

I smile at the memory. It was my first overseas shoot and I was so green, but excitement overtook my nerves then.

"What'd you do all day?" Jimmy asks, picking up my baggie of weed.

I fill him in on Mina's earlier phone call, diffusing his anger.

"Lilah, that's amazing!" He pulls me in for a hug, baggie of pot forgotten.

"Yeah."

He pulls back, his hands holding my shoulders. Lines scrunch on his forehead. "Aren't you excited?"

I shrug.

"Hey…" He places his finger under my chin and forces me to face him, but I'm reluctant to meet his gaze until he gently tucks a loose strand of hair behind my ear. "What's the matter?"

"It's huge and I'm probably going to screw it up."

"You're not going to mess it up, okay? You're going to go to that meeting, wow them, and they're going to sign you."

I nod.

"I mean it. You got this."

Jimmy used to calm me and make me believe I could do anything. His pep talk is nice, but I'm not sure it did its job.

"Should we celebrate?" I gesture to my weed and papers on the table.

For a split second, disappointment flashes in his eyes, but he recovers quickly with one of his million-dollar smiles. "Sure. This definitely needs to be celebrated."

I smile and rise from the couch to make us some drinks while he rolls us a joint. Jimmy doesn't partake in anything other than alcohol very often, and the truth is, I'm jealous of his ability to stop and start whenever he wants. I return with a vodka soda for me and a beer for him. He's already lit the joint and taken a haul.

"Thanks," he says, blowing out a stream of smoke and leaning forward to grab his beer.

I hold my hand out for the joint, the skunky scent pulling a Pavlovian response from me. "I need this. I'm so nervous about meeting with the House of Carlisle." I inhale from the joint, and the smoke in my lungs is heaven before I slowly let it fall out my lips.

"Want to go over it?" Jimmy asks.

"What you mean, like, act it out?" I scrunch my forehead. "I'm not an actress."

"I know," he says, leaning forward to grab the joint from me. "But practicing your answers to the hard questions can't hurt."

I think about his offer for a second. "You're right. Okay, let's do it."

We spend the night role playing my interview. Not sure how well we do after smoking another joint, but it's nice to be with the old Jimmy. The best part came afterward, when we did a different kind of role playing in bed.

* * *

I WAKE to the feel of lips pressed against my shoulder, followed by a scratchy beard nuzzling into my neck. I moan, gathering my bearings as I shake off the last of my sleep. I roll over onto my back. Jimmy's lying on his side, his head in his hand, gazing down at me. His dark hair is curled up at the ends and mussed, resembling a younger Jimmy.

"What do you want to do today?" he asks in a raspy morning voice.

I wrinkle my forehead before I remember that he has the day off because of the rain. I look over my shoulder at the wall-to-wall window. Rain clouds loom over the dark ocean. "I don't know. What do you want to do?"

"To be honest, nothing. Just chill with you, catch up on some movies I haven't seen."

"Okay, let's do that then." I smile. In my mind, I calculate how many pills I have left, trying to come up with an excuse to slip away to grab some weed and oxy.

"Great. Why don't you relax, and I'll make us some breakfast?"

I run my hands through his hair, and he turns his head to kiss the inside of my wrist.

When we were younger, he used to make me breakfast if my dad forgot to get food. Twelve-year-old Jimmy was already the responsible man he is today. His situation wasn't much better than mine, but he had a mom who tried to keep food in the cabinets. I can still smell the burnt eggs from the first time he tried to make me scrambled eggs in their old cast iron pan. Their stove was ancient and never worked properly, so the one burner only pumped out heat full blast regardless of where you set the dial. The whole place filled with smoke. I remember the awe of gratitude that he'd even tried to help me. Unfortunately, with the good comes the bad. Jimmy's dad returned from his midnight shift, and I listened from the front room as Jimmy took a beating.

He taps my temple. "What's going on inside there?"

"Nothing," I say softly.

He kisses my forehead. "Relax for another half hour. I'll call you when it's ready."

He rolls out of bed, wearing his black boxer briefs and looking every bit the superhero he's playing.

After he's gone, I slip out of bed and sneak out of his room to "my room," the one my stuff is in. When I agreed to stay with Jimmy, I insisted on having my own room, something he wasn't happy about but agreed to. I don't want him to think that I'm ready to have a real relationship, because I'm not. I'll probably never be ready. With anyone.

* * *

I TIPTOE into my bedroom and to the walk-in closet. My hands shake as I root around the bottom of my purse for the small container of oxy. I breathe a sigh of relief, counting that I have enough to get by today, but I need some for tomorrow for sure. I swallow one pill, close the container, and push it to the bottom of my purse, covering it with tampons and receipts.

"What are you doing?"

I spin around to find Jimmy behind me, holding a spatula.

"I'm picking out some clothes. Figured I'd have a quick shower before breakfast." It's scary how quickly lies pop into my brain.

His gaze dips to my purse then back to me. "Do you want your eggs scrambled or fried?"

"Fried please," I say with a smile.

"Coming right up. Don't take too long in the shower," he says and walks down the hall.

I sag to the floor, exhaling a breath in relief. Jimmy knows I'm no angel, but I don't know how he'd feel if he knew I need to pop a pill on a regular basis now.

After a minute or two, I shake off the panic and head to the bathroom to shower and wait for the pill to take effect.

Chapter Eleven

LILAH

The next day, Jimmy insists I join him on set, since it's only ten minutes down the beach from his place. Even though the need to get to Derek's runs over and over through my mind in the most obsessive way, I agree to follow him. He has to go over the script changes for the day and see hair and makeup first.

At eight o'clock, I drag myself out of bed, pop my last pill, and brush my teeth and hair. Deeming myself good enough, I walk down the beach. The sand wiggles between my toes and brings up memories of Jimmy and me, two desperate deserters, arriving in Los Angeles with next to no money but determined to make it. We were so different then.

The set for the day comes into view. It's blocked off by security, but men with cameras are hanging around the perimeter.

Shit. I hadn't even thought about the paparazzi.

I duck my head as I make my approach, knowing it's a useless endeavor. These guys are better than the FBI at identifying one of their suspects. It's as if their brains have an entire catalogue of celebrities, from the A list all the way down to the Ds.

I stay as close to the water as I can, away from where most of the paps stand. When the bulky security guard spots me, he walks the length of the temporary fencing to meet me.

"Sorry, ma'am. They're filming today. You can't get through."

I lift my head and smile. "I'm here to see James Crawford. My name is Lilah."

He gives me the once-over then reluctantly pulls his walkie-talkie off his hip. "You got a Lilah on your list for James?"

The click of a camera shutter sounds to my left. The paps have figured out who I am. Who knows what kind of juicy story they'll cook up to go along with these photos.

I turn my back on them, but it's no use. They walk down to where I am.

Something garbled comes through the walkie-talkie that I can't understand, but apparently the guy in front of me can, because he says, "Right this way," and steps aside, allowing me through the fence.

"Thanks." I move as quickly as I can over the shifting sand.

"He's just finishing up in makeup."

I give him a wave and keep walking toward the parking lot where the trailers are set up. I've been on enough sets to know the deal, so it only takes me a few minutes to find his trailer. I give a quick knock and peek my head inside.

Jimmy sits in the makeup chair with the script in his hands. Adelaide Sheridan sits in the chair across from him, doing the same. She's laughing, and he's smiling. A sour queasiness fills my stomach as I watch the two of them. The fact I opened the door and he's yet to notice bothers me.

"Hey, Jimmy."

He looks away from Adelaide and smiles, his mocha eyes sparkling. "Hey, come in." He stands and meets me halfway, giving me a hug hello. "Lilah, this is Adelaide."

"Hi," I say, giving her a short wave and an even shorter smile.

"Hi, nice to meet you."

She's pretty. Not glamorous or anything, like a lot of Jimmy's previous coworkers, more the girl-next-door type. Honest and fresh-faced.

"Same." I nod.

There's a bit of an awkward silence which Jimmy quickly fills. "We were just running our lines for today, since we're done with hair and makeup."

"So I don't get to see you in the superhero suit?" I tease, poking his stomach.

"Not today, sorry. We're doing the climax of the B plot today."

The itchy anxious feeling I'm so familiar with crawls across my skin. I know that the B plot in a superhero movie is code for the love story.

"Oh? What's going on in the scene today?" I ask, doing my best to sound genuinely interested. I wonder how long it will take for me to get to Derek's with traffic.

"Today is our first love scene," Adelaide says. "Always awkward."

I can't tell if she said that deliberately to piss me off, or whether she's truthfully not looking forward to it. Unless she's dating some other LA heartthrob, I'm sure no one looks at Jimmy and thinks, man, the last thing I want to do is roll around in the sand with him.

I give her a small smile and look at Jimmy.

"Yeah, they changed it. We were supposed to be in studio for our love scene next week, but when the sides came, we saw that they'd changed it."

I've known Jimmy long enough to see the apology in his eyes. He never would have invited me had he known. Regardless of the fact that we're not anything official and everyone here is a professional, there's nothing pleasant about watching someone you have feelings for dry humping another person.

"When are you due on set?" I ask, thinking maybe I can have a quick visit and bolt, but there's a knock on the door as the last word leaves my lips.

A woman with a headset on pokes her head in. "They're ready for you."

"Great, thanks," Jimmy says.

Adelaide hops off her chair and heads toward the door. "It was good to meet you. I'm sure I'll be seeing more of you."

I mumble a, "You too," and smile at her.

Jimmy steps into me so that we're chest to chest. "I understand if you want to leave." His hands rest on my hips.

I feign indifference with a shrug. "No worries."

His hands drop to his sides. "I forgot, you don't really care if you're not the only woman in my life."

He's picking *now* to have this fight?

"It's not like that and you know it," I snap.

He settles his hands on his hips. "What's it like then?"

I squeeze my hands into fists at my sides, resisting the urge to scratch at myself because that feeling, the one I hate, is back and it's like bugs crawling under my skin. "Why do you keep pushing me on this? You know I'm not girlfriend material. You know better than anyone the issues that would ruin us."

He grips my shoulder and using his other hand to brush his knuckles along my cheek. "You're so much more than you think. I wish you could see that."

Our gazes connect, my blue to his deep brown, and a part of me wishes I could sink into him, believe what he sees in me. But there're things about myself I hide, and I'll only end up hurting him worse than I already am.

I sense the day coming, the day when I'll have no choice but to dislodge the anchor of me and let him move on with his life. I owe him that much at least. But I can't bear to think of how hollow my life will be without the one good thing I have left in it. One day I'll find the nerve.

I wrap my hand around his wrist and pull it from my face. "You'd better get on set."

His lips thin and tilt down, but he doesn't argue. "You gonna stay?"

"Yeah, I'll stay for a bit."

He nods, and we both head for the trailer door.

Once on set, Jimmy is so busy and enthralled in Adelaide—or the scene they're filming—that I slip away unnoticed fifteen minutes later.

I can't handle watching him and Adelaide kissing and carrying on, but sadly, that's not the only reason I hightail it out of there.

Chapter Twelve

JIMMY

"**M**ake yourself at home. I'm just gonna run and change," I tell Adelaide as I head down the hall.

I invited her back here once we wrapped on set. Not for me exactly, but because Tripp is supposed to drop by tonight and I think he and Adelaide might get along.

Lilah wasn't in the living room or out on the deck when I came in, and she's not in the bedrooms either. I'm relieved she isn't home, because I have no idea how she'd react to Adelaide being here and she and Tripp can't be civil. Still, I can't help worrying about where she is and what she's doing. I do my best to put it out of my mind while I change. I texted Tripp before we left set, so he should be here soon.

Adelaide is on the couch in the living room.

I pour her a glass of wine in the kitchen. "So tell me, Adelaide, how come you don't have someone in your life?"

She joins me, sitting on a stool across from me at the island. "Why are any of us single in this town?" She shrugs and sips her wine. "This job is demanding and it's hard to find someone who will put up with your schedule. Dating in LA is a cesspool. Most men are more interested in getting into my pants than my heart."

I pull the chicken from the fridge and rinse it. Thankfully, my back is to her, I'm not sure what to say to that since it's true. "Maybe you'll like my buddy Tripp when he gets here. He's a good guy."

"Maybe. Why are you single?" she asks, then seems to think better of her question. "*Are* you single? Or is Lilah your..."

"Me and Lilah are complicated."

She presses her lips together and gives a big nod. It comes off a bit skeptical, so I feel the need to explain.

"We've known each other since we were kids. Been through a lot together."

"So you're what? Friends with benefits?"

I place the chicken on a large cutting board and pull the meat tenderizer from the drawer in the island. "I don't think there's a word for what we are. We're sort of like two planets orbiting the sun. Sometimes we're close to each other, and other times we're on opposite sides of the universe."

I grab some plastic wrap and cover the meat, so the juices won't splatter all over us while I beat it. I bang the tenderizer on the meat, relieving some of my frustration about the topic of Lilah and what we are to one another. Adelaide seems content to watch me, and I grow uncomfortable under her gaze, as though she senses more than she should. When I finish, I place the tenderizer in the dishwasher and toss the plastic wrap in the garbage.

"Well, I think she's foolish if she doesn't see how good she has it with you." She smiles and sips her wine again. A smile tips the corners of her mouth over her wine glass.

She does see too much.

"Trust me, I'm no angel." I give her a friendly wink and move the chicken to a plate before I head to the sink to wash my hands.

Thankfully, Tripp joins us then, walking right in as usual.

"Hey, man." I give him a nod.

"What's up? And who is this lovely lady?" he asks, knowing full well who Adelaide is.

"Adelaide, this is my friend Tripp." I motion between them with my hand.

"Good to meet you," he says, taking her hand.

"Same here." She smiles and gives him the once-over.

"Well, you two get to know each other. I'm going to warm up the barbeque. Be right back."

I listen to them chitchat as I walk across the living area and out the sliding doors onto the deck overlooking the ocean. After lighting the barbeque, I look inside the house to judge how it's going. Tripp and Adelaide are engaged in a conversation, and my mind fills with the thought of what it would be like if Lilah and I ever did something so normal as have a night in with another couple. You know, were Lilah and I are officially a couple ourselves. My hope that that will ever happen is vanishing every day.

No matter how much I push, she won't budge and give us a real chance. Sure, sleeping with her is great. But I want her to clean up her shit, move on from the past, and *really* be with me. As a couple.

But I learned early in life that you can want something, but you might never get it.

* * *

A COUPLE OF HOURS LATER, I've cleaned up from dinner. Adelaide and Tripp are getting along well enough, but I'm not sure there's enough spark for a love connection.

I'm enjoying myself too. I'm on my fifth drink, lying to myself that it's not because Lilah hasn't shown her face. I texted her an hour ago, and so far, I've heard nothing back.

Tripp hasn't mentioned Lilah at all tonight, which is a blessing, but we've all had a few and the conversation won't go as nicely as it would if I were sober.

"Where's Lilah tonight?" he finally asks, as though he can hear my thoughts.

I shrug and lean farther back into my lounger.

"What, is your GPS tracker not working?" he teases.

"Fuck off." I guzzle a fair amount of whiskey. I moved on to the hard stuff after my first beer.

"Did James tell you that he's Lilah's official babysitter?"

I roll my eyes but say nothing. He's half drunk, and there's nothing he likes more than to bust my balls.

Adelaide giggles. "He mentioned that he and Lilah are 'complicated.'" She puts air quotes around the word complicated.

"Yeah, that's one word for it. He's more of a glutton for punishment, if you ask me," Tripp says with a laugh.

"Not sure if you noticed, bro, but no one did ask you." I finish off my drink.

"Not like you'd listen anyway." He turns his attention to Adelaide, whose gaze is ping-ponging between the two of us. "Do you know how many times I've tried to tell him to ditch the bitch? She's been dragging him down since I've known him, and he just keeps going back for more."

Adelaide's worried gaze bounces over to me.

"He could be getting any girl he wants—hell, probably you—but instead he's trying to set me up with you, and he keeps going back to that drug addict, waste of skin—"

"That's enough." I pin him with a stare and rise up from the lounger. "I'm going to get us all another drink, and when I come back I don't want to hear her name from your mouth again, got it?"

I've reached my limit and Tripp must know it because he puts his hands up in a placating gesture. "Whatever you say, man."

I walk across the deck, my empty glass clutched tightly in my fingers. He needs to let it go. There's no way he could possibly understand the history Lilah and I share, even if he knew all of it. You have to live it to understand it. I pour myself another drink and grab a few shot glasses of tequila. After I've placed them all on a tray, along with a lime and some salt, I click the button on my phone on the island to see if Lilah texted back.

Nothing, but there are a few missed calls from my agent, Keane. I wonder what that's about. It's not ideal to call him back while half in the bag, but if there're problems on set or something has come up with the *The Regulator* shoot, I need to know.

"Hey, James, how are you?" he asks. The sound of clinking dishware and the murmur of a room full of people fill the background.

"Good, the shoot went well today. How are you?"

"Same old." I hear shuffling and he says, "Excuse me for a second," to someone before the background noise dies off. "Listen, normally I wouldn't bother you with something like this, but it seemed kinda strange, so I thought it was worth mentioning."

The hair on the back of my neck stands up.

"Some woman named Darla keeps calling my office, looking for you. My secretary thought it was some crazed fan at first, because she called a few times a week for a month straight, but the thing is, this last time she called, she said she was your mother."

The earth drops out from under me like when you go down the first big hill on a roller coaster. Except there's no exhilaration that follows. My stomach pitches, and I grip the counter to remain upright.

"James, you still there?" Keane asks.

"Yeah, sorry, bad connection."

"Anyway, yeah, she says she's your mom, which I told my admin isn't possible because your mother passed away, but this woman insists that she wants to talk to you."

My mouth is drier than a desert. "Did she say what she wants?"

"Nah, just insisted that she was your mother over and over again and demanded to speak to you."

"Do you have her number?" I ask, regaining my composure. I have no choice but to handle this before it scatters out of control.

"Well… yeah, I'm sure my secretary probably wrote it down."

"Send it to me. I'll take care of it." My voice is devoid of any emotion.

"Are you sure? I can take care of it if you want. Should I call the cops to see if we can get a restraining order?"

"I said I'd take care of it," I snipe.

"Okay, man, I'll send it over when I'm back in the office tomorrow."

"Thanks." I lift a shot of tequila from the tray and tip my head back, downing it in one swallow, without the lime.

"You sure you don't need me to do anything?" Keane offers.

"Nah, I'll take care of it."

"All right. I'll get it to you tomorrow."

I hang up and put the phone back on the counter.

The only question in my mind is the most obvious one. What the hell does she want?

Chapter Thirteen

LILAH

I stumble up the stairs to Jimmy's front door. It's dark, and I'm hoping Jimmy's asleep already.

A few voices float out from the other side of the house. Shit. Using my key, I open the front door and look at the empty living room. I spot him and a couple people out on the deck. Adelaide and Tripp. My two least favorite people.

"Ah, the prodigal daughter returns," Tripp says when I open the sliding glass door, and he laughs, almost falling off the lounger, which spurs him to laugh harder.

Tripp's obviously drunk. My gaze darts to Jimmy. He's slumped back in a lounger, staring at me with half-lidded eyes.

"Hey, what are you guys doing?" I walk toward an empty lounger in their little semi-circle, doing my best not to stumble.

"Same thing you've been doing," Jimmy says.

I plop down on the seat and lean back. "Hey," I say to Adelaide and give her a nod.

What the hell is she doing here?

"Hi," she says with a little wave.

"Where have you been?" Jimmy asks in an accusing tone.

I whip my head in his direction. "I had some things to do."

He smirks.

"How did it go on set today?" I ask to steer this conversation anywhere but on me.

"It went well. I think we nailed a couple of the takes," Adelaide offers.

"I'll bet. Rolling around in the sand with Jimmy must be really hard."

Adelaide stiffens.

"Relax, Lilah." Jimmy brings his drink to his lips, but dribbles fall onto his T-shirt.

"How much of that have you had?" I ask.

"*You're* going to ask him that?" Tripp scoffs.

"Piss off." I open my purse and pull out a set of rolling papers, a baggie of weed, and roll a joint.

They all remain quiet. Have they been like this all night, or is it just my company that makes everyone a mute?

Once I roll and light the joint, I take a couple tugs off it and hold it out to offer to the others. Jimmy reaches for it first. After he takes a couple of pulls, he passes it to Tripp. When he's done, he offers it to Adelaide, who waves it away.

"What's wrong, princess? Does it offend your sensibilities?" I ask, laughing.

"Chill out, Lilah," Jimmy says.

"What crawled up your ass?" I ask, because something is definitely up with him tonight.

"Nothing, you just don't have to be such a bitch."

"I'm sorry, did I hurt your girlfriend's feelings?" I use the voice of a child.

"Whatever. Do what you want. You will anyway." He lifts his drink to his lips and finishes it.

Pissed off, I bolt up off the lounger and storm into the house. I'd rather hang out with myself in my room than these lame asses. I stash the recreational substances I picked up off Derek today and flop back onto the mattress. What is Jimmy's problem? Has he finally tired of me? Found someone more redeemable in Adelaide?

That thought both frightens and elates me in equal parts. I'll never have the courage to push him away on my own.

I don't know how long I lie there, drifting between emotions, before the sound of my door smacking open startles me. When I whip into an upright position, Jimmy stands in the door frame, hands clenched into tight fists, breathing heavily. The expression on his face is a mixture of desperation, regret, and anger.

"What are you doing?" I whisper.

"Why do you do that?" He steps into the room.

I stand from the bed. "Do what?"

He shakes his head and steps toward me. There're only a few inches between us now, and my skin tingles at the thought of touching his.

"You always do that," he says.

"Always do what?"

He stares at me.

"Forget it. I'm not doing this with you. I'm tired. I'm going to bed." I turn to climb back into bed, but his arms wrap around me from behind, pinning mine to my sides.

"Jimmy, what are you doing?" I struggle to free myself from his hold, to no avail.

He dips his head to my neck and inhales. "Do you know you always smell the same? Whether you're sober or drunk, high or pissed off, happy or sad? It's one of the few constants about you. I always feel better after I smell you."

He sounds sad and more hopeless than I've ever heard him. What the hell happened to make him feel this way?

I stop struggling and lean into him. "Are you going to tell me what's going on?"

He shakes his head. "I just need you right now. I need to feel you all around me. I need to lose myself in you."

He eases his grip a bit, and I turn in his arms. Our gazes lock, and I'm not prepared for the emotions swirling in his vision. He hasn't looked so torn apart since we were back in Virginia. My heart clenches at the pain in his eyes, and I brush his dark hair away from his forehead.

"Whatever you need," I whisper.

His shoulders sag.

My hands move to the hem of his shirt and I lift it over his head until he stands shirtless in front of me. I pepper kisses over his hard pecs, and his hand sinks into the hair at the back of my head. His eyes fall closed.

Ever so slowly, I drop to my knees in front of him, then I undo his belt and pull down his jeans and boxer briefs.

He stands in front of me in all his glory, looking every bit the man he is. Anyone can see that Jimmy is beautiful on the outside, but not everyone knows how brightly his soul shines within.

I grip his hard cock at the base and jerk my hand up and down a few times to the sound of his quick gasps.

"I want to look at you," he says, brushing a hand over my head and gazing down at me.

"I'm right here."

"I want to see all of you." He reaches for my free hand and pulls me to my feet.

He does nothing at first, cupping my face and leaning in so our foreheads touch. My eyes drift closed, and I savor the feeling of the connection we share. There's no one else in the world who will ever know the true me.

Jimmy pulls away and undresses me with a note of desperation to his movements. When I'm completely naked in front of him, he wraps a hand around the back of my neck and tugs me forward, resting his chin on my head. I wrap my arms around him, my cheek pressed to his hard chest.

"You know what you mean to me, right?"

I can feel the vibration of his voice in his chest against my cheek. "I know." I squeeze my arms tighter around him.

"You know I'd do anything to protect you."

I pull back to see his face and nod slowly. He's already proven that to me. "I know."

"You need to know that no matter what, I'll take care of you and protect you." His voice is fierce, and his eyes burn with emotion.

"You're starting to scare me. Why are you saying all this?"

Seeing him like this is unsettling. Jimmy is my rock. He's always been my rock. Even if that's not fair to him, that's the way it's always been.

"No one is going to come between us." He leans in and claims my lips in a fierce kiss.

I moan when our tongues touch, and he draws me into him again, our naked chests meeting. His hand is at the side of my head, directing me which way he wants me, and in a couple of minutes, we end up on the bed. Jimmy poises himself at my entrance and stops, meeting my gaze with a questioning look.

I know what he's asking.

"It's fine," I say, holding up my pinkie finger.

He loops his pinkie around mine.

When his hand is placed back beside my head, he slowly pushes into me.

It feels different. Like when we were younger and all of our feelings for one another took over our minds and controlled our hands as we slowly explored our sexuality. Except this time, there's the bad with the good.

All the doubt and disappointment I've brought him.

The anguish and the fear I've caused us over the years.

Every time I've torn him apart and pieced him back together.

The times he's saved me.

It's suffocating, and I can't get enough air to fill my lungs. I grip him tighter, afraid one of us will disappear and I'll miss out on this moment.

His eyes stay trained on mine as he rocks in and out of me, whispering words of endearment. Words I know as his truth, but not mine. For this brief moment, I push away my self-deprecating nature and let him speak from his heart.

"You're everything to me." He grinds his hips and my eyes roll to the back of my head. "That will never change. No matter what happens, believe that. My past." He kisses my forehead. "My present." He kisses the tip of my nose. "And my future." Jimmy steals my mouth in a rapturous kiss that hits me all the way down to my soul.

He lets his head drop so that our foreheads touch. My eyes drift closed, and I concentrate on the sensation of him rocking into me, the feeling of him *loving* me. Sweat makes our chests cling together, and soon it's all too much.

Too much physical sensation.

Too much emotion.

Too much of everything.

When my climax peaks, I cascade over the waterfall like a rush of water, tumbling down and not wanting to find the bottom. To live in this state of euphoria forever. The high I'm always chasing.

Moments later, he bucks against me in an unsteady rhythm and comes inside me on a groan. My nails drag up and down his back while he catches his breath and my legs drop to the side.

I can't find the energy to get up and clean myself. I'm too content and tired. Jimmy rolls off me to the side, and I slip under the covers. He instantly joins me, spooning me from behind.

No words are needed. This is what he needs, and so do I.

I lie there, drifting off, listening to the gentle inhale and exhale of our breaths until Jimmy's voice pulls me from sleep.

"My mom's been trying to reach me," he mumbles.

Every muscle in my body tenses, waiting for more information, but when I roll over to look at him, he's passed out.

Chapter Fourteen

LILAH

I toss the empty Red Bull can on the passenger side floorboard of my car. I popped an oxy before I left the beach house for downtown Los Angeles and need something to give me a boost before I go into the meeting with my agent and the House of Carlisle representatives.

The four of us are lunching at a trendy LA celebrity hot spot named Vice. Nerves have my stomach rolling over—there's no chance I'll be able to eat anything while I'm here. But I raise my head high and strut into the restaurant like I am Lilah Robbie, the hottest model in LA.

Landing this campaign will be huge for me. A giant stepping stone in my career. I can't afford to squander the opportunity.

The hostess is the typical LA wannabe model/actress—high cheek bones, plump lips that have seen a filler or two, and a botoxed forehead that barely moves when she smiles.

"Hi, I'm here to meet some people. The reservation is under Mina."

She glances at her list, and when she raises her head again, she gives me a quick once-over before turning on her heel. "Follow me. Someone from your party is already at your table."

I hope it's Mina. We planned to meet here a little early so that the two of us can go over our game plan before the House of Carlisle representatives arrive.

When the hostess bypasses the main dining room, I realize that Mina must have booked us the private room in the back. The girl, who is probably only a few years younger than me, leads me to a room with glass on three sides. The other wall features a floor-to-ceiling wine rack.

Mina sits at the table, her bright red—and most certainly from a box—bob covering the majority of her face since she's looking at her phone.

The hostess doesn't enter but stops at the glass door and waves me in.

"Thank you," I say.

When Mina hears my voice, she raises her head and smiles. "You look fabulous."

"Thanks. I figured wearing one of their pieces for this meeting made sense." I glance down at the blue patterned dress I'm wearing before hanging my purse on the back of the chair beside her.

"Good choice." She sets her phone aside and shifts in her chair so she's facing me. "They should be here soon, so let's go over how we're going to approach this. Whatever they offer you in this meeting, if they do make an offer, don't give them any reaction. Leave the negotiation to me. If they've reached out to you, you can bet that they want you."

I nod.

"Next, we need to figure out how we're going to respond to some of the bad press you've gotten." She stares at me meaningfully until I feel the need to defend myself.

"Can't we just tell them that's all behind me?"

"Is it?" she asks with raised brows.

I shift in my seat. "I'm here, aren't I? Do I seem like anything is wrong with me?"

She studies me, and I do my best to look relaxed and not paranoid.

"Look"—she leans in as if we're sharing a secret—"you and I both know half the models in this town are using one thing or another. I don't care. Hell, the clients don't care. As long as it doesn't interfere with your work and stays out of the press. Can you manage that much?"

I think back to Jimmy's words last night and what that could mean. He was out of the house already when I woke up this morning and hasn't returned my calls.

Not sure if I believe it myself, I nod anyway. "That won't be a problem. I can keep it on the straight and narrow."

"Excellent," she says with smile.

We chat for a bit before the director of marketing and the CEO of the House of Carlisle arrive. All in all, the meeting goes well, and I sell them on the fact that my troubled past is behind me. I leave the meeting feeling as if I stand a genuine chance against whoever else they're considering.

When I reach my car, I text Jimmy again, but he still doesn't respond.

My anxiety level rises and all I want is to blow off some steam, so I track down Trina and Courtney and head over to their place.

JIMMY

We don't wrap on set until almost ten o'clock at night, and after a shower in my trailer, I can no longer put off thinking about what I've been avoiding all day—my mother.

Why is she calling after all these years? Where has she been?

My dad used his fists to settle any disagreements and that included ones with my mother, so I shouldn't have been surprised she took off when I was fourteen. What surprised me was that she hadn't taken me with her.

I expected her to return home for days that turned into weeks. Finally, after a few months, I realized she was never coming back and that I had been left to deal with my dad on my own.

My dad didn't take kindly to her leaving and took it out on me more than a few times. The teachers saw the bruises. They had to have—one time he gave me a black eye and a swollen jaw— but they never asked me about it. I probably would've lied anyway, knowing that social services would take me out of my house. That would have left Lilah to fend for herself and we were inseparable, even then.

I plop down on the leather couch in the trailer, palming my phone. Keane sent me the number to reach her. I haven't seen or spoken to Darla in fifteen years—I can't imagine what she has to say.

With my elbow on my knee and my head in my hand, I stare at her name on my phone, feeling... I don't even know what. A mixture of trepidation, anxiety, and anger.

Before I can stew any longer, I press the number and hit the button to call her. As I put the phone to my ear, my knee bounces over and over.

A woman answers with a cigarette-rippled voice I'd recognize anywhere. "Hello?"

"It's me." I don't want to call her mom. She doesn't deserve the title anymore, as far as I'm concerned.

"Jimmy?"

I cringe. Everyone called me Jimmy when I was younger. These days, only Lilah refers to me as Jimmy and that's how I like it. It's something special between the two of us. Hearing Darla say the word tarnishes that somehow.

"It's James now," I say with spite in my voice.

A chuckle rings through the line. "That's right. I forgot you're a big Hollywood hotshot now. Congrats, my boy."

"What do you want?" Being on the phone with her, even for this short amount of time, isn't good for me. I feel as though the past has swallowed me whole.

Is this what Lilah feels like all the time? I'm able to push away everything that happened on that mountainside most days, but she never can.

"Can't a mom call to catch up with her boy?"

The phone makes a sound under the tight grip of my fingers. "Not when she abandoned him as a teenager and left him alone with an abusive asshole for a dad."

Her response is silence.

Silence I'm not filling. She's the one who reached out to me. She had to know this wouldn't be a happy reunion.

"I want to apologize for that." Darla sounds sincere, I'll give her that.

"What did you think was going to happen after you left? Who do you think he took it out on?" I seethe.

"Jimmy, I—"

"James."

"James, right. You know what he was like. I couldn't take it anymore. I had to get out of there, and I had nothing. Nothing to provide for you with. I had no idea where I was going or how I'd survive. I just knew that if I didn't leave, I was going to end up dead."

Standing from the couch, I pace. Whether she's right or not, you don't leave your child alone with someone like that.

When I don't respond, she continues, "You only had a few years left before you were an adult, and you were getting bigger every day. I knew that soon your dad wouldn't be able to push you around anymore."

Pain settles into my palm and I stop pacing, looking down to see that I'd been clutching my hand so hard, my fingernails had dug into my skin.

"None of this shit matters anyway. As nice as this stroll down memory lane has been, you must've called for a reason. What is it?" I resume my pacing through the small trailer.

She releases a long-suffering sigh. "I need money."

Any chance of reestablishing a relationship with my mom dies with those three words.

"Get a job," I bite out.

"I had one, but I got laid off. Things have been hard lately."

"Sorry to hear that. My life was hard after you abandoned me."

"Jim—James, I'm sorry for the past, but I can't change it. I really am proud of you, you know. I had no idea my boy was a big movie star until I saw a poster at the mall last year and you were on it. It took me a few minutes before I really believed it was you. I hadn't seen you in so long, but your eyes haven't changed, and your hair still curls at the end if you let it grow too long. When you were a baby, I'd—"

"I'm not doing this with you, Darla."

She sucks in a big breath when I use her name.

"You're right about the fact that we can't change the past and what's done is done. I've moved on with my life and you're not a part of it. Go find some other schmuck to give you money, because it's not going to be me."

She's quiet for so long that I think she hung up.

"You know, I didn't stay away from the mountain... I went back about five years ago..." She lets her words hang in the air.

"Glutton for punishment?"

"Nah. I caught wind that your father had died, so I went back when I was traveling through Virginia. I don't know why. There were some good times too."

Her words knock the wind out of me.

My dad is dead?

It's not as though I care about the son of a bitch. I've tried really hard not to think of him since I left. But I always assumed he was still out there, just as miserable as ever. I'm not sure how to feel now that I know he's dead.

"I take it you didn't know your daddy was dead?" Darla asks.

"No, I... I didn't keep tabs on him after I left." I sink into one of the chairs at the small kitchen table.

"Well, he's dead. Didn't leave much behind. The old place was still standing when I got there, but just barely."

"How did he...?" I don't know why, but I need to know what finally took out the prick.

"Not really sure. Ol' Willy found him. Went by to get him so they could check the stills out in the forest. It was moonshine season. Found him sitting in his chair, dead as stump. You know how it is up there. They don't call the cops or anything, just bury you on your property and put a marker on it."

I do know how it is. It's as backwoods as you can get. People on that mountainside don't typically report births or deaths, file taxes, or do anything else that involves the government. Hell, Lilah and I had been lucky to go to school in the first place. My mom's the one to thank for that. She pushed for it because she knew it had been important to Lilah's mom. They'd been best friends before she died in childbirth.

"I guess he's running around hell now then."

"I suppose he is," she says. "But that wasn't my point. You should know, the people there still keep to themselves, but they talk. Heard all about you in high school. Heard a lot about Lilah and her dad too."

My lungs contract and all the air leaves them in a rush.

"So like I said, I need some money." Her voice has a smug tone now, as though she knows she's got me. And maybe she does, maybe she doesn't.

Confronting the inevitable, I ask, "How much are you looking for?"

"Thatta boy. I knew you'd come around. I'm thinking twenty thousand should get me by for a bit."

I know, without her saying it, that this is only the beginning of her shake-downs. "Why don't you tell me what it will take for you to go away forever?"

She chuckles and the sound is grating. "Feeling generous, are you?"

"I'm feeling like this is the last time I want to speak to you. What's it going to take to make that happen?"

I can almost envision her trying to figure out the best way to play this. She used to get a look on her face when I was younger, when she was trying to figure out how to deal with my dad in a way that wouldn't set him off.

"I don't want to be greedy, so how about three million?"

I squeeze my eyes shut. I've done well for myself—hell, I own a beach house in Malibu—but I can't pull three million out of my ass. It'd put a dent in my finances that I'd feel for sure. "I'll give you one point four. A hundred thousand for each decade you raised me."

"Two and a half," she counters.

"One and a half."

"Two million," she says, and I detect the growing excitement in her voice.

"One point seven and that's my final offer." I hold my breath and wait for her response.

"Done."

"If I give you this money, I don't ever want to hear from you again. I don't want you talking to the press—nothing."

"Sure, sure, whatever. When can you get it to me?" she asks, showing how eager she is.

"I mean it. I'm going to have my lawyer draft up an agreement that says that if you do any of those things, you have to pay me back in full immediately."

"Trust me, kiddo, you send me that money and I'm like the wind."

No surprise there. She was able to leave me when she had nothing. Why wouldn't she be able to do it when she's newly rich?

"It's going to take me some time to get my lawyers to draft an agreement and for me to get the money together. I'll call you next week to get the details from you."

"Don't take too long. I might get chatty."

I fist my hand over the steering wheel. "Don't forget your end of the agreement. I'll be in touch."

With that, I press the red circle on my phone and toss it onto the couch where it thankfully bounces across the cushions and doesn't fall to the floor.

"FUCK!"

"Is everything all right?"

I whip my head in the direction of the voice to find Adelaide standing in the entrance to the trailer, wide-eyed.

"What are you doing here?" I ask.

"I had a conference call with my manager when we were done shooting, so I took it in my trailer before I left for the night. Are you okay?"

I blow out a breath and run my hand through my hair. "Yeah. Sorry, I'm fine."

She gives me an unsure smile. "If you say so. Anything I can do to help?"

"No, really, I'm fine." I stand from the chair. "What did you think of Tripp last night?"

We haven't really had time to discuss last night. As soon as we arrived on set, we were both whisked off to makeup, and since then, we've always been around someone. This is the first time we've had any privacy today.

Adelaide steps farther into the trailer. "He was nice. I'm not sure there's a love connection there, but I appreciate you trying your best." She chuckles.

I shrug. "It was worth a shot. He's a nice guy and you're nice, so I thought maybe..."

"Nice guys are hard to find in this town, so I appreciate you pointing one out when you see him."

I smile, but I don't think it reaches my eyes. "You headed home now?"

She adjusts the strap of her bag on her shoulder. "Yeah, I think so. It's late, and even though we don't have an early call time tomorrow, I'm still kinda recovering from last night."

I chuckle. "I hear you. Tequila is not my friend."

"I guess that's why they call it To-Kill-Yah."

"True story." I shove my phone in my back pocket and reach for my keys and my wallet on the counter. "Come on. I'll walk you to your car."

"Thanks, I'd appreciate that." She smiles at me in a way that might be more than just a general appreciation of me doing a nice thing for her, but I ignore it. She knows how messed up my personal life is.

"About Lilah last night..." I say as we make our way out of the trailer.

Adelaide waves me off. "Don't worry about it. It's obvious she has issues." Judgment colors her tone, and I hate it.

"She's a good person."

"I just meant... I've heard the rumors, seen the press. I know she has some...."

I don't say anything to that because, how could I? It's the truth.

We reach her car, and she pulls her keys from her bag. "Anyway, I'll see you tomorrow, I guess?"

"I'll be here." We're back at the studio tomorrow to finish shooting the scene we started today.

"Okay then…" She unlocks her car and opens the door then tosses her bag across so that it lands on the passenger seat. "I didn't mean to upset you with what I said about Lilah."

I push my hands into the front pockets of my jeans. "It's fine. Nothing I'm not used to."

Her lips tip down at the corners.

"I'll see you tomorrow," I say, walking backward with a wave.

At the moment, people's perceptions of Lilah are the least of my problems. I have one point seven million dollars and a contract to get together.

LILAH

I stare at Jimmy while he sleeps. He looks so peaceful and relaxed. Meanwhile, my blood is on fire and adrenaline courses through my veins. After I arrived at my friends', I'd told them about my meeting with the House of Carlisle, and we celebrated the way only models can—with buckets full of champagne at the trendiest LA club and a nose full of cocaine.

The Uber back to Malibu cost me a fortune, but I wasn't up for crashing at someone's place tonight. I need to know what Jimmy meant when he said his mom called him.

Still, even in my state, I feel a small amount of remorse for having to disturb his peaceful sleep.

I slide under the covers with him and grip his strong shoulder, nudging him. "Jimmy, wake up." He doesn't twitch a muscle, so I do it again, this time with more force. "Jimmy, c'mon, wake up."

He groans and rolls toward me, his eyes slowly opening.

"We need to talk," I say, sliding up the bed to rest my back along his headboard.

"Are you okay?" He pulls himself up and runs a hand through his dark hair, yawning.

"Yeah, I'm fine." I run my hand down his arm, entwining my hand in his. "Why did your mom call?"

He blinks a few times. I've caught him off guard.

"What time is it?" he asks, glancing at the clock on his nightstand.

My gaze falls on it as well.

"Two thirty in the morning? Seriously, can't this wait until the morning?"

"You know it can't. You didn't return any of my texts today." I tighten my grip.

"I was busy on set." He yawns again.

"Just tell me why your mom called."

He's stalling, which is a horrible sign. He's hiding something, I know it.

"Are you fucked up right now?" he asks, swinging his legs around so his feet reach the floor at the side of his bed, disengaging from my hand.

"Just answer the damn question!" I say with more force.

Jimmy walks over to me and places his hands on my shoulders. "I shouldn't have said anything. I was drunk."

"You can't do that. You can't expect me to act like you didn't say it." I stare him in the eyes, willing him to tell me and not leave me in the dark.

He blows out a breath and drops his hands from my shoulders. "Maybe we should talk about this when you haven't been railing coke all night." He brushes by me and out into the hall toward the kitchen.

I have no argument, because if he's clued into my earlier activities tonight, there's no point in lying.

"Stop changing the subject. What's going on?" I stomp down the hallway, my sympathy over what the call did to him turns to anger over him treating me like a porcelain doll.

By the time I reach the kitchen, he's got a glass of water in his hand. I take the glass to kick away his distraction technique, but it slips from my fingers right before I can set it on the counter. The glass smashes on the hardwood, shattering into pieces and water puddles.

"For fuck's sake, Lilah!" Jimmy screams.

It's the first time he's yelled at me in a long time. Jimmy doesn't lose his patience with me. He's the most patient person I know, which means whatever is going on with his mom is bad.

Tears form in my eyes staring at the broken glass. I turn to head to the laundry room to get a broom to clean up the mess, but his hand wraps around my upper arm, stopping me.

"Be careful. Don't cut yourself."

I nod and slowly step backward, investigating the area I walk to make sure I don't step on any jagged glass. Once I've made it into the safe zone, I meet Jimmy's gaze.

He still stands near the island.

"Go have a shower and clean yourself up. I'm gonna clean this up, then we'll talk." The resigned tone in his voice says he's accepted that he'll have to share with me whatever is going on.

I nod slowly, my lips pressed together. I head down the hall to my room, not ready to hear what Jimmy has to say but knowing I have to.

* * *

I DRY off and put on my grey cotton sleep shorts and tank top and exit the bathroom to find Jimmy sitting in the chair in the corner of my room, staring straight ahead. I sit on the edge of the bed across from him, waiting for him to tell me.

His chin tips up and his sorrow-filled eyes meet mine. He doesn't want to tell me, and I fear I'm hurting him by forcing him to do so, but he cannot handle this news on his own. I don't break eye contact because I want to show him I'm strong enough. Strong enough to help him through this. God knows he's helped me through enough shit.

"My mom has been trying to track me down through Keane. He called to let me know, thinking it was a hoax. He said she'd called a bunch of times and demanded to speak to me because she was my mom."

My hand flies to my mouth. "What did Keane say?"

Jimmy's told every interviewer that his mom died, and no one has ever called that into question.

"I haven't filled him in on everything yet, but I will." His jaw clenches. "Anyway, long story short, she wants money."

Hate fills my chest and burns like an open sore. "I hope you told her to go fuck herself."

"I did at first." His voice is ominous, and it sends a chill down my spine.

"What changed?" I ask slowly.

"When she told me she'd gone back to the mountain and that people are talking, filling her in about what went down after she left." He stares into my eyes so I understand what he's talking about.

Of course I know what he's talking about. I might be a druggie, but I don't have amnesia.

I suck in a quick breath. "She doesn't know…"

He shakes his head. "I don't think so. But I don't want that to change, so I'm going to pay her."

I squeeze my eyes closed for a moment, hating that he has to do this while knowing he has no choice. It must kill him to give money to the woman who abandoned him. A woman who did nothing to help him achieve his found success.

"How much?" I whisper.

"It doesn't matter." He stands from the chair. "So there. Now you know."

I stare at the floor, unsure of what I can say. Another predicament I've put Jimmy in. If he hadn't… if I hadn't… he could have told her to fuck off.

I always liked Darla—until she left her son. With an abuser who beat him more often after she left. She wasn't *my* mother, but she was the only example I had of any kind of mother growing up. Sadly, I'd looked up to her.

"How can you be sure she doesn't know?" I ask.

"Just the feeling I got."

I bite my bottom lip and draw in short puffs of air.

Jimmy crouches in front of me with a hand on my thigh. "Lilah, it's going to be fine. We have nothing to worry about. I'm going to pay her, and she'll go away. End of story."

I want to believe him. I really do. But so often in my life, things don't go the way they should.

"Okay," I whisper, unable to meet his eyes.

He dips his head, not accepting my dismissal. "I mean it. Don't let this derail you. We both have good things happening for us right now. The past is far behind us."

My eyes snap to his gaze, and I nod to appease him.

"I'm not going to let anything happen to you." He leans forward, circling his arms around my stomach, his head falling into my lap.

I smooth my hand through his hair. The poor boy who freed himself from a life of poverty and abuse will never stop hurting.

He draws back and stares into my eyes. "Come sleep with me?"

I slide back onto the bed, pulling the covers down as an invitation.

A gentle, loving smile crosses his lips and he climbs in under my blankets. I hold him to me, his hands lazily running up and down my back, comforting me. I kiss his sweaty forehead and run my fingers through his hair. Eventually Jimmy's breaths slow and his hands stop running along my skin.

I shut my eyes, but visions of my life on that mountain roll like a film reel through my brain with no stop in sight.

I suck in deliberate breaths until sleep overcomes me.

Chapter Seventeen

JIMMY

"And cut," Scott says. "That was great, you two."

"Thanks," I say.

"Why don't you guys take a quick break while we set up our next shot?" he says.

"Perfect. I need to use the facilities," Adelaide says.

We smile at each other and she heads off, which is perfect for me.

I left Keane in my trailer when I was called to set early and I'm hoping he's still there so we can finish our discussion. I jog off the soundstage and step out into the bright California sunshine. I race up my trailer's steps and look inside to see Keane is right where I left him. Sitting on the leather couch, typing something into his phone. The man probably set up his office while I was away.

"Good, you're still here," I say, pulling a water from the fridge. "Want one?"

He shakes his head. "Of course I'm still here. It's not every day you call me down to set, insisting that we talk right away."

"True enough." I chug some of the water before catching the dribbles on my chin with my sleeve.

"What's happened? You knock up the director's daughter? Piss off Bernie Butler?" he asks, sliding his phone into his interior suit pocket.

"Not exactly."

His forehead creases. "What is it then?"

I bite the bullet because Keane is my guard. He'll be able to navigate us through the shitstorm of my life with a clear head. "How much do you know about my childhood?"

He shrugs. "Only what you've told me, which is next to nothing." Keane raises a brow.

"True enough."

I pause, unsure how much I should reveal. I trust Keane implicitly, but the last thing I want are looks of pity. Besides, it's not just me giving this confession. By proxy, it's Lilah too.

I explain my mother leaving and her reason for doing so. I leave out the dirt-poor living on a mountainside part of my history and I mention none of what Lilah had to deal with. Instead I focus on why my mom has been trying to contact me.

"Shit, man. That's harsh." He leans forward in his seat, his elbows on his knees.

"Agreed. But I'm not telling you this so you'll feel sorry for me. I need something from you."

"Say the word."

"I need a good lawyer who can draft an agreement that will force my mom to keep her trap shut if I give her what she wants. Then I want an investigator, someone who can keep their mouth shut too, to look into what she's been up to since she left." I set the bottle on the kitchen counter and lean back against it with my arms crossed.

"You sure you want to pay her? People don't usually go away after the first payment." He pulls out his phone because Keane works fast. A quality I hired him for.

"You let me worry about that. I'm going to make it worth her while." I push off the counter. "I had better get back to set."

Keane rises from the couch. "I'll take care of both for you."

I clap him on the shoulder. "This is why we work well together. You're a smart guy."

He rolls his eyes. "Yeah, yeah. I'll text you when I have something."

"Sounds good."

I head back down the trailer steps and out into the sunshine. Now all I have to do is get in touch with the bank and sell off some of my investments to get the cash for the payment.

Hopefully after she has her money, my mother will be the same way she was before—a distant memory.

Chapter Eighteen

LILAH

A couple of days pass without me seeing Jimmy. He's working constantly, but I think he's avoiding me too. Not that I care, with me drowning my anxiety and memories with alcohol and pills anyway. Yesterday I woke up on the couch at nine at night and couldn't recall how long I'd been there.

Darla's reappearance into Jimmy's life set off a string of reactions in me—panic, fear, self-loathing, and guilt. I trust that Jimmy will handle the situation, but a small part of me worries she won't go away.

My phone rings and I pick it up off the table, my vodka soda almost knocking over in the process. My phone fumbles in my hand. "Hello."

"It's Mina. Have I got news for you!"

Through my haze, I register that she's excited. "What's up?" I attempt not to slur, but I'm not sure I pull it off.

Shit. I'm more fucked up than I thought.

"The House of Carlisle called, and you got the job. You're their new rep for next year!"

"Really?" I sit up, my head circling until I zero in on the television to set myself straight.

"Believe it. They said they liked everything you had to say and want to be a part of launching you into the next phase of your career."

Her excitement should be intoxicating, and I'm excited, but that self-loathing side of me knocks down the happiness. Guilt arrives to our party right after. I owe Jimmy—again. I couldn't have done it without him prepping me.

"That's great."

"Listen, I can tell you're not clearheaded right now. You need to cut that shit out. You're representing the House of Carlisle now, and they won't put up with your antics."

"I got it, Mina. Jeez, relax." She's such a dictator. This is money in her pocket too.

"Lilah, this is a turning point for you if you let it. It's an amazing opportunity."

I stick my tongue out at the phone and raise my hand as if it's talking nonstop. "I said I got it."

She blows out a long-annoyed breath. "Well, make sure you do. Be at my office at nine a.m. the day after tomorrow to sign the papers."

"Aye, aye, Captain."

"Smartass," she mutters, and the line dies.

I toss my phone on the couch and lie down, a slow smile crossing my lips.

I did it. I'll be representing the new line of one of the fashion world's most prestigious houses. Tears spring to my eyes and my hands cover my mouth in disbelief. Is this how Jimmy felt when they asked him to be The Regulator?

I pick my phone up off the coffee table and click on Jimmy's name. He's the only one who will be as excited as me.

I hit the green circle and wait while it rings.

"Hey," his smooth timbre answers.

"You're not going to believe this. House of Carlisle chose me for their campaign!"

"Really? That's amazing! I told you you could do it." His smile comes through his words and spurs a happy dance inside me because, for once, I'm the one to bring him happiness.

"Thanks. You're always my biggest cheerleader."

"We should celebrate," he says.

Usually he's the one telling me to stop celebrating.

"What do you have in mind?" I ask.

"Why don't we head to Santa Monica Pier tonight after I'm done on set? It'll be like old times, back to where we started?"

I smile. It's our spot and I love that he suggested we go there. "I like it."

"Okay, I'll send a car for you and meet you there. That way you can ride back to the house with me."

"Perfect. What time should I be ready?" I ask.

"I'll text you about an hour before."

"'K, see you then."

I hang up with a sense of hopefulness brimming with possibility. Good things are happening. Maybe I need to learn to accept them. On my way to my room, I repeat my mantra—*don't fuck it up.*

Chapter Nineteen

JIMMY

"See you tomorrow," Adelaide says as we head to our cars in the studio parking lot.

"Yeah, sure thing." I pull my keys from my pocket.

"You sure you're okay?" she asks, stopping and hiking her purse farther up on her shoulder.

"I'm fine. Just have some things on my mind, that's all."

Namely my mom. The private investigator did some digging and found out that she bounced around a lot after she left my dad and me. Seemed to move from one man to the next and they all supported her. No record of any drug or alcohol abuse and no arrests. Meaning, she's not an addict or a criminal, just an opportunist.

Adelaide frowns. "Anything I can do to help?"

"Nah. It'll work itself out."

"Okay then, have a good night."

"You too." I walk over to my car, using the remote to unlock it.

Once I'm seated inside, I stare at my phone in my hand, attempting to rein in my temper over the fact that I have to pay off my own mother. I can't let her know how desperate I am for her to go away, otherwise she'll dig up more dirt and come back for more. I'm giving her enough to set her up for the rest of her life if she's not stupid with the money.

I press her number and listen to it ring through my car's Bluetooth.

"Hello?" she says on the second ring.

"Hey."

"Son, how are you doing?"

I cringe at her referring me to as her son. "I have the money for you."

A sigh of relief sounds through the speakers of my car. "I knew you'd come through."

"You didn't leave me much choice." My knuckles turn white as I grip the steering wheel.

"Now, now. Don't be like that, kiddo."

She's fucking delusional!

"I also had my lawyer draw up an agreement that you won't contact me or Lilah ever again. Nor will you speak to anyone else—including the press—about either of our pasts."

I had my lawyer throw Lilah in there as even more protection. I don't want her getting around the contract on a technicality, nor do I want her messing with Lilah. My mom's sudden reappearance is screwing with Lilah's head. Half the time, she's passed out when I return home. She's using more than she used to, and that's why I wasn't going to suggest the Regent to celebrate her contract with House of Carlisle.

"Still playing Superman to your Lois Lane, are you?" Her tone of boredom, like I'm a moron for watching out for Lilah, irritates me.

"Don't you worry about what I'm doing. Just know that if you violate the contract, not only will you owe me every penny back, but I'll sue you for extortion and you'll be eating cat food under a bridge for the rest of your life. You get me?"

"That's no way to speak to your mother!"

The bitch sounds offended. Hello? Left me with abusive father. I shake my head.

"You stopped being a mother to me the day you left. Get a lawyer, text me with the info, and I'll have the contract sent over. Once you sign it, I'll transfer the money. You've got forty-eight hours." I check my rearview mirror and back out of the parking spot.

"I know you're angry with me, but thank you," she says.

I hit End Call on the steering wheel, driving to the studio gates.

She'd better keep her word after she receives the money. If not, she's going to figure out how far I'll go to protect the life I'm building for myself and Lilah.

Chapter Twenty

LILAH

It's been two weeks since I got the contract for House of Carlisle and other than Jimmy's mom, things have been mundane in our lives. For Jimmy's birthday, we go to Santa Monica Pier. We spend the day together and have dinner. As a way to say thanks for everything he's done for me over the past months, I planned a surprise party at his place after dinner. We still have some time to kill until we can show up, so I suggest a walk on the beach.

We walk hand in hand away from the craziness of the pier, listening to the sounds of the waves hitting the shore and the kids' squeals from the rides in the distance.

"You should know that I settled all that shit with my mom. She won't be bothering me again."

My body tenses. "Really?"

He stops and turns to me. His hand cradles my cheek and he stares into my eyes. "She signed an agreement. She can't bother either one of us or talk to the press unless she wants to pay the money back. It's over and she's out of my...our lives for good."

My hand covers his and I squeeze. "I'm sorry."

He shrugs and kisses my forehead.

Before he can slide away, I wrap my arms around his waist and step into his warm chest. I want to say how sorry I am that his mom extorted money from him. That life isn't fair that his mom left him only to return because she wants a piece of what he's made of himself. Reassure him that I love him and he's an amazing man despite his horrible childhood. Jimmy doesn't like to show me any weakness and it's his birthday, so I don't want to rehash things with his mom or the past tonight.

We walk a bit more in silence.

"Did you have fun today?" I sit down in the sand, which is cool, and a welcome relief compared to how scorching hot it was earlier.

He sits beside me and takes my hand. I lay my head on his shoulder. "Of course I did. I spent it with my favorite person."

I smile. "I wanted to do something nice for you for your birthday. I'm glad you liked it."

"I want one present from you?"

I draw back, my eyebrows furrowing.

"I want us to be a real couple. No more of this on-again-off-again, are-we-or-aren't-we bullshit."

"Jimmy..." I wiggle my toes in the sand. He's caught me off guard.

"I want you to get clean so we can build a life together." There's a hint of desperation in his voice that I can't ignore. We're coming to a head and it's leaving my insides raw. He places his finger under my chin, forcing me to meet his gaze.

"Look at me. Just say you'll give us a chance. A *real* chance. Don't you love me the same way that I love you?"

My eyes burn from the tears building. "You know I do... but I can't do what you're asking." I blink, and a single tear rolls down my cheek, falling to the sand below.

"Can't get clean or can't be with me?" he whispers.

"Both." My chin falls to my chest and he drops his hand.

"That's bullshit," he says, pulling his legs to his chest and wrapping his arms around them. "If you wanted to, you could. You've never even tried. Am I not enough for you to try?"

"Of course you are. Don't you see? I'm broken. And if we're together, really together... I'll break you too."

He shakes his head, his vision focused on the dark ocean. "So, what's your plan? Are we just going to keep fucking when the mood strikes you? When you get scared I'm moving in my own direction, you'll pull me back in? How long will that last? Into our late thirties? Forties? Because at some point you're either going to kill yourself by overdosing or I'll move on. There're things I want in life, Lilah. Are you too messed up to realize that?"

His words are like a closed fist to the face, but they don't surprise me. Not really. They've been a long time coming, and Jimmy wore velvet gloves with me for years. The iron fist is due, but that doesn't change the fact I need Jimmy in my life and if we cross that line, he won't be anymore.

When I don't say anything, he grips my shoulders. "Tell me why. Tell me why you won't be with me after everything we've been through together. I know you love me. You can deny it if you wish, but I know you do."

I shake my head; my chest constricts and tears stream from my eyes. Why is he pushing this so hard? "I can't be with you because I care about you too much! We both know I'll mess it up, and once we've crossed that line, there's no going back. And then I won't have you in my life at all! I'll ruin you if I let you get any closer to the real me. I'll destroy you and break your heart and it'll never be the same between us again."

Tendrils of anger weave throughout my body. At the same time, relief winds through.

He pushes himself up off the sand and looks at me with his arms out at his sides. "Are you fucking blind? You're already gutting me here. Things are already changing between us and I know you feel it too."

I grab my purse from beside me and stand as well, meeting him head-on. "Things don't have to change! You're the one who's trying to change them."

"Don't you ever get tired of this shit? Of running from all your problems? Of drowning them with alcohol and drugs? Haven't you figured out yet that that doesn't work?"

My hand raises. His vision shifts to my open palm and back to me. I lower it knowing that as bad as I want to slap him, I never will.

"You don't know what you're talking about," I snap.

"Hand me your purse." Jimmy stretches his hand out between us. "Give it to me."

"Why?" I step back, feeling as though I'm back in my child-hood bedroom and the walls are slowly closing in around me.

"Give it to me." He leans forward and reaches behind me to grab it.

"No!"

I don't have time to move out of the way before he springs forward and snatches it from my hands. I reach to get it back, but he holds it up over his head. I jump up and down, trying to snag the strap, then I pull on his bicep, but he's got six inches and a hundred pounds on me. I stop my hysterics and stand in the sand with my arms crossed, watching as he opens it and roots through my belongings.

"Christ, you've got an entire pharmacy in here." He tosses bottles to the sand, one after the other. "I thought you said you were cutting back on all this shit?" He runs a hand through his hair, pulling at the strands.

The anger inside me reaches a boiling point. "Fuck you! You have no right to judge me. I wouldn't be like this if it wasn't for you."

Jimmy's face drops. The smallest hint of guilt and regret flash in his eyes before anger slashes all his features.

The second the words left my mouth, I regretted them. But I won't take them back. I won't show an ounce of remorse.

"That's low," he grinds out. "You know if I could take it back I would."

Back when we were teens in Virginia, Jimmy dealt in order to make money. He'd head into town on foot, or hitchhike, whatever it took in order to sell to the townies. It's how we paid for our bus tickets to LA in the first place. It's also how I was introduced to weed, which eventually moved to coke and pills.

Jimmy was able to take them or leave them, but I instantly craved the sweet relief from the thoughts and memories I'd regurgitate in my head over and over. I know he feels guilty for it, I know that on some level he blames himself, but we've never discussed it and I've never gone so low as to use it against him.

Until now.

I'd still have my demons regardless of whether he'd put the first joint in my hand and I still would've found a way to drown them out. But he's the one who's pressing the issue about us.

"It's not low, it's true. If it weren't for you, I never would have been introduced to that world, so don't sit on your high horse and judge me. You're not exactly squeaky clean yourself," I spit out.

From his scrunched-up forehead, I'd say he's not sure if I'm referring to the drugs now or something more. Does it really matter?

"I did that for you. I had no choice." His hands clench into fists at his sides and the artery in his neck throbs. For the first time, I might have pushed him too far.

Regret douses the fire raging inside me. "Jimmy—"

"Thanks for a great fucking birthday." He pushes off the sand and walks toward the parking lot.

I want to chase him and apologize.

I'm trying to make him understand.

I didn't mean those things, but he cornered me. What did he expect me to do? Admit that I might have a problem and he's not enough for me to stop using? That would hurt him more.

* * *

WE RIDE BACK to his place in silence, and though I wish there wasn't a house full of people waiting, it's the most accessible way to tie one on and forget all this shit.

We'll make up. We always do. But I can't deny I'm a little scared. This fight felt different. He openly called me an addict and I blamed him for my being one.

Jimmy pulls into his driveway, slams on the brakes, and exits the vehicle without a word. I follow him, happy to see that even after everything else went wrong, at least the partygoers manage to pull off the surprise.

He unlocks and whips open the door while I'm still ten paces behind. Instead of witnessing it, I hear "Surprise" yelled.

He stops in his tracks, turning to look at me, a half scowl marring his handsome face. "Did you know about this?"

"I planned it."

I step past him without another word and head straight to the kitchen to pour myself a giant tumbler of the first bottle I see. Jimmy gets caught up saying hello and accepting congratulations from his friends.

I pour whiskey into one of the glasses and sit on the kitchen island stool. I slide a hand into my purse and pull a pill from the inside pocket, then I toss it to the back of my throat and chase it with whiskey.

I sense someone's eyes on me and glance to my right to find Jimmy's coworker, Adelaide, watching me. I hold her gaze for a moment, adding no friendliness to my own, until she looks away.

Jimmy hugs her, and she wishes him a happy birthday. He smiles and shoots her his Jimmy smile. Not one of his practiced, James-red-carpet ones. They must be getting chummy.

I pour more whiskey and chug it, relishing the burn as the alcohol slides down my throat into my stomach.

Might as well enjoy the party.

Chapter Twenty-one

JIMMY

I take a hit off the joint and pass it back to Tripp in the lounger next to me by the pool. My birthday party has been in full swing for a few hours now. Everyone is having a blast, especially Lilah. She's the life of the party. She always is, with a little help from her best friends—alcohol and drugs.

I've only seen her drinking tonight, but I'm not naïve enough to think she isn't on something. Lately, I see her on something more than sober. Downers, uppers, party drugs... whatever. She's not particular. Anything to alter her natural state.

"You want some more, man?" Tripp holds the joint out in front of me.

"Nah, I'm good."

I'm hoping the joint will mellow me. My anger with Lilah from our conversation at the pier isn't fading and we're not done discussing us, but it's none of these people's business. My breaking point is close, I'm ready to blow, but still... she's Lilah.

Lilah steps out of the sliding glass doors, heading to the other side of the deck with a group of people.

"You wouldn't mind if I asked Adelaide out then?" he asks.

"Knock yourself out. But I don't want to be in the middle of any lovers' quarrel and I don't want it to affect me on set, so don't fuck her over."

Tripp doesn't exactly do commitment, but Adelaide is a big girl. She can figure that out for herself.

"I'm just messing with you." He claps his hand on my shoulder and shakes me. "I was just testing the waters, seeing if you had a thing for her."

My forehead wrinkles. "Why would I have a thing for her?"

He inhales another hit of the joint. "You two just seem like you get along, that's all."

"Well, she's cool and we've developed a friendship, working together these past couple of months. But we're only friends, nothing more."

"Does she know that?" He laughs, smoke trailing out of his mouth.

"What's that supposed to mean?" I sip my whiskey.

Tripp shakes his head and looks at me as though I'm a dumb fuck. "I swear you're clueless half the time. She obviously likes you, man. Just watch how she looks at you."

"Bullshit."

He chuckles again. "I'm telling you, she does."

From the other side of the deck, Lilah lets loose a loud laugh and places her hand on Jerome, who's apparently a stand-up comic tonight. Jerome is a decent enough guy. I've known him for a couple years, since we worked on a smaller production together. But seeing Lilah with her hands on him has my fist clenching in my lap.

"What's going on with you and Lilah?" Surprisingly, Tripp's voice is void of the usual derision it holds when he mentions her.

"What do you mean?" I sip my drink again and shift in my seat to get more comfortable.

"It's obvious you two are avoiding each other. What gives?"

I'm not in the mood to get into it with him over Lilah tonight. I've had enough bullshit for one birthday, thanks.

When I don't answer, Tripp shifts in his seat and faces me. "Look, I'll admit I'm not her biggest fan, but it's not because I don't think she's a decent person. I just think she's needs to get her shit together before she drags you down with her. That's all." He tips his beer to his mouth. I open my mouth to respond, but he puts a hand up between us before I can speak. "I know, I know, she's had a hard life, I have no idea what she's been through, blah, blah. Well, let me tell you, my life wasn't a fucking picnic growing up either, but you do what you have to in order to get past it."

Listening to him voice all the excuses I've made for Lilah over the years brings the anger back to the surface. For the first time, I hear how pathetic I sound and what a fucking idiot I am for chasing a girl who I've done the unthinkable for and she still doesn't want to be with me.

"Like bang groupies on tour buses and backstage?" I make light of his words, not wanting to further deteriorate my mood at my own party.

He claps a hand on my shoulder again and shakes me. "Now you're getting the idea! Come on tour with me and work her out of your system." He laughs, but his offer is tempting.

"Us actors aren't like you rock stars. We don't have the luxury of being in a different city every night."

He grins. "True dat. The best part about being a musician is that you're leaving town the next morning. No chance of developing a stage-five clinger."

We laugh together and sip our drinks.

"Any idea when you're headed back out on tour?"

"Nah, man. I've been writing a bit lately, but nothing is really gnawing on me and pushing me into the studio, you know? Until it does, there'll be no new album and no tour." He leans back into the lounger and glances around the patio. "Until then, I'll have to settle for LA pussy and hope I don't attract any bat-shit-crazy girls."

I roll my eyes and finish my drink. We sit in comfortable silence for a bit, but my gaze keeps lingering on the group of people Lilah's sitting with. No matter how badly I don't want to be reminded of her rejection, I can't seem to stop myself from looking at her.

Maybe I do understand more about addiction than I thought.

LILAH

I felt Jimmy watching me as I laughed with Jerome. All night, we've played a game of cat and mouse, catching each other stealing glances at one another, but not speaking. I'm confident that we'll be made up by tonight.

Right now, I'm the good-time girl and fucked up enough to push everything Jimmy said earlier to the back of my mind. I miss him though, and the more I drink, the more I want him.

"Feel like going for a dip?" I ask Jerome.

His gaze meets mine, his eyes hooded. "Damn straight. We doing this with or without clothes?"

I laugh and lean forward to touch his shoulder. "Let's start with our clothes on."

Without waiting for him, I scream, run, and jump into the pool.

He follows me, doing a cannonball into the deep end. The minute he surfaces, he swims over to me, but I escape his grasp, playing a game of keep away, garnering the attention of everyone on the deck.

Jerome grips my wrist and tugs me back into his body. I laugh as he raises me up over his shoulder before tossing me back in. I sputter a bit as I stand and pull my hair off my face. A couple of other people jump into the pool, fully clothed, to join the fun.

My eyes seek out Jimmy sitting in a lounger. Adelaide is sitting where Tripp was moments ago. Jealousy flares so deep, I swear if you cut me open, my blood would be green.

I have no right. I gave him his walking papers hours earlier at our sacred place.

* * *

HOURS LATER, Jimmy and I have flipped spots. I'm on the pool deck, my clothes almost dry, and Jimmy is horsing around in the pool. He and of his friends are playing a drunk version of Marco Polo. Adelaide is with him. Of course she is. She hasn't left his side all night.

I hate the way she looks at him.

It's pitiful really.

He catches her because she purposely moved into a corner where she couldn't escape. He wraps his hands around her and she laughs and squirms in his hold, loving every minute of it, I'm positive.

Bitch.

"Okay, Adelaide, you're it!" one of the other guys calls.

"I'm gonna get myself a drink. Anyone else?" Jimmy asks, swimming over to the stairs.

No one takes him up on his offer. Adelaide stares at his bare chest and every other part of his body while he emerges from the water. He grabs a towel to dry off and talk to Tripp for a minute before heading inside.

I glance at the passed-out Jerome next to me. *Lightweight.*

I walk through the sliding glass doors, heading inside.

Jimmy's not in the kitchen or the living room, so I walk down the hallway to his bedroom. He's tossing the wet shorts over his glass shower wall.

Perfect.

I close the door behind me, securing the lock.

He turns around. "What are you doing?"

"Do you care about her?" I ask, pulling my shirt over my head and stepping in his direction.

His gaze darts to my black lace bra. "You know I don't. Not like that."

"How do you like her then?" I ask, slipping my skirt over my ass so it slides down my thighs and pools at my feet.

"As a friend." He swallows hard, his eye scorching the closer I get.

I'm drunk on the power surging through my veins. For most of my life, I've been powerless. It's only during times like this, when I can bend a man to my will using my body, that I have control over what happens.

I shrug, stepping out of my skirt. "We're just friends."

"We've never just been friends and you know it."

"So there's nothing between you two?"

We're almost chest to chest. I've purposefully left an inch of separation between our bodies. His body heat projects toward me like a magnet drawing me closer.

"I swear to you, there's not." He sticks out his pinkie finger.

I wrap my own digit around his and the panic that consumed me watching the two of them eases out of my pores. He flings our hands to the side and wraps his arms around me, dragging me against him. His lips press to mine.

Our kiss is passionate but laced with anger as our tongues duel for control. His hands run up and down my back until he unclips my bra, slides his hands down my back, and squeezes my ass until a satisfying moan slips from my lips.

Just as we're getting started, he rips his lips from mine. "Don't you ever try to manipulate me with your body again. You already own my heart and soul."

I have no time to respond before his lips are back on mine with fire and fury. I clutch at his skin, trailing my nails down his back, claiming him as mine. We kiss, and Jimmy works my bra straps off my shoulders before inching back from me so the delicate fabric can slip to the floor between us. My hard nipples press into his muscular chest and a groan from deep in his throat escapes. He's always loved the moment our chests first meet when we undress.

His hand roams between us, dipping past my panties to find me hot and wet. His groan turns to a growl. I moan as he uses his index finger to play with my nub in slow circles. The sensation is too overwhelming and my knees buckle, but Jimmy uses his strength to keep me upright.

He pushes one finger in, then two, while his thumb manipulates my clit. There's no tenderness in his actions. His movements are raw and uncoordinated and desperate. I hold his eyes as he studies my face while manipulating my body. My muscles tense in anticipation of my orgasm, but he doesn't relent, working me endlessly.

Just when I can't handle any more, just when I'm shaking my head and begging him to stop, he pushes down on my clit with his thumb and I gasp, detonating like he wishes. White heat races up my spine and between my legs. I am everything and nothing all at once as I scream his name. He rips my panties down my legs, lifts me by my ass, presses my back to the wall, and pushes inside me.

"Why do you have to always push me?" he roars in my ear, driving into me.

He removes one hand from my waist and forces my chin up to make me look at him. He stills inside me, waiting for an answer.

But I don't have one to give.

Recognition flashes in his eyes when he realizes he's not going to get an answer from me. "Sometimes I think I hate you as much as I love you."

His words cut deep, and a small part of me welcomes the sick sense of satisfaction when they leave his lips. If there's hate, it will be easier for him to leave me one day.

He thrusts inside me again, over and over, with anger and desperation driving him. Jimmy fucks me as though I'm a whore who means nothing to him, rather than the girl he's saved his entire life.

His face tucks into my neck and I grip his shoulder, my other hand clutching at the hair at the back of his head while he pounds into me. There's no concern for my own pleasure. He's taking what he needs, and I don't fight him because isn't this what I was trying to push him to do in the first place?

With a few uncoordinated movements and one final thrust, he empties himself into me. His cock jerks inside me as he rides out his climax.

Neither of us moves or says a word. Our heavy breathing is the only sound, the scent of our sex the only smell. It's the messed-up relationship between Jimmy and me.

Once he regains his normal breathing, he pulls out of me and gently sets me on the floor. He doesn't say a word and doesn't look at me while he swipes a new pair of shorts out of his dresser and steps into them.

For the first time, it's awkward after we have sex. I'm not left with the security of love and feeling cared for and wanted. I feel used and cheap and dirty. Three things I have *never* felt in Jimmy's presence.

Covering my breasts with one arm, I retrieve my undergarments from the floor. He waits until I'm fully dressed to speak.

"I think it's best if you leave," Jimmy says in a flat voice.

My blood, heavy and thick, slows in my veins.

"Okay." I turn and leave.

"I think…"

The pain in his voice is the only reason I turn back.

He stares at me with wetness in the corners of his eyes, wearing his pain as clearly as if it were a shirt. My very transparent Jimmy, vulnerable in front of me.

"I think it's better if you don't come back." He squeezes his eyes shut and runs a hand through his hair, shaking his head to himself.

Oxygen sucks from my lungs and I stagger back a step. "Wh-what?"

He opens his eyes and his expression is a mix of disappointment, desperation, hurt, and anger. A complexity of emotions I know well from my own existence. "Everyone is right. You'll ruin my life if I let you."

"You don't really mean that," I whisper.

But he does. Otherwise there would be no hurt and disappointment in his eyes. He means every word. I've pushed him to his final breaking point, strung him along for too long, dangled the carrot long enough.

"I do mean it. For most of my life, I've tried to fix you. And I'm tired. So tired." His shoulders sag. "I can't do it anymore. I can't be your Mr. Fix-It. I can't be the one to clean up your messes. I can't be the person who cares more about you than you care about yourself. It's too painful to watch you spiraling to nothing."

"But I love you." The words slip out. Words I've held off saying to him for most of my life for fear that saying them would strip him away from me.

"How could you possibly love me? You don't even love yourself."

I laid myself out and he threw my words back at me.

Well, I'm not going to stay and fight for someone who wants me gone.

I turn, and I run.

Chapter Twenty-three

JIMMY

"I can't be sure, but was that a smile?" Adelaide raises her eyebrows.

I push her shoulder lightly, and she loses her footing for a moment.

"What? It's been a long time since I've seen you smile unless the script dictated it."

She's not wrong, but I roll my eyes. It's been a month since I kicked Lilah out of my house. The longest we've ever gone without speaking. Sure, we've gotten into some rip-roaring fights in the past, but one of us always came crawling back.

That's not the case this time. As painful as it was to speak the words, I meant them. It took way too long to reach the conclusion that I can't save her—she has to want that herself.

Life hasn't been easy since then. Not an hour goes by when I'm not thinking of her and wondering what she's doing. Whether she's taking care of herself, supporting herself, and where is she living? Will the questions and concerns for Lilah endlessly haunt me?

"I haven't been that bad, have I?" I ask, attempting to act normal. I grab a cookie from the craft service table.

Adelaide picks up an apple and shrugs. "You haven't been unbearable, but it's been clear that something is bothering you. Want to talk about it?"

I sip my water. "It's been tough. We've known each other forever."

Her lips turn down at the corners. "I'm sorry. I've lost a lot of friends due to this business."

"Yeah." I look at my water bottle, tilt it to my lips, and finish it. "It was a long time coming." I crush the bottle in my hand and shoot it into the recycling can.

"Maybe you guys will sort out your differences." She reaches across the table and places her hand on mine.

It's a purely platonic move, but I'm man enough to admit that having someone comfort me feels good. What I don't tell Adelaide is Lilah is, or was, my family.

"Maybe." I shoot her a smile that says I doubt she's right. "The ball is in her court."

Adelaide nods, probably understanding the undercurrent of what I'm not saying. Or maybe not. Who knows? The more I've gotten to know her, it's clear that she's the complete opposite of what this town chews up and spits out. God only knows how Adelaide remains intact in Hollywood. This city is full of sharks ready to devour anyone at the first sign of weakness.

"Well, I hope it all works out," she says with sincerity and finishes her apple.

One of the production assistants approaches our table. "Mr. Butler is here and wants to see you both in Jimmy's trailer."

What the hell is Bernie doing here?

"Okay, we'll be right there," I say.

The production assistant nods and scampers away.

"Any idea what that's all about?" I ask Adelaide.

Her eyes are wide with reservation. "None."

"Well, let's get this over with." I rise from the table, taking another water with me, and wait while Adelaide throws away her apple core. "I don't like this," I say to Adelaide as we walk across set.

Nothing good ever comes when Bernie makes a surprise visit.

"I'm going to head to the bathroom quick. I'll meet you at my trailer." I step toward the bathroom.

"Oh, I'll wait." She stops alongside me.

"No, go, Adelaide. I'll only be a few minutes and you know Bernie, he doesn't like to be kept waiting."

She glances around and then leans toward me. "I'd just prefer to go with you."

The scared look in her eye clears up what she's saying under her words. "No problem. I'll be a few minutes."

Her smile isn't as big as I'm used to seeing, but she pulls out her phone while I disappear into the bathroom.

* * *

WE STEP INTO THE TRAILER, and Bernie sits with his arms and legs spread like king of the fucking world. Which I suppose in this town, he is.

"There's the guy who's going to make this studio a shit-ton of fucking money when this movie releases."

"Hey, Bernie. How are you?" I sit in the chair across from him.

Bernie motions for Adelaide to do the same, though he says nothing to her. "Never been better. I've looked at the dailies, and things look like they're going well. Chemistry is sizzling."

He sounds way too happy. Did they hire a double?

"Yeah, Scott seems happy with them, don't you think, Adelaide?" I turn my head in her direction, and she glances at me, nodding silently.

"And how are you two getting on?" Bernie points between us.

"No problems on my end," I say.

"What about you?" Bernie asks Adelaide the first question since she walked in.

"James has been really easy to work with." Her voice sounds shaky. If I didn't know better, I'd say she's scared.

"Great, great." He claps once and somehow manages to lift his rotund frame up off the couch. "I got some news yesterday, and I've been trying to figure out a way to make the problem go away." He paces the length of the trailer, his forearms resting on his stomach, his fingers steeped.

Unease creeps up my spine. "What's up?"

"I got word that Vanguard Studios is putting out a new super-hero series based on Malcolm Treader's books. They're fast-tracking release so it beats our movie to the box offices."

Malcolm Treader's books are a huge hit and sat on the *New York Times* bestseller list for close to a year, so I'm not surprised that a studio optioned the rights and is making a movie. The timing couldn't be worse though.

"Shit. That's not good. What do you have in mind?" I ask.

"I've already talked to Scott and the production team, and there's no way we can move up our release and do the film justice. So we're going to have to be creative. Creative enough to make sure our movie appeals to the public more than Vanguard's does."

I glance at Adelaide. She sits quietly, watching with wide eyes as Bernie paces in front of us.

"What's your plan?" I ask.

Bernie stops between Adelaide and me. "An on-set romance. Not original, but nothing grabs people's attention and gets them talking more than a romance between costars."

I stare at him. Foolishly, I expected him to say they were going to double the marketing budget or bring in a big-hitter to do a cameo.

"You want Adelaide and I to date?" My forehead creases, and I glance away from Bernie to see Adelaide's reaction.

"Date. Don't date. Fuck. Don't fuck. I don't really care. But as far as the world is concerned, I want you two to appear like the happiest fucking celebrity couple out there. I want the paps making up a stupid celebrity couple moniker for you two, and I want teenage girls scribbling Mrs. James Crawford in their notebooks, you follow?" He crosses his arms and stares down at us. It's an order, not a request.

We both nod.

"What is it you want us to do exactly?" I ask.

He tosses his hands up in the air. "You don't have to do much now, but maybe get coffee or let Adelaide pick out an outfit for you on Rodeo Drive. Let them think something's happening even if it isn't. But closer to Vanguard's release, you'll have to be been seen together a lot. Let the press trickle questions in their magazines, on their blogs, on their shows about whether you are or aren't dating. Eventually, let them snap a picture of you two kissing to really fuel the rumors. It's not rocket science, for fuck's sake."

"How long are we supposed to pretend?" I ask, since Adelaide is strangely mute.

Bernie shrugs. "Who knows? We'll see how it goes. Just wanted to make sure we have an understanding."

I blow out a breath and push my hand through my hair. Though I hate the idea of pretending anything to the press, he has a point. Couples sell movies. Whichever film is able to capitalize on the organic interest of the press and the public's appetite for scandal will come out on top. Hollywood is a strange place, where it's good for business if people are talking behind your back, and it doesn't matter whether it's truth or lies.

"I assume this isn't up for discussion?" I ask, looking at Adelaide, who's playing with her hands in her lap.

"There's nothing to discuss," Bernie snipes. "We've all got a lot riding on this film and this has to happen. You're both the leads."

My jaw tics, but I nod.

"Adelaide?" Bernie questions.

She looks up from her lap and nods.

"Good." He slides his hands over his stretched-out shirt. "I'm glad to see that we're all on the same page. Go grab a couple of meals together off set, make sure the press can easily snag a couple shots, and the rumor mill will start."

Adelaide and I are silent as he walks past the kitchen to the door of the trailer.

The sun streams in as he stops on the first step, looking at us over his shoulder. "This does mean that any fucking you two do with other people needs to be behind closed doors."

My thoughts go to Lilah. Old habits die hard, I guess. I still hope she'll get her shit together so that we can be a couple.

"Understood." I nod, and the door slams behind him.

Moments later, a production assistant pops his head in the door. "You're both needed on set."

"Coming." I step in front of Adelaide and offer her my hand.

She accepts it with a small smile, and I lift her from the chair.

Once we're out of the trailer and walking back to set, I look at her. "You were quiet in there."

"He gives me the creeps. You know how he is with women. I prefer not to be on his radar."

It's true. Bernie does have a reputation for being a misogynistic ass. I've been at parties and heard the way he speaks. He openly talks about hooking up with various women, even though he's married.

"Gotcha. I think it's best to stay off his radar—man or woman."

"Agreed. What do you think of his plan?" She stops walking and looks at me, her big hazel eyes wide with uncertainty.

"If I'm honest, I don't like it." Her expression falls, and I'm quick to correct my mistake. "I don't mean because it's you. It has nothing to do with you. I just don't like pretending for the press. Lies always catch up to you."

That fateful night on a Virginia mountain gnaws at me and I suppress a shiver.

"I get it. I mean, how do you think I feel? I have to pretend to be involved with James Crawford." She rolls her eyes playfully.

I push her shoulder gently. "Imagine if Gregory Fox was the one costarring with you."

Gregory is a rough-looking actor in his late fifties who's well-known for being a little too handsy with his costars.

Adelaide throws her head back and laughs. "Yeah, I guess it could be worse." We stare at each other for a minute before she looks away and gestures to the large building in front of us. "I guess we should go."

"Yeah, I guess so. I'm sure we'll find some way to stand being around each other even more than we already are."

"I hope so, or these next few months are going to be hell."

She punches my shoulder. I grimace and grip the spot in mock pain.

"Let's go, you." She pulls me forward by my hand until my feet start moving.

I follow her through the door, and a small part of me feels guilty that I enjoy how easy it is to be with Adelaide.

Chapter Twenty-four

LILAH

Jimmy's been spotted around town with his costar. The press snapped pictures of them eating together. They were even out dancing together at the Regent.

Jimmy.

Jimmy.

Jimmy.

He's all I can think about. It's been two months since I've seen or spoken to him, but he's still on my mind every day.

Wondering what he's doing. Who he's doing. Wondering if he's falling in love with his costar and agonizing over how easily he replaced me.

I toss the stupid tabloid on the table in front of me and grab the half-full bottle of vodka.

I've been crashing with Derek since Jimmy kicked me out of his life. It's not that I can't afford a place of my own—I can. As much of a mess as I am, the House of Carlisle pays well, and I've managed to book another couple gigs too. We've shot the spring campaign, and we're due to shoot the summer one in a couple days.

I'm at Derek's because I don't want to be alone. Jimmy was such a huge part of my life and then—poof—he was gone. Being alone leaves me too much time to think, too much time to spiral.

My grip on the bottle tightens and I chase my desperate thoughts with another punch of vodka to my system.

"Hey, what're you doin'?" Derek steps into the small living room from the bedroom.

"Getting drunk." I offer him the bottle.

He snatches the bottle and downs a healthy swig, but instead of handing it back to me, he puts it on the table. "I'm gonna chase the dragon, you in?" He tosses the tinfoil and heroin on the table.

I read online that Jimmy and Adelaide are walking the red carpet and presenting an award together at the Oscars tonight. It's not atypical for actors of what is expected to be next year's big hit to present at this year's awards ceremonies, but I know it's more than that. If I wasn't such a masochist, I wouldn't watch, but I have a sick fascination with torturing myself. And I want to see Jimmy, so I know I'll watch.

I glance at the instruments of my destruction on the table, desperate for the oblivion they'll give me from this empty feeling inside me. It won't ever leave. If you scrape through one layer of the black sludge that coats my insides, there's only another waiting. "Sure, why the hell not?"

Derek sets up everything, spreading out the piece of aluminum foil with a slight curve to it. He places the heroin on top and passes me the straw. He flicks the lighter and heats the bottom of the foil while I wait with the straw. When the heroin bubbles and vapor wafts off the top, I use the straw to chase it around, sucking hard to inhale.

I pass the straw to Derek and grab the lighter, moving it around underneath the foil. He sucks in a hit. When the heroin is burned off, the straw and the foil drop between us onto the old couch. I toss the lighter toward the coffee table, but I miss. I fall back into the cushions and close my eyes, letting the dragon consume me.

My head feels light and my limbs tingle. My chest is heavy, and I feel as if I'm floating on a cloud. Finally, peace.

Sometime later, I feel hands on me and I stir, cracking open one eye. Derek's hands are on either side of my leggings, pulling them down my legs. I shift and attempt to pull my legs up and away from him, but they're heavy and my arms are as useful as Jell-O.

Derek's glazed eyes soak me in. "C'mon, let's have a little fun. I love fucking when I'm high." His gnarled teeth peek out with his smile.

I lift my hips so he can slide my leggings and underwear down my legs.

"Condom," I rasp, my eyes closing as another wave of oblivion crashes over me.

"You got nothing to worry about," he says, unbuckling his jeans.

I manage to get my arm out to place a hand on his chest. "Condom."

He glares at me with narrowed eyes for a moment before standing and almost cracking his head on the television. He walks a few steps to the bedroom door, and my eyes close again.

Jimmy and I aren't a thing anymore, but it's still the one promise, probably the only one, I won't break.

I must have passed out, because the next thing I know, he's pushing inside me. Panic flares inside me for a moment but retreats when I feel a condom between us.

I'm in the same position on the couch as I was before, my legs spread wide, my ass at the edge of the cushion. I look at Derek as he moves in and out of me, and I close my eyes, waiting for it to be over. I lay there, limp and numb, while he uses me for his pleasure. He squeezes my breast so hard I cringe.

I let him use me. My body is all I'm good for anyway. All I've ever been good for.

He finishes with a disgusting groan and one final thrust. Derek stands, pulls the condom off himself, and chucks it in the garbage.

My eyes drift closed again, trying to find the place where nothing matters, where my loneliness lives.

"I've gotta do a pick-up. Be back later."

Derek's voice stirs me, and I open my eyes. He's dressed again, standing by the apartment door with his hand around the handle. I'm still on the couch with my legs spread, bare from the waist down.

"Do what you gotta do," I say.

He leaves, and I lay there for another minute, coming down from my high. Eventually I sit up and pull on my leggings, not bothering with my underwear. I spot my phone between the couch cushions and check the time.

The red-carpet event for the Oscars already started. I reach for the channel changer and click on the TV. It's seen better days, but it works, and I flick through the channels.

I grab the bottle of vodka that's still on the table and nestle into the corner of the couch. Ten minutes go by as the usual celebrity A-listers and their dates stop to talk to the interviewers about what they're wearing and how they're here to support blah-blah-blah.

I chuckle when an actor everyone adores steps out of his limo, because I know for a fact we shared a dealer at one point.

The bottle tips to my lips when I spot *him* in the background. The air rushes from my lungs. My heart shrivels. My eyes sting.

Jimmy looks so good. Healthy and happy. A part of me is glad he's doing so well, and another part of me rages over the fact that he can so easily move on without me, while I sink further and further into a black hole.

I am nothing.

I am no longer anything to anybody.

He was all I had left, and now he's got the girl of his dreams.

I chug gulps of vodka as the realization hits me. My stomach churns at the invasion of alcohol, but I ignore the choking reflex, my gaze transfixed over the shoulder of the woman being interviewed. My grip on the neck of the bottle tightens while I watch Jimmy lead Adelaide along the red carpet, his hand on her lower back.

I stalk the area, begging cameramen who can't hear me to turn one way or another, watching for a glimpse of Adelaide's red dress in the background of every interview.

Eventually, the happy couple walks past the man interviewing everyone and stops for their turn. She smiles at Jimmy as though she's had him. Of course she has. They're a couple. He's waking her up with kisses to her shoulder blades. Making her eggs. She's the deserving one.

I hold my breath and tears prick the corners of my eyes.

"Everybody, I'm excited to get to talk to James Crawford and Adelaide Sheridan, the costars of *The Regulator*, which is set to release next year. How are you both?" the host asks.

"Good," Jimmy says with the most charming of smiles. "A little overwhelmed." He glances behind them at the throng of people and chuckles. "But excited to be here."

"How about you, Adelaide?" The host puts the microphone in front of her.

The camera zooms in. She's stunning in her red gown and large diamond drop earrings. Her hair flows in soft waves down her back, and her smoky eye makeup is sexy and alluring.

And she's the one standing beside Jimmy, being interviewed on the red carpet.

I always thought it'd be me.

I lift the bottle to my lips. Alcohol slides down my throat.

"This is my first time attending, so I'm a little nervous. I think I need a drink."

The three of them laugh.

"Well you don't look nervous. In fact, you look gorgeous tonight in this dress. Tell the viewers at home who you're wearing."

Jimmy's face lights up with pride as he holds her hand above her head, and she spins before she tells the host about who fashioned her look for the night.

"Doesn't she look stunning?" Jimmy replaces his hand on her lower back.

She'll survive without your touch for two seconds, Jimmy.

The host nods while Adelaide lovingly stares at him and smiles with a twinkle in her eyes.

"Speaking of..." the host says. "You know I can't have the both of you here without asking the obvious. There're rumors out there about an on-set romance between the two of you. Can you confirm for us here tonight whether or not that's the case?"

Adelaide smiles and defers to Jimmy.

I stand with the vodka clutched in my hand, waiting on tenterhooks to hear his answer.

"Nice try." Jimmy winks. "I prefer to keep my private life just that—private."

The host waves him off. "Okay, okay. You can't blame a guy for trying."

Jimmy smiles. Even drunk and stoned, I don't miss Adelaide looking at him as though he's a god.

"How's filming going? I hear you guys are almost ready to wrap it up?"

"We've got a few weeks left before everything will move to post-production," Adelaide answers.

"And how has it been working together? This is the first time you've worked together, am I right?" the host asks.

"It is," Jimmy agrees. "Working with Adelaide has been fantastic. She's a complete professional and treats everyone on set with respect. It's been a great experience."

The host moves the mic in front of Adelaide. "I agree. I wasn't sure what to expect when I signed on to this project but working with Jimmy is a dream come true."

The bottle slips from my hands and clatters against the floor.

She called him Jimmy. Only I call him Jimmy! Only I have ever been allowed to call him Jimmy!

I bend over with my hands on my knees, trying to catch my breath.

I assumed they were sleeping together, but I didn't realize, didn't even bother to think that they were serious enough that he'd let her call him that.

He was always insistent that it was *our* thing.

I can't.

I can't handle this.

Hate, rage, pain, shame swirls inside me, forming a toxic cocktail until I vibrate with the need to stop the pain.

I grab my purse and riffle through it, desperate for anything. I dump it over, my lipstick, wallet, and tampons scattering to the floor. I glance at the empty bottle of vodka.

I cry out and scratch my nails down my face, desperate to push it all away.

I only have myself to blame. I can't be who he needs me to be. I'm the one who pushed him away, who drags him down. And now he's happy... with someone else.

How long until Derek gets home?

However long it is, it'll be too long.

I rack my brain for the nearest dealer when it dawns on me that I know where Derek keeps his stash. Maybe he has something in there. I'll pay him back. He'll understand.

My body ricocheting from one wall to the other, I stumble to the bedroom. I drop to my knees in front of the beat-up bedside table. I pull out the bottom drawer, the one with the false bottom, and work the thing until I figure out how to access the bottom part.

When the wood lifts, my panic dissipates. He has a few rocks of heroin, along with a few needles and a baggie of weed. Weed isn't going to cut it for me right now, and neither is the vapor. I wrap one hand around a needle, second-guessing myself. I may be a fuck-up, but I've managed to stay away from needles so far.

What the hell do I care? I have no one. No one truly cares what happens to me.

I snatch the needle and the heroin and stumble around the apartment, scrounging up the other instruments I need. I may be a newbie with needles, but I've watched enough of my friends.

The heroin is in the needle and my shirt sleeve is rolled up when the overwhelming urge to reach out to Jimmy and admit my feelings becomes too strong to ignore.

He once did the unthinkable for me. He deserves to know how I really feel before I do this and set myself on a path I'll never be free from.

Setting the needle on the table, I turn over my phone, type in the password, and hit his number, pressing the speaker button. The call goes straight to voicemail. After the beep, I plunge the needle into my vein.

"I really did love you."

A rush of white heat envelops my body and my eyes drift closed. I fight against the pull to get out my last few words.

"As much as I was able to."

I slip away and lose myself to the sweet oblivion of the darkness, where nothing can hurt me.

Chapter Twenty-five

JIMMY

Our presentation at the Oscars goes well and Adelaide and I are at an after-party, sipping on drinks and making small talk with some industry insiders. They're filling us in on some of the drama going on over at one of the big entertainment agencies in the city.

I observe how Adelaide gives each person her undivided attention. In spending time with her these past couple of months, I've come to realize that she has the unique ability to put people at ease and make them feel important because she grants all of her attention to whomever she's talking to.

She catches me watching her and smiles with a blush in her cheeks. It warms her face, and without thinking, I brush my thumb over her soft skin. The man who's speaking clears his throat, and I drop my hand.

"Sorry, gentlemen. Would you mind if I stole Adelaide for a moment?" I say to the group.

"Of course, you two young things go have fun," one of the older executives from the studio says.

I nod my thanks and lead Adelaide away by the arm. When we reach the corner of the room, I stop her, strategically blocking us from view with a large gathering of helium balloons rising up from weights on the floor.

"You know earlier when you called me Jimmy?"

Her eyes crinkle. To her it's probably nothing.

"To the reporter on the red carpet."

"Oh." She nods.

"Could you stick to James?" How do I word this without offending her?

"OKAY," she says, but it's clear in her tone she doesn't understand what the problem is.

"IT'S JUST... Jimmy's my past and it's a childhood name and—"

She places her hand in the air and smiles. "You don't have to explain. James it is."

"Thanks." I release a breath, thankful she took the news so easy.

I step closer to her. "I think we did a pretty good job up there tonight. What about you?"

"I agree. We make a good team." Her gaze dips to my lips.

Something has grown between us in these past few months. It's not the overwhelming and crazy chemistry Lilah and I always had, more of a mutual respect and fondness for one another. But it's obvious we're both curious what would happen if we took the leap and actually tried dating for real.

"We do make a pretty good team," I say, leaning in another inch.

"Let's hope the box office numbers think so, too." She follows my lead and raises her chin so that our lips are only an inch apart.

"Adelaide, what would you say if—"

"James! Christ, finally."

I turn my head and crease my forehead when I see Keane twenty feet away and racing toward us.

"What the hell is going on?" I ask.

He stands with his hands on his hips, gasping for breath, before he speaks. "I got a call." He inhales a deep breath. "It's Lilah. Apparently she ODed and—"

I haul him to me by the lapels of his tux jacket. "Is she alive? Is she okay? What hospital?"

He shakes his head. "I don't know anything other than that she ODed and she's at Sinai."

"Fuck!" I drop my hands from his chest and push through the crowd.

The valet approaches me outside the hotel, looking starstruck and a little wary at the same time. "Can I help you, sir?"

I didn't drive here myself. I was dropped off by a driver, but I'm not waiting around for that. "I need a cab or an Uber... something."

He nods quickly, obviously responding to the urgency in my tone, and jogs to the podium near the doors the porters use, where he picks up a phone. He exchanges a few words with whoever he's speaking to and hangs up. "They're going to let a cab through. Should only be a minute."

I nod and pace. I push both hands through my hair and stop walking, pulling on the strands. It's all my fault. If I hadn't pushed her away, I could've kept an eye on her, made sure she stayed above surface level.

Desperation claws at my insides while I wait for the fucking cab.

I yank my phone from my inside pocket to check the time and find a list of missed calls.

Damn it. I forgot to take my phone off silent when we left the awards.

Using my thumb to open the screen, I pull up the missed calls and see a bunch from Keane, my manager, and one at the bottom from Lilah. My heart seizes as I press the voicemail button and bring my phone to my ear. Lilah's message plays first, since hers is the oldest, and I listen, my heart constricting at the desperation in her voice.

Her words, sounding so hopeless, reverberate through my head and I collapse to my knees on the concrete.

If she isn't okay, I don't know what I'll do. I realize now that if I thought I can survive without her, I was kidding myself. Lilah is as much a part of my life as the cells that make up my body. And if she's gone, there'll be nothing left for me.

Chapter Twenty-six

JIMMY

The cab doesn't come to a full stop in front of the Emergency Room when I toss a hundred-dollar bill in the front and push the door open. I race through the sliding doors.

The place is packed with people. Some old, some young, babies sitting on their mother's laps. I spot the desk in the far corner and push past a woman escorting an elderly lady with a walker. I startle the nurse when I come to an abrupt stop in front of the desk, and she narrows her eyes.

"I'm looking for Lilah Robbie. She was brought in here by ambulance," I say, panting from a mixture of rushing here and stress increasing my heart rate.

She purses her lips. "Are you related to her?"

"No, but I..."

The corners of her lips tip up, and instead of judgment, her eyes now hold disbelief. She's figured out who I am.

"Oh my God!" she screams, then leans forward as if we're sharing a secret. "Are you James Crawford?"

It's clear I'm going to get further with this woman if I play to my celebrity status, so I smack on my most charismatic smile and do what I love—act. "Can you keep a secret?"

She nods with vigor.

"I am."

The nurse, whose name tag reads Leslie, bounces off her seat. "I knew it. Oh, I loved your last movie—where you played that soldier? You were so good in it. I can't believe you're standing here in front of me right now. James Crawford!"

I glance behind me to see if anyone is paying attention or has their cell phone out for a picture, but everyone here appears too deep into their own misery to be concerned. "Thank you, that's very nice of you. Now do you think you could tell me where my friend Lilah Robbie is? She was brought in by ambulance."

"Anything for you," she says and turns her attention to the computer, typing away on the keys. "Yes, she's here. I don't know her status, but she's still in this unit. She hasn't been moved yet."

"Is she going to be all right?" I lean over the desk, my hands splayed in front of me.

"I have no idea. Why don't I slip back and see if I can get an update for you?"

Relief worms through me. "I'd really appreciate that."

"Okay, give me a second." She heads farther into the unit behind her until she turns down a hall and I can't see her anymore.

I push up off the desk and undo my bow tie. Unable to stand still with all this nervous energy and anxiety rolling through me, I pace with one hand gripping my hair and the other on my waist. *She has to be okay. She has to be okay. She has to be okay.*

The false assurances I give myself do nothing to make me feel as if she will.

A couple minutes later, Leslie returns with a grim look on her face. I stand in front of the desk, not moving, barely breathing, afraid to ask.

"She's still alive," she says with a matter-of-fact tone. "If you want, I can bring you back so the doctors can talk to you."

"Thank you, thank you!"

Leslie points at the large set of swinging doors to the right of her desk. "Head through those. I'll buzz you in."

Wasting no time, I move to the door.

The energy back here is completely different. While outside in the waiting room, the feeling was morose and stagnant, behind these doors, there's a not-quite-frantic feeling permeating the air.

Leslie approaches, smiling, and I return it with an awkward one of my own.

"Follow me."

I wish she'd pick up the pace. It's as if she's out for a Sunday stroll, and it's all I can do not to put my hands on her shoulders and push her to move faster.

She brings me to the very end of the row and stops outside a curtained-off space. "Nurse Rangefield?" she calls through the blue fabric.

An older woman with shoulder-length, curly brown hair appears around the curtain. She's all business and glances at Leslie reproachfully before setting her gaze on me.

"This is him," Leslie says. "This is James Crawford." Her eyes are wide again.

"So I see," Nurse Rangefield says, not looking as impressed as her coworker.

"How's Lilah? Is she going to be okay?"

She opens her mouth then looks back at Leslie. "Shouldn't you be back at your desk by now?"

Leslie startles as if she was woken from a trance. "Oh, right. Sorry." She grips my forearm. "It was really great to meet you."

I shake off my irritation at her lack of self-awareness—this is not the time or the place—and smile anyway, then I nod and turn back to Nurse Rangefield.

"She was unconscious and barely breathing when the ambulance arrived. According to them, there was evidence of heroin use, so they administered Naloxone. That helped, but she still hasn't regained consciousness. Her pulse and heart rate are unstable still, and because we don't know if she stopped breathing for any period of time before the ambulance arrived, we'll have to do some tests to make sure her brain function is fine. It's not likely she stopped breathing and regained the ability on her own, but since she was alone, there's no way to be sure."

I try my best to understand everything she's telling me, to examine its meaning piece by piece, but I'm rolling over the same word over and over again. "Heroin? Are you sure?"

"That's what the EMTs reported. Said it was pretty apparent."

I push a hand through my hair, the lump in my throat increasing. "What are her chances of being okay?"

This woman has been hardened by her job, that much is clear. But for a moment, I swear I see pity in her eyes. "She's not out of the woods by a long shot. Right now, we're trying to get her stable so we can run some more tests. These next few hours are critical as far as her long-term prognosis."

My chin falls to my chest and I suck in a shaky breath. "Is there somewhere more private I can wait?" I know it's far-fetched to think that somehow the press won't get wind of this and show up here.

"Sure, this is LA after all. There's a private waiting room for your type just down there." She points behind me, and when I turn, I see the door she's referring to.

"Thank you."

She turns to head back behind the curtain.

"Can I see her first?" I ask, needing to set eyes on her to see how bad she looks.

"I'm afraid that's not possible right now, Mr. Crawford."

"If anything changes though, you'll come find me?" I ask with raised brows.

"I will." She gives a curt nod and ducks back behind the curtain.

I stand, unmoving for a moment, stunned by the news. *Heroin?* I'd understand cocaine, alcohol, but Lilah has always stayed away from the really hard stuff. I foolishly took that to mean she had *some* self-control and *some* desire to turn her life around.

Then again, why wouldn't she? What was left in her life to keep her afloat?

She'd lost me.

Slow steps lead me to the waiting room. Because I know if something happens to Lilah, the guilt and loss will shackle me for the rest of my life.

Chapter Twenty-seven

LILAH

The first thing I notice is the taste in my mouth. Funny that something so ridiculous would be my strongest anchor. My neck twitches and my head aches.

Something feels weird on my arms, and something warm is on my hand. I try to move my arm, but a pinch on top of my hand stops me.

"Lilah?"

Something about the voice, some quality to it, makes me feel safe. I want to figure out who it is, but I'm so tired.

* * *

THE NEXT TIME I WAKE, I want to move. My entire body aches and my hip hurts in this position. I gather all my strength and try to shift my body, but I can't.

"Lilah, can you hear me? That's it, baby, see if you can open your eyes."

That voice speaks again.

A squeeze on my hand alerts me, and I try but fail to squeeze back.

"Lilah, wake up, honey."

The voice is so familiar...

Jimmy.

Jimmy is here.

I might not smile on the outside, but I smile inside. He came back for me.

I open my eyes and light filters in for a moment before the demands I've placed on my body take their toll. Sleep calls to me again. Even though I want to see Jimmy, I'm not strong enough to fight off its hold.

* * *

I NOTICE the soft sound of equipment around me. A small hum and an intermittent beep. I'm not lying flat on my back; my front half is raised. I think I'm in the hospital.

The same grip that has been present on my right hand every other time I tried to wake up is still there. This time, rather than wasting energy trying to move my body, I concentrate on opening my eyes.

After a few tries, I pry them open into small slits, but I close them immediately from the glare of the overhead fluorescent lights. After a few seconds, I open them again, better prepared this time.

Jimmy sits in a chair beside my bed and holds my hand, leaning forward, asleep.

He looks awful. There are bags under his eyes and his clothes are rumpled. His hair is mussed and not in his sexy, effortless way. In a way that makes me think he hasn't seen a shower in a while. Even so, it's been so long since I've seen him that I can't help letting my gaze travel up, down, and all over him.

I open my mouth to say something, but my throat is so parched, it's painful.

I squeeze his hand. I'm so weak.

I swallow the little saliva there is in my mouth and croak, "Jimmy."

His eyes fly open and he sits straight up. He's looking at me as if I'm a figment of his imagination.

I force a small smile. I'm not sure why I'm here, but what I am sure of is that we haven't seen or talked to each other in a long time.

"You're awake."

The relief in his voice makes my eyes well with tears.

He leans forward, hands extended as though he wants to cup my face, but he stops and glances at the equipment. "I should let the nurse know. They told me to let them know when you wake up."

He seems unsure of what to do. Not at all like the man I know, who's always so full of confidence and self-assuredness.

He disappears through the door, which gives me a minute to examine my surroundings. The hospital is clean, and my stay here must be on Jimmy's dime. It's a private room with a living room suite to my left and a full bathroom to my right.

I look down at my body. I'm hooked up to IVs and other equipment. I try to remember what brought me here. Was I in a car accident? I don't think so. I don't seem to have any casts or anything.

Before a recollection forms, Jimmy returns with a nurse who looks a few years older than he is. She gives me a professional smile as she approaches the bed and looks over the equipment. "Hi, Lilah, my name is Julie and I'm your nurse. I'm going to give you the once-over and call the doctor to let him know you've woken up, okay?"

I nod numbly.

Julie proceeds to poke and prod me while making idle chitchat. "I bet you're thirsty aren't you, darling?"

I nod again.

She looks over her shoulder at Jimmy. "James, can you please grab Lilah here a cup of water with some ice and a straw? You can ask one of the nurses at the station for help."

How long have I been here that she's talking to Jimmy like she knows him?

"Sure thing."

I've been watching him, and he's had his gaze on her the entire time, as if he can't look at me. But why would he be here if it pains him to look at me?

Julie finishes whatever it is she's doing and smiles at me. "You take it easy. James will be back with your water soon. Small sips when you get it. I know you probably want to guzzle it, but that'll only make it come back up. You haven't had anything solid in your stomach for a while now, so baby sips."

I nod because it's too painful to talk.

She smiles, squeezes my shoulder, and leaves the room.

A couple minutes later, Jimmy returns and sits beside me. I try to sit up so I can better hold the water, but it's too exhausting, so I lean back against the pillow with my eyes closed.

"Here, let me."

I open my eyes and see him holding out the cup, pointing the straw at my lips. I move a little forward, wrap my lips around the straw, and sip slowly. The cold liquid coats my tongue and cools the fire in my throat. Julie was right—I find myself desperate to finish the whole thing, but I do as she says, not wanting to experience what would surely be the painful process of bringing it back up.

After a few minutes and enough to relieve the worst of the sting in my throat, I lean back against my pillow.

Jimmy's gaze meets mine, and there's desperation in his eyes that I haven't seen since that fateful night.

"What am I doing here?" I ask in scratchy, low voice.

His breathing stutters as he sucks in a big breath. "You don't remember anything?"

I shake my head, afraid of what he'll say.

"Derek found you at his place. You overdosed on heroin."

His words shock me. I try, through the dull ache in my head, to pull up the last thing I did. Jimmy must realize I need a minute because he sits silently at my bedside, letting his words soak in.

I recall being at Derek's, though I'm not sure if what I'm remembering is the last time I was there. The days and weeks have been a blur. A memory of him leaving forms in my mind, almost like walking through the fog and seeing something ahead but being not quite able to make it out.

Then what?

A TV. Something about a TV. Was I watching TV?

A beautiful red gown comes to mind and I know it's Adelaide's. I pick at that memory, trying to pull up the corners so I can see what's underneath the picture of that dress. A minute goes by until the image is vivid in my mind, but finally I see Adelaide in that dress, standing beside Jimmy.

They're on a red carpet. The Oscars! It's the Oscars and I was watching it on TV... the word *Jimmy* echoes through my mind, but it's not my voice saying it. It's Adelaide.

And then it flashes in my head. She called him Jimmy. She called him Jimmy as though he was hers to do so, and then I...

I tense, and Jimmy squeezes my hand. I glance at him, and all the raw pain I felt rushes forward.

Jimmy clutches my hand in both of his and leans forward, holding mine to his lips. "Did you do it on purpose?"

I open my mouth to deny his unspoken accusation but shut it. "I don't know."

He cringes and tips his head down so our hands press to his forehead.

"I just wanted the pain to go away."

His shoulders shudder and a sharp sob escapes.

This is what I do to him. This is why he's better off without me.

All the joy of seeing my best friend, who is more than my best friend, washes away as the tide of shame bowls me over from the sight of him so undone.

"I'm sorry, Jimmy," I whisper as tears tumble down my cheeks. "I'm so sorry."

He shakes his head but doesn't raise his face to look at me.

"I'm sorry," I say again, this time giving in to my emotions and saying it through a sob wrenched from the depths of my soul. "I'm sorry for everything."

He sniffs and raises his head, wiping his eyes with the backs of his hands. "You need help, Lilah."

He meets my gaze with determination because we both know my answer to his declaration will either be the bedrock or the quicksand that we rebuild our friendship on.

I squeeze my eyes shut and nod.

There's no way I can go on like this. The constant pain is too much to bear, and the fact that I'm inflicting that same pain on him will be my undoing. I need to deal with my issues instead of running or pushing them away with sex and drugs. Rather than avoiding feeling anything at all, I need to be willing to fight my demons in order to truly live my life.

"Will you get help?"

The thought absolutely terrifies me. I've been to a few NA or AA meetings over the years when I thought I wanted to try to better myself, but they never stuck. The idea of being isolated somewhere, unable to interact with the outside world and talking about everything that's wrong with me in front of a bunch of strangers, isn't appealing.

But neither is the idea of living with this feeling of worthless-
ness and shame forever.

"I will," I answer.

Relief floods his features. "I'll make some calls and get you
into the best place possible. I promise."

I open my mouth to argue that he doesn't need to do that—
he's already done so much—but I don't. I can give him this
one small thing because it will make him feel useful.

"Thank you." I yawn, trying to keep my eyes on him. It's been
so long since I've been with him.

"You need to rest. I'll make some calls, but I'll be right here
when you wake up again."

I nod, and the weight on my eyelids becomes too much and
they drift closed.

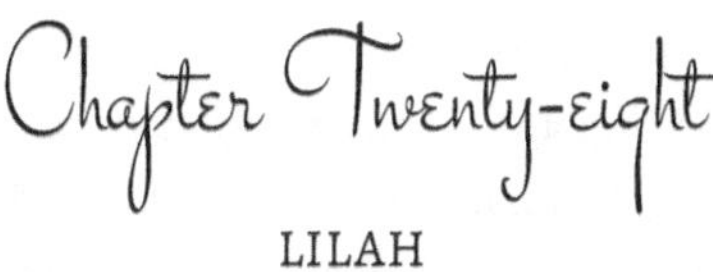

Chapter Twenty-eight

LILAH

It's been a week since I woke up as weak as a newborn calf.

Today I leave for rehab.

I process that realization for a moment.

I've almost bailed about a hundred times. All I want is to disappear out the front doors of the hospital and return to my old life. Then I look at Jimmy and the reasons why I won't surface.

I need to do this for myself or there's no chance of me getting clean. I understand that fact. I really do. But right now, I'm going for Jimmy, because I can't see again the pain I caused him when I woke up in this hospital bed.

House of Carlisle fired me. I expected it, but it stung just the same. Jimmy tried to keep the news from me, but sobriety is refreshing in that I notice what the hell is going on. Not to mention if I have a chance of getting straight, he can't hide things from me.

Jimmy knocks on the bathroom door, drawing me from my thoughts. "Lilah, there's someone here to see you."

"I'll be right out."

I pull my shirt over my head and smooth out my hair. It looks as good as it's going to using hospital shampoo and conditioner. I debate putting it up but decide to leave it down. Photographers always said positive things when I had it down. I want to make a good impression on the woman escorting me to the rehab facility in Utah. Maybe she'll cut me some slack if I'm put-together when she meets me, instead of looking like the jittery, nerve-racked girl I am.

Drawing in a calming breath, I open the door and step into the hospital room, where Jimmy speaks in low murmurs to a woman in her mid-fifties. I can tell she dyes her short auburn hair, because no one has a natural color that shade of maroon. I'm guessing she's a little shorter than I am, based on her height in relation to Jimmy, and she focuses with great concentration on whatever Jimmy's telling her.

The light thump of the bathroom door hitting the door stop draws their attention, and they turn in my direction. The woman splashes on a big, positive smile, giving the "we're all in this together" impression, while Jimmy can't stop fidgeting in the chair. A trickle of cold sweat travels down my spine. The time has come to deal with my shit.

"Lilah, this is Ruth." Jimmy motions to the woman.

She steps forward with her hand outstretched. "It's good to meet you, Lilah. I'm going to be accompanying you to Desert Vista in Utah."

Why do they always try to make rehab joints sound like country clubs? There's no spa with daily massages. Not even a tennis court.

I shake her hand. "Hi."

"We need to leave soon in order to catch our flight. Do you have everything you need?"

"I don't know. Any chance you have some weed or opioids in your purse?" I say, trying to lighten the weight in the air, but it falls flat.

Jimmy cringes, though I can tell he's trying not to, and Ruth's lips tip down at the corners.

I've already disappointed both of them.

I peer down at my shoes. "I was just kidding."

"It's okay. I know you're nervous and scared. That's completely normal, and everyone deals with it in their own way." Ruth's voice is soft and nurturing. I think she must have kids, because a woman who has a voice that calming should definitely have kids they tuck in at night.

"Ruth, do you mind giving us a minute to say goodbye before you guys leave?" Jimmy asks.

"Sure, I'll wait out in the hall. But don't take too long."

He nods and waits until she closes the door before he eats up the space between us. "I'm so proud of you." He puts his hands on my shoulders.

His touch feels so good, so comforting, that my eyes drift closed, and I nod. We haven't discussed what led to our falling out, the things he said to me or my behavior. There's been a silent understanding that we'll deal with the issues between us after I've dealt with my own. I'm just thankful for his support. I have a clearer head than I have in years, but I fear the urge to numb myself will forever be the beast clawing at my back.

"I know you can do this," he continues. "I know you can. You just need to believe that yourself, okay?"

I open my eyes, and unshed tears burn at the corners. "I'm scared." Terrified really, but I don't need to put more weight on Jimmy's shoulders.

His hands slide down my arms, and he grips my hands. "I know. And that's okay. That means you're ready to get clean."

I nod. "What if it doesn't work? What if I'm too broken to fix? What if the pieces don't fit back together?"

Full-on tears run down my face as I voice my biggest fear.

He pulls me into a hug and lets his warm arms do the convincing that he believes I'm strong enough and that I will be put back together. His grip around me is like a vise, and I sense that my leaving might be hard for him too. At least I can hope.

There's a knock on the door and Ruth peeks her head in. "We have to go, Lilah."

Jimmy pulls away, and emptiness rises inside me. "You got this, Lilah. I believe in you."

"Will I be able to talk to you?"

His chocolate eyes soften. "I'll be there whenever I'm allowed. But I don't think that will be for a while."

"Okay. You promise you'll be there?" I hold out my pinkie finger.

He glances at my hand with a melancholy expression, but he doesn't hesitate to link his pinkie finger with mine. "I promise." He leans forward and kisses my forehead.

A soft knock sounds on the door again, and Ruth pushes it open slowly. "I'm sorry, but we've got to get going if we're going to catch our flight."

"That's okay. She's ready," Jimmy says.

I'm glad he believes in me, because right now, ready is the last thing I am.

Chapter Twenty-nine

JIMMY

It's been a month since Lilah went to Desert Vista—the longest thirty days of my life.

Every time my phone rang, or a text came through, my stomach dropped, anticipating someone notifying me Lilah had bailed on rehab. But she is still here. That has to be a good sign.

Today is the first day she's allowed visitors, so I'm here.

My palms are sweaty, and my heart is racing. Will she be different? I'm so used to seeing her half-fucked on pills or alcohol that I hardly remember what she's like sober. Maybe she'll refuse to see me? Maybe she'll hate me now for what I did.

Those thoughts kept me up all night in that dingy hotel room. A decade ago, it would have felt like the Ritz. I'll blame the bags under my eyes on the lumpy bed and pillows, but truth is, I'm terrified we won't be the same Jimmy and Lilah.

I walk through the doors of a rehab facility that specializes in helping addicts who have a history of childhood trauma. I did research before deciding on where to send her. If she was gonna have any shot at success, it had to be a place best suited to her needs.

It's disguised as an oversized contemporary dwelling in the middle of the Utah desert, but the inside is spacious and decorated with ivory, beige, greens, and blues. It has a rustic Sahara vibe. Calming music pipes throughout, soft enough that it's not intrusive.

I step up to the woman behind the desk. "Hi, I'm here to see Lilah Robbie."

"You must be Jimmy." She extends her hand, a big smile on her face.

"I am." I shake her hand.

"Lilah's looking forward to seeing you."

I smile and nod, not familiar with people calling me Jimmy, not James. They're so different from one another.

"She's waiting for you in the reading room. Straight down the hall, and it's the last room on the right."

"Great, thanks." I start to head down the hall but turn back to her. "Is there anything I should or shouldn't say today? I don't want to set her back or anything."

She tilts her head, and a soft smile forms across her lips. "You can say anything you want. Part of these visits is allowing the real world to intrude a bit. She needs to learn how to deal with her emotions in a productive way and interacting with the people she's hurt in the past is part of that. We'll be here after you leave to help do that."

I nod then make my way to the library. All I wanted to know was if it's okay to ask about her treatment and therapy or if I'm supposed to ignore the pink elephant in the room?

My footsteps echo as I walk over the hard tiles. I pass a dining room, where people sit around the table and play a board game, but other than that, I see no one.

Sweat breaks out on my temples as I reach the end of the hallway. I inhale a deep breath and prepare to see Lilah. I'll admit it's been nice this past month to know she's safe every night when I go to bed. The worst part of her addiction was the questions that plagued me when she wasn't around. Where she was, who she was with, did she need me?

Now new questions set me on edge. Will she be pissed that I sent her here? Will she blame me for setting her on this road in the first place?

I push a hand through my hair, draw my shoulders back, and step into the library.

She sits on a chaise lounge with her back to me, facing a large window that looks out over the burnt-orange rock formations jutting up on the horizon. The room is lined with white bookcases full of books of varying colors and sizes.

I'm mesmerized. Only a few steps away from her. A soft, contented sigh escapes my lips, making her turn toward me.

My chest clenches when I see her face. Our eyes lock and my stomach knots until she smiles. It's small and tentative at first, but it grows the longer we soak one another in. Tears fill my eyes. She's as beautiful as always. Her face rounder, her body healthier, her skin tone rosy. I haven't seen her like this since... well, ever.

She walks quickly toward me, and I anticipate her running into my arms. But she slows and stops in front of me, her hands clasped, and looks at her feet.

"Hey," I say.

"Hey." She glances at me and I can't get enough of her healthy glow.

I told myself to let her lead today. *Don't suffocate her.* But I can't hold myself back—I pull her into a hug. "C'mere."

Lilah expels a big breath of air and wraps her arms around me, squeezing tightly. "I missed you."

"I missed you too."

I relish the simple fact that I can touch her again, feel her, that she's here with me, living and breathing. I know the statistics. Most addicts relapse. But hope blooms inside me like a small seedling bending toward the sun.

When we pull apart, her eyes glisten, but tears never fall. "Come over here and sit." She leads me by the hand to the oversized chaise she was sitting on.

The novel she was reading is discarded to the side. I don't think I've seen Lilah read a book since we were young. Thinking back, I don't think I've seen her pick up a book since before...

Shaking my head to purge that thought, I sit beside her. "Are you reading again?"

Her cheeks flush. "Yeah. It's one of the few activities we can do here with our free time." She shrugs. "I forgot how much I like escaping into other worlds."

I wrap her hand between mine. Now that I'm near her again, the impulse to touch her is too much for me to ignore. "What have you been doing here?"

"The first couple of weeks were tough. Physically. I never want to go through withdrawal again. They're getting easier, but it's a different game now. It's mental." Her lips tip down at the corners.

I squeeze her hand. "That's okay. You can do it."

She exhales a rough breath. "I'm trying. I really am."

"I'm so proud of you. I can't say that enough."

"I do, I do know that. To be honest, I came here because you believed in me." She lets a sad sort of laugh escape. "I'm trying to make myself proud now. Believe in myself."

I hoped for so long to hear her say words like that, and I can't help but do a happy dance inside. All the times I thought she'd die and never understand who she could be without the drugs... "How is it going here? How's therapy?"

She pushes her hair behind her ears. "Excruciating."

I frown.

"It's okay. The first few weeks, I wasn't willing to really open up. You know, go as deep as they want you to. But they helped me understand that if I was here, I might as well do the work. I'm tired of hurting all the time. And this process is painful—more than that really—but I keep telling myself that once I'm on the other side of it, it'll be easier to resist the urge to use again. I'll be able to stop self-medicating."

This is a whole new Lilah. One I've never known.

"That's great, Lilah, really."

"Enough about me. Tell me about what's going on in the real world. How is filming going?" She crosses her legs and wiggles to get more comfortable.

She's never really asked about my day, and when she did, there was no eagerness to hear the details.

"We just wrapped actually. I think it's going to turn out well."

"You're going to be an A-lister soon... just remember the little people." She smiles and giggles. Is she genuinely worried I'd leave her behind?

I cup her face. "I'm never going to forget you, you know that."

Her shoulders sag in relief. "Guess you're stuck with me then."

"Guess so."

Our gazes hold for a moment before I let my hand drop.

We chat for a bit about what else is going on in the world, mostly mundane stuff, before a man pops his head into the library.

"Lilah, group session is starting in a few minutes," he says.

"Okay." Sadness blankets her features.

"Guess I have to go."

"Yeah," she says. "Thanks for coming all this way to see me."

"You don't need to thank me. How much longer do you think you'll be here?" I ask.

"I wanted to ask you... they gave me the option to stay another thirty days, thought I could use it. But..." Her lips straighten.

A proud smile stretches my lips. "Whatever you need. As long as you want."

"Thank you, Jimmy. I'll pay you back."

"Don't worry about that." I'll continue to pay as long as she's getting the help she needs.

"I'm sick of being stuck here, but I know it's what's best."

"I'll be here waiting when you get out. Whenever that is."

We stand and she steps forward wrapping her arms around my waist. I rest my chin on her head, close my eyes, and inhale her scent.

I didn't tell her what I wanted to today. Maybe next time. She's so at peace, I can't bear to strip that away from her. But one thing's for certain—if we're ever going to move on with our lives, we need to make peace with the past. Lilah's doing her part. I'll need to do mine.

LILAH

It's been four weeks since I've seen or talked to Jimmy.

The past month has been so painful at times that it's hard to stay with these memories. My walk down memory lane isn't a fond one. A mother who died when I was young, a father who abused me, growing up dirt poor, my own sexual escapades over the years and... the one thing I'll never discuss with my counselor.

I never will.

That secret goes with me to my grave.

It's the least I can do.

I'm making progress though. And that's something. Hell, that's something I haven't done in more than a decade. Baby steps.

Jimmy's visiting today, and I'm giddy like a little girl waiting in line to see Santa Claus. Every minute ticks by slower, so I decide to go for a swim to keep my mind sane.

Desert Vista has a large outdoor pool that's more like a hot tub because of the desert heat. Since I've been here, I've started swimming laps. Exercise is good for my body, but even better for my mind. It clears my head and puts me in a meditative state. When I'm swimming, the outside world slips away and I only concentrate on proper pace and breathing.

I'm about to turn and push off the wall to do another lap when something catches my eye. I stop and lift my head to inhale, then I pull my goggles off my face. Jimmy stares at me with a serene smile.

I wipe the water from my eyes. Trying to catch my breath, I look at him and enjoy the feeling of being home that warms my body when he's around. It was always there, dulled by the effects of drugs and alcohol before. Now it's like a living, breathing entity of its own.

"You're early," I say, keeping the smile on my face so he knows it's not a problem. The counselors have warned us about families being worried and walking on eggshells. I never want Jimmy to fear I'll use again because of something he did. I've put way too much blame on him already.

"Guilty as charged. The flight left a little early and the pilot said we made good time with the winds."

"Just give me a second to get dried off."

I push up on the side of the pool and exit the water. Once I'm standing, water dripping off my sport bikini, I sneak another glimpse at Jimmy. The last time he came here, it felt like a dream after. I want to soak up as much of him as I can.

Heat flares in his eyes when they flow down my body, but he quickly snuffs it out.

Heat rises to my cheeks and I'm not sure why. This man has seen me without my clothes on more times than I can count. But I had no idea how different the world would look without drugs. So vibrant and full of color.

"You look great," he says, breaking the silence. "I mean, you always look good, but you look healthy."

"Thanks. Just let me dry off, then we can sit and catch up." I grab my towel off the lounger and dry myself.

I wrap the large towel around me and gesture for Jimmy to follow me. I lead him to the large circular lounger that has an overhang to keep off the blinding rays of the desert sun.

"Let's sit here." I crawl up and lean back against the cream-colored cushions, letting my legs extend in front of me.

Jimmy does the same, sitting to my left. He's wearing a pair of camouflage shorts with large pockets and a T-shirt that fits him snuggly. Something stirs low in my belly and I recognize it as desire. I'm surprised—shocked really. I haven't felt desire since I got sober.

I've always needed Jimmy, but this is the first time in forever that I'm aware of wanting him. Only for pleasure. Not to use sex to numb myself, or because it's what he wants, or I want to manipulate him like that fifteen-year-old girl in my bedroom again.

I push that feeling aside. It will only complicate things right now. We're trying to mend the damage I've done to our friendship.

"How are you?" he asks, shifting so that he's facing me, leaning against the lounger, holding up his head with his hand.

"Better than the last time I saw you. I really think I'm starting to get somewhere in my therapy. The past isn't as scary to talk about now."

He trails his index finger down my jawline, and my eyes fight the desire to close. "I knew you could do it."

"At least one of us did." A dry laugh falls from me. "I'm not saying it's easy. It's not. I still have days when I know if there was anything I could get my hands on, I wouldn't hesitate to self-medicate. But I'm more confident now that I can tackle my issues. For so long, I shut down as soon as anything from my past showed up in my head. I'm finding better ways to deal with stuff than making myself numb."

"You're a survivor. One day you'll look back on this and it will be a distant memory."

I shake my head. "No, I need to remember the pain I caused you, the pain my father caused me. If I forget, I'll end up back in that place where I didn't care whether I lived or died."

He blanches. The old me would've backtracked, but the new me knows that I have to say what I'm feeling. I have no chance of staying sober if I repress my feelings.

"Lilah." He takes my hand. "I'm so sorry I wasn't there for you. I never should have pushed you away." His voice breaks on his last few words.

A sharp, stabbing pain cracks in my chest. "It's not your fault." I squeeze his hand.

His gaze darts away from mine.

"Jimmy, look at me."

He does, but his eyes are sad.

"You were right to do what you did. I was a mess, and I was screwing up your life. If you had been there, I might never have ODed, and I might never have gotten here."

He shakes his head before I'm even done speaking. "No, I should've pushed you harder to stop. I should have sought help for you. Instead I cast you off with nowhere to go."

"You know as well as I do that I wouldn't have listened to you. We'd still be going through the same unhealthy cycle—you giving me everything and me taking advantage of you." He opens his mouth to say something, but I cut him off. "No, I needed to hit rock bottom and almost die. I should be thanking you, because if you hadn't done what you did, I would still be a lost girl who had no value for herself or her life." Tears well in my eyes, but I refuse to let them fall. I didn't think I had any more tears left.

"Do you know that now? That you have value?" Hope fills his eyes.

The counselors warned us of this too. Our loved ones hoping rehab was like a Band-Aid and when we leave, we're all healed up and ready to start our life. Sixty days isn't long enough to make me love myself. The hope in his eyes makes me want to lie, but there've been too many lies between us.

"I'm working on it."

He presses his lips together and nods.

"There's something else I want to say... you can say I don't need to apologize for pushing you away and what it eventually led to, and that's fine. I'll never feel that way, but I won't bring it up again if that's what you want. But there is something else I need to apologize for." I slide my hand away from his, but he grips it harder. "Back in Virginia—"

"I don't want to talk about that night. We promised we'd *never* talk about it."

"I know, I know. It's not that." His eyes search mine. "I need to apologize for getting you into drugs in the first place. If it wasn't for me, you never would've gotten a taste for it and your life would have gone a different way."

A short burst of laughter escapes me.

He drops my hand and looks away.

I take his hand, and it lays limp in my palm. "I'm sorry, I'm sorry, but do you honestly think I never would have turned to drugs or alcohol to numb myself? It was inevitable. It's not your cross to bear."

It's true, I did smoke my first joint with him and try some party drugs, but he isn't the reason I'm an addict. I'm an addict because I chose to numb myself rather than deal with the repercussions of my abuse.

"Lilah, because of me—"

"Stop. Enough. My addiction issues are not your fault. End of story."

His eyes flare open from the bite in my tone. "Okay, okay. I won't bring it up again if it bothers you."

Here's what the counselors were talking about. He's scared to agitate me because he thinks it will send me over the deep end. I hate it just as much as they said I would.

"The only thing that bothers me about it is you thinking I'm here because of you."

His eyes flick away from mine for a second before meeting my gaze again. "There're a lot of things I regret."

I pull him in for a hug. "I know that everything you did for me was out of love. I know that." A tear trickles down my cheek.

Admitting that someone loves me is as hard as loving myself. Whether or not I think I deserve his love, I know that he's only ever tried to help. Selling drugs wasn't just a means to an end for him; it was for my survival and to help get us out of that hellhole.

He sniffs and turns his face into my neck. We stay in one another's arms, trying to heal from circumstances kids should never have to deal with. We were young and did what we had to in order to survive and free ourselves from abuse. Whether or not it's genetics that I got hooked and Jimmy didn't doesn't matter. Our lives are as entwined as the roots of a large oak tree.

Eventually we pull apart.

"I'm glad you came today. Thank you," I say.

"You know there's nowhere else I'd rather be."

And with that, we talk about other things. Anything other than our shared past. I find myself wishing that this is how it will be when I'm out of here.

I've decided to stay another thirty days. The real world is a scary place, and I'm not sure I'm ready. Whether I'll be able to handle staying sober once life interferes. Here, I'm focused almost one hundred percent of the time on working on myself. Out there... there's a job, an apartment, money, food, survival to worry about.

The other part of me wants to stay until I'm as strong as I can be. Because when the world tries to crush me under its enormous weight, I'll be standing on my own, weathering the storm.

Chapter Thirty-one

JIMMY

The lights of the photo shoot shine down on me, heating my skin. You'd think by now I wouldn't squint when thousand-watt bulbs are pointed directly in my face, but I still do.

"That's it, move a little closer to him, Adelaide. Wrap your arm around his waist," the photographer says in his Australian accent. "Perfect."

We're here to shoot some promo for the film. It's still in editing, but the studio wants to push it well in advance of release.

I don't know how Lilah did this for a living. It's arguably one of my least favorite parts of the job.

Just the thought of Lilah makes Adelaide's arm slung over me feel wrong. But ever since Lilah's overdose, there's been no question of something other than friendship between Adelaide and me, and Lilah and I aren't romantically involved at the moment.

"Great. I want to get some shots of the two of you looking at each other."

I turn my head down and meet Adelaide's gaze. She bites her lip to stop from laughing. I told her this morning how much I hate these things and she must see my displeasure on my face. The right corner of her lips quirks up a bit then a bit more, and now I'm biting back a smile. When a short burst of laughter escapes her mouth, I can't help but laugh back. Soon we're caught in a laughing fit about nothing specific.

Lilah refers to it as "we've got the giggles."

The thought stops my laughing, and after a couple of seconds, Adelaide stops too.

I swivel my head to search out the photographer behind the blinding lights. "Think we can take a break?"

"Sure thing, mate," he says, staring at his camera.

"Thanks."

Without looking back at Adelaide, I head to where I got ready. Normally I'd soldier through. I never want to be known as hard to work with. That tanks careers in this industry. But it's been three months since Lilah left for rehab and she's been on my mind a lot.

I haven't heard from anyone at the rehab about my monthly visit. Usually by now, Ruth would have contacted me to let me know I'm able to visit. Which makes me think maybe Lilah's seeing my apology in a different light now and has decided I *am* to blame. Maybe she no longer wants to see me.

That fear keeps me up at night, sipping on whiskey to relax my mind enough to fall asleep.

I sit in the makeup chair and check my phone to see if I've missed any calls while I was on set. There's nothing but a text message from Tripp, asking if I'm up for a night on the town tonight.

As if. I haven't done much since Lilah's overdose. Everything I do is mostly business-related stuff that I can't weasel out of.

My thumbs are on my phone to respond to Tripp when heels click behind me. I glance up through the mirror to see Adelaide approaching. We formed a definite friendship while working on the film and I'm sure she's only trying to be a good friend right now, but I really wish she'd leave me alone. Didn't I say I needed a break?

"Hey," I say.

She comes to stand beside me and watches me in the mirror. "I wanted to make sure you were okay. It seems like maybe something is bothering you." Adelaide's assessing eyes meet my gaze.

"I'm good."

Her lips tip down in the corner. "If you say so..." She lets her sentence hang there, waiting to see if I'll offer her more information.

I do need to talk to someone about Lilah. Tripp has never been on #TeamLilah, even though he seems to respect the fact that she's getting help for her issues. Adelaide and I have developed a friendship and she is a good listener.

I shift in my seat so I'm facing her and place my phone on the makeup table in front of me. "I'm concerned about Lilah is all."

Adelaide's shoulders sag right before a concerned look appears in her eyes. She leans in and covers my hand with hers. "How is she doing in rehab?"

"That's the thing. I wouldn't know. I mean, she's still there, so that has to account for something, right?"

She nods.

"Normally by now I've gotten a phone call to arrange my visit, but so far I've heard nothing. It's making me crazy, wondering whether maybe she doesn't want to see me for some reason." I'm not going to get into our history together with Adelaide, but I've said enough to give her an idea of what's going on.

"Why wouldn't she want to see you? From everything I've seen, you've been nothing but a rock for her." She squeezes my hand.

"Trust me when I say she definitely has her reasons."

"Maybe she's just going through a hard time there and they—"

Adelaide's attempt at making me feel better is interrupted by my phone vibrating on the table. I grab it, and relief mixed with uncertainty wraps around me when I see the rehab's number on the screen.

"That's the rehab place. Give me a minute?"

She presses her lips together and nods, turning to walk away.

I don't wait for her to be out of earshot before I slide my thumb to the right. "Hello?"

"Jimmy, hey."

Adrenaline surges through my veins when Lilah's voice sounds through the phone. "Hey, you. How are you?"

"Good. I'm good… actually, that's why I'm calling."

I'm on alert with the hesitation and unsureness in her voice. "What's going on?" I lean forward and rest my elbows on the makeup table, looking between my legs at the concrete floor.

"I'm coming home… well, see that's the problem. I don't really have a home and I'm not sure where I should—"

"I'm your home." I shake my head. I don't want to pressure her, if she'd rather me pay for a place. "I mean, my house is open."

A rush of breath leaves her. "Are you sure? I was hoping you'd offer, but after everything that happened, I wasn't sure whether that would be okay, or what your… situation is right now…"

The fact she isn't fighting me makes me forget the uneasiness I felt before she called.

"Of course, Lilah." I don't even bother addressing her other concern. I can't believe that she thinks I would be dating anyone while she's getting herself together. Will she ever understand and accept the depth of my feelings for her?

"Thanks. It won't be forever. Just until I can figure something out and get on my feet."

"You know you're welcome as long as you want. I have to ask though, are you leaving because it's time or are you…" I wait for her to fill in the blank.

"No, no, I'm not bailing. My therapists all agree it's time I get back to the real world, and I think so too. As scary as it is."

"You know I'm here for you."

"Jimmy?" I straighten up and turn to find Adelaide behind me with an apology in her eyes. "Sorry, the photographer wants us back."

"Tell him I'll be there in a minute." Without waiting for her to respond, I turn back around. "When are you leaving? I'll charter a plane and come get you."

"Was that Adelaide?" she asks.

"Yeah, we're just on set, getting some promo pics shot for the movie. Enough about that though, when will you be back?" My leg bounces.

"The day after tomorrow. And no, I'll take a commercial flight home and meet you at your house."

"You don't need to do that. I don't have anything going on that day. I can come get you."

"Jimmy, I know you love to save me, but... I need to do this on my own" She chuckles. Hopefully that means I have nothing to worry about.

I run a hand through my hair. "If you're sure."

"I am."

I want to push my agenda, but I let it ride. I need to let her run her re-entry into the world, so I let the topic go. "All right then."

"I'll text you the details of when I'll be there. I have my phone back." The delight in her voice is clear to hear.

I grip my phone tightly. "I can't wait to see you."

"Me either," she says.

"I'm here for you, you know."

"I know you are. You always have been. Talk to you soon."

She clicks off and I sit in the chair for a second, nerves and excitement colliding in my blood. In two days, she'll be here, and I hope we can form something even more special.

Chapter Thirty-two

LILAH

The Uber pulls up in front of the gate at Jimmy's house. My hand drifts unconsciously to my stomach. It rumbles with nausea.

"You can let me out here," I instruct the driver.

He grunts something unintelligible and puts the SUV in park before exiting to retrieve my bags from the back.

With my hand on the door handle, I inhale a deep breath and push the door open. Here goes nothing.

The driver has my suitcase and carry-on waiting for me when I reach the back of the truck.

"Thanks," I say, grabbing the handles.

"You sure you don't want me to help you to the house with those?" he asks.

I shake my head. "I can manage."

Dragging my luggage across the driveway to the house will be the easiest thing I do all day. I'm worried about memories and triggers. Jimmy's is the safest place I can come to and that's why I'm here, but there could be expectations and I hate disappointing Jimmy.

"All right then. Have a good one." He gets back into the car.

I wait for him to pull away before I punch the code into the gate and pull my luggage behind me as I head toward the house. Just setting eyes on this place frays my nerves. The last time I was here, I lived an entirely different lifestyle.

Before I reach the door, the gate closes.

He knows I'm here.

Butterflies flutter in my stomach. I'm more nervous to see him now than when he visited me in rehab.

The front door opens, and he appears.

I stop, taking him in. He's gorgeous with his movie-star looks, wearing a pair of black athletic pants and a fitted white tee that sets off his dark hair. It curls at the ends because it's longer than the last time I saw him. His eyes glisten with emotion as he looks at me.

One thing therapy helped me to sort out was my feelings for this man. I've always loved Jimmy—I know that now. I resisted giving him the words for the longest time. According to my counselors, that's what happens when your mom dies and your dad... does what he does. You think that everyone you care for will hurt you. But Jimmy's proven to me over and over that isn't the case.

My newfound emotions make this homecoming harder though.

I don't know anything about his life or what he's been doing these last three months. Having been cut off from the outside world, I have no idea if he's seeing anyone, dating, or what.

I need to be honest with him about my feelings. Honesty is my new policy in life. It's the only way I'm going to stay sober. Bottling up my emotions is a toxic endeavor and I've worked so hard to get where I am. I don't want to waste my chance.

"Hey," I say.

My voice startles him out of his daze. He bolts down the steps toward me.

I abandon my luggage and meet him halfway, where we crash into each other, squeezing tightly.

He turns his head into my neck and murmurs against my skin, "You're home."

"I missed you so much."

He pulls away and cups my face, gazing down at me with a smile that fills my heart with so much joy. "You have no idea, Lilah. Every day, every day I wished you were here, even though I knew you were where you needed to be."

I step into him again, my arms around his waist.

"Let's get in the house."

We untangle from one another, and Jimmy clutches my luggage. Everything inside looks the same as it once did. I don't know what I expected, but in one way, I was gone forever. At the same time, I never left.

"So what do you want to do? I have nothing going on today. I'm all yours," Jimmy says with his arms out to the side.

I want to run to him and wrap myself around him. He's my safe place. Always has been. But I know that if I want to do this—really stay sober and start over—I have to learn to rely on myself, not Jimmy. "I wouldn't mind unpacking and maybe going for a swim."

"You're really liking swimming now, huh?"

I shrug sheepishly. "It keeps me centered, disperses a lot of the toxic energy and thoughts I still have."

He nods. "Maybe I'll make us a late lunch while you're doing that then."

"Sounds good."

"What do you want to eat?" From his expression, you'd think he has no idea what my likes and dislikes are.

"Whatever you decide on is fine. I'm not going to spiral because you didn't have what I want on the menu."

"I didn't—"

"It's okay, Jimmy. I'm not that damaged." I smile and head down the hall with my large suitcase.

I pause at the master bedroom door. When I first came to stay here, I put up a fuss about having my own room. I now know it's because I wanted to prevent any true intimacy from seeping into my relationship with Jimmy. Now, I'd do almost anything to share that bed with him.

One step at a time though. I need to get acclimated to everyday life. Then he and I can sit down and have a conversation where I'm truthful for the first time since we were teenagers.

Chapter Thirty-three

JIMMY

It's been a week since Lilah returned from rehab, and from the outside, she's doing well. She attends a meeting every day—either NA or AA, sometimes both. And she's always sure to fit in her laps in the pool. Watching her, I can understand why it helps her. When she's swimming, she's completely focused on what she's doing, and when she's done, there's a calm aura around her, one I've never seen before.

I try to be home as much as I can, but we've had more photo shoots for promo for the movie and I've had to do some voice-overs in the studio in LA. But all that is done, and I have the next three days to myself before I have a meeting with my agent in the city.

The sun glistens down on my pool and the ocean beyond. I watch her dunk her head under the water as she moves her arms in smooth strokes and kicks her feet. She's getting better every day. She's gotten faster and built up her endurance since I saw her in rehab. Pride swells in my chest. Immediately followed by the stirring of my dick in my shorts when she stops in the shallow end and stands.

She's wearing a sporty bikini, but it dips low at the front and reveals an abundance of her cleavage, and her nipples poke through the fabric. My eyes draw down to the curve of her waist and the swell of her hips. She's so beautiful and sexy and stunning. Since she quit the drugs and alcohol, she's gained the weight she desperately needed, and all her swimming has defined her womanly curves.

I've been jerking off every morning to relieve my desire for her. I'm starting to feel like a teenage boy.

Lilah pulls the goggles off her face as my cell phone rings on the table beside me. I pick it up as Adelaide's name flashes on the screen.

"Hey, how's it going?" I answer.

For some reason, guilt punches my stomach when Lilah looks at me. I can't hold her gaze, so I pick at a piece of lint that isn't there on my shorts.

"I'm good, but I was calling to see how you were doing. It's weird not seeing you every day now, and I know Lilah is home, so I thought you might need to… talk."

I appreciate Adelaide's concern, but I won't be confiding everything about our complicated past to her. My gaze flicks to Lilah. She's out of the pool and walking toward me. Probably to grab her towel from the lounger beside me. My eyes stay trained on her as her hips sway with each one of her steps.

"James?" Adelaide recaptures my attention.

"What? Sorry, yeah, things are good. Lilah's doing well."

"Oh, that's good to hear." Her words hold an undercurrent of disappointment.

My forehead wrinkles. "Yeah, speaking of… I can't really talk right now. Is it okay if I call you later?"

"Sure thing," she says. "Take care of yourself."

"Will do." I hang up and set the phone on the table as Lilah runs the beach towel down each of her arms.

This is ridiculous. I'm jealous of a fucking beach towel.

A rush of air leaves my nostrils, and I shift in my seat to hide the growing bulge in my shorts.

"Who was that?" Lilah asks, patting the towel down her abdomen.

I want to offer to lick off each drop of water. "Adelaide. She just called to see how you're doing."

She tenses but continues drying herself. "That was nice of her."

She drops the towel on the lounger and squeezes out her long blonde locks. Locks I'd give anything to have fisted in my hand as I pump into her from behind.

Jesus, I need to shower.

"Are you two friends now?" she asks, but there's trace of what she *really* wants to know.

"We are friends. There's something I need to tell you, but we are *just* friends."

She presses her lips together and nods before lowering herself to sit on the lounger beside me. "What is it?"

I sit up so that I'm facing her and enclose her hands in mine. "Bernie Butler asked Adelaide and me to pretend, or at least put it out there, that there could be something between us."

She huffs.

"For the sake of the movie. Another director and studio are putting out a superhero movie a month before ours, and he figures a romance between us would be good for sales."

It sounds so stupid, but with Bernie, my hands are tied.

"Oh." She slides back in the lounge chair.

I lean forward, squeezing her hands harder. "You know Bernie, there's no choice, and with our fight and..." Not wanting to go into everything we've decided to leave in the past, I move to what I'm going to do in the future. "That's over. Screw him. But I wanted you to know."

She faces me, leaning forward with her elbows on her knees, her hands under her chin. "Okay. Do you want to... be with her?"

"*No!*" I grip her hands tighter. "Not at all. It was all a ruse for the press. I promise."

She's silent for an excruciating minute, her eyes on our hands. She weaves her fingers through mine, running them along the length, watching as we come and go together. "Can we talk for a minute?"

My heart thumps. I don't know how I know—maybe it's that I've known this girl my entire life—but this isn't going to be a throw-away conversation.

"Of course, what do you want to talk about?" I pick up the bottle of water I have on the table and take a sip. I'd kill for a beer right about now.

"Us."

One word. Two letters. Yet so profound.

"Us?" I clarify.

She nods. "First, I want to say thank you for arranging rehab and letting me stay here afterward. I fully intend on paying you back for the cost of sending me to Utah, once I figure out what it is I'm going to do with my life."

I shake my head. "Lilah, you do not need to—"

"I do though. I need to pay you back. It's important to me."

I'm never going to accept her money, but I nod, figuring we can save that argument for another day.

"I also noticed that you removed all the alcohol from the house... thank you." She whispers the last part. "I hope there'll eventually be a time where I can be around alcohol and not have it be an issue, but I'm not there yet."

I grip her chin and squeeze it until she straightens up. "I'd never knowingly put you in a position that would make it harder for you to cope. I know how hard you've worked to get this far."

She nods. "I have worked hard. I have. And it's still a struggle, but one I'm committed to getting through. Which leads me to my next point..." She lets my hand go, straightens her back, and puts her hands on her knees. I can't help the way my gaze dips to her chest when she does that. "You have to stop walking on eggshells around me."

The line between my eyes deepens. "What are you talking about?"

"Jimmy," she sighs. "You walk around here like the place is loaded with land mines and if you say or do the wrong thing, everything is going to explode in your face."

"I just want to make this as easy as possible for you."

She places her hand on my cheek for an all-too-brief moment. "And I love that about you. But I need to learn to deal with life —real life—and also be sober. For the longest time, my coping mechanism was to numb myself. It's important that I use the skills I learned in rehab, so they become my new normal."

I bundle her hands in mine. "All right. I get it. I do."

She smiles, and it reminds me of the way she used to look at me when we were kids—as if I hung the moon and stars.

"There's something else I want to talk about," she says in a low voice.

My gaze locks with her. "Okaaay..."

Her hands twitch in mine and I can tell that she's nervous. I have no idea what the hell this is about.

Drawing in a deep breath, she closes her eyes for a moment. "The first thing I want to do is apologize for all the damage I've done over the years. There're too many things to list them all, but we both know what they are."

I want to cut her off and protect her from the guilt about the past. I don't care about any of the shit she did. But a part of her recovery is making amends with the people she's hurt, so I press my lips together and let her continue.

"I've done so many selfish and hurtful things—some unintentionally and some on purpose to hurt you when I was lashing out."

My mind drifts over her more biting comments. Visions of her messing around with other guys in front of me to get a rise out of me pummel my brain, but I force them back. We're starting over.

"For that, I'm truly sorry. If I could take it all back, I would, but the best I can do is tell you that I'm committed to not being that person—the addict—anymore. The only thing I control going forward is my behavior, but I won't let you be hurt because of me any longer. I vow to you that I will do whatever it takes to make sure that's the case."

I seize her pause as my opportunity to speak. "Thank you for the apology. I'm glad we're getting this fresh start."

Her shoulders fall. Was she honestly worried I wouldn't forgive her? "I'm glad to hear you say that, because I want to talk about our relationship going forward and what I'd like it to look like."

I try not to let my disappointment show. I know what she's going to tell me—that I'm a trigger for her and we can no longer be together in any kind of romantic way. I understand that. I do. I'll even support it, but it's hard to sit here and hide my utter devastation while I wait for her to deliver the hammer to something I've wanted for so long.

My eyes are set on our hands because I can't look her in the eyes.

"The first thing you need to know is that I love you, Jimmy."

My gaze flicks up to meet hers.

"I've always loved you. I know I didn't speak the words until it was too late, but you need to know that I did mean them. You're the most important thing to me, and I only want your happiness."

I swallow, unable to speak because I can see—hell, I can feel—that she means what she's saying. The moment is surreal. Running away from Virginia, becoming an actor, getting the part of The Regulator. All of those were dreams I hoped for but doubted could happen, but Lilah admitting she loves me? That always seemed more impossible than all the rest.

"I did love you in the past and I love you in the present, and if you'll have me, I want to love you in the future. The way normal people do. A real relationship. I want to be with you, Jimmy, and I can't be here with you and pretend otherwise any longer."

Elation bubbles in my blood. I cup her cheek and smile until a realization dawns on me. My smile falters and I remove my hands from her, standing from my chair and running my hand through my hair.

She's a recovering addict. They're not supposed to have any romantic entanglements for at least a year after becoming sober. So even though I'm being offered what I've waited a lifetime for, I can't accept it.

I pace as Lilah sits silently.

"You don't feel that way about me anymore. I've done too much damage." The pain in her voice is clear, but at the same time, she sounds resigned.

"No, that's not it." I shake my head. "What about your sobriety?"

She walks over to me. "What about it?"

"Aren't you supposed to not be involved with anyone until you've been sober for at least a year?"

She glances at her hands. "That is something they recommend, though it's not a hard-and-fast rule."

"Listen..." I step into her, holding her face. My bare chest almost brushes against her damp swimsuit, but I deny myself

LILAH

He crushes his lips to mine, lust and desire emanating from his kiss. His tongue slides against the seam of my lips and I open for him, truly tasting him for the first time in forever. He groans as our tongues meet, and he pulls me into him. My nipples peak against the bare skin of his chest.

He pulls away for a moment and brushes the strands of loose hair off my face. "God, I missed this, missed you."

He runs his tongue from the base of my neck to my earlobe. My eyes drift closed, and my head falls back as the coarseness of his short beard brushes against my skin in opposition to the soft caress of his tongue and lips as he travels to my other ear.

"Lilah, you're everything to me. Do you know how hard it's been to watch you swim in this every day?" His thumb brushes over the peak of my nipple through my swimsuit, and a bolt of electricity zings from my breasts to my center. "Every time I see you out here, I want to strip this damn suit off you, lay you out on one of the loungers, and feast on you for days."

He tugs on my nipple. Without warning, he pulls back and slips both straps of my bikini top down my arms, so it hangs underneath my breasts, exposing me to him.

Jimmy examines me with pent-up lust, my skin sizzles from his gaze. The warm rays of the sun heat my skin, reminding me that we're out on his deck, but before I can say anything, he kneads my breasts and sucks on a nipple. My hand pushes into his dark hair, the curls at the end spilling out around my fingers.

He tugs on my nipple with his teeth before sucking on it and swirling his tongue over the rigid tip. My fist tightens in his hair and he squeezes my other breast, rolling the nipple between his thumb and forefinger.

Was it always this good? This on the edge of orgasm the entire time?

I moan when his hand drifts down my stomach and dips into the front of my swimsuit. We need to move inside before we're screwing for all to see. His finger coasts over my swollen nub.

"Jimmy, we need to take this inside." I pant. There's no conviction in my words. I'd let him have his way with me right here if he refused.

But my words clearly cut through the fog of his desire, because he straightens out, taking a second to eat up my body with his eyes while he squeezes his straining length in his swim trunks. "You're right. What I plan on doing to you, no one should see."

I giggle. The promise of his words makes my womb ache, and all I can think of is him inside me.

Without warning, he picks me up and puts me over his shoulder.

"Ah! Jimmy!" I laugh, holding onto the fabric of his shorts.

"What can I say, you bring out the caveman in me." He closes the sliding glass door and heads across the living room to the hallway that leads to the bedroom.

Once we reach the master, he slowly slides me down the length of him until my feet touch the floor. I meet his gaze and gone is the lighthearted mood from moments ago. The lust from the deck releases in the solitude of his room.

His knuckles brush along my cheek and his eyes lock with mine. All the love seeping from him to me drowns me. It's us, Jimmy and Lilah, but at the same time, it's not.

Neither of us has to verbalize the words that we're about to have a first. A first at true intimacy with one another.

I've never made love with anyone. Never wanted to. Until now.

Fear tries to poke holes in my happiness, and the itchy feeling on my skin I so often associated with the need to numb myself commences.

No.

I won't let it win.

Jimmy loves me, and I love him, and our love is enough.

I push the negative thoughts from my head—the ones that tell me he only wants to use me for my body and the pleasure it can give him. The ones that say I'm worthless, the ones that make me believe I'll never be enough for a man like Jimmy. I put them all into a pile in my mind, douse them with gasoline, and light a match.

I reach for him, and even though he doesn't know it, I'm giving him more than my body in this moment. I'm giving him my soul.

Our tongues slowly tangle in a tender kiss. His hand's in my hair, mine in his. He slides down the bottom of my bathing suit with care, followed by pulling the top over my head. I push his shorts down his hips until they fall to the floor, careful not to catch his straining erection.

We stand with our hands linked, drinking in one another.

I've never been embarrassed or insecure about my body, but laying my soul and heart out there is a lot harder. Those are more precious. I want to cover myself up, but I don't. I force myself to remain under his gaze because it's not my body I'm afraid to let him see; it's the me that sits inside my outer shell. But I need him to see it. I need him to see *me* and accept me.

His gaze, filled with love and acceptance and most importantly forgiveness, finally meets mine. Wiping our slate clean.

He leads me to the bed and I crawl up. There will be no foreplay in our coming together this time. We're beyond dirty words and physical sensations.

He crawls over me, and I breathe a sigh of relief with the familiarity of his weight as he lowers himself just enough to make contact with my skin. His warmth seeps into me, and I brush the hair falling off his forehead.

Jimmy kisses me slowly and languidly, with a relaxed comfort. Our tongues meet and neither of us vies for control. The kiss draws to its natural end before he props himself up on his elbows over me, cupping my cheek.

"I love you, Lilah. I've always loved you and I always will. That is my promise to you."

My chest swells, and tears spring to my eyes. His gaze never wavers, giving me his patience as I collect myself before I can speak.

"I love you, Jimmy. And I promise you I'll never stop. No matter what happens. I'll always protect you the way you've protected me for so long."

Our lips meet, and I open my legs for him, welcoming him inside me.

He pulls back for a beat, silently asking if we're still safe without a condom. I haven't been with anyone since I entered rehab and I had a full physical there, so I know I'm safe. I don't care to know if he's been with anyone while we were apart. Nothing matters except this moment.

I give him the smallest of nods and he pushes inside me, his eyes drifting closed. I try to keep mine open as long as possible, but I too close my eyes as he fits himself perfectly inside me. He drags his length out and I open my eyes, needing to see the pleasure in his expression. When I do, he's watching me.

Our gazes never waver as he slides in and out of me. Every thrust is like a promise to love, protect, cherish, and accept.

The grind of his hips when he's fully seated rubs against my swollen clit and my orgasm builds. It's slow, as if we're repairing us brick by brick every time he pushes in.

Words don't leave our lips, but it doesn't matter. What we're sharing is more intimate than any words could express. Emotion swells between us and eventually I cry out, close my eyes, and press my head back into the bed as my climax washes over me. Jimmy comes moments later, and I watch the pleasure in every twitch of his face and groan from his mouth.

He's not quick to get up. Instead, our lips tangle and mesh as our hands lightly run over each other's body.

When he pulls out, the evidence of his pleasure leaks out of me, but I don't care. I don't want to leave this bed or the serenity we've created.

He rolls onto his back and pulls me into his side, stroking my arm with his hand. I close my eyes and squeeze him, truly the happiest I've ever been in my life.

"I want you to move your things in here. If we're doing this—really doing this—I want you sleeping in my bed *every* night."

I place my chin on his chest and look up at him, my hand stroking his cheek, and nod. The delight and surprise in his eyes when I don't put up a fuss like I did months ago warms me, and there's not a doubt in my mind that I made the right choice by telling him my feelings.

For the first time, my future is bright.

JIMMY

Most of my time these past few weeks I've spent trying to keep Lilah busy. The Pier being our go to place since it offers the privacy as long as we're wearing disguises.

She's forming her own routine—swimming every day, sometimes twice, attending daily meetings, and reading a lot of self-help books. Outwardly it appears she's great, but I sense she's hiding how hard recovery really is for her.

A couple of times I've woken in the middle of the night to find her sitting on the deck. She says she's listening to the sound of the waves rolling in because she can't sleep. I worry on those nights, and even though she sends me back to bed, saying she's fine, I lie awake, hoping she's not slipping out to meet one of her old dealers.

Then we have mornings like this one, where she's eager to learn how to cook.

"Here you go." I slide her omelet onto a plate.

"You make it seem easy."

"You'll get it."

"Maybe I need to start with scrambled eggs." She laughs.

I kiss her forehead. "Lesson tomorrow."

"Thanks."

I nod and return to the stove to make my own omelet. Ten minutes later, I'm sitting beside her while she's finishing hers. We've been honest and open with each other since she returned from rehab, but I'm still nervous to ask her what I need to.

"It's so good. I think you're becoming a better cook," she says.

"Well one of us has to be, otherwise we'd starve."

Lilah knocks me with her shoulder and giggles. "Touché."

Cutting into my omelet, I think I might just be getting better. "I wanted to talk to you about something." I shift on the stool to face her. "Feel free to say no if it's too much."

"Okaaay..." Her hands clench into fists on her lap.

"I have to go to a movie opening next month. The same studio that's doing *The Regulator* is doing this one, and I want you to be my date?"

You'd think I was a seventeen-year-old boy asking a girl to prom the way my heart is racing, and my palms are sweaty. Not that I know what a boy feels like in that situation. I never went.

"Of course I want to go with you." She squeezes my wrist.

"We'd have to walk the red carpet. There's a chance a reporter might ask you about rehab."

She contemplates my words and inhales a deep breath. "That's okay. I can't avoid it forever."

Lilah's overdose and subsequent trip to rehab made headlines. I'm not sure she's aware—she'd have no way of knowing unless she's googled herself since she's returned—and since she hasn't asked, I haven't offered the information. Who wants to hear their name was trashed all over gossip magazines? No one.

"Are you sure?" I cover her hand with mine. "I don't want to push you to do something you're not ready for. I can go stag."

She places her hand on my cheek and runs it over my short beard. "If it's too much beforehand or when we're there, I'll tell you. I can always slip out if I need to."

I nod, and she places a soft kiss on my full lips. She smiles and pushes her plate away.

"You know, us showing up together is going to lead to some questions about the status of our relationship," I add.

Lilah shrugs. "They can think what they want as long as we know what's between us."

"I agree, but we should probably decide how we're going to approach the topic."

She swivels in the stool to face me with a grin. "Do you *want* to confirm our relationship to the press? What about Bernie's plan with you and Adelaide?" She rolls her eyes.

"Fuck Bernie and his plan. He won't be happy, but too bad. As for us, I wonder if we're better to confirm it for the press rather than face months of speculation about what's going on."

Though we've spent a lot of time together in the weeks since she's returned. We stick around here, other than the few times we've driven north to hike trails or to the pier. It's no small wonder there have been no pictures of her going to meetings yet.

"They're going to hound us either way, but it might be worse if they're speculating rather than have confirmation," she says.

"So, are we officially coming out to the press?" I can't fight my smile, which spurs Lilah's smile.

Neither she nor I have ever discussed our relationship with the press. Over the years, there's been talk about us on and off again, but we've never confirmed or denied anything.

"I say we do it. We're leaving the past behind. This is part of that."

I kiss her, slipping my tongue between her lips briefly before drawing back. I smile when I pull back. "It's official then. *We're* official."

She slips off the stool and straddles me, wrapping her arms around my neck. "We should celebrate." Her lips mash with mine and her center grinds along my growing dick.

"I like how your mind works." I pick her up and carry her to the couch.

I'm not hungry for an omelet anyway.

* * *

LATER THAT EVENING, I'm sitting out on the deck, watching Lilah do her laps in the pool, as has become our routine. The sun descends as though it's suspended in midair, painting the sky in streaks of orange and amber. Although it's warm out, a cooler breeze picks up off the water. Peace and contentment fall over me.

Lilah is in the early stages of her sobriety and the future isn't certain, but this is how it always should've been. What our future will be. In my head, a decade from now, we're married with maybe a kid or two. Me at the top of my game and Lilah doing whatever it is she wants to do. I smile from the visual.

Between the two of us, I'm the planner. The one who looks into the future and figures out the path to get where I want to be. Lilah was always a "don't hold me down" girl. I'm not sure the sober Lilah is the same way, and confessing my hopes for our future could scare her. So, I'm content for now, keeping things how they are between us as boyfriend and girlfriend.

The sound of water dripping pulls my vision from the sky. Lilah's stepping out of the pool. I want to chase every drop of water running down her smooth, tanned skin with my tongue.

She's a vision as she steps toward me, not bothering with a towel. "I've been thinking..."

"That's never good," I joke.

She lightly slaps my shoulder before she joins me on the double lounger. "Har, har." She presses into my side and wraps her arm around my waist.

"You're getting me all wet." I lean away and she squeezes me tighter, draping her leg over me.

"Well I'm always wet around you, so we're even," she whispers into my ear.

My dick twitches in my pants, and she laughs.

I roll my eyes. "You were saying?"

"Part of my recovery is righting my wrongs and apologizing to the people I've hurt. I was thinking that it might be a good idea for Tripp and me to have a conversation. I know I didn't ever do anything specifically to him, but he helped you clean up a lot of my messes and I owe him an apology."

Pride fills my chest. Tripp's my closest friend, besides Lilah.

"I think he'd really appreciate it." I kiss the top of her head.

"We might never be best friends, but for your sake, I hope we can figure out a way to be in same room without ripping each other's head off."

I chuckle, and she rests her chin on my chest, looking up at me.

"That's the criteria, is it? Just to be able to be around one another without killing each other?"

She smiles. "Ideally, we'll eventually grow to like one another, but baby steps. With our past, it'll take time for him to trust me. He saw me hurt you so many times... now that I have a clear head, I don't blame him. He was only being a good friend to you."

The guilt and shame in her voice cuts me with a dull knife.

"Hey." I tuck a piece of hair behind her ear. "Fresh start, remember?"

She nods and digs her chin into my chest, which makes me wiggle to the side because it half hurts, half tickles.

"Are you ticklish?" She grins, rising over me and straddling me. "How did I not know you're ticklish?"

Her grin shines from ear to ear. She tries to get her hands under my arms, but I fight her off. She shifts gears to my neck, but I squeeze my chin down. We both laugh, and I tickle her ribs until she's laughing so hard she can't catch her breath and falls into my chest.

All her jostling on my lap excites my dick, the hard length straining the confines of my shorts now. While she's pressed against me, catching her breath, she notices and purposely grinds into me.

"Careful. Don't start something you can't finish," I say in a ragged voice, my hands gripping her ass.

"I always make sure you finish." She lets out a soft moan, circling her hips.

The soft pants of her breath on my neck, her tits pressed into my chest, and the friction she's causing leaves me with undeniable desire. My balls ache for release as she speeds up her pace.

I reach down between us. She lifts up, allowing me to undo the button of my shorts and unzip them. Boy am I ever glad I went commando today.

"Here?" she asks, her eyes growing wide.

"It's getting dark and the lights aren't on." I pull out my cock, and Lilah licks her lips.

Fuck, I love how she's always as hungry for this as I am. And her need is genuine now—not once since she's been home has she used sex as a distraction or to avoid her feelings.

My fingers slide her bathing suit aside and she sinks down over me. My eyes roll to the back of my head from her warmth and wetness. I force them to face her, getting off more on watching her. Her eyes flutter closed as she presses down, and when I'm fully inside her, she lets out a rush of air.

She's so tight, and I'm so deep inside her when she's right up over me. Without any encouragement, she rides me, slow and steady.

I'm underneath, watching her steal her pleasure from me, owning me and taking everything she craves, biting her lip and moaning softly. Slowly, she's losing the battle to be quiet. I bring my thumb down and circle her clit, and her cries of pleasure mix with the sound of crashing waves.

I wrap my arms around her, pulling her into me, wishing we could stay here forever.

Chapter Thirty-six

LILAH

Today is not a good day.

I don't know why. Some days, it's easier than others to resist temptation. Some mornings I wake up knowing I'll make it through the day without a drink or using, and others it's a struggle before I have my morning coffee—like every minute of the day drags on like an hour and each second, I'm thinking of ways to score.

Today is one of those days.

The fact I'm alone in the house, since Jimmy had a meeting with his agent this morning, doesn't help. I've swum my laps, cleaned the house, had a shower, and prepped the chicken like Jimmy told me to. Anything to keep my hands and my mind busy. None of it is working. The familiar need claws inside me like a hungry beast demanding to be fed.

There's not a meeting for another hour and I'm afraid if I leave early, I'll just end up at a bar rather than a church base-ment. I contemplate calling the leader of the NA group I usually go to. Since I've yet to find a sponsor I really connect with, he gave me his number.

So, I sit with my legs pulled up to my chest and my arms wrapped around them, rocking back and forth on the couch, trying to will away the need.

Eventually I decide to try using some of the meditation practices they taught me in Utah. I don't bother to move off the couch and sit the way you're supposed to, too afraid that I'll reach for my car keys if I move an inch. Instead I attempt to retreat to the silent, peaceful place inside of myself—the one I found when I was there, away and free from distractions and stressors.

After I don't know how many deep inhales and long exhales, I do eventually find peace.

A hand lands on my shoulder and I rear back.

"Sorry." Jimmy waves his hands.

My hand flies to my chest, and I exhale a short breath to ease my racing heart. "I didn't hear you come in."

"What are you doing?"

I frown. I hate that I might disappoint him by telling him the truth. "I'm having a hard day. I was meditating."

He matches my frown and sits down beside me. Guilt flares inside me for worrying him, but instead of pushing away the unwanted feeling, I allow myself to recognize it. I have to be honest with him on this journey if we have any chance of making it to the other side together.

"What can I do to help?" he asks, taking my hands.

"Nothing." I give him a small smile. "This is all me."

The crease between his eyes deepens. "There must be something I can do."

"Well, you can drive me to my meeting so I don't make any random pit stops."

His worried eyes say my joking tone didn't gentle the delivery. "Done."

My shoulders sag in relief that he doesn't want to talk this out. "Thanks."

He squeezes my hands. "Did something happen that upset you?"

I shake my head. "No, not at all. Some days are just harder than others. Some days it's like I'm torturing myself and it's easy to forget the why."

"Hey." He raises his index finger to my chin and nudges me to look at him. "Do me a favor, as cheesy as this is going to sound. Close your eyes."

I raise my eyebrows.

He rolls his eyes. "Just do it."

I do as he asks.

"I want you to picture ten years from now. Picture yourself, how you look, where you're living, who you're with... what kind of life are you living?"

I've never been one to look too far ahead. Eventually I do see an image of myself nearing forty. My hair is shorter and I'm in good health, which shows with a few more curves. I'm not in California, but I don't know where I am. I'm happy and content. A man and two kids are running around a huge yard.

"Do you see it? Do you see the life you want?" he whispers.

I nod slowly. I suck in a breath, the visual clearing like a camera focusing. Jimmy's smile as he chases and pulls a child in a fit of giggles into his arms. Another one latches onto his leg. All three look back at me, waving. All the current sins and destruction of our past are long behind us.

I blink open my eyes and meet his gaze. "I saw it."

"That's why you're doing this. Any time you find yourself wondering that or struggling to push away temptation, picture that future. *That* is your why."

* * *

I DROP the tin foil and it falls to the kitchen floor. "Shit."

"Everything okay in here?" Jimmy walks into the kitchen.

"Yeah, the steam from the lasagna just got me when I took the foil off." I close the oven door and pick up the tin foil.

"Can I do anything to help?" He leans over me, taking the foil from my hands and kissing my neck. "It smells delicious."

I swivel my head to look at him. "Are you talking about the lasagna?"

He laughs, circling me with his arms. "No." I lightly slap his chest, and his arms grow tighter. "Damn Tripp."

I shake my head. "Take the salad out to the table on the deck."

"Sure thing." He kisses me one more time, his lips falling down my neck. "I love you."

"I love you too." I sink into his strong arms for a moment. "Now, go."

He laughs.

I remove the garlic bread from the packaging. "Oh, and leave the Saran Wrap on until we're ready to eat!"

"Aye, aye, Captain."

"Smartass," I mumble.

Tripp is coming over tonight, and if my hands would stop shaking, that'd be great. I've been too afraid to ask Jimmy whether Tripp was receptive to coming here tonight. All I can control is me. At the end of the day, he doesn't have to accept my apology. He's entitled to his feelings.

I shove the wrapper into the garbage and place the frozen garlic bread on a baking sheet. My eyes land on the clock on the microwave. Tripp will be here any minute.

Lasagna is a little hearty for California, but it's one of the few dishes I can make. I have enough on my mind today, and I didn't want to stress too hard on dinner.

The doorbell rings, Tripp having let himself in through the gate. I glance at the sliding doors. Jimmy is out on the deck, on his phone. Guess it's time.

I will my racing heart to settle down, reminding myself to control what I can control. I grip the doorknob, inhale one calming breath, and I open the door. Tripp stands there with a wary expression, which I'll concede as a good sign since it's not his usual scowl when I'm around.

"Hi, Tripp."

He nods and steps into the house. "Lilah. How are you doing?"

"Good... better..."

A small smile tilts the corner of his lips and he shoves his hands into his shorts' pockets. We stand there awkwardly for a moment, neither of us saying a word.

"Come on in. Dinner is almost ready. Jimmy is on the phone, but I'm sure he'll be done soon." At least I hope so. God, this is so awkward.

"Something smells good," he says, following me into the kitchen.

"I'm making lasagna." My cheeks heat. It's completely ridiculous to invite someone over for lasagna in the middle of summer. "I know it's weird to have it in the summer—"

"Are you kidding me? Do you know how long it's been since I ate a home-cooked meal?" He sits at the breakfast bar while I open the oven door.

The weight on my shoulders lightens. He's trying. That knowledge eases the anxiety creeping over my skin.

"Jimmy mentioned that the band has been back in the studio, working on a new album?" I close the oven and turn around to face him.

"Yeah, the record company wants something new out by the end of the year."

"How's it going?" I walk over to the fridge.

"We've been able to lay down a few tracks. Nothing that's going to go platinum though."

I open the fridge door and spin to face him. "Do you want something to drink? We don't have..."

Tripp waves me off. "Water's good."

I grab two bottles of water and place one in front of him. The sound of the sliding glass door opening causes us both to look into the living room.

Jimmy walks in with a forced smile. "Sorry, man. Adelaide called, and we were catching up."

I tense. Jimmy's been clear that they formed a friendship while working together and I'm secure that Jimmy and I are more solid than we've been in years, but the insecurities and jealousy plague me whenever he mentions her name.

He and Tripp do that handshake thing guys do when they kind of hug but not really. Then Jimmy comes around to my side, wraps one arm around my shoulder, and leans in to give me a chaste kiss on the lips.

"No worries, Lilah and I were just catching up."

Jimmy nods. "How's recording going?"

"Meh." Tripp shrugs. "How's Adelaide?"

"All right, I guess. She was telling me about a movie role she's been offered. Wanted to run it by me and see what I thought."

Neither Tripp nor I ask for details. I've been around long enough to know that loose lips sink ships in this business and nothing is final until the ink is dry on the contract.

"Lilah, did James ever tell you how he tried to set me up with Adelaide?" Tripp laughs and sips from his water bottle.

"You did?" I look at Jimmy.

"I thought maybe I could get this guy to settle down, but neither one of them was into it."

I mock astonishment. "You mean the great Tripp Savage, rock god, couldn't win over a woman? Has hell frozen over too?"

"Right?" Tripp grins, and Jimmy laughs.

Our conversation turns light and easy through dinner, which is more than I could have hoped for.

Then again, I haven't gotten to the hard part yet.

Chapter Thirty-seven

JIMMY

I didn't hold out much hope that Tripp and Lilah could be civil to each other tonight. So, I'm shocked that we manage to finish dinner without either of them snipping at the other.

When I invited Tripp to join us, I explained the reason why and urged him to come with an open mind and be ready to start over. He seemed receptive. Wonders never cease.

"That was great, babe, thanks," I say, leaning over.

She meets me halfway to share a chaste kiss, and before our lips meet, our eyes lock and I notice the undercurrent of nerves.

The time is here.

"Thanks." She leans back in her chair, looking across the table at Tripp. "I'm assuming Jimmy mentioned why I wanted you to come by tonight?"

He nods slowly. "Yeah." He crumples his napkin and tosses it on the table.

"Before I say what I need to say, I want to explain a few things." She takes a deep breath and reaches out in front of her, using her hands to steady herself.

What the hell is she going to say?

"The first time my father sexually abused me, I was eight."

Bile rises up my throat and I swallow it back. My hand shoots out and grabs hers, squeezing. "Lilah, you don't have to do this."

Tears prick her eyes and her lips press together when she looks at me. "I do."

I glance across the table at Tripp, whose face is pure white.

"I don't know how much of our past Jimmy has shared with you, but growing up, all we really had was each other. My mom died in childbirth, and his mom left when he was young. We lived on the side of a mountain in the Appalachians. It was its own little community of sorts, but no one had any money. We were lucky we even got to catch the bus and ride almost an hour to school every day.

"Anyway, like I said, I was eight the first time it happened. Jimmy was the only bright spot in my life. Without him, I never would have survived. If I was hungry, he scavenged for food for me to eat. If I was cold, he lent me some of his own outdoor gear to stay warm. If I was upset about stuff going on at home, he'd drag me out of the house and force me to go on an adventure with him."

For the first time, she makes eye contact with Tripp. He hasn't interrupted or even looked as though he wants to. It's clear she needs to say whatever it is she's leading up to here.

For a second, panic grips my insides, turning them cold—surely, she'll stop before... no, there's no way.

I squeeze her hand, silently urging her to continue.

"I didn't tell you all of that to excuse my behavior, not at all. I'm the one who made the choices I did, no one else. I told you so that you'll understand why it was impossible for me to let him go. He's a part of me. You might as well have been asking me to cut out my heart, because living without him would have killed me."

"I'm so sorry that all that stuff happened to you. No one should ever have to deal with that," Tripp says, and the sincerity in his voice rings true.

"I'm the one who owes you an apology. You helped Jimmy clean up so many of my messes, and you were the one to console him when I would hurt him time and time again. Thank you for always looking out for him and for taking care of him when I couldn't." A tear trails down her face, and she swipes it away with the back of her hand.

"You should know that I'm committed to my sobriety. It's not easy. Some days I'm so close to calling one of my old contacts and going on a bender, it's scary. But then I imagine my life years from now and what I want it to be"—she glances at me with a small smile and squeezes my hand—"and I do what it takes not to cave into my base instincts to numb myself. And I'll keep doing whatever I need to to get through each second, each minute, each hour, until I'm stronger."

"I'm so proud of you, babe." I lean in and cup her face.

I don't fucking care if Tripp's here. It takes a lot to lay yourself out like that, and the fact that she can even talk about her past with Tripp here, when she wouldn't discuss it *at all* before, shows me the progress she's making. I kiss her softly, letting the love I have for the strongest woman I've ever known pour through me and into her, willing her to feel it too.

The sound of a chair scraping across the deck draws our attention. Tripp's risen from his chair and comes around to her other side, reaching for Lilah's hand and helping her up. He pulls her into a tight hug. Something about that act undoes Lilah, because she sobs into his chest.

He rubs her back and rocks her. "I'm happy you're working to get better. I know how much James cares about you." He pulls back and holds her out from him by the shoulders. "Anything I ever said to you was out of concern for him, but I have to apologize too. There are times that I said some things that were way offside. Why don't we start fresh from this point forward?"

She nods, and they share another hug.

Christ, so much weight lifts from me that I think I could fly. Everything is coming together in my life. I have a movie that's going to change my career, the woman I've loved forever is finally healthy and committed to sobriety, and my best friend made amends with her.

That "anything is possible" sensation fills me just like the day Lilah and I first walked Santa Monica Pier. Life only gets better from here.

Chapter Thirty-eight

My mascara wand shakes as I raise it to my eyelashes. "Shit."

I place my hands on the counter and stare at myself through the mirror. I can do this. If I need to leave at any time, I can. If it becomes too much, Jimmy will understand.

The pressure of accompanying Jimmy down the red carpet, effectively announcing our relationship to the world, builds. I would rather not face all the people in the industry who know, or think they know, what I've been through. I'm not naïve enough to think my name wasn't splashed all over the press after my overdose. Not when Jimmy ran out of the awards show party.

Jimmy and I have gone out to eat locally a few times, but this will be the first time I've been around alcohol since the night of the overdose. With triggers all around me and easy access, I'm testing an atomic bomb.

The proximity to the stuff shouldn't matter since I ebb and flow all day, every day between wanting a drink and getting by without one.

"There." I put my mascara back in my makeup bag and survey myself. Not bad. My hair is pulled back in a loose bun, and I've opted for a simple cat eye with red lips.

Jimmy offered to have someone come and get me ready, but I insisted on doing it myself. I didn't want to make small talk, knowing I'd already be nervous.

I step out of the bathroom and into the walk-in closet to slip on my dress. We went shopping in Beverly Hills last week and found me a red-and-ivory Monique Lhuillier gown. I've been lucky enough to wear a lot of designer clothes over the years, but nothing has made me feel more like a beautiful princess than this one. Something I never felt when I was using, no matter how great my makeup looked or what designer I wore.

I step into the gown and pull the zipper up as high as I can, then I step into my silver heels before leaving the closet. "Can you do my zipper the rest of the way?"

Jimmy's hands fall from his bow tie, his mouth hanging open. I can only compare it to what a child might look like spotting Santa Claus—complete wonder and awe.

"Do I look okay?" I ask, self-consciousness creeping in.

He steps forward until we're inches apart and cups my face. I lean into his warm touch and close my eyes.

"You look stunning," he says, his voice soft and chock-full of emotion.

I slowly open my eyes, and they lock with Jimmy's. Old habits die hard though. I want to look away from the intensity in his eyes, so I force myself to hold his gaze.

"Thank you," I whisper.

"I mean it. You're a vision." His thumb traces over my cheek, sending shivers down my spine.

"You're really laying it on thick tonight." A nervous laugh escapes me.

"Don't do that." A crease forms on his forehead. "Don't push the compliment away because it makes you uncomfortable."

I wrap my arms around his neck. "It's still hard to hear good things about myself, let alone believe them."

"I know." He kisses my forehead. "But you need to work on it because I'm going to be saying those things to you for eternity."

A warm awareness spreads through my chest, and I smile. His hands snake around my waist, and he slowly raises my zipper the rest of the way.

"I'd really prefer to stay here all night and strip you out of this beautiful dress, but we should get going. Are you ready?"

I nod, unable to speak past the nerves racking my body.

"Limo is here, so I'll meet you in the foyer in a minute."

"Okay, I'll grab my clutch."

Jimmy insists on supporting me in my sobriety by not drinking himself. I hate that he needs to do that, but I hate it more that I'm probably not ready to be around him while he casually drinks. One day hopefully, but not today.

Snagging my purse off the dresser, I steel myself for the onslaught of questions I'll face tonight. I hope that for once in my life, I don't crumble under the pressure.

* * *

"READY?"

I nod. "As I'll ever be."

Jimmy knocks on the tinted glass, and the driver opens the door to let us out. Jimmy steps out first, turning to extend his hand to me. With my hand safely in his, I step onto the red carpet. The press is snapping pictures and calling our names on one side of the blocked area, fans screaming behind them. On the other side is the large wall of fabric advertising the movie.

Just pretend you're on a shoot. Play the role.

I put on my best smile and hook my arm through Jimmy's waiting one.

Fans scream his name as we step up the carpet. The sea of red is already sprinkled with a few other celebrities I recognize. Jimmy waves with his best movie star smile.

God, he was made for this role.

One of the handlers approaches and asks us to stop for some pictures, first with us as a couple, then each of us on our own. This part I can do. It's second nature. It might have been a bit since I've been on a modeling shoot, but I've still got it.

After we've smiled for a few rounds of photos, the reporters call us over. Jimmy wraps my hand in his, and we step toward the pack of wolves. The first few keep it short and sweet, asking questions about Jimmy's movie and the one we're here to see tonight. I smile at his side, my eyes fixed on Jimmy.

I should have known it wouldn't stay that way.

Once we reach the reporter from Celebrity Hot Shots and she's finishes asking the usual questions, she glances at me. "Lilah's overdose and recent stint in rehab has been much publicized. How's she doing today?"

Jimmy's smile wanes, but as he stares at me, his smile returns. He looks back at the reporter. "Well, she's standing right here. Why don't you ask her yourself?"

"Of course," the mini pit bull says with a fake smile and moves the mic in front of me.

Jimmy squeezes my hand.

"I'm taking it one day at a time and I'm focused on my sobriety right now. Things are going well." I smile, hoping to give the impression that she didn't unnerve me.

"That's good to hear. And since you're here together and holding hands, can we assume that you two are, in fact, a couple?"

She shifts the mic back over to Jimmy and I stare at him. Why, I don't know. We discussed this and how we'll handle the question, but maybe he'll change his mind now that he realizes he'll be answering questions about my sobriety and overdose until the press forgets.

"I can confirm," he says. "We are together, and I am madly, irrevocably in love with this woman beside me."

He brings our joined hands to his mouth and kisses my hand. Tears prick my eyes and I look at him as though he's my prince, which he is.

He gives me a chaste kiss on the lips. "Lilah is working so hard to gain her sobriety, like millions of other Americans whom I'm sure can relate to her struggle. Watching the strength she has, has been nothing short of awe-inspiring."

The reporter flounders for how to respond before thanking us and sending us off.

Jimmy squeezes my hand again as we walk away. We share a relieved a smile, both happy that the announcement is out there. After years of dodging the question and never giving into the are-they-or-aren't-they chatter, our relationship is public and official.

Though it's scary and my heart is beating out of my chest, when I stare at Jimmy, there's relief and excitement for our future too.

* * *

THE MOVIE HAS ENDED and we're out in the large Art Deco lobby of the theater at the after party. Luckily, I haven't had any run-ins with any more members of the press, and most people who approach us are more interested in talking with Hollywood's up-and-coming hot new star than me. I smile, nod, and laugh in all the appropriate places.

Everyone around us sips on alcohol—wine, champagne, beer, hard liquor.

Calder Fox and his wife, Francesca, approach us. Jimmy greets them and introduces me. They're both a big deal in this city and fell for each other on the set of a movie they were working on a few years ago. One that ultimately won Calder an Oscar. He's had his fair share of trouble and was front page news after a car crash left his friend dead and him in rehab.

After the three of them chat about studio stuff, Calder turns to me. "So, how are you doing?" The concern in his eyes and the sincerity in his voice reveal he's looking for more than a surface answer.

I shrug, glancing at a waiter who walks by with a bunch of half-empty wine glasses on his tray. "Hanging in there."

"It gets easier." Calder takes Francesca's hand. "I hated these things when I first got sober, but I've gotten used to attending them without a drink in my hand. I just don't stay as long as I used to."

The four of us chuckle. It's somewhat comforting that I'm not the only one sober here tonight.

"My time away was good for me. Something had to give." I shrug.

Jimmy wraps his arm around my waist and pulls me into his side. "Lilah's been working really hard. I'm proud of her."

Calder smiles, and I'm reminded of exactly why he's a movie star. It's hard to look away. Just like Jimmy. "That's great. Keep working the program. If you ever need someone to talk to who understands, I'm only a phone call away."

"Thanks, that's really nice of you."

"I mean it. In fact, give me your phone right now. I'm going to program my number in, so you have it." He holds his hand out between us.

"Better just do it. He's not going to quit badgering you until you do," Francesca says and rolls her eyes.

"Okay then." I pull my phone from my purse, seeing that my agent has called again.

I've been avoiding Mina because she wants to discuss some type of game plan for my future, but the truth is, I'm not sure I want to model anymore. I have too many bad memories attached to that work, too many triggers waiting to drag me back down. I clear the notification, open my phone to my contacts, and pass it over to Calder.

He adds himself and hands it back. "There you go, and don't hesitate to use it. I mean it. Day or night."

I give him a grateful smile. "Thank you."

Truth is, it would be nice to have someone to talk to who understands the pressures of this town and how they make it harder to navigate sobriety. Maybe he's willing to be my sponsor.

"Well, we'd better work the room before we leave. You know how it is," Calder says.

Jimmy chuckles. "I do. Good to see you guys again. Have a good one."

They smile and disappear through the cluster of bodies surrounding us.

Jimmy turns to me, wrapping both arms around my waist. I raise my hands to circle his neck, my evening purse dangling from one hand.

"How are you doing?" he asks, concern lacing his face and voice.

"Pretty good. But I think I'd like to go soon if that's okay."

He nods, his forehead creasing. "We can go right now if you're finding it too hard."

"It's not that. Well, not entirely." I rise to my tiptoes so I can whisper in his ear, "You look so good in this three-piece suit that I want you all to myself."

He growls, and I draw back to meet his eyes. "I've been undressing you all night. This dress looks killer on you. I can't decide if I want to fuck you while you're still wearing it or strip it off your body and have you just keep the heels on."

Desire flutters low in my belly, and I suck in my bottom lip. His dark eyes turn molten with promises of the things to come when we get home.

I open my mouth to speak, but the sound of his name has me snapping my mouth shut.

"James!"

We turn to see Adelaide making her way over, smiling as though she didn't interrupt an intimate moment. *Great timing.*

She looks beautiful as always. Her long dark hair hangs past her shoulders in soft waves, and she's wearing a cream-colored gown that hugs her small curves.

"Hey, stranger," she says leaning in to air kiss his cheeks. Once they're apart, she turns her attention to me. "Hi, Lilah. How are you doing?"

The condescending way she asks smarts me a bit, but I can play the game. I put on a smile. "I'm doing well, thanks. How about you?"

She ignores my question. "How's sobriety going? Rehab did you good?"

Jimmy takes my hand. An action Adelaide notices since I don't miss the way the corners of her mouth tense a bit.

Hmm. Jimmy might look at her as a friend, but I'd bet my last dollar that little Miss Adelaide wants more than friendship. *Too bad, sister—he's mine.*

"Rehab did put some things in perspective for me, yes." I give Jimmy a loving glance and hold his gaze. "I know what's important, and I'm going to do everything in my power not to lose it again."

He kisses my cheek.

"Oh... that's great." She falters but recovers quickly, turning her attention back to Jimmy. "Rumor mill says that you might be getting an offer for Truman's new movie. Any truth to that?"

"Sorry to interrupt, but I'm going to visit the ladies' room. I'll leave you two to talk, then we can head home and finish what we started?"

Jimmy's eyes flare with heat, leaving no room for Adelaide to wonder what that might be. "Can't wait." He kisses my lips and lets my hand go.

"It was good to see you again, Adelaide."

I smile, and she gives me an insincere smile back.

"Yes, good to see you."

I spin on my heel and weave through the crowd to the women's restroom on the other end of the lobby. I'm more than halfway there when someone grabs my upper arm, pulling me to a halt.

"Lilah." It's Bernie Butler, head of the studio for the *The Regulator* movie Jimmy is in.

"Mr. Butler, hi, how are you?" I retract my arm from his grasp.

I've only met the man a few times in passing, and every time, he gave me the creeps. As a user, I've hung out in some less-than-stellar places and met some nasty people. No one unsettles me the way he does.

"Please, call me Bernie." He smiles, and his pockmarked cheeks rise, making him look as though he's squinting.

"Okay."

"I saw you here with James." He allows his statement to hang there.

"Yes, we're here together." I want to brush him off and bolt, but this man holds a lot of power in the entertainment industry and therefore a lot of power over Jimmy and the trajectory of his career, so I force myself to smile and be polite.

"I hope you're not going to cause any more trouble for him? He has a big movie coming out next year."

I squeeze my purse. "I promise I'm not. I spent ninety days in rehab and I'm sober now. Doing better."

"Good, glad to hear it." He squeezes my shoulder. My eyes follow his grubby hand on my skin before looking back at his bloated face. "I wanted to catch up with you anyway and set up a meeting at my office."

I blanch. "About what exactly?"

After I glance at his hand again, he drops it from my shoulder. "There's some issues that have landed on my desk."

"And I can help?"

"It pertains to James. The two of you being so close, you're probably the best person to help me." The ice in his glass clinks as he circles it, motioning to the crowd.

"What is it?" My heart hammers in my throat. No way he knows, but I'd rather clear it here than have a meeting.

He shrugs. "Nothing we want to discuss with so many ears around."

I step back and look through the crowd. "Let me get James and we can—"

"Maybe you're not understanding the severity here." He touches my arm again and I turn around.

Our gazes lock, and there's an undercurrent of something I can't decipher in his eyes.

"Well, I'll tell James and we can schedule a meeting."

"No James," he says abruptly.

I pull my head back.

"Trust me, Lilah, we don't need to add more weight to James's plate. The movie is enough and with all the magazines and gossip circles after you overdosed, I think he's got enough going on. This is your opportunity to help him out for once."

I inhale a breath. His jab hit its mark. He's clearly not going to accept no as an answer, and I don't want to cause any more problems for Jimmy than I already have. "Sure, okay, let's set something up."

"Great." He smiles like a wolf who knows he's caught his prey before actually catching it. "I'll have my secretary call and set something up." He lifts his glass to me and nods before taking a sip.

The urge to rip the glass from his hand and down the remaining contents is fierce, but I push away the impulse.

"I'll see you soon then." Without waiting for a response, I spin on my heel and head toward the bathroom.

The itchy feeling on my skin intensifies with each step. I'm almost lost to it before I remember what Jimmy said. When I reach the restroom and enter my stall, I lock it, lean back against the cool metal door, and exhale, picturing the reason for my suffering right now. I can see me, healthy and happy, in the future, married to Jimmy, with a child or two running around in the grass. All of us laughing with full hearts.

That's why I'm doing this. That's why I will not numb myself. I want *that*.

I keep breathing, and after a few minutes, the tension eases until I no longer want to peel out of my skin.

When I step out of the bathroom, Jimmy's waiting for me, his hands in his pockets and a look of concern directed my way. He gives me a head-to-toe sweep with his eyes, assessing me.

"Everything okay?" he asks, pushing off the wall.

"Yeah. I had a moment there, but I got through it."

He cups my face. "That's my girl."

I kiss him, holding on to his wrists. *This is why I'm doing this.*

"You ready for me to take you home and ravage you?" He winks.

"More than ready."

With my hand in his, he leads me through the crowd.

It wasn't a perfect night, but the most important part is that I got through it.

Another step in the right direction toward my new life.

Chapter Thirty-nine

JIMMY

I'm close to signing a contract for another movie. If I do, it'll be my first eight-figure deal. All the buzz around *The Regulator* has worked in my favor, and I'm more in demand than ever.

I jog up the steps and enter my front door, eager to tell Lilah. The house is dark and quiet. I walk to the living room, and the excitement bubbling in me bursts.

She sits in a chair with her back to me. The TV isn't on, and for a moment, I think she might be asleep. But she shifts and pulls a blanket up to her shoulders. I must be imagining the grim atmosphere in the house.

"I've got good news," My feet eat up the final few steps around the chair, and I come to a halt, soaking her in. "What's wrong?"

I drop to my knees in front of her chair. Her damp hair lays over her shoulders, and she's fresh-faced and makeup-free while wearing her sleep cami and shorts. I wouldn't think much of it except for the red tint around her eyes and her desolate expression.

She bites her bottom lip and tears pool in her eyes.

"Lilah, what happened? What's going on?" Taking her hands, I bring them to my lips and kiss her knuckles as my insides clench.

I'd mentally prepared myself for her to fall off the wagon—or I'd thought I had.

"Just a rough day, that's all." Her voice is scratchy, as though she's barely used it today.

"Did you..."

She shakes her head vehemently. "No, I'm still sober." Her eyes squeeze shut. "But I want to use so badly right now."

I wrap my arms around her, squeezing her tightly, letting her know I'm here. I can't fight her internal battle for her, but I'm here and willing to do whatever I can to get her past this momentary rough patch.

"What can I do?" I murmur into her hair.

"Nothing." She pulls away. "Tell me your great news." She rubs her eyes and gives me a pleading look, obviously wanting to forget whatever demon she's fighting.

Although my enthusiasm has waned, I figure it will distract Lilah. "I'm close to signing on to another movie. And if things go as planned, this will be my first eight-figure deal."

Her smile grows. Though she's clearly happy for me, there's still a glimmer of sadness in her eyes. "That's amazing. All your hard work, all the sacrifices are paying off. I'm so happy for you."

"For us, Lilah. Be happy for us," I say, because for me, it's not I, it's we.

"I am." She places her hand on my cheek and kisses me softly, tenderly as she opens her mouth for my tongue to slide in. She closes the kiss sooner than I'd like. "Will you make love to me?"

I pull back and meet her gaze. A depth of emotions swim in her eyes—love, pain, remorse, shame, and most importantly, hope.

"Always."

I drag her forward on the chair until she slips off and onto my lap, straddling me. Cupping her face, I meet her lips with a kiss fueled by desire and desperation.

Lilah needs to savor my love for her right now.

After a few minutes, I lead her to our bedroom, where I strip her bare and worship her body with my mouth.

"You're everything to me," I say, twirling my tongue around her nipple.

"You are my past, my present, and my future," I whisper into her inner thigh.

"You are all that matters," I promise her before sucking on her clit.

Once I've sated her with my tongue, I push inside her with our eyes locked. I force myself to keep my eyes open despite the pleasure coursing between our bodies. She must need the connection too, because her eyes never wander.

"You are the best thing that ever happened to me," she whispers.

I want to respond, but she climaxes soon after. The pulsing of her center sends me over the edge, and I spill into her with ecstasy in my body and love in my heart.

Afterward, she lies in my arms and falls asleep. I hope I was able to show her how loved she is.

* * *

THE SUN IS FALLING in the sky and I flip my page, waiting for Lilah to come back out so we can decide about dinner.

The sliding doors open behind me. "I'm going to run out for a while."

I turn away from the ocean view to see Lilah stepping out of the sliding doors. "Where are you headed?"

"I'm meeting Mina in the city. She wants to discuss what my next steps are, if there are any."

I sit up from the lounger and place my feet on either side. "You've decided to go back to work?"

She shrugs. "I'm not sure. We're going to discuss it."

Up until now, she's told me she has no interest in returning to modeling. What changed?

"Okay. I'll come with you and then we can grab dinner?"

"No, I'm good to go on my own. I'll call you on the way back. It'll be late, but maybe I'll stop at that Thai place you love and bring some home for us as a late-night snack and we can watch a movie or something?"

I sit back and stare at her. The last thing I want is to pressure her. At the Al Anon meeting I went to, they said I can't control Lilah and shouldn't try. "Yeah, okay, sounds good."

"Great." She smiles, but it's not the one I've seen since she returned from rehab. In fact, she's as cagey as she was when she used.

"Are you sure everything is okay?" I ask.

"Promise," she says.

"Pinkie promise?" I hold out my hand with my pinkie finger extended.

The anxiety churning in my gut has reached a boiling point. I need to know she's okay, that we're okay, and she would never lie to me on a pinkie promise. It may have started as a silly game between kids, but it's developed into a solemn vow—one I know neither of us would ever break.

Leaning in, she places a chaste kiss on my lips before cupping my face and meeting my gaze. "I love you." She hooks her pinkie finger to mine.

She withheld the words for so long that every time she says she loves me, it's a precious gift. A morsel of relief eases some of the tension racking my body.

"I love you too. Always."

Rather than love reflected back at me, her blue eyes shine with sadness.

"I'll call you," she says and heads back into the house to leave.

I watch her until she's out of sight.

Why can't I shake the feeling that the perfect future I envision is about to be ripped away?

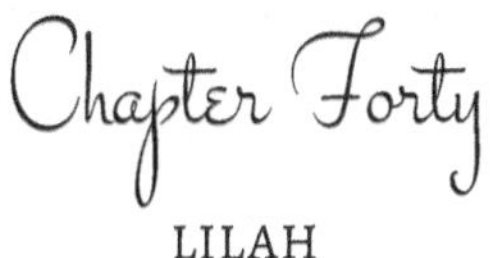

Chapter Forty

LILAH

fter the movie premiere, Bernie's secretary called the next day to set up a meeting for the following week. A helluva lot sooner than I'm prepared for.

Keeping the secret from Jimmy that I'm meeting with Bernie almost put me in a tailspin, but it's time for me to be the strong one in our relationship.

I enter the lobby of the building all the studio executives work in, make my way through security, and get into the elevator, where I hit the button for the top floor. I step off the elevator, and in my Esperanza heels and sundress, I approach the reception desk. A young blonde who looks as though she could be my sister is packing up her bags and shutting down her computer.

"You must be Lilah," she says.

"I am."

"Mr. Butler is expecting you. You can go right in. His door is at the end of the hall."

"Thanks." I smile and head down the hall.

Most offices are dark, and everyone I pass in the hallway has their jacket on, their bags on their shoulders. As I draw near his office, my footsteps are the only sound—besides my thundering heartbeat. I feel as though I'm walking toward the gates of hell. God knows evil lurks there.

I knock on his door.

"Yeah."

I twist the handle and poke my head in. "Hi, I'm a little early, I know."

He puts down the stack of papers he's riffling through and turns to face me. "Come on in." He waves me in. "Close the door behind you."

The hairs on the back of my neck spring to attention, but I shove away my unease. The door was closed when I arrived.

I close the door, then I turn to make my way over to his desk and find his eyes glued to my ass. That gut feeling inside me says something is off, but with a tentative smile, I sit in the chair across from him. He looks at me with a grin, saying nothing. I wiggle in my seat, allowing my eyes to focus anywhere but on him.

"So... what did you want to discuss with me today?"

His lascivious gaze roams up my body one more time. "I got a call a few weeks back from a woman who claims she's James's mother."

My stomach flips, and my eyes scan for the nearest trash can. I'd forgotten all about her. Last I knew, Jimmy hadn't heard anything from her since he paid her off. "Well, that's crazy. As you know, Jimmy, er... James's mom died."

He quirks his lips into an expression to say, *is she really?* "Whoever this lady is, she had some interesting things to say." He leans back in his chair and steeples his fingers in front of him.

"I'm sure she did since she's a complete loon. I can assure you, James's mom died." My heart pounds with the lie.

"She said James isn't the The Regulator he's playing in the movie. He was a drug dealer throughout high school—"

"Well, that's funny since his real mom wasn't even around then." My defense of Jimmy comes as second nature to me.

Bernie shrugs. "People talk. She said she's back in whatever hick town it is you two are from."

I cross my legs, and his eyes fall to the movement. His Adam's apple bobs and his eyes flicker back up to me.

"Don't you find it convenient that a woman claiming to be his mom calls at the same time the movie that's going to propel his career is due to release? You're a smart man, Bernie." Part of me feels slimy from going back to my old mind games, but they worked well when I was trying to score, back in the day.

He huffs. "I did find it very suspicious at first. I didn't even accept her calls until she used the word blackmail."

"So you paid her?" At this point, I stop arguing that the woman isn't Jimmy's mom.

"Fuck no." He stands and looks out through his window. "She can try to blackmail me all she wants. She's right though… having this kinda shit come out right before the movie's release could tank it. James's mom is smart, even with only the fourth-grade education you guys get in the mountains." He turns to face me with a leer that makes my skin crawl.

"I told her she can go fuck herself. That I'd drag her through court for extortion and take whatever measly scraps she has left from the money James paid her—yes, she told me about that. When I was done with her, she seemed to get the point." His pupils glitter with menace, almost as if he gets off on this sort of thing.

"She's a lying psychopath."

His eyes land on me again. "Let's stop the charade. I'm not an idiot and I've been in this business a long time. The lady who called me is James's mom." There's certainty in his voice.

I swallow, trying to coat my dry mouth. "You don't know the whole story. She doesn't deserve—"

He holds up his hand. "Stop fighting and just say thank you."

"Th-thank you." My voice is shaky with surprise. "If you took care of it, why am I here?"

I tense as he slinks around the desk and comes to stand in front of me. "Just wait, I'm not done."

I shift in my seat to face him, craning my head back to meet his gaze.

"I can't afford to have any surprises upend this movie, so I had my PI do a little digging of his own. The upbringing you and James had... well, pathetic is the best word. Not surprising why you ended up a hot mess."

Fear thickens my blood until it's like sludge pushing through my veins.

No, no, no.

If someone is poking around in our past, they might find out about that night.

My breathing becomes shorter and faster. I don't think he knows—how could he? But if he continues to dig around, he will.

I attempt to keep a lightness in my voice. "There's nothing to find there except people who have no idea there's a world outside of theirs and some cheap moonshine."

He pounds his fist on the table. "Stop acting like I'm an idiot!"

I slide as far back as I can in the seat, gritting my teeth. "What do you want?"

I'm not here to help him protect Jimmy. I know a shakedown when I see one.

"How about a drink?" His anger dissipates, and he walks over to his small bar.

"I don't drink."

"Oh, that's right. You're really convincing the press. It's funny, what with the whole fake relationship I had James and Adelaide put on, but maybe it's your happily ever after that will sell my movie. I forgot how much the world loves a happily ever after." He pours a hefty amount of scotch into his glass, looking back at me while he drops in an ice cube. "Then again, the press does love heartbreak just as much."

I swallow the lump in my throat, my body falling to its old habit of fear. I stand from my chair, tightening my purse over my shoulder, preparing to leave. "Just tell me what you want."

"Who says I want anything?" He wanders over to his leather couch and sits down, patting the spot next to him.

"You're delusional."

"Am I?"

I'm on the other side of the room, our eyes locked in a show-down until a hollow laugh falls from him.

"James—or Jimmy, right?"

I say nothing.

"He's done a lot over the years to help you. I'd say he could have already hit it big if not for you. He's sacrificed everything. You know what's funny about small towns?"

My stomach gurgles and I grip the edge of the desk to hold myself up. I say nothing.

"Money is king. It wouldn't cost a lot for my PI to find out everything there is to know about Lilah Robbie and James— or excuse me, Jimmy—Crawford. I can see the headline now." His hands are in the air. "'The Regulator sold drugs...'"

He pats the seat next to him.

I shake my head.

"You're really on that whole staying clean and not letting every shithead-fuck-you-in-the-bathroom thing, huh? Good for you. How long do you think it'll last? If I were a betting man —which I am," he laughs again, "I'd say you wish you could score right now. Well, top drawer on the left." His eyes shift to the drawer.

My eyes follow his.

"Come on, Lilah, grab the blow and let's party." He pats the leather seat again. "Oh, on second thought." He opens a drawer in the table next to him, pulls out a baggie and tosses it on the circular table in front of him.

"No. Just tell me what you want. Money? I'll get you some."

His head falls back onto the edge of the couch. "Money? I'm the richest guy in this town."

I could argue he's not, but this isn't the time.

He opens up the baggie, plucks a business card out of a holder on the table and divides it into six lines. My eyes don't stray from the powder that would allow me to disappear from what's happening in this room.

"Then what?"

He opens the drawer he got the coke from and pulls out an already rolled up hundred. Staring up at me, he snorts a line and holds the rolled bill out to me.

Another cynical laugh ruptures out of him. "Oh, that's right, you're sober now."

I fight my bodies urge to rip that hundred out of his hand and inhale all five lines left. I close my eyes briefly, remembering Jimmy's words, our future, why I won't listen to the temporary craving of oblivion. "Can we move this along?"

"I used to think I wanted you out of James's, or Jimmy's, life." He shoots me a condescending smile. "Prepared to pay you off maybe, but with this clean Lilah now? I'm not sure that's the wisest choice." He sips his scotch. "Come sit and we'll talk."

I don't move, my eyes on the door. I've been in this position before, with dealers and the first man in my life who should have been protecting me. "You realize that if you bring Jimmy down, you're only hurting your own studio. You've invested hundreds of millions in his film and if its star gets on the shit list, you'll make zero money at the box office."

Bernie stares at me blank-faced for a moment. I think that maybe I've gotten somewhere, but then he bursts out laughing. "You're smarter than you look. Everything you say is true, but you forget that my studio can afford to lose money on this film. We've had a great year, and yeah, it would hurt our bottom line, but we'd recover. Besides, all the blame would fall on James's head, not mine." He opens his legs, leaning back on the couch. "When I want something, there's *nothing* I won't do to get it. Not to mention, I'm sure you've heard the saying bad press is better than no press."

"You're sick," I spit at him, rage boiling.

"Maybe. Maybe not. The fact is, you have something I want." His gaze takes a lecherous trip down my body and he leans over the lines of coke snuffing another line. "And I have something you want—to keep quiet about James's past and to quit digging into it. You're not going to let your savior fall when you could have prevented it, are you? After all he's done for you?"

I step one foot forward.

"That a girl. Jimmy would be so proud. You actually doing something for him. All those meetings when he sat there at the end of the table like a pathetic love-sick boy who couldn't walk away from someone self-destructing right before his eyes. Someone who didn't love him. You didn't love him, did you?"

"Yes, I did. I do." My feet stop in front of the small table in front of the couch.

"Of course you did. Everyone around him tried to get him to leave you and he never did. Never wavered. Now it's your choice to repay him. Or not."

I sit on the couch.

I'm not fully settled on the couch before he leans in. The smell of his cologne brings bile up my throat. He runs his finger up my arm, and I swallow it back down.

"Just tell me," I choke out.

"Do I really need to be more specific?" He slides closer.

The bile rises back up my throat when my eyes spot his erection tenting his pants. He brushes his hand over himself.

"You think I'm going to fuck you?"

"Yes, I do." His forwardness knocks back my snarky self.

My dad was the same way. Took what he wanted regardless. He might have been the poorest man in our town, but he always took what he wanted from me.

"That's what it will take? Me fucking you to not out Jimmy?"

"Yes."

I turn my head away as memories of the girl hiding under her bed rush forward—the shame and dirtiness coating me like paint on my skin.

"I won't sleep with you," I say to the door.

"You will if you want your precious James to continue to work in this town. I can ruin anyone's career with a few phone calls."

He allows his response to linger around us. My fists clench in my lap. He's right. We both know it.

The phone next to him rings and I'm surprised when he picks up the receiver.

"Yeah."

Another one of his twisted smiles forms. "Sure. Five minutes."

I move to stand.

"Where are you going?" His hand takes mine and leads me back down on the couch.

"I thought…"

"Five minutes is long enough."

I shake my head. "You're kidding."

"What sells headlines better than the latest heartthrob crashing down from stardom? I can see the magazine in ten years —'Where is James Crawford now?'"

I whip my head around to meet his gaze.

All his hard work, all the sacrifices and the things he's done would be for nothing.

Unshed tears burn my eyes, but I push them back. I will not show him weakness.

"I'm sure if I did some more digging, I could find even more fun facts about Hollywood's good guy. Like I said, money gets a lot of information."

Alarm bells blow in my head. No, if anyone found out about… no. That would change his life in catastrophic ways. One of my tears breaks past the dam and slips down my cheek. I open my mouth to speak, but I lose my voice.

He grabs my hand and covers his dick with it. "Don't you want to repay him for all the times he saved you?" He undoes his belt and his pants.

He situates himself on the couch, his eyes falling to his dick, not shy about asking for what he wants. With tears falling, I drop down and let my purse slide from my shoulder to the floor.

Bernie pulls out his erect dick and strokes himself.

I squeeze my eyes shut. I'm doing this for Jimmy.

"Open your eyes, sweetheart, and suck back those tears. I want you to look like you're enjoying it as you suck me."

I flutter my eyes open, trying to calm my shaking body. His breathing becomes more and more labored.

"Let me see those gorgeous tits."

His gaze is like acid burning my skin. I allow the numbness to seep in. It was always my best defense when I was young, and now it falls like a curtain over me. It offers a small amount of relief, keeping me one arm's length separated from reality.

I slowly lower the straps of my sundress. His sausage fingers pull down my bra cups.

"Come here." He grips the back of my head to pull me forward.

The closer I get to his small dick, the more strength I gain. I'm not an eight-year-old girl anymore. I can go to Jimmy and we'll figure this out together. Screw Bernie.

"I can't do this." I place my hands on his knees, resisting his pull forward. "I won't do this to Jimmy. I can't. Do what you want, but I won't betray him this way."

A knock on the door shocks me and I stare at Bernie.

"Come in," he says before I have a chance to get up.

"What..."

It all happens in slow motion. The door opening and Jimmy appearing, looking irate and devastated at the sight of me between Bernie's legs with his pants wide open.

I've done things I can never undo.

No matter how much I wish I could, sometimes the wounds I inflict are too deep, too catastrophic, too septic to heal. As I look into the eyes of the only man I've ever loved, I know I've gone too far. I've finally crossed the line.

Even if he knew my reason for doing this, he'd never forgive me.

He always puts my needs before his own.

This was my time to protect him and I failed him again.

None of that matters though, because the betrayal and disgust in his eyes reaches deep into his soul. There's no coming back from this.

He will forever be tainted by what he's seen, and he will never forgive me.

Chapter Forty-one

JIMMY

I must have blacked out, because the next thing I know, Lilah's sitting on the floor, my knuckles are throbbing and Bernie's holding his eye with his limp dick hanging out. I cannot be seeing this.

I knew something was off with Lilah, so I followed her into the city, thinking that maybe she'd slipped and was off to see her dealer.

But this... I never could have predicted this.

When she parked her car, I was confused at first. Why would Lilah come and see Bernie?

"Jimmy!" Lilah gets up off her knees.

Oh God, she's on her knees. Tears stream down her face and the cups of her bra hang down, revealing her tits.

I glance behind her at Bernie, who's slipping his cock back into his pants.

I can't fucking be here.

Turning without a word, I bolt down the hall to the elevator. I stab the button, but it takes too long, and Lilah calls for me down the hall. Pushing my hands through my hair, I look around until I see a stairwell. I race to the stairwell door. I can't be around her right now. I'm afraid, for the first time ever, that I might hurt her.

I'm out of breath by the time I reach the bottom floor, pushing through the door that opens to the back part of the lobby.

Lilah is waiting for me. She must have ridden down on the elevator I called.

"Jimmy, just wait!"

I push past her and speed walk out of the lobby, ignoring the security guard calling out to say goodbye.

"Jimmy, wait." She tugs on my shirt after I clear the doors to the building,

I can't hold back my anger. "That sure didn't look like Mina."

"Please listen to me. I can explain." She sobs, hanging on to the front of my shirt.

"I know what I saw!" I rip her hands off me because I can't stand for her to touch me with hands that were almost wrapped around Bernie's dick.

The thought makes me wretch, and I step to the side of the walkway and puke into the garden. Straightening, I wipe my mouth with the back of my hand and glare at her. The sight of her pulls more bile up my throat.

"You don't... it wasn't..."

"It doesn't even matter whatever cokehead lie you're about to tell me."

"What? I didn't..."

"I saw the lines on the table. Don't fucking lie to me. Don't treat me like I didn't see what I did. You think I'm stupid?" I yell.

She grabs on to my shirt again, not letting go.

I unclasp her hands off me finger by finger, her tears shattering my heart to pieces.

"I can't witness you like this anymore. Don't you understand how much I love you? We were here." I raise my hand over my head. "and in one swoop, I'm here." I lower my hand below my waist. "You're killing me. You do realize you lied to me on a pinkie swear?" I run my fingers through my hair. "I worried you might lose your sobriety, but even when you were so high you literally thought you could fly, you never lied to me on a pinkie swear."

The more I recount the scene in my head, the more my anger calms but sadness seeps in. This is really the end of us because I can't keep saving her.

"I didn't."

I hold my hand up in the air to stop her. I can't bear to hear her bullshit. "You've finally done it, Lilah. For years you tried to ruin us. Congratulations, you finally did."

"No." She drops to her knees on the sidewalk, begging me with her eyes as tears tumble down her face.

Before rehab, this would have been par for the course, but this time, I thought she was all in, done with the games, done with ruining everything good in her life. I believed her—heart and soul. Only for her to break me again. Break my trust that she loves me just as much as I love her. The trust that I mean as much to her as she does me. Maybe I could have handled a relapse. But this is a betrayal.

Well, I'm the fucking fool, aren't I? She'll never change.

Grief and anger well up inside me and spill out. "I'm not doing this anymore. This cycle has to stop. You've stolen everything from me! Do you understand? I have nothing more to give!"

"Jimmy..." she says through hiccupping sobs.

"There is no explanation that will make this okay." Something tickles my cheek, and I reach up and realize that tears are running down my face. "I want you to get your shit out of my place."

Her hands drop from her face, and she looks at me in complete shock before pain lances through her features. I push away the impulse to console her, to fix the situation for her. Give her a hug and tell her it's okay.

The definition of insanity is doing the same thing over and over again and expecting a different result. No more. I'm done with this asylum.

"I love you," she whispers.

I lean in, my face contorted with rage. "No. You don't. Find some other schmuck to clean up your messes."

I stalk away, trying to push the pain of betrayal from my mind, but it's like a thousand-pound cinder block stacked on my heart. I slide into my car peel out of the parking lot, leaving behind the woman who was my everything, but instead took everything from me.

Chapter Forty-two

LILAH

"**Y**ou gonna stare at that thing all night or drink it?"

Glancing at the bartender through puffy, sore eyes, I say nothing.

I have no idea how I got here. I mindlessly scraped myself up off the sidewalk, though I do have a vague memory of walking aimlessly through the streets.

The bartender shrugs and walks off to help another customer.

Pain stabs my chest when I remember the look on Jimmy's face in Bernie's office.

I want to shrivel up and die.

He will never forgive me. There's zero hope for reconciliation.

I grip the shot of whiskey. Whiskey because it reminds me of *him*.

What will the fallout be from what happened tonight? Will Bernie leak the info on Jimmy? Does it matter? I've done him more damage than anyone else could ever do anyway.

A lone tear slides down my cheek, burning as it snakes a path over my raw skin.

The fragment of my heart that held out hope that we'd share a future withers and dies. I stop fighting my demons and give myself over to the darkness clawing within.

Gripping the shot glass hard, it looks like salvation from the crippling feeling that I destroyed the one person I loved the most.

I pick the shot glass up off the lacquered wood bar top and bring it to my lips. My mouth waters as the scent wafts into my nose.

Fuck it.

I toss back the shot and revel in the burn that coats my throat, down to my stomach, and pushes away all the helplessness, the shame, the pain.

This is nothing more than I deserve.

I have nothing.

Part Two

ALMOST SIX YEARS LATER...

Chapter Forty-three

JIMMY

The California sun beams through the large window, and I slowly open my eyes. I lie there half asleep for a minute until a small hand wraps around my waist. The light catches on her diamond, casting a light show on the ceiling. I roll over to chestnut-colored hair sprawled over the pillow, her eyes still closed.

Six years and some mornings when I first wake, I still expect to find Lilah and her bright blue eyes staring back at me. Like those people who lose a limb and say they still feel it years later. That's what removing Lilah from my life feels like—losing a piece of me.

So even though I'm a shit fiancé, I resolve my guilt by telling myself that I'm not to blame. Eighteen months with Adelaide can't instantly erase the half of a lifetime I spent with Lilah.

"Morning." I rub her shoulder.

Her mouth forms a small smile, but her eyes remain shut. "Morning." Her voice is rough from a sound night's sleep.

"What do you have on your schedule for today?" I guarantee something wedding related. It always is.

Ever since we got engaged, the laid-back, easygoing, take-it-as-it-comes-and-don't-stress-the-small-stuff woman I proposed to, has been swallowed up by the hyper-focused perfectionist lying beside me. I hope it's a temporary change, but what would I know? I'm a guy. We're just told what to wear and when to show up. Women man the reins and make sure the whole day is pulled off without a hitch. And when you're A-list celebrities like the two of us, the pressure of perfection is greater.

Adelaide opens her eyes, her content gaze meeting mine. "I have to meet with the wedding coordinator about the flowers. Then I'm having lunch with some of the girls. How about you?"

"I've got a call scheduled with Keane around lunch to talk about what's next for me. I'll probably work out after that. Why don't I make us dinner?"

"That would be great." She places a chaste kiss on my lips.

"Anything in particular you feel like having?" I ask as she rolls over and sits on the edge of the bed.

"Yes, a leaf of lettuce. I have to fit into my wedding dress."

I scoot up the bed to rest my back against the headboard. "You look fine. Quit with that shit."

She looks over her shoulder, rolling her eyes. "Says the guy who can eat almost anything and keep a killer bod." She stretches her arms over her head and stands, heading into the ensuite.

"You have a killer bod. And why isn't my opinion the only one that matters?"

"Because our wedding picture will be plastered over every magazine and tabloid for years to come. Every time they make up a story about us having problems or 'is she pregnant,' they'll post a picture from our wedding. And I for one want to look good."

Thankfully, she's in the bathroom, otherwise she'd see me rolling my eyes.

"Fine, whatever. Eat like a rabbit."

I roll over and stand from the bed, adjusting my morning wood in my boxers. My dick begs for some action, but my fiancée doesn't enjoy morning sex. Regardless, her mind is on the wedding twenty-four seven, not on getting me off.

I leave the master bedroom and head down the hall to the other bathroom to relieve myself. I cannot wait to put all this wedding nonsense behind us and start our lives.

In my opinion, which counts for nothing as far as this wedding goes, the wedding is one day—everything that comes after that is what really counts.

* * *

I set myself up in my office, pull up Skype, and wait for Keane.

I just wrapped a movie, and though I'm taking a small break until after the wedding, it's time to figure out my next role.

When *The Regulator* released six years ago, my life did a one-eighty. I became a household name, so now I get to pick my projects. After all the shit that went down with Lilah, I threw myself into my work, traveling from country to country to film movie after movie. Otherwise I would have cracked and searched for her.

Thankfully, I chose my projects well and I'm rewarded now by getting offers for more serious work, rather than the romantic lead in rom-coms or the tough guy in action films.

My computer rings, dragging me from my thoughts. I click the button, and Keane's smile pulls up on the screen.

"Hey, man."

"Hey." He looks to his left and gives his assistant instructions before looking back at me. "Sorry about that."

"No worries."

"How's your fiancée?"

"Busy with wedding plans."

"Sounds about right. I never understood how the wedding industry was a billion-dollar industry until I got married. Who knew you could charge so much for flour and eggs?"

"I just try to stay out of the way."

"I still can't believe you're getting married." He shakes his head.

That same line has been on repeat from my friends. I can't blame them. A couple years ago, I only cared about work and playing hard. And playing hard meant banging any willing and available female as long as they weren't blonde.

But after a few years, I grew tired of having women sleep with me just to say they had. That's when Adelaide's and my friendship rekindled. Soon my playboy days were over, and I was enjoying an easy relationship with Adelaide.

"I could've said the same thing when you tied the knot."

Keane chuckles. "True enough. Seriously though, I'm happy for you. You're very calm and content with Adelaide."

"Well, she's a calm and content kinda person." I smile.

"All right, enough of this personal shit. Let's get down to business."

I shift in my seat, eager to hear who's expressing interest in working with me. "What do you got?"

Keane shuffles a few papers on his desk. "A script came in from Dedrick Walker, but it's shit. I'll send it your way if you want, but I know you'll pass on it."

"I trust your judgment. If you think it's shit, I will too."

"Good enough." He tosses the paper aside. "Dreamcast Studios is working on a reboot of the *Three's Company* sitcom. Before our time. They're planning to modernize the concept and make it a feature-length film, but that one is for streaming services, not theaters."

"I'll pass. Not because it's not theaters, just because I'd like to work a dramatic role."

"Got it. Okay, that means these three are out..." He shifts more papers and pulls up another one. The muscles in his jaw tighten, and he hesitates.

"What is it?" I lean back in my chair.

He blows out a breath and looks up from the sheet. "This one is from Freelance Studios. It fits what you said you wanted to work on next."

Anger stabs my chest like a hot poker. "Fuck that."

"I know how you feel and that's why I hesitated to bring it up, but the script and role could be award-winning. I just couldn't not tell you about it."

"I could never work for him." I wrap my hand around my water bottle, and it crinkles under the pressure of my grip.

"You know Bernie stepped back after his heart attack. He's not involved in the day-to-day anymore."

"It doesn't matter. I told you six years ago that I will never work for that studio again and I meant it."

What happened six years ago still makes me want to hunt Bernie down and beat the shit out of him. Will I ever be over it?

"You've never really told me what all went down, but—"

"I'm not discussing it."

"Don't cut off your nose to spite your face, James, that's all I'm saying. It's a good script. It has a good director attached to it. It's going to be a successful project."

I lean closer toward my laptop because maybe Keane is somehow missing how serious I am. "I will *never* work for that bastard again. Don't bring it up—*ever*."

He holds up his hands in a placating gesture. "All right, all right. I got nothing then. I'll put some more feelers out for the kind of project you're looking for and let you know if I find anything."

I nod, unable to speak because my jaw is clenched so tight.

"I'm sorry I brought it up. It's just... it's been years and you've moved on with Adelaide. I just thought..."

I say nothing to fill the silence.

"Anyway, keep in touch. I'll let you know when I have something."

"Great." I push the laptop closed without saying goodbye.

My mood is shit now thanks to the mention of that asshole, Bernie Butler. I won't lie, when I heard he'd suffered a heart attack a few months back, I was disappointed the thing hadn't killed him. His heart is black anyway.

I push a hand through my hair and stomp down the hall toward the living room, but when I get there, I look around, unsure what to do with myself.

Deep down, I'm aware how messed up it is that that night can still rile me up until I can't think clearly. It's just a reminder that I have no idea why Lilah did what she did.

I haven't spoken to her or Bernie since that night. When he approached me at *The Regulator*'s premiere, I made it clear that I had nothing to say to him and if he didn't want another round of plastic surgery, he'd better stay the hell away from me.

Pacing doesn't help me gain control of my emotions, so I head back down the hall.

Best decision I made after Lilah's abrupt departure from my life was turning the guest room into a gym. I quickly change into shorts and a T-shirt, ready to spend the next hour and half using my anger to fuel my workout, until my muscles ache and my clothes are drenched. If I'm lucky, the image of Lilah and Bernie on that couch will disappear.

* * *

I TURN up the temperature on the oven, so it'll stay warm until I'm ready to put in the salmon. I decided on baked salmon for dinner, along with asparagus and quinoa. All wedding-diet-approved items.

Adelaide called to say she'll be a little late for dinner. Apparently, the wedding coordinator had a lead on the perfect chair covers for the reception.

I grab a beer from the fridge, pop off the cap, and sit on the couch, clicking on the TV to kill time. I flick through the channels to find something interesting, but it's mostly just news, given that it's six o'clock. I settle on a national news channel. I should know what's up in the world anyway.

Probably a glutton for punishment since I've been in a crappy mood since this morning. I curse myself for even thinking of Lilah in the first place. She'll leave my head before I marry Adelaide, won't she?

Ten minutes into the broadcast and nothing has changed since the last time I watched the news—people in the world are still horrible to each other, our president still has top billing, and politicians continue to abuse their power. Great.

I sit up, my thumb on the power button of the remote, when a story catches my eye. A serial bank robber the FBI had on their most-wanted list for the past few years was apprehended and is in custody. I lean back down, extending my feet onto the coffee table. At least justice will be served. This sounds promising.

The report goes on to say that he was arrested after robbing a Kansas bank when someone stole his getaway car. I guess he'd left the keys inside. Idiot. I remember when I was doing an FBI role two years ago, our source of knowledge on how to act told me all criminals get caught because they're stupid.

They roll footage of the outside of the bank. People are huddled together. Some crying hysterically. Others silently weeping. Many clinging to one another.

And then time stands still.

My beer slips from my grasp, falls onto me, hits the couch, and lands on the floor. I lean forward to get a better look at the TV.

I grab the remote and rewind. Thank God for modern technology. I watch the same woman crying and pleading. The man trying to hold her up. I hit pause as she walks out of the building.

All the oxygen leaves my lungs as if I'm hooked up to a machine.

There she is.

I'm sure it's her.

I'm ninety percent sure it's her.

It's a little hard to tell, because she's walking and the freeze frame is blurry, but I've mesmerized every angle of her face and body. I'd bet my next big box-office hit it's her.

The sound of the front door closing drags me out of my daze. I hit the power button on the remote. The TV clicks off and I stand, realizing my shorts are wet from the beer spilled.

"Shit."

"What's wrong?" Adelaide carries in a few shopping bags, smiling as she sets them on the kitchen island.

"Nothing, I just spilled my beer." I avoid her gaze and walk over to the stove, reaching for the dishtowel to clean up my mess.

"Are you okay?"

"Yeah, I'm fine. Why?" I blot at the wet spot on the couch, soaking up most of the liquid, then return to the kitchen for a washcloth, feeling Adelaide's gaze on me the whole time.

"You look pale. Are you sick?"

I squeeze the washcloth of excess water and walk back over to the couch, happy for the distraction.

"I told you. I'm fine." I head back to the kitchen with the washcloth, walk around the other side of the island to Adelaide, and give her a kiss. "You have nothing to worry about. I'm okay."

Or I will be. Because I refuse to allow Lilah any more of my headspace than she already has. She will not ruin my future.

"You ready to eat? I have to cook everything, but it won't take long." I toss the washcloth toward the sink in the middle of the oversized island.

Adelaide steps toward me. "You're the best fiancé. Have I told you that lately?"

I smile even though I feel anything but at the moment.

But I will live up to her words. One glance at Lilah will not undo all my efforts to move past her. Who knows if it was even her? I probably conjured her up in my mind.

Chapter Forty-four

JIMMY

Forgetting the past is easier said than done. My past is like a splinter stuck five layers deep. If I move in the smallest wrong way, a sharp pain assaults me.

Seeing Lilah on the television was the splinter puncturing my skin, and I haven't been able to remove the sucker. She's always in the background of my mind, always making herself known. Our shared past nags and irritates me.

Last night, I tried to push aside all the plaguing questions, but it's impossible.

Was it really her?

What is she doing with her life?

Has she finally straightened herself out?

Does she have someone special in her life now?

And what pisses me off more than anything is the fact that I'm relieved nothing happened to her during the bank robbery.

My first instinct is still to protect her. In what universe is that okay? I'm marrying another woman.

With Adelaide out of the house, I give Tripp a call. He's out on tour and might not be able to answer, but he'll put my head back together.

"Hey, man. The ball and chain let you out for the day?"

I chuckle. "Whatever, asshole."

Tripp likes to bust my balls about getting married. We all laugh at the fact that I had set him up with Adelaide all those years ago.

Tripp's laugh rings through the phone, and I hear his band-mates and bottles clinking. I have no idea how he lives in a twenty-four seven party.

"You busy?"

"Nah, man. Just headed over to the venue for tonight's show."

"Where you guys at?" I push open the sliding glass door and step onto the deck.

"London, baby." He uses his best British accent. "When are you joining us?"

I roll my eyes. Tripp is always trying to convince me to go on tour with him and Savage Revolt. The last time I did, I ended up in the tabloids in every language. Keane would kill me if I did it again. "I'll have to keep missing out if I want my wedding to happen in a few months."

"True enough," he says with a chuckle. "So what's shakin'?"

I head down the stairs of my deck until my feet sink into the warm sand. "You got a few minutes to talk?"

There's a moment of silence, but I think Tripp's realizing I didn't call to have a friendly chat. "Sure, man. Give me a sec." I hear something shuffling. "Be a doll and get up, would you?" A female voice complains. There's more movement before the sounds of partying lower. "Sorry. I'm in the shitter on the bus now. What's going on?"

I sit on the bottom step, squinting from the sun glistening off the blue water. "The bedroom wasn't available?"

"Nah, Jericho's in there with some groupie right now. Thank fuck we're sleeping in hotels and not buses on this tour."

"Yeah, I get it."

"So what's up?"

I dig my big toe into the sand and wiggle it around, designing a nonsensical pattern. "I saw Lilah a couple days ago." I rush the words out, but I'm surprised by the relief I feel after finally saying them out loud.

"Fuck me. That bitch is trying to get back into your life?"

I knew Tripp would be pissed. It's one reason why he's my go-to person when it comes to Lilah. He saw me after I kicked her out of my life. He saw the depression. He saw the destruction she caused.

"Not in person. I was watching the news. The Feds arrested some bank robber and they rolled some footage of the bank and Lilah was there. At least I think it was her."

He's quiet for a second. I get it. It took me time to wrap my brain around the fact that after six years, she just appeared like a dream or a nightmare. I'm not sure which.

"Okay, so you saw her on TV. Big deal."

I blow out a breath and push my fingers through my hair. "It is a big deal because..." I squeeze my eyes shut. Tripp doesn't want to hear the truth that claws at my insides.

"Because what?" His voice is monotone and void of emotion.

"Because I can't stop thinking about her. I can't help wondering what she's doing, whether she's clean or not, if she's done something with her life and..."

"Why she did what she did," he finishes for me.

A large sigh slips from me. "Yeah, I'm an idiot."

"Nah, you're human."

We stay on the phone for a minute, neither of us speaking. The sound of the waves doesn't relax me like it usually does.

"What are you going to do?" Tripp asks.

"What can I do? It's not like I want her back in my life. I'm with Adelaide now. What went down between us... nothing can ever erase that."

"Can I be straight with you for a minute?"

My chin falls to my chest. "You know you can always be straight with me."

He sighs. "What I'm gonna say is probably going to surprise you. When all that shit went down, you were a mess and you did everything and anything to push away dealing with what happened. Don't get me wrong, you were a great wingman."

I chuckle.

"But you never really dealt with what went down. You cut Lilah out of your life, yeah, but she disappeared before you ever got answers, and Bernie's a prick, so he was no help. You just pretended it didn't happen, and any time I tried to bring her up, you got pissed. Eventually I respected that it was your business and stopped asking. But you're getting married in a few months. And I know you love Adelaide, I'm not questioning that. But if there's lingering questions about the past, maybe you need to get the answers so you can start the next chapter in your life with a clean slate."

I get what he's saying but I can't help but worry that if I open this door, I might not be able to close it. What Adelaide and I have is uncomplicated. After the roller coaster life with Lilah, I'm enjoying uncomplicated a lot.

"I get what you're saying but what if instead of giving me closure, it drags me back to the past?"

Tripp's the only one I trust with my real fear. My fear that seeing Lilah again will ruin the life I'm trying hard to build. It might not be the life I envisioned, but things and people change.

"I can't guarantee that won't happen. You and Lilah share something most people don't. But if you don't address it now, do you really want to say your wedding vows to Adelaide when your mind isn't free from Lilah?"

"Fuck, I hate it when you're right." I stand from the step and turn to head back up the stairs.

"It's a gift." He laughs.

"Yeah, well, I wish you were a dumbass who just told me I'm an idiot and to move on with my life."

"Sorry," he says, turning serious. "It's only fair to Adelaide and you."

"Do you think I should mention all this to her?" I slide open the door, and the air conditioning chills my body.

"Fuck, no. I might be sounding all hearts and flowers right now, but do *not* tell her."

"If I do this without telling her, I'm a liar, and you know how I feel about liars."

"Man, I get it, but telling Adelaide will only upset her, and the whole point of you putting the past to rest is so you don't have to upset her in the future."

He's right. I know it, but after being the one deceived for so many years, I hate deceiving others.

"Maybe I'll start with hiring a private investigator to track her down and decide from there."

"Good idea."

"All right. Thanks for the chat."

"No problem. If you need an escape, you know you can always join us on tour."

I chuckle, remembering the month I toured with him and the band after Lilah and I split. "Yeah, I almost died the first time I took you up on that offer."

"Ah, but what a glorious way to go, right?" He laughs. "Come on, we'll call it your bachelor party."

"I'm sure Adelaide would love that."

"Say hi to the ball and chain for me."

"Will do. Talk to you later."

I hit End on my phone and place it on the kitchen counter, staring at it.

I still have the number of the private investigator I used when my mom called to hustle me for money. I wonder if he's still in business. The question is, do I really want to use it?

There's no going back.

Tripp's advice flows through my brain. He's right in the fact that Adelaide deserves a husband who is one hundred percent committed to the marriage. I'd be a liar if I said Lilah doesn't continue to occupy a part of my brain. And yes, I'm sure a lot of the reason why is because there was no closure after she betrayed me. Within minutes, we were finished, and I couldn't bear to listen to any of her excuses.

Before I can talk myself out of it, I pick up the phone and scroll through my contacts until I find the PI's number. I'll tell him I want him to locate her. I just want the address of where she lives, and no more information.

This is either one of the smartest or one of the stupidest decisions I've ever made. I hope it's the former.

Chapter Forty-five

JIMMY

A week later, I'm sitting in a small cake shop off Melrose, understanding what Keane was saying about flour and eggs. The cakes are pretty, but all you get to remember it by is a picture.

"I'm thinking the lemon cake for the top two tiers, red velvet for the bottom, and vanilla with a butterscotch swirl for the other two tiers. What do you think, honey?" Adelaide's hand presses on my thigh.

I blink. "Sorry, what?"

I zoned out again. I've yet to hear from the PI about Lilah, and she still won't leave my mind.

A small pout forms on Adelaide's lips. "For the cake. Are you feeling okay? You haven't been yourself lately." She smiles, gripping my thigh tighter, and giggles off any true concern. Surely these people aren't surprised to see a groom who doesn't give a shit about the cake they're about to spend a fortune on. "Are you okay with those layers?"

I glance at the wedding designer and the celebrity cake designer looking on in anticipation.

"Whatever you want." I grab her hand on top of my thigh and squeeze it.

"Are you sure? I want you to be happy too." She leans her head on my shoulder, shooting me dreamy puppy dog eyes. It's been her go-to move lately with anything wedding related, as if she needs permission.

"I don't care about the cake. I just want to marry you."

She beams and kisses my cheek. Before we can share any moment, she faces the pair of women sitting across from us. "It's decided then. That's what we'll go with."

"Excellent," the wedding designer says, sharing a smile with the cake designer.

I'm sure she has a pretty nice commission tied into the price of the cake.

"Do you need anything else from us?" I ask, sitting up straighter.

"That should be it," the cake designer says.

We stand and shake hands with the women, exchanging our goodbyes, then walk out. I slip my sunglasses off my head and onto my face, then I take Adelaide's hand as we walk toward the car.

"You hungry?" I ask.

"I could eat a bit. I'd love a lunch with my fiancé." She smiles.

I let her hand drop when we reach the car, and I walk around to the driver's side. "You want to stay in town or grab something in Malibu?"

I press the key fob for my car, and we both climb in.

"Let's head to Moonshadows," she says.

I smile because that's where we went on our first official date.

Shortly after things went down with Lilah, Adelaide made her feelings for me known, but I rejected her. She took it hard, but I wasn't in the headspace to be serious with anyone. Our friendship drifted and things got awkward. Until we saw one another at a premiere years later. She forgave me and accepted my dinner offer. We haven't been to Moonshadows in a long time, and I worry that she's noticed I haven't been completely present the last couple weeks and wants to remind me why we're getting married.

"I think Moonshadows is a great idea." I reach across the console and bring her hand to my mouth then kiss her knuckles.

For most of the hour and a half ride, thanks to LA traffic, we listen to music. Adelaide stares out the window. We're always able to have a comfortable silence, and it's nice.

We pull into the parking lot and are seated within a few minutes.

We're at one of the tables near the glass railing overlooking the ocean. The salt air blows Adelaide's hair around, so she secures it in a ponytail. After we order our meals and drinks, I relax back into my chair, sipping on my beer. Adelaide is always trying to get me to become a wine connoisseur like her, but that's not me.

"How are you feeling about the wedding?" I ask.

"Let's talk about something else. There's still so much to do. I can't even think about it right now. It's too stressful." She shakes her head and waves.

"All right, does your agent have anything in the works for you?" I lift my beer to my lips and take a sip, relaxing more when the cold liquid hits the back of my throat.

"A couple things, but nothing I'm excited about."

"Same," I say, planning to expand on that, but my phone vibrates on the table in front of me. I pick it up and turn it over. The PI's number flashes on the screen and I quickly send him to voicemail.

She leans forward for her wine glass. "Who's that?"

"Tripp." The lie falls from my mouth faster than I'd like. "I'll call him later."

She sips her wine. "How is America's Rock God?"

"You know Tripp. Work hard. Play hard."

Adelaide laughs. "Sounds about right."

She sets down her wine glass and looks at me. There's tension in her muscles that wasn't there a second ago.

My heartrate skyrockets. Did she see it wasn't Tripp? Or is she suspicious because I didn't answer? Most of time I put him on speaker when Adelaide's around. Fuck, this is exactly why I hate lying.

"Speaking of agents... mine mentioned that there's a rumor Freelance Studios is courting you for a big upcoming production."

Thank fuck. She saw nothing.

I lock eyes with her, and my fingers tighten around my beer. "I already told Keane to forget it."

Adelaide knows full well where I stand on the matter of working for that studio again, and she *should* know this is a conversation I don't want to have.

I told her what went down between Lilah and me, or as much as I know, since I don't have the answers as to *why* Lilah would do what she did. I have no doubt she had her reasons, but I can't get over the fact that whatever they were, she didn't trust me to help her deal with them, and in the end, she shit all over our most sacred vow when she locked pinkie fingers with me earlier that day.

"I heard it's an amazing script, the studio is going to pour money into marketing it..."

I down a healthy gulp of my beer, giving me a moment to collect myself so I don't direct my anger at Adelaide. I set my beer on the table in front of me a little harder than necessary and the liquid sloshes in the glass. "You know I won't work for that asshole again."

Adelaide's lips purse. "It's been six years. I would've thought you'd have cooled off a bit by now."

Lilah is a taboo topic. We don't discuss her—ever. So I'm surprised she's bringing the topic up now.

"You know how I feel, Adelaide. That's the end of it."

She looks at the ocean briefly then around the restaurant. I'm assuming to see if anyone is paying us attention. She leans in. "Is this about *her*?"

I meet her narrowed gaze. "It's about her, it's about him, it's about me not putting another dime in that asshat's pocket. I did what I had to do to fulfill my contract when *The Regulator* came out, but I won't willingly put myself in a position to help that man ever again. I don't care how good the script is."

She leans back in her chair and studies me for a moment. So much for our romantic memory-land dinner date. "Do you still love her?"

Fuck. I huff and lean forward. Taking her hand, I rub both sides and look into her eyes. "I love you. I'm going to marry you."

Thankfully, she smiles and covers our entwined hands with her free one. I don't want to hurt Adelaide, and she would be hurt if she knew that the truth is that part of my heart will always belong to Lilah. We went through too much together —things that connect us for the rest of our lives. But that doesn't mean I'm *in* love with Lilah or that I want a future with her—or even have her in my life.

"Okay then. I'll drop the subject, but I think you should at least consider the role. It would be great for your career."

"My career is already great, but thanks."

"Okay, okay." She dislodges our hands and puts her hands up in a placating gesture. She grabs her phone and puts her hand back between mine. "Let's do that again for our Instagram friends."

Since our engagement, there's been a shift in Adelaide's attitude. She was always a driven and focused woman whose career took precedence. When the press revealed our engagement, the news was on the front page of every industry magazine and tabloid. Whereas before, our relationship was all about the two of us, lately Adelaide's focus is on what everyone else thinks. Her image on social media, and what the public will say and how they'll react to anything having to do with us, is forefront on her mind.

"Let's forget social media and have a nice dinner, okay?"

She nods, but she bites her lower lip which means there's still more she wants to say on the subject. "Can we at least get the waiter to take a picture of us? The fans love it when they see us doing something romantic."

I groan and lift my beer to my lips again. "You know I hate when you post that shit of me online. I saw the pic you posted of me running on the beach."

She smiles. "I think that was my most-liked pic. It was a nice surprise for me to wake up and see you from the deck. I thought I should share how great my life is."

The public gets enough of me. I don't feel the need to give them any piece of my personal life, but Adelaide is almost obsessed.

"Come on, James. I have almost thirty million followers. I'm trying to get there before the end of the week, and pictures of the two of us together always get the most likes and comments." She puts her hands up in front of her in a prayer pose.

Whether it's the guilt that another woman is taking up my head space or not, I find myself waning. "Fine."

She can see I'm not happy, but she squeals and waves over the waiter. After she instructs him through at least twenty different pictures, she takes her phone back and buries her head in the screen.

"'Spent the day wedding planning and now I'm enjoying dinner with a sunset view with my love,'" she says as she types her caption. "'Hashtag 3 months and counting, hashtag true love, hashtag best guy ever.' There." Adelaide sets her phone facedown on the table. "Now we can enjoy a nice dinner together."

"Finally," I say with a practiced smile that feels forced. My phone is like a bomb in my pocket and the timer is slowly ticking down until it blows everything to pieces.

* * *

WE ENJOY a nice dinner and head back to my Malibu beach home rather than Adelaide's condo in Los Angeles. Although she prefers the condo to the beach, because it's more accessible to everything, I spend as much time in Malibu as I can because of the seclusion it offers.

No one would think we're A-listers if they saw our nightly ritual. We lounge on the couch before heading to bed. She changes into her sleep set, and I put on a fresh pair of boxers. We both slip under the covers. We lean into the middle of the bed, and I give her chaste kiss.

"Night," she says, and rolls over so her back is to me. She can only fall asleep on her right side, but only if she's on the right side of the bed.

Sometimes I feel an inkling that we should have the passion I shared with Lilah. Is something amiss because we're about to get married and it doesn't take a lot of fingers to count how many times we sleep together in a month? But what I have with Adelaide is steady and predictable. Maybe that's why the passion with Lilah was so intense. We were always hurdling over peaks and falling into valleys. There was never a time to just be.

I lie on my side, wide awake, staring at my phone on my night-stand. After dinner, I didn't have an opportunity to slip away and call the PI back, at least not without raising Adelaide's suspicions. Something I can't afford to do since I'm doing this for her in the long run. She'll never understand why I need to shut the door completely with Lilah.

Once her breathing turns slow and steady, I slip out of bed, grab my phone, and head down the hall. I bypass the living area and quietly slip out the sliding door and onto the deck. I look behind me to make sure I didn't wake Adelaide before I pull up the missed call. It's just before eleven thirty at night. Not too late to call. I hope. I hit the PI's number and suck in a deep breath.

Maybe he never found her, and she'll finally slip out of my mind.

"Hello?" His tone suggests I didn't wake him.

"Hey, it's James. I missed your call."

"Yeah, hey, James. I found her."

Oxygen rushes from my lungs and blackness accosts me for a minute. I sit on a lounger to collect myself.

"You were right about her being in Kansas."

I swallow the lump in my throat. How did I think he wouldn't find her?

"You still there?" he asks.

"Uh... yeah. Sorry." I push a hand through my hair. "Just text me the address. I'll make sure the rest of your fee is transferred over in the morning."

"Sure thing."

"Pleasure doing business with you, James. Call me if you need anything else."

He hangs up, and I lean back into the chair. Adelaide recently changed out all the patio furniture, saying we needed to upgrade. Honestly, I liked the pieces I had, but it wasn't worth an argument. I did put my foot down for a lounger to stay. Of course, she got new cushions for it.

Kansas? What the hell is in Kansas?

I have no idea why it feels so surreal. I knew she was still out there somewhere—or at least I assumed she hadn't managed to kill herself yet. Surely some pap would have picked up on that. But now, knowing her exact location is about to come up on my phone, my body surges with energy to find her. The exact reason I doubted this decision in the first place.

My phone vibrates in my hand and I look at the text with her address.

I fist my free hand and let out a breath. My head is like a tornado, feelings good and bad swirling around without coming to a conclusion to the question of what to do next. My heart led before when it came to Lilah, but this time, I have to let my head lead. Otherwise, she could do what she did before—rip it from my chest and stomp on it until it's a bloody pulp.

Chapter Forty-six

JIMMY

"You look terrible. You sure you're feeling okay?" Adelaide raises her hand to my forehead.

"Does that mean no pics for your followers today?"

She drops her hands and stares at me.

I blow out a breath. "Just a shitty night's sleep, that's all."

"Well, don't go getting sick on me. Remember we have that photographer coming to shoot us for the *Hollywood Journal*. They might use the headline, 'Hollywood's Power Couple,' can you imagine?" She beams, putting her hands out in front of her.

I wish I was as excited as she wants me to be, but I don't have any energy to fake it today. Sometimes I wonder if Adelaide knows who she's marrying? All I ever wanted was to be at the top of my game so I could make enough money to earn my freedom and pick projects that really mean something to me. I hate the press. I hate the paps. I hate anything that hinders my privacy.

And I've made it in this town without compromising my personal life as much as I can.

You don't see Leo out doing photoshoot after photoshoot for shit like this.

But I don't say that to Adelaide because this crap makes her happy and I already feel like a bad fiancé for hiring a PI to find an address for an ex. So I smile and nod. "Don't worry, I'll have my game face on."

"Perfect." She kisses my cheek. "I have to leave now to head into the city. God, I hate traffic. We really need to talk about selling this place and moving full-time into my condo or buying a place of our own."

"Don't start," I say, sleeplessness getting the best of me.

She blinks, and her eyes widen.

"I'm sorry. I'm just exhausted. I don't want to talk about it right now."

"Okay then. I'll be back by dinner. I'm shopping with the girls on Rodeo. We need some cute clothes for my bachelorette weekend."

"Isn't that in two months or something?" I absentmindedly grab an orange from the basket in the middle of the island.

"Men. You have no idea how much effort it takes to put the perfect outfit together." She rolls her eyes in a playful manner.

"Okay, well, drive safe."

"Have a good day. Take a nap or something so you're not so grumpy tonight."

I nod while I'm looking down and peeling my orange, then I hear her leave.

Finally, a moment to get my thoughts in order.

I abandon the orange on the island, taking my phone back out onto the deck. The fresh air wafts off the ocean. I inhale and exhale a large breath. I'm not sure I'll survive not experiencing the early morning air here, no matter how much Adelaide's happiness means to me.

I've thought of nothing but this text for the past nine hours, and still, I'm torn as to whether seeking out Lilah is a good idea. My sensible and rational side tells me nothing good can come out of seeing her face-to-face. Even knowing that, a part of me is pulling me in her direction, telling me I need to hash it out with her in order to be done for good.

There's nothing I want more than to leave her one hundred percent in the past and cast away the many what-ifs that have plagued my mind over the years. It took me years to want to date someone else after Lilah. I wasn't a monk during those years but sleeping with a woman and trusting a woman enough to open up to her, giving her the power to hurt me, are two entirely different things.

Adelaide is the first woman I opened up to, but not completely. She knows hardly anything of my past in Virginia. She'd never understand what it was like growing up there. I've never admitted to her the terrible things I did in the name of survival, nor would I now. She knows me, but she doesn't *know* me the way Lilah does. Truth be told, she knows James. I'm not sold she could look at me the same if she knew me as Jimmy.

"Fuck," I yell to the seagulls circling above.

I plop down into the lounger and pull my phone from my cargo shorts pocket. Scrolling through my contacts, I hit Tripp's number.

"This better be good," he answers.

"Sorry, man, is it morning where you are?" I ask, mentally calculating what country he should in right now.

"Nah, man. But when you party until six a.m., does it really matter?"

I chuckle. "Guess not. Listen, I'll make it quick. The PI I hired found Lilah. She's living in Kansas. That had to be her that I saw on the news."

"Wow. Kansas, huh? Seems way too down-home for her life-style." There's rustling and murmurs from a woman's voice, then a door clicks shut. "So what are you gonna do?"

"I think I need to see her."

I hate the way my stomach pitches when I say the words out loud, as if some sick part of me is actually looking forward to the idea. This is a means to an end, nothing more.

"Agreed," he says. "Just make sure you remember why you're there. Don't get sucked into her vortex again."

"No worries." And I mean those words. It took every last miniscule of willpower in me not to hunt Lilah down the first couple of years. I have no interest in putting myself through that torture again—not when it would jeopardize my future with a wife who cares about the life we're making.

"I know this is going to be hard, man, but I wouldn't encourage you to do it unless I really thought it was best for you. Lilah's been like an albatross around your neck the entire time I've known you. You're close to ditching that albatross, and I, for one, couldn't be happier."

"Me too."

I've always wondered if there'd be a day I no longer thought about my past and the what-could-have-beens, letting calm and peace settle over me and the rest of my life. Yeah, seeing her will be tough. But I'll get the closure I need to finally move forward without the weight of what Lilah and I once shared weighing me down.

"All right, man, I won't keep you. Sounds like you had company," I say after a short stretch of silence.

Tripp chuckles. "That's okay. A rock god like myself can only handle so much pussy and booze."

I roll my eyes and laugh. "Yeah, poor baby."

"You call me if you need someone to set your head straight after you see her."

"Thanks." I hit End on the call and reflect for a moment.

A minute later, my phone vibrates in my hand. Adelaide.

Guilt swarms me like barbed wire. Knowing what I'm planning to do and why I'm keeping her in the dark. She won't understand that I just want to be able to give her all of myself, and I can't do that without closure from Lilah.

"Hey," I answer.

"You're not going to believe it!"

She must still be in traffic because she's screaming through the Bluetooth of her car.

"What's wrong?" I ask, noting the edge of hysteria lacing her voice that only comes when she's really worked up about something.

"I just got a call and I have to do re-shoots in Vancouver for *The Bully.*"

"Shit, that sucks."

It's not that surprising really. When they wrapped months ago, she told me she didn't have high hopes for the project.

"Yeah, I guess test audiences felt something was missing in the B plot and they want us to shoot some more scenes to insert into the final cut. Can you believe that?"

"When do you have to go?" I bypass agreeing with her. This happens all the time with movies.

"I have to be there in three days! They're sending me the sides this afternoon."

Pushing a hand through my hair, I lean back in my seat. "Well, I can help you run lines tonight."

"That'd be great, but my bigger problem is now I have to rearrange my meeting with the venue. We were going to go over how to set-up the ballroom!"

I grip the bridge of my nose while she prattles on about all the small decisions she's yet to finalize for our big day. The thought of what a circus our wedding will be is making my head hurt. I want the marriage. I don't give two shits about the wedding.

"Listen, it's a bunch of chairs. How hard can it be to put them around tables?"

She sighs.

"What?"

"You just don't get it. You don't seem to understand that our wedding might be the event of the entire year." She honks her horn at someone. "You should see this guy who just cut me off."

"De-stress a little. We'll get this handled. We always do." No need to piss her off about the wedding right when I've figured out a time I can slip away from LA.

"You're right. Thanks."

"Don't mention it," I say with a small smile. I'm not unused to having to talk Adelaide off the ledge, and it's easy to do. She always comes around fairly quickly.

"Okay, I'm gonna roll. I have a bunch of calls to make to juggle everything around."

"All right. See you later."

She hangs up, and I clutch my phone.

Adelaide flies to Vancouver. I fly to Kansas. This lying thing is becoming too easy.

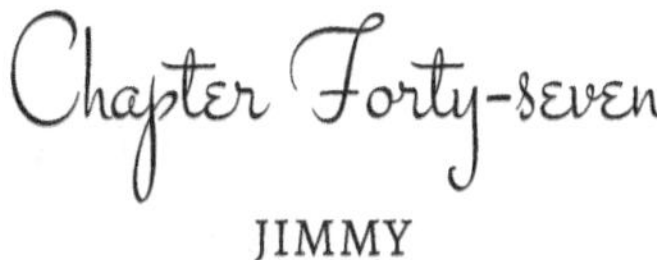

Chapter Forty-seven

JIMMY

The two-and-half-hour flight felt more like twenty hours.

The private plane touches down. From the looks of it, there's nothing here. At least the rental I arranged is waiting for me. Money has its perks, because I needed this to be as quiet as possible. If anyone got wind that I'm in Kansas, it would be splattered all over the online gossip channels and I'd have to answer a lot of questions.

The closest airstrip we could land at is twenty minutes away from the small town Lilah now calls home. My stomach rolls over with each passing minute, the fear still consuming me that I'm opening Pandora's box.

Adelaide is shooting in Canada for at least five days. There was no use in telling her I was leaving town since the pilot is waiting around to fly me back to LA tonight. She won't know the difference, except when she returns, I'll be freer.

I punch Lilah's address into my phone and place it in the console of the rented SUV. Estimated arrival is eighteen minutes.

Never has time felt so short and yet so long.

I take a deep breath and drive out of the airfield.

I have no idea what to expect when I find her and that's somehow almost as nerve-racking as the idea of seeing her again.

Will she be strung out, living in some dilapidated shack like we both grew up in? Or did she manage to scrape together some sort of life for herself? From the quick glimpse and fuzzy pause on the television, she looked like she did out of rehab. Healthy and happy.

Shit. She could be married. How did that idea never occur to me? I could barge into her new life and stir up crap from our past for my own selfish closure. Although I tried and failed to move on, that doesn't mean she wasn't successful in forgetting me.

My grip on the steering wheel tightens.

I'm not here to upend her life. If a guy answers the door, I'll make up a lame excuse about being lost.

I stew on that thought for a moment, picturing Lilah happy and living her life with another man. Him being able to kiss her good night. To snuggle with her while they watch a movie. The way her small body would wind its way around mine. She could do that with him. And I shouldn't care. Adelaide, I remind myself. But the uneasiness that surfaces suggests what I already feared—I'm fucked.

Pushing away that entire line of thinking, I check out the area as I drive. All I've driven past are flat, empty fields, until a small downtown area comes out of nowhere. It's a small Midwestern town. The buildings have clearly been around for a while but are neatly decorated with awnings and signs for the businesses.

I follow the GPS as it tells me to make a right-hand turn right after I've passed through town. Then I make a couple more turns through a modest neighborhood until I've arrived. I park the SUV across the street and look at the house that matches the address the PI gave me. She could be in there. Living her life as though I'm not about to upheave whatever happiness she's found.

If someone told me six years ago that this is where Lilah would be, I never would have believed them.

It's the picture of America. A small white bungalow with a wide front porch sits in the middle of a large lot that boasts a well-manicured lawn and colorful garden. Flower pots are positioned at either side of the steps that lead to the front door and hanging baskets dangle from the awning. A mid-sized sedan is parked in the driveway, and the front door is open, though the closed screen door prohibits me seeing inside.

I study everything I can about the place as if it will grant me knowledge into what I'm about to find.

It's gut-check time.

I put on the baseball cap and aviator sunglasses I brought with me. Wiping the sweat from my brow, I open the SUV door and step out onto the street. My heart is in my throat and my palms are sweaty. Shit, I haven't been this nervous since I accepted my Oscar.

Before I talk myself into turning around and forgetting this, I walk across the street, up the cute interlock path, and up the stairs to the front door. My hand clenches as my eyes fixate on the doorbell. I need to do this, I remind myself. This will give me closure and make the life I'm building with Adelaide better. No matter what, Lilah will not drag me back into her life. I'm here for answers and nothing more.

With a deep breath and my heartbeat nearing heart attack territory, my knuckles rap on the side of the door, shaking the screen door slightly.

"I got it!" someone calls.

Before I know it, the owner of the voice pushes open the screen door.

"Hi," the little girl says, looking up at me with a smile. Her wavy blonde hair hangs past her shoulders, and her hands are covered in an array of colors, suggesting she was playing with markers.

She's definitely Lilah's.

She's the spitting image of her mom except for her eyes. My throat closes up when I stare into her brown eyes—the same ones reflected back to me in the mirror every day.

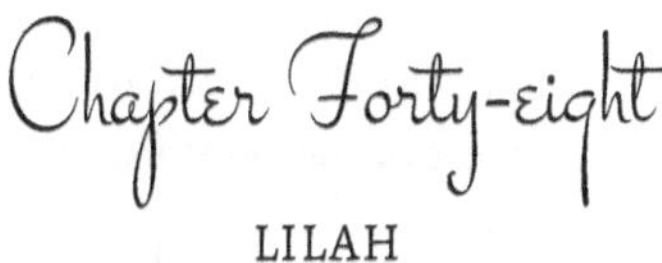

Chapter Forty-eight

LILAH

"**I** got it!" Her words are accompanied by the pitter-patter of my whirling dervish daughter's feet slapping against the hardwood as she races down the hall toward the front of the house.

I slide the cut-up chicken into the frying pan. "Hold on!"

"Hi," she says to whomever is at the door.

Shit. I frantically pump the anti-bacterial soap out of the dispenser, rub it all over my hands, and rinse them off. Grabbing a dish towel off the handle of the oven, I pat my hands dry while heading to the front door.

"How many times have I told you that you can't answer the door without Mommy..." I look up from my hands, and the weight of emotions cement my feet to the floor as my words die on my lips.

I blink, doubling-check that the day I have put off since the moment those two pink lines appeared on the pregnancy test is here.

Jimmy stands at the other side of the screen door, his hat and sunglasses on. One sliver of silver lining is that there's not a mass of media behind him, ready to point me out as the villain.

Six years should change me. Change him. Change us. But his soul still calls to mine. Although his arrival can only mean terrible things, a small part of me sighs that he's here.

His eyes are laser-focused on the five-year-old in front of him, and I stand halfway to the door, watching the scene unfold. Our daughter's eyes volley between us. She's way too young to understand how her life has just shifted. That the daddy she asks me about has been delivered to her doorstep as though it's Christmas morning.

He slowly removes his sunglasses. His eyes seek answers from mine as his face transforms with shock, pain, and betrayal. All feelings he has a right to. Shame coats me like a thick layer of tar, and I strip my eyes away, concentrating on the floor.

"Hey, you're that man from the magazines my mom always buys at the grocery store," Monica says.

My cheeks should heat from embarrassment as my daughter exposed the fact I keep up with Jimmy's life as though I'm the president of his fan club, but I have bigger problems. Much bigger problems.

Ice-cold fear snaps me out of my daze. The fear that she'll be taken from me makes me check on Monica on rare nights. The fear that there will be payback one day for me keeping her from Jimmy. That nightmare is here—except this time, there's no waking up.

"Kiddo, why don't you go play in your room for a bit?" I place my hands on her shoulders.

Jimmy's gaze flits from me down to her.

"I wanna stay here," she says.

"I know you're curious, but Mommy has to speak to this man in private. It's grown-up stuff." I wrinkle my nose to suggest she'd be bored if she stayed.

She sags her shoulders a bit and waves at Jimmy. "Bye."

Before he can respond she spins and races down the hall to her room.

Before I can open my mouth, Jimmy speaks. "Tell me this isn't what it looks like." Unshed tears rest in his accusatory eyes.

"I can't," I whisper, and my eyes find the floor once more.

"Jesus Christ."

I look up. He turns away from the front door and stares at the street with one hand on his hip, the other pushed into his dark hair. I glance behind me to make sure Monica isn't spying, then I step out onto the porch. The screen door bangs shut behind me.

"I have a daughter," he says to himself.

"We can't talk about this right now. I know you're angry, but—"

He whips around, spearing me with a look that could cut through bone. "Angry? That's the half of it—"

"I get it. But we can't have this conversation when she's ten feet away. She's curious by nature and if she overhears..."

"I wouldn't know, since I don't know her."

In all the years, through everything we've been through, even the night everything between us blew up, he hasn't looked like he hates me as much as he does right now. I can't say I wouldn't feel the same way.

"I know."

He stares as me unblinking, his breathing calming. "Okay, you're right."

I almost relish the fact he hasn't changed. He was always able to compartmentalize his way through a crisis.

The smoke alarm blares through the screen door.

Shit. The chicken.

I spin around and race inside, waving my way through the billowing smoke. The chicken is stuck to the pan, but thankfully there's no fire. I flip on the fan over the oven and put the pan into the sink. The pan sizzles as water rushes over the charred chicken and burned oil. I open up the back door and the window, then I wave the dish towel under the smoke alarm until it stops.

Small whimpers catch my attention and I toss the dish towel back on the counter. Monica is in the hallway, her fingers in her mouth, crying.

I pick her up. "Shhh, it's okay, kiddo. It's done now. Mommy just burnt the chicken." I rub her back until she stops trembling in my arms. "I'm sorry it scared you, honey. You okay now?"

She nods into my neck, and I set her down. Cupping her face, I wipe the tears from her pudgy cheeks.

"Why don't you go play while I finish talking to the man at the front door, and then we'll decide where we're going to go grab dinner since Mommy burned ours?"

Excitement lights up her cocoa eyes. She gives me one big squeeze before running back to her bedroom.

I look at the door, expecting Jimmy to be gone. That he's left to contact an expensive lawyer to take me to court for custody. But he's watching from the other side of the screen. He shakes his head when he notices I'm staring at him.

"Why don't we meet for breakfast in the morning?" I say.

I have a million questions for him—How did you find me? Why are you here? Where's your fiancée? What are you going to do now that you know?—but they can wait until my daughter isn't within earshot. Plus, I have a lot more difficult questions to answer.

I figure he'll argue to stay. Jimmy was never one to patiently wait to clear the air. But he nods.

"Great. There's a diner on Main Street. Let's meet at eight fifteen."

He nods again, looking through the screen with such a mix of emotions I'm not sure what he's thinking. Without a word, he turns and heads down the steps. When he reaches the bottom, he turns back to me. "What's her name?"

My stomach flips over, and I swallow past the painful lump in my throat. "Monica."

Pain slashes his features, but the tiniest of smiles forms before it disappears. "Like the Santa Monica Pier."

I nod. "I'll see you tomorrow."

I watch until he drives away in his SUV. Then I shut the door and lock it.

Chapter Forty-nine

JIMMY

J immy

Driving away from Lilah's without any answers might be the stupidest thing I've done. A normal man would demand she explain why she hid his daughter for five years. Hell, she probably would have hidden her for longer. What would have happened if I hadn't come knocking on her door today?

I drive down Main Street and pull into the parking lot of a small motel with a vacancy sign. Using my hat and sunglasses, I pay cash because if the paps find me in Kansas, they'll find out I have a daughter with Lilah Robbie. That just upped the ante on making sure none of this hits the press.

It's not until I'm inside the stale-smelling, modest, but clean room that the reality of what has happened crashes down on me.

I fall onto the bed and replay the entire sequence in my head.

A daughter.

I have a daughter.

And she's beautiful.

She has my eyes.

And has Lilah's blonde hair.

A hot, stabbing pain of anger burns in my chest.

And I didn't know until now.

I push up off the mattress and pace the room. My body overflows with adrenaline as every thought runs through my head over and over again. How could Lilah keep her from me?

Never in my life have I thought of laying my hands on a woman, but after Lilah admitted she was my daughter, I briefly wanted to grab her shoulders and shake the answers out of her.

How dare she deny me the right to know I had a child!

I slam my fist into the wall, leaving a hole in the drywall. Rather than shaking out my hand, I enjoy the distraction of the burn that settles in my knuckles from the toxic swell of emotions.

Continuing my pacing, I glance at my watch. It's nearing seven o'clock.

Shit. I have no overnight bag with me. I have to call the pilot and tell him this one-day jaunt has turned into two days. I can't imagine there are any twenty-four-hour stores in this town, so I head out.

A half hour later, I'm back in my room with bags filled with crap I could have brought with me. I was able to get everything I needed, and thankfully no one recognized me. At least, they didn't approach me if they did. A few people gave me weird looks for wearing my sunglasses into the stores when it's dark outside, but no one commented.

I texted the pilot and told him to head back to LA. I'll figure out later how I'm getting home. I'm not sure what Lilah's thinking will happen tomorrow, but I'm not leaving until we figure out how I can have a relationship with my daughter.

The adrenaline coursing through my body is scattering my thoughts and making it hard to stay still, so I decide to go for a run to clear my head and exhaust my body. Maybe then I can get some sleep tonight.

I change into the plain grey T-shirt and athletic shorts I bought. I have on running shoes that are more suited for fashion than running, but they'll work. After grabbing my headphones from the small bag I did bring with me, and putting my hat on just in case, I head outside. My feet hit the concrete and I run away from Main Street and out toward the country surrounding the small town.

Eventually I'm running at a good pace, sweat trailing down my face.

Monica.

My daughter's name is Monica.

Weird that I have a daughter.

Lilah named her after the spot that meant so much to us.

Why?

She obviously didn't want me in Monica's life.

I run a little harder as the anger refuses to diminish. The more my muscles burn, the harder I push my legs.

There's so much I've missed. There's so much I don't know about her.

My feet pound harder on the pavement.

Will Monica even like that I'm her father? If she doesn't resent me now for being away for five years, she could resent me in the future for the time away while filming. The last thing I want is for her to become one of those self-entitled celebrity spawns who spiral out of control. My world is no place to raise a daughter.

Adelaide?

Shit, how did I not think about her reaction until this moment?

Sweat coats my entire body, but I increase my speed to a punishing pace.

I'm a father.

A dad.

Dad.

Dad.

Dad.

That word echoes in my head with every footstep slamming on the pavement.

Dad.

Dad.

Dad.

I picture that beautiful little girl's face in my mind—the innocence, the purity, the curiosity—and I choke back a sob.

She's mine.

And Lilah's.

The love we had produced a beautiful creature.

A foreign feeling fills my chest. A love so unbelievably pure.

Creed's *Arms Wide Open* blasts through the headphones and the lyrics reach inside me, twisting all the emotions from my soul like a wet dish rag.

Tears burn behind my eyelids, and I push them away until the swell of emotion is too much to contain and it overflows. I stop and bend over on the side of the road, heaving for breath, tears streaming down to the pavement. I lower myself to the curb, my heavy head falling into my hands, and I cry.

I cry for what could have been.

I cry for all the memories I've missed.

I cry for the impending pain on the horizon.

Mostly though, I cry tears of joy.

Because I have a daughter.

When I was with Lilah I had hoped we'd marry and have a family, but with her constant drug abuse and the emotional turmoil from our past haunting her, it seemed like an unrealistic hope. Adelaide is firm on not wanting children, so I figured fatherhood would never happen. Monica is the gift I never thought I'd receive in this lifetime and I'll do everything in my power to love and protect her.

Chapter Fifty

LILAH

Later that night, long after I finish my nightly ritual of putting Monica to bed, preparing her lunch for tomorrow, tiding up around the house, and double-checking that the locks are secure, I lie in my bed, staring at the ceiling.

It's no surprise sleep won't come. What can I possibly have a nightmare about? Mine just came alive like some twisted Hollywood movie.

I haven't had the itchy feeling on my skin in years. The one that used to cause me to turn to anything to numb myself. But the minute Jimmy landed on my doorstep, it returned. Which means I'm going to have to work harder on my sobriety than I have in a long time.

Tomorrow morning, I'll figure a good time to attend a meeting and see if Eileen can watch Monica.

I roll over, the covers cinched in my tight fists.

I could put Monica in the car. We could drive through the night and be in a whole new city with two new identities by morning. Jimmy might have found me now, but I was stupid not to change my name.

The thought of avoiding Jimmy is nice. To not have to risk him taking her away from me. But as I'm about to roll out of bed and pack our suitcases, Jimmy's face flashes in my head. Him sitting in the diner's booth, waiting for me. And when he finds out I've fled, the despair that will land on his features is enough to keep me under the covers. At least for tonight it is.

All these years. Why now? Why would he search me out?

The forced smile I put on display all night didn't hide my panic from my sweet baby girl. Numerous times, she cuddled up to me, asking if I was okay. With her curious nature, she has the ability to be hurt the most by this situation, and I need to triple-check that she remains the sweet, caring girl who thinks life is a beautiful playground.

I swipe the tears from my eyes.

There's no doubt she *will* find out Jimmy is her father, and I wish I had a magic ball that told me how she'll react. Jimmy isn't a guy who'll throw us some money and jet back to his celebrity life. He'll want to be a part of her life—a *major* part of her life. He has the power and the money to make sure she's in his life more than mine. A new town and a new start is sounding better the longer my eyes stay wide open.

* * *

It's funny how people don't change when they're not around you. I step into the diner and glance to the back, finding

Jimmy in the farthest booth with his back to the door. Never one who wants to be recognized.

"Hey, Lilah! How's Monica?" Misty asks as I walk toward Jimmy.

I give her a wane smile. "She's doing good. Excited for story time on Saturday."

"It's Dr. Seuss day. I've been practicing my voices." She slides a cup of coffee to a customer at the counter.

"She'll be excited." I smile and murmur hellos, hoping no one makes a huge deal out of me meeting a guy who is clearly not from around here in the back of the Farmhouse Diner.

Every step depletes my energy as if my feet are stuck in cinder blocks.

My only saving grace is we're in public and Jimmy rarely causes a scene. Well... except for those fights that were in my honor. Shit, maybe I should have rethought this.

"Hey." I slide into the booth across from him.

He stares at my left breast, where my name is embroidered, before shifting his attention to my eyes. From the bags under his eyes, he looks as if he got as much sleep as I did. Hard for him to look shitty though.

We sit across from one another, taking in the other . Six years and so much change. I'm no longer the thin-framed model. I've had a baby. He has much more muscle. Which means I grew soft and he grew hard. Hard.

"What can I get you guys?"

Thank you, Misty, for stepping in before my thoughts traveled away from the reason I'm here.

"Just a coffee for me please," I say.

"Same." Jimmy doesn't spare her a glance.

"Boy, you guys are easy. Coming right up." Misty makes her way around the counter, pours the coffee into two white cups, and brings them over. "Cream and sugar are on the table."

I smile my thank you. Her smile fades slightly as she looks between Jimmy and me before she leaves the table.

I wrap my hands around the warm mug and meet Jimmy's gaze over the rim of my cup. He opens and closes his mouth as though he's not sure where to start.

My body feels at war with itself. Part of it wants to throw the coffee in his face. Tell him to leave me alone. Another part wants to relish the enjoyment that we have a child together. The last part wants to slide over to his side of the booth and draw comfort from being close to him.

"Why didn't you tell me?" he whispers, staring at his coffee mug.

My gaze drops to my own coffee. The lowness of his tone reflects how deeply I cut him this time. "That's hard to answer."

"Well, try." His voice has an edge. He has a right to be angry, but I'm petrified of the action that anger will provoke.

"Can we not do *that* here? You deserve answers, I agree. But can we save that argument for another time? I need to know what you plan on doing now that you know."

He blinks, looking surprised, but after a moment, his expressions turns earnest. As though he might not want to touch that subject right now since it means talking about that night.

"Fine," he bites out. "I don't know what I plan." He leans across the table. "I found out less than twenty-four hours ago that I have a kid."

I drop my gaze to the table once more, no longer able to look into his scorned chestnut eyes. It's been so long that I forgot how easily his contempt can cut me.

"One thing I can tell you," he continues, "is that I plan to be in her life."

My entire body seizes as if I got touched in a game of freeze tag. Air struggles to fill my lungs, and tears prick my eyes.

"Are you going to take her away from me?" I whisper, and one lone tear streams a path down my face.

Damn it. Where is the woman from the pep talk in the car? The one where I said we were going to stand strong and not let him mess with us?

His eyes slash with shock and hurt. "Of course not... unless there's a reason to." He sips his coffee, looks outside and back at me. "I can't believe you think I'd do that—rip a child away from the only parent she's ever known." He shakes his head. "I'm still the same Jimmy. The one who—"

"I don't know who you are anymore." As hard as it is to accept, that's the truth.

He's promised another woman his future. I recall the magazine I picked up in the store a couple of weeks ago. Adelaide had given an interview and gushed about the behemoth of a wedding they're planning. The Jimmy I knew would've hated that. But time has passed, and people change. I'm the best example of that.

He says nothing. What can he say really? It's true.

"I want to see her," he says.

I take a sip of my coffee to buy time. It's only logical he does. I've been trying to figure out the best way to introduce Monica to her father. "I know. She doesn't know about you."

His grip tightens on his mug, his knuckles turning white. "That's your doing."

"If you want, you can come for dinner tonight. I'll introduce you as my old friend. We can start there."

He stares at me for a couple seconds, his nostrils flaring. Isn't this why I brought him to a public place? To keep his temper in check.

"I have to fly back to LA in a couple of days."

"Okay." I pause to not lightly approach my next topic. "Listen, you have every right to be pissed off, but when we're in front of Monica, can we put that aside? She's a smart girl and has a lot of changes headed her way. If she feels the tension between us, it will only make this more difficult for her."

He stares into his coffee mug. For a moment I worry he's going say no. "Sure, yeah."

"Thanks." I release the breath I was holding because he could very well bulldoze into our life and tell Monica how I took her from him. He can make me the monster and him the hero. I shouldn't have doubted he wouldn't put our daughter first though, this is Jimmy after all.

"How long have you lived here?" Jimmy asks at the same time I ask, "Why did you come here?"

We both laugh awkwardly, but before either of us can answer, Parker catches my eye.

Shit.

"Hey, doll. We still on for tonight?" he says a few steps before reaching the edge of our booth.

I glance at Jimmy. He's looking down at the table and away so Parker will only see the top of his ball cap.

"Hi, Parker. I've been meaning to call you. Something came up and I'm going to have to reschedule."

A slight frown tilts the corner of his lips, and he spares a glance at Jimmy. "Sorry to hear that. Everything okay?"

I purposely spill my coffee, the dark liquid gushing over the edge of the booth. "Yeah, everything's fine. I'll text you later this week and we can figure out another time, okay?"

He bends down with napkins and Misty rushes over to clean up the mess.

Parker smiles, standing. "I'm gonna hold you to that." He knocks his knuckles on the table twice, winks, and heads to the door

"Thank you, Misty. I'm such a klutz." I help her with all the paper napkins from the table.

"It's fine. I'll bring you a refill." She smiles and walks away.

I can already feel Jimmy's gaze on me before I turn my head to him.

"Who's that?"

"No one. Don't worry about it. Now tell me why you came here."

"I will worry about it if he's around my daughter," he snaps.

I barely hold back my own tone. "Thanks, but I've looked out for Monica pretty well over the past five years. You don't need to worry about that."

"Yeah, well, I wouldn't know that, would I?"

I rub my temples, pissed at myself that I walked into that one. There's no defending the fact that I kept Monica away from him.

"So who is he?" he asks again.

"Just a guy I've gone on a few dates with. He hasn't even met Monica. She thinks I'm going out with my friend Amanda. Happy?"

He nods, his lips pressed firmly together.

"And before you ask, I'm sober. Have been since I went to the treatment center in Utah."

Minus the one shot at the bar that night, which I promptly forced myself to throw up. But that's none of Jimmy's business.

The tenseness in his muscles eases a fraction, suggesting he was worried I'd been raising his daughter while high on coke. "I'm madder than hell at you, Lilah, but I'm happy to hear that you were able to stay sober."

An unwelcome surge of warmth blossoms in my chest at the sound of my name on his lips. It's been too long since I've heard it in that deep timbre of his.

I can't get railroaded by a lust that has yet to diminish over the years. He's an engaged man, and not only that, he despises me.

"I should get to work." I reach for my purse beside me.

"What is it you do?" He nods at my name on my scrubs.

"I'm a dental hygienist."

"Huh." He pauses to soak in the information. "Good for you."

His response comes off half patronizing, though I don't think he means it to.

"Well, we can't all be Oscar-winning actors." I slide to the end of the booth and stand, my hand on the strap of my purse. "I'll see you for dinner then? Six?"

"You can count on it."

"Great," I say.

It doesn't feel great at all.

In fact, it feels more like my happy little bubble is about to pop.

Chapter Fifty-one

JIMMY

The second time I walk up the stairs of Lilah's house, my mind is worlds away from where it was a day ago.

Yesterday, I was brimming with the need for answers, closure, retribution.

Now I'm filled with nerves and uncertainty and curiosity.

What if Monica doesn't like me?

How am I supposed to talk to her? I know nothing about kids.

What if I screw this up?

What's her favorite toy? Her favorite food? Her favorite color?

I'm so mad at Lilah for stripping the years away from me, it's hard to look at her. She looked healthy and happy though. The people at the diner referred to her by name. She's made a life here with Monica. A life I would have liked to be a part of.

Focusing on one thing at a time, I bring my mind back to the fact I get to spend the evening finding out the answers to the questions about my daughter. This moment means nothing to Monica, but tonight is a night I'll never forget.

I knock on the screen door, and Monica peeks around the corner from the back of the house. Her eyes light up when she sees me, and her little feet clap against the hardwood as she flies down the hall.

Lilah pokes her head out of the kitchen and follows, looking way less enthused than her daughter. Wait, *our* daughter.

Monica pushes the door open for me. "Hi!"

"Hey." I beam down at her.

God, she's as beautiful as her mom. Her eyes sparkle as she stares up at me with a smile from ear to ear. She's cute as a button in a pink, one-piece short-and-tank set with silver stars printed on it. Her hair is pulled back into a ponytail at the top of her head, and her wavy blonde hair hangs down her back. She's definitely the most beautiful kid who ever existed.

"Sweetie, you remember Mommy's friend Jimmy from yesterday? He's going to have dinner with us tonight."

"Yay!" She takes my hand and pulls me into the house. "Do you wanna come see my Barbies? I have lots. We can play with them."

I blink a couple of times, taken aback by her enthusiasm and energy. Lilah bites her bottom lip, and I ignore the subconscious pull to her that always enticed.

I smile.

Lilah doesn't.

"Dinner will be ready in ten minutes."

Monica drags me down the hall to her room, which is painted a soft purple and has cream furniture. A filled bookcase is against the wall, a large bean bag chair nestled beside it. A tiny chandelier hangs from the ceiling in the center of the room, and her mermaid bedspread matches her walls.

Looks like she has everything. So different from how Lilah and I grew up. It's nice to see she hasn't gone without.

"This one is my favorite. But you can play with her if you want." Monica sits down near a toy box in the corner of her room, holding up a Barbie with long blonde hair similar to hers.

I sit beside her and take the Barbie. "Thanks. Does this one have a name?"

"It's Cecilia."

"Cecilia. That's a good name. I like it. Suits her."

She smiles at me. We've only been playing for a little bit, but I swear I feel this girl tether to my heart and wrap herself around my finger.

"What clothes do you want her to wear?" she asks, stripping the brown-haired Barbie in her hand.

"Hmm. I'm not sure. What are my options?"

She takes the top off a small plastic container and dumps small dresses and plastic shoes between us.

I chuckle. "Wow, you have a lot to choose from."

Monica nods enthusiastically. "My favorite is this one." She holds up a silvery ball gown with sparkles. "But she can't wear that right now."

"Oh, why not?"

She looks at me, and her expression implies I'm missing the obvious. My breath seizes at how similar her expression is to Lilah's when she was young.

"Because she's going to work, not to a party!" Her tone matches her expression, and I attempt to hold in my laughter.

"What kind of job does she have? That might help me pick the right outfit." I struggle to remove the bathing suit on my Barbie.

"She's a teacher." Monica picks a red dress out of the pile and dresses her own Barbie.

"A teacher, huh? Okay..." I move around some of the clothes in the pile before grabbing a navy dress with polka dots. "What do you think of this?"

She peers up from concentrating on getting Barbie's arms in the dress and twists her mouth to the side, appraising my choice as though she's the judge of *Next Top Model*. "That's good."

She's so adorable.

We spend the next few minutes acting out a scene between the two dolls. Something, to my surprise, I'm pretty good at. Probably because of my job.

I stretch forward to grab the little miniature dog that's Monica's Barbie's pet and notice Lilah from the corner of my eye. She's leaning against the doorway, arms crossed, and watching us. Our eyes lock and she's awoken from her mesmerized state.

She clears her throat. "Dinner is ready if you guys want to wash up."

She turns and heads back down the hall, not waiting for either of us to answer.

"All right, let's go wash our hands." I stand.

"Okay, I can show you where the washroom is." She springs up and takes my hand, pulling me out of the room.

She drags me down the hall to the bathroom we passed. I let Monica wash up first, and by the time I reach the kitchen, she's already seated at the painted wood table. There's a place setting beside her and one across from her. Since Lilah is at the stove, getting dinner on everyone's plates, I slide into the seat beside Monica.

I'm nothing if not eager to soak up all the time and proximity I can.

Monica gives me a conspiratorial grin once I'm seated, and my heart explodes. She's happy I took the seat next to her. The feeling that the two of us are sharing something steals the air from my lungs. After only an hour, there's no going back to a life without Monica. A firm line has been drawn in my life. Before Monica and After Monica.

I return her smile as Lilah places a plate in front of me. "Thanks."

Chicken, rice, and a baked potato fill the plate, and my eyebrows shoot up in surprise. After the near kitchen fire when I was here last night and her lack of culinary skills back in the day, I figured when she said dinner, it would be a frozen meal.

"I see you've learned to cook," I joke to ease the tension.

If we're going to do this and make it work, then we have to get comfortable with each other too. Lilah and I have to be adults. She was right about that.

"I had to learn." She nods in Monica's direction and sets a smaller plastic purple plate in front of our daughter. "I've learned a lot, but I still consider it a necessary evil." She turns to retrieve her plate from the counter.

"Did you know…" I lean to the side, closer to Monica. Her eyes grow wide and eager, waiting for me to tell her a secret. "Your mommy didn't know how to cook at all back when I knew her?"

"Really?" She looks to Lilah for confirmation.

She sits in her chair. "Yep. Completely true."

"But Mommy makes all my food. It's good. Except I don't like the green stuff."

Lilah looks at me. "Pretty much the vegetables."

I wrinkle my nose and look at Monica. "I eat a lot of vegetables."

"That why you're so big?"

Lilah laughs, positioning her napkin on her lap.

"Definitely. Like The Hulk?" I boost myself up, but my daughter should think I'm a superhero.

"The who?"

Lilah laughs again. Who would have thought we'd be laughing so quickly?

"Oh, I see we have boy territory to zone in on." I put my napkin over my lap.

"Boys are yucky." Monica picks up her fork.

Lilah shrugs. I shake my head, not offended.

"Okay, everyone, dig in."

The awkwardness rises again during dinner. We eat in silence and it's clear my being here has changed the dynamic.

"Monica, eat some of your chicken please," Lilah says.

"I don't want to," she whines. Her shoulders sag and she tilts her head to the side.

"Drown it in ketchup if you need to, but if you want a popsicle after dinner, you need to eat your chicken."

To her credit, Monica doesn't argue with her mom. She sticks out her bottom lip in a sulk and reaches for the ketchup. She struggles to get the lid open before I offer to help.

"Need a hand?" I hold out my hand.

She nods, frustration on her small face. After taking the ketchup bottle from her hands, I squeeze some onto her plate into the spot where she's pointing. Who knew a small act, like helping my child get ketchup on her plate, could make me feel so wanted?

Lilah and I make forced conversation through the rest of dinner, and I try to engage Monica as best I can. Although I feel as though Lilah is studying me like a delinquent parent who can't be left alone with his own child. I hope she remembers I'm an absentee parent because of her doing.

Monica ends up eating the majority of her chicken after covering every single piece with ketchup.

She's sucking on her popsicle when the bark of a dog sounds from outside. "Mommy, can I go play with Charlie?"

"Who's Charlie?" I ask.

"Our next-door neighbor's dog. Monica is in love with him and the lady who lives there watches Monica for me sometimes." She moves her attention from me to Monica. "You can go play with him for a bit, but I don't want any arguments when it's time to come in for your bath."

"Pinkie swear," she says and sticks out her hand with her pinkie finger extended.

I suck in a breath, rearing back in my seat.

Lilah looks guiltily at me quickly before she locks fingers with Monica. "Come on, I'll take you over and make sure it's okay with Eileen. I'll be back in a minute."

They leave the kitchen and head out the front door. I sit there by myself for a minute and look around the room, trying to picture their daily life. Does Monica stand on a stool so she can reach the butcher board counter and help Lilah make cookies? Where do the two of them normally eat? Is it different tonight because I'm here? What cereal does Monica like for breakfast?

These are all questions I don't know the answer to because Lilah kept her from me. I'm not usually an angry guy, but it keeps rushing up my throat like indigestion. Nothing, then all of a sudden, bam, I'm about to go ballistic.

I push back from the table and gather the plates, bringing them to the counter. I need something to occupy my mind before I can't control my anger. The last thing I want to do is to explode on Lilah in front of Monica. The little girl will cast me as the villain.

I'm rinsing off the plates and stacking them in the dishwasher when Lilah returns.

"Sorry I took so long. Eileen was digging into me about who my company is." She shrugs. "Small town."

"What did you tell her?" *Did you tell her that he's the father of your child and you kept from him knowing about her for six years?* But I don't say that, knowing it will take us down a path we won't veer off of tonight.

Tonight, all I want is to spend time with my daughter.

"Just that you're an old friend who came to visit. You don't have to do this. Why don't you go sit and I'll clean up?" She steps up to the sink with her hand out for the dish in mine, but I ignore her.

"I'm perfectly capable of loading a dishwasher."

"Oh, you don't have a housekeeper and personal chef who do your bidding now that you've made it big time?" She attempts to pass off her comment as a joke, but the bite in her tone keeps the humor from coming across.

"We have a housekeeper who comes once a week, but I'm not waited on hand and foot."

I don't tell her that Adelaide wants someone there full time and I had to fight her not to hire us a personal chef. I enjoy cooking. I don't want that taken away from me.

"Speaking of your home, how is Adelaide?" She picks up the condiments and places them back in the fridge.

My phone rings in the back pocket of my shorts, and I pull it out to look at the screen. "Speak of the devil. Mind if I take this out on the porch?"

Her head is in the fridge, but she shakes her head.

I texted my fiancée last night to say that I was exhausted and heading to bed before she wrapped on set for the night, not sure how to explain to her where I was and what was going on. I'm still not sure, but I don't want her to worry needlessly, so I have to take this call even if the timing sucks.

"Hey," I say, wandering toward the front door.

"Hi, sweetie, how are you?"

"Good. You? How're re-shoots going?"

"Ugh. Not bad, I guess, but the weather isn't cooperating. I swear, does it have to rain every day in this damn city?"

I chuckle. "I sense some frustration."

"Just a bit." Her small laugh sounds through the phone. "Anyway, I have a few minutes before I'm back on set. Distract me. What are you up to?"

"Nothing much. Just about to go for a run I think." I push my hand through my hair, a sick feeling coating my skin. Another lie to mark on the tally, but I can't tell her, "Oh hey, your soon-to-be-husband is a father." That needs to be done in person.

"I wish I had time to jog. I haven't been able to get any workouts in since I arrived. I'm going to have back fat in my dress at our wedding."

"You're going to look beautiful. You don't need to change anything." I step over to one of the rocking chairs on the porch and sit.

"You have to say that, you're my fiancé."

"I'm saying that because it's true. Now when do you think you'll be home?" Nausea rolls my stomach because once again,

I'm asking so I can beat her back to LA, not because I'm an eager fiancé waiting to see his would-be bride.

"Well, despite the delays we've had with rain, I should still be home by the end of the week. If it changes, I'll let you know."

"Good. I'm glad." And I am. I haven't really had time to miss her, with everything going on over the past couple of days, but I'm looking forward to seeing her. Just not the part where I have to admit why I sought Lilah out in the first place and what I discovered once I did.

"I hope you're ready to get down to all the wedding details once I return. We have a lot of decisions to finalize."

"You just give me my marching orders and I'll make sure it gets done."

"You're the perfect fiancée, you know that?" She giggles. "I've gotta run, they're calling me back to set."

"Okay, break a leg. I'll talk to you tomorrow."

"Love you."

"I love you too." I hit the red circle on my phone and slide it into my pocket.

I've officially crossed a line in my relationship with Adelaide. I've never lied to her before. Yeah, I never confessed to how horrid the conditions were growing up and what I had to do to survive back then, nor will I ever tell her about that night on the mountain... but I always considered that to be more withholding information than outright lying.

Now I'm a liar, which doesn't make me much different from Lilah.

Chapter Fifty-two

LILAH

When Jimmy leaves to take the call from Adelaide, I peek out of my bedroom window to make sure that Monica is still next door with Eileen, playing with Charlie. A breath of relief leaves my lungs when her blonde ponytail flits behind her while she runs around the yard. I'm not sure if she's chasing Charlie or if he's chasing her, but she's smiling and laughing.

Normally I wouldn't feel the need to check on her, but Jimmy's reappearance in my life has me wanting to keep her close. Jimmy thinks I should know he wouldn't take her, but kids are game-changers. I should know. I never thought I'd keep my child from her father.

I head back into the kitchen and concentrate on cleaning the counters and table. Turning on the kettle, I pretend I'm not bothered by the fact that he's out on my porch, talking to the woman he's going to marry in a few short months, if the tabloids are telling the truth. The woman who, six years ago, he swore he had no feelings for. Does she call him Jimmy now?

Once their relationship was officially in the press, a barrage of questions hit me. Did he care for her when we were together? Was something going on between them back then? What does he see in her? Does he feel more for her than he ever did for me?

All those same questions push at me now, demanding to be answered. I grit my teeth, centering myself to remember he's not mine and never will be.

The kettle whistles. Jimmy's not back yet, so I pour hot water into two mugs with the tea bags, not sure if he'll want one or not but trying to be a good host. By the time I've done a final wipe of the counter, he still hasn't returned, so I pour some milk into the mugs and carry them out to the front porch.

His back is to me, his front leaning against the railing with his hands out to his sides. His position bunches the muscles in his arms and his upper back, causing a flutter to wobble in my stomach—something I haven't felt in longer than I can remember.

He's an engaged man.

But our falling-out had nothing to do with me falling out of love with him, so rather than feel guilty about the feelings I still have for the man in front of me, I ignore them. "I brought you a tea."

He faces me, his straight-line brow suggesting he's worried. "Thanks."

Our fingers brush against one another's for a split second during the exchange, and our gazes meet. I look down and back away, sitting in the rocking chair on the far side of the porch. Jimmy follows, sitting in the one beside it.

"Things okay with Adelaide?" I ask when I shouldn't. It will only bring up my own agitation over the fact they're engaged.

His head jerks to the side, and he holds the mug steady in front of his lips. He sets his tea on the small table to his left without taking a sip. "Yeah, things are good."

Good to know I can still read him. Which is scary, because that means he can probably still read me.

"Does she know you're here?" I ask, voicing my suspicion.

"No."

I take a sip of my tea. After a minute of silence, I ask the question that's been plaguing me since I saw him on my front porch yesterday. "Why are you here, Jimmy?"

And what are you going to do about it now that you know you have a daughter? I *don't* ask—too afraid of the answer.

"That's not important." His tone is curt, so I don't push the topic.

"How long are you planning to stay?" I grip my mug between both hands on my lap as though it's anchoring me.

He shrugs. "Don't know. A couple more days, I guess. From there, we'll have to figure something out."

Well, that's better than him telling me he's going to sue me for custody of Monica. But it doesn't mean we won't end up in a courtroom, arguing over holidays and weekends. I don't want to anger him further, so I decide to forget the details for now and turn things to a happier subject.

"Is your wedding really in a few months like the press says?"

He sighs, his gaze shooting to the yard next door. "Yeah. Lots to do still though."

I nod. "So, you and Adelaide... how did that happen?"

Gah, someone get some duct tape and shut me up. Could I come off any more jealous?

He stands abruptly. "I don't want to do this."

I set my mug on the table. "Do what?"

"Sit here with you and try to catch you up on the last six years of my life while we ignore the bigger issues. But I'm not ready to talk to you about them yet, so let's just leave it for now."

"Okay, whatever you want." I stand from the rocking chair. "Why don't I go get Monica so you can say goodbye?"

"Yeah, fine." He blatantly ignores my existence, and that itchy feeling begins.

I want to scream from the tension between us. The uncertainty of where his head is at. The not knowing what he has planned. We were lovers yeah, but we were friends too. As afraid as I am of the outcome, I need to fast-track us to the part where he lays his cards on the table and tells me what he wants and how far he's ready to take it.

"Tomorrow is my day off. Monica will be at school. Why don't you come over for lunch and we can have a real conversation about everything?"

He grips the back of his neck with one hand and looks at the porch floor.

"We have to do this, Jimmy. Let's air everything out, because this living in limbo isn't working for me." I step on the stair down from the house, waiting for his response.

He slowly turns his head in my direction. "Okay, what time?"

"I'm going to drop off Monica at school, go for a swim, then I'm headed to a meeting. So, say... twelve thirty?"

"I'll be here."

I nod and make my way down the porch steps to go fetch Monica.

"You still swim?" he calls.

I swivel around and nod, walking backward.

"I guess some things don't change."

I step across the grass, wondering if that's a good omen or a bad omen.

Chapter Fifty-three

LILAH

A knock sounds on the door and I jolt. Not sure why I startle since I was expecting him. Neither the laps in the pool nor the AA meeting this morning have kept my anxiety about this conversation in check.

My chest is tight and struggling to inhale a full breath. I clench my hands on the way to the door before spreading my fingers open to will myself to relax.

Jimmy stands on the porch wearing his ball cap and sunglasses, a plain T-shirt stretched across his hard chest, and a pair of cargo shorts. I have no idea how no one has spotted him in our small town. He emanates that "I'm someone special" quality without trying.

I open the door and step aside. "Come on in."

My eyes close for a second when his fresh, clean, manly scent follows his entrance. The same scent that I attributed to safety and security for the majority of my life. I hope our conversation doesn't sour Jimmy's smell to me.

He removes his sunglasses and ball cap, running his fingers through his hair. He's overdue for a haircut. Or maybe he's growing it out for a role. A dull ache hits me with the reminder that I know nothing about his life. Well, nothing that no one else who can read does. I've gone from his confidant to his hidden stalker.

"Has anyone recognized you yet?"

He shakes his head and stuffs his hands into his pockets. "Except the store the first day, I haven't really gone anywhere. Been living off food deliveries mostly."

I nod with the hope it remains that way. His fame is another puzzle piece we have to figure out. My hand falls to my stomach when I think about Monica's face on those magazines. One day she'll be old enough to read horrific things about her mother's past, but I won't sit idle and let the paps ruin her life with lies.

"I'm not sure you'll be too thrilled with lunch then. I had the diner make up sandwiches for us." No way do I have any ability to cook an edible meal today.

"As long as it's not pizza, I'm happy."

"I hope you still like roast beef."

I walk into the family room. I wanted somewhere comfortable and private for what's about to go down. We sit at opposite ends of the couch, and I'm surprised he didn't take the arm chair to be farther from me.

"I thought we'd eat here." I pull his sandwich out of the bag and pass it to him.

"Thanks." He unwraps it and takes a large bite. "It's good."

I give him a small smile and remove my turkey on rye from the bag. I open the wax paper and place the sandwich on the coffee table. Gathering courage I didn't think I had, I shift on the couch so one leg is under me, one dangling to the floor, and face him. *You can do this.*

"We might as well get right to it. I want to start off by saying that I'm sorry I didn't tell you I was pregnant." He opens his mouth to say something, but I raise my hand and he allows me to continue. "I know sorry doesn't cut it. Nothing I say will. I just want you to know I truly am. It's a decision I've second-guessed a lot through the years. If things had been different..."

"When did you know?" He abandons his sandwich on the coffee table.

"After that night when you told me to..." My gaze falls to my hands in my lap, unable to see his expression when I reference the night that sent our lives in opposite directions.

"I don't understand why you wouldn't have told me." He stands from the couch and paces in front of the coffee table. When I don't answer, he spears me an angry look.

"After... what happened, I went straight to a bar. I didn't even think, and I barely remember getting there, I was such a mess. All I knew was that I wanted to numb myself from the fact I'd lost you. I could tell you really meant those words and we wouldn't come back from the mistake I'd made."

His fists clench at his sides when I say the word mistake.

"I sat on that bar stool for so long before I took a shot."

"I thought you said you'd been sober since Utah? Just another lie?" he sneers.

"As soon as the alcohol hit the back of my throat, I knew it was a mistake. I ran to the washroom and forced myself to throw up. Then I called Calder."

His forehead creases, and he looks at me for a second before piecing the information together. "Calder Fox?"

I nod, my hands clenched in my lap. "Remember when we met them at that premiere? He put his number in my phone and told me to call if I ever needed someone to talk to. He picked me up. He found me an Airbnb to stay in, got me to a meeting."

His hands rest on his hips as he shakes his head. "I've seen him a few times since then and he's never mentioned anything."

"I made him promise not to. You guys aren't really friends. At least not close friends. I think he understood me since we share the same problem. Anyway, those next few months were a blur. I barely left the house except to get food and go to meetings. Sometimes two or three a day. Anything to fill my time so I wouldn't use or take a drink. I spent hours and hours in bed, crying over the things I had done. By the time I came out of my haze, I realized I couldn't remember when I'd had my period last." I pull my legs up to my chest and wrap my arms around them, resting my chin on my knees.

He sits on the arm chair as though standing takes too much energy. His hands are clasped between his legs and he stares at me, waiting for more answers.

"I thought there was no chance, but I took a test. I sat on the bathroom floor shaking as I stared at those two pink lines." I pause, but there's no sympathy for me in Jimmy's eyes. Not that I should expect any. But as terrified as I was on that bathroom floor, doubting my ability to be a mother, I'm more terrified now that Jimmy could strip motherhood away from me.

"That's the part when you should've called me."

I sigh. "Yeah, I should have. I was already four months along by the time I found out. Too far to have an abortion—not that I would have anyway. I kept telling myself that once I got used to the idea, I'd call you and tell you. Days passed, then weeks. Then she started moving inside me, and this love sprung for the little being I was growing. The way you looked at me that night... the hatred in your eyes." I shake my head and clutch my stomach as though Monica is still in there. "I was petrified you'd take her from me."

Wetness burns my eyes and one tear escapes, rolling down my cheek before another one tumbles after it.

"I changed my phone number, started off in Texas before landing in Kansas. The further along in my pregnancy I got, the more I knew she was my meaning to life. She was my turn-around point. My start over. I'd do everything in my power to give her the life she deserved."

"Why would you ever think I'd take her from you?" Jimmy growls.

I wipe the tears from my cheeks and suck in a deep breath, willing myself to say the words. "I think you're forgetting how much you hated me the last time we saw one another. I was the used-up junkie you'd taken care of your entire life. If you found out I was pregnant, you would have never trusted me with her. You had the money, the great lawyers. Your big break happened, *The Regulator*, and there you were, Hollywood's golden boy. I had nothing. I had a bit of money saved from modeling, but I didn't have the kind of cash at my disposal that you did, and I certainly didn't have the clout or backstory working in my favor."

I stop, all of it sounding like excuses now. "I figured that if I had the baby and waited a few months, I could show you I could handle things on my own. Build the trust I broke so many times. But then one month went by, then another and another, and the fear of you taking her away became more and more real and I couldn't risk that I'd never see my daughter again because... I knew I wouldn't survive if that happened."

A sob rips up my throat and I bury my face in my knees. My body shakes as my fear, my betrayal, and the uncertainty of our future comes to a head.

I suck in a breath, wipe my tears, and gather another ounce of courage I didn't think I had. I look at Jimmy—the man who was my everything, the man I've kept everything from for six years. He looks at me with clenched fists and an anguished expression.

"Were you ever planning to tell me?"

The salt from my tears burns my cheeks. I nod slowly. "I only ever wanted what was best for her. That sounds backward, I know, since I didn't tell you about her. I was going to reach out a little over a year ago because... it's become clear to me that she needs a dad in her life."

"And why didn't you? You were obviously sober and able to make this home for her. What's your excuse this time?"

"You started dating Adelaide."

His eyes close. He opens his mouth, but I hold up my hand to stop him.

"I know that's not an excuse either, but I'd see you on the tabloids or on television, smiling with her and I thought…" I shake my head.

"What?"

"That I'd be ruining your life all over again." I refrain from mentioning the hurt I felt when I saw them together because that's not on him, it's on me.

He stares at me, unspeaking, and I shrink into myself. But I have to reap what I've sown, so eventually I meet his gaze.

"I truly am sorry for the years I stole from you. There wasn't a day that went by that I didn't question my decision, but every time I'd think of telling you, the fear that you'd take her from me was paralyzing and I'd tell myself I was doing the right thing. She's all I have." I pull my eyes from him. So much for being courageous.

When the couch dips beside me, I turn my head to look at him.

"I don't know if I'll ever be able to really forgive you for keeping her from me. I'd like to think that if you'd told me about her back when you were pregnant, I wouldn't have tried to take her from you, but the truth is that I don't know what I would have done. What you did… it ripped me in two. I was so angry and hurt. Maybe I would've lashed out at you and felt you weren't stable enough to raise a child. I'd like to think I could've put our differences aside and seen things objectively, but who's to say. Not trying to cast stones, but six years ago, I would have doubted you could make this life for you and our daughter." His head falls into his hands.

"Are you going to try to take her from me?" I whisper, and my breath dies in my throat.

His lips press into a thin line. "I don't want to do anything to hurt her. No. She obviously adores you and you've built a good life for yourselves here. But I am going to be in her life, there's no question about that."

Relief swells through me. I wrap my arms around his neck and hug him. "Thank you."

His scent envelops me and I die a little, remembering this feeling of safety and security that I've gone without all these years.

He doesn't return my hug, so I pull away, heat flushing my cheeks. "I'm sorry. I'm just so relieved."

He clears his throat and stands. "It's fine. I have to fly home tomorrow morning, but I want to see Monica before I leave."

"Okay, sure. Do you want to come for dinner again tonight?"

"I don't think that's a good idea. I'll come by after to play with her before she goes to bed."

I nod.

"Okay then." He stomps out the front door without a backward glance.

I hear his truck start up and drive off. I sit in the corner of my couch and let the conversation sink in. For years I've dreaded what just happened, my actions like a shackle around my neck. The load was too heavy to carry at times, but my selfishness always made excuses for my decisions.

I'm still wary. I'm still uncertain. Having Jimmy in my life without actually *having* him will be a new weight to bear, but the joy for my daughter to have a man like Jimmy be a real father to her overrides the burden.

Chapter Fifty-four

JIMMY

The moment she pressed her body to mine, I had no choice. I needed to get out of her house. There was nothing sexual about her hug, but my body reacted. My arms almost welcomed her back. Nuzzling my head into her neck and allowing some closure to the past would have been easy. I consoled my guilty conscience by telling myself it was all psychology—a Pavlovian response to her. Especially when I'd been away from my fiancée for so long. But it's a lie. It's all Lilah.

I'm not worried about overstepping the line. I would never do that to Adelaide. My head is fucked up enough without adding another layer of deceit. I *am* worried about co-parenting with a woman who still holds some power over me.

I drive straight to my hotel room and lie on the shitty hotel bed with my arm over my forehead, staring at the popcorn-painted ceiling and going over every fact Lilah told me. A part of me understands why she didn't tell me about Monica, but it doesn't excuse it. Then again, Lilah was always one to run from problems. If she found herself in the same situation now,

I'm not sure the new Lilah I've seen in the last two days would do the same thing. Despite everything, it's clear our daughter's well-being is her top priority.

One good part about having crappy parents and a shitty life growing up, you learn not to steep in anger until you're toxic. I'll force myself to find a way to be around Monica without showing animosity to her mother. I'm going to have to put Lilah in the category of "daughter's mother" and nothing more.

"This is so fucked up."

With the issues of Lilah sectioned off in my mind, Adelaide slips into her spot.

Shit. I have to tell Adelaide on Friday.

I wish time would slow down. How will Adelaide react? She doesn't even want to be a mother—something I begrudgingly accepted because I love her and thought eventually her feelings might change. Will she accept the role of stepmother?

Rolling over, I grab my phone off the nightstand. I press Tripp's name.

He answers on the first ring as if he's telepathic and knows how badly I need to talk to him. "Hey, man. You take care of that thing we talked about last time?"

He must not be alone.

"I did."

He moves the phone away and tells whoever he's with he'll be back. I hate that I keep interrupting his tour with my bullshit. "Sorry, I'm grabbing a bite at a restaurant in Paris before the show. How'd it go?"

The sound of a noisy restaurant dims.

"Not as expected."

"Stop being so fucking cryptic." A flick of his lighter and a deep inhale. I could use a cigarette right now and I don't even smoke.

"I have a daughter." The words rush out with an uncontrollable need to put it all out there. A strange sense of relief and pride fills my chest.

Tripp coughs into the phone before gathering himself. "The fuck? We must have a bad connection. Did you just say that you have a daughter?"

I sigh. "Yep. When I got here, she answered the door. I knew as soon as I saw her."

"Lilah was pregnant and she never told you?" he yells.

"Pipe down. The last thing I need is someone eavesdropping and putting two and two together."

"This is unbelievable. What a bitch!"

Here's one instance where we see eye to eye in regards to Lilah.

"I was shocked. As was Lilah when she saw me standing there."

"Unbelievable. You're a dad?"

"I'm a dad." The word is starting to feel more comfortable. Not completely.

"So what's she like? Tell me about her. I'm assuming you've talked to her?"

"Yeah, I had dinner over there last night and I'm going back tonight. She's amazing, man. You have to meet her. Her name is Monica and she has Lilah's hair—long, blonde, and wavy—but my brown eyes. And she's smart. And so happy all the time. When she smiles, her cheeks puff out and her eyes sparkle. She's the cutest kid ever."

He chuckles. "She won you over."

"Can't lie, she's going to wrap me around her finger before I know it."

"No doubt. I remember when her mother had the same effect on you."

"Whatever." I act as if there's no truth to his comment.

"Did you guys ever get to the whole reason you went there in the first place?"

"Nope. Yet one more thing to figure out, along with how I'm going to tell Adelaide about Monica."

He blows out a stream of air. "Fuck. I don't want to be you."

"No shit. I'm gonna break the news to her when she's home on Friday. Any words of advice?"

"Wear a jockstrap."

I laugh. This is why Tripp's my best friend.

"Let me know how it goes. I'll be back in Cali in a few weeks."

"For sure. Thanks for listening."

"Always, man. I gotta roll. My brother's about to lose it on the waiter."

"Go."

Tripp's brother, who is basically his Lilah, er... who Lilah was six years ago, is always causing problems for the band, but I'm not sure Tripp realizes how toxic he is.

"Hey, you know what I just realized?" he says.

"No, what?"

"I'm an uncle. Uncle Tripp." He laughs and hangs up before I can form a rebuttal.

I hang up with a smile. That lasts about a second before reality sets in.

* * *

I SIT on the front porch, waiting for Lilah to put Monica to bed. Another moment when I had to put my wants aside because Monica doesn't need a strange man tucking her into bed. Once she knows I'm her daddy, all this waiting on the sidelines is over. I've missed too many tuck-ins. I'll know her nightly routine just as well as Lilah.

Lilah was nice after dinner and made herself scarce. Monica and I played outside with chalk. She showed me how she could ride her bike and told me about some friend at school who told her she had baby training wheels. Yeah, we'll be rectifying that situation immediately. I never wanted to beat up a five-year-old before. That daddy label is starting to saran wrap itself around me.

She really is the happiest child I've ever seen—not that I've had a lot of experience with kids, except for on set.

It's hard not to jump ahead and think of what the future will bring, all the places I want to take her, all the experiences I want to give her.

The sound of the screen door shutting draws me from my thoughts. Lilah sits in the rocking chair to my left.

"You tired her out. She went straight to sleep, no fuss."

I give her a small smile. "Let's get down to it, okay? What's the plan?"

She plays with her hands in her lap, unable to meet my gaze. "You tell me. What do you want to happen?"

What I want to say is, "Why didn't you ask me this question six years ago? We should be raising her as a couple. I should be up there reading her a story and tucking her under the covers." But I don't. We can't go back. The damage is done. Decisions were made. The best thing I can do for Monica is look forward.

"I want to get to know my daughter, and when the time is right, I want us to tell her who I am. But before I do any of that, I have to tell Adelaide."

Her gaze flicks up to meet mine. "How do you think she'll react?"

"I'll worry about that." Mine and Adelaide's relationship is none of Lilah's damn business.

"I have to worry about it because it has the potential to affect my daughter. I'm not going to let someone treat my daughter—"

I raise my hand to stop her. "Enough. I'll deal with Adelaide. I'd never put my daughter in a situation like that."

She nods. "Okay."

"What's your work schedule like?" I ask.

"I have Wednesdays and Sundays off."

I roll that over in my head and come up with what I think is the best idea. "This weekend is off the table, but I'll fly into town on Fridays and watch Monica while you're at work on Saturday. I'll fly back out on Sundays."

"Sure, yeah, okay," she says in a small voice.

Standing from the rocker, I face her. "Probably best if I put you in my phone so I can text you if need be."

I pull my phone from my pocket, type in my password, and pass it to her without thinking. She holds it and hurt flashes across her features. The background screen is a selfie of Adelaide and me on the beach outside my Malibu place.

I shouldn't feel remorseful, but I do. Old habits die hard. I haven't done anything wrong and she's the one who put herself in this position.

Her thumbs run over the screen and she passes it back.

"Will it just be you coming next weekend?" Her eyes still won't meet mine.

"I won't introduce Monica to Adelaide until she's used to the idea of who I am. Let's take it one step at a time."

She stands from her rocking chair. "Well, let me know what time you'll be here Friday. You can come for dinner."

"Do you need anything before I leave? Are there any expenses for Monica you need help with?"

Her eyes narrow. The woman who looked lost a minute ago straightens her back like a prize-winning bull ready to play a game of chicken. "I don't need your money, Jimmy."

Without another word, she brushes by me and retreats into the house.

I remind myself it's only day three.

Chapter Fifty-five

JIMMY

delaide arrives home earlier than expected and immediately peppers me with wedding details that need to be finalized. She doesn't notice my fake enthusiasm when my preoccupied head is everywhere but on our wedding.

We eat on the deck, unwinding with a glass of wine for her and a beer for me. The sun descending is like a clock in my head. The deeper it falls below the horizon, the heavier the secret weighs on my shoulders. My palms are clammy and sweat dots my forehead as the secret seems to get heavier and heavier on my shoulders. I wipe my forehead with my napkin and run my palms down my shorts.

I have no idea how she'll react, and that realization leaves an uncomfortable feeling in my gut. Shouldn't I know my fiancée well enough to predict how she'll feel about this? Then again, this isn't an everyday couple problem.

I refill her glass of wine and set the bottle on the table.

"Thanks, honey. I've needed this, though I can only have one more if I want to look my best on our wedding day. I'll savor it though."

I smile at her and watch her take a tiny sip. Sometimes she feels like a different woman than the one I met on *The Regulator*.

"There's something I need to talk to you about." I grip the arms of the chair until my fingers ache.

"Uh oh. That sounds ominous." She sets down her wine glass and frowns.

I release my grip on the armrests and push a hand through my hair.

"James, what is it?" She reaches over but never makes contact with me.

"I saw Lilah while you were away."

She stills and backs up in her seat, the caring gesture stripped by one woman's name. That doesn't surprise me. "She's back in town?"

I shake my head. "A couple weeks ago, I was watching the news and I thought I saw her, which got me thinking about where she ended up and whether she ever got her shit together. It's something that's been on my mind more and more lately. Not because I have those feelings for her anymore." I try to put all my jumbled thoughts in a logical order so she'll understand this was all for her. "But I think because we were on and off for so long and I always thought that at some point in my life, it would be her I'd be marrying."

Well, shit, I didn't intend for that to come out.

Adelaide's mouth hangs open. I'm as surprised as she is. But it's the truth, and if I'm going to do one thing for our marriage, it'll be that there are no untruths between us.

"Go on." She grips the stem of her wine glass, circling it on the table.

"I wasn't feeling like I missed her romantically, but I never got answers as to why she betrayed me. I never got the closure I needed. When I saw her on TV, it sent my curiosity into overdrive. I called Tripp to tell him how I was feeling about everything and he suggested finding her to hash it out."

"Remind me to thank him," she deadpans.

"Adelaide." I reach across to the table to take her free hand, but she places it in her lap. My chest constricts. "I only wanted to get answers because I want to move into this marriage with a clear head and heart. I didn't want anything from my past lingering in my psyche. And the reason I didn't tell you was because I was doing all this to not hurt you. I know It sounds stupid when I say it out loud, but it made sense at the time."

She's quiet for a minute. I meet her gaze, willing her to see the truth.

"And how is sweet Lilah these days? Still giving blow jobs for a bump?" She raises the wine glass to her lips and takes a sip.

I blow out a breath and look at the sunset for a moment. As mad as I am at Lilah, I hate it when Adelaide says shit about her.

"Actually, she has her act together. She's been sober since I last saw her." Even I can't deny there's pride in my tone. No matter how pissed off I am at her, what she did with her life, the way she turned it around, is amazing. Many have tried and failed. I heard all the sad stories of death and prison and diseases when I was attending the Al-Anon meetings. Lilah beat the odds.

"What are you trying to say, James?" Her voice holds anger, but her shaking wine glass says she fearful.

I suck in a deep breath before I really lay it on her. "Not what you're thinking."

"What I'm thinking is that my fiancé snuck off to see his ex while I was working and figured out he still has feelings for her!" She pushes out her chair and stands, leaning toward me with her hands on the table.

"It's not that."

"Then what is it?" she asks between clenched teeth.

"I have a daughter."

Her eyes widen and she inhales a deep breath that, for a moment, I think might come back out shooting flames. The veins in her neck are about to pop. She pushes off the table and stands by the glass guardrail.

I wait to say anything else. Let her mind wrap around the news. I make my way over and stand beside her, both of us facing the ocean.

"How can you even be sure she's yours?" The anger has already evaporated from her tone.

I whip my head in her direction, ready to defend my right to be in Monica's life, but it's a reasonable question to ask. "She's mine. She has my eyes."

Her lips press harder together. "You need to have a DNA test done to be sure."

I take her hand. "I will, but Adelaide?" I wait for her to look at me, which she does with wetness coating her eyes. "She's mine."

Her shoulders sag, and her head falls to her chest. "What does this mean?"

"It means you're going to be a stepmom."

She cringes and drops my hand. "I don't even want my own kids."

She can't be thinking I'd walk away from Monica? I mean… the woman I'm about to marry would never want that of me. I'm sure of it.

"I get it, but the child is mine. I've already missed five years with her. I'm not going to miss any more." My voice hardens with the unspoken accusation she's asking me to do something I'll never do.

She turns to face the ocean again. "Why didn't Lilah tell you?"

"She says she was afraid I'd try to take the baby from her."

"Pfft. Typical."

I agree, but unlike me, Adelaide won't let her anger disperse as easily as I did. I can guarantee that fact.

We stand in silence for a few minutes, the awkwardness between us growing.

"So what's your plan?" she asks.

I fill her in on what Lilah and I discussed before I left Kansas and bring her up to speed on what Monica and Lilah's life is like.

"Great, so in the months leading up to my wedding, I'll be left to fend for myself every weekend and make all the decisions on my own. Perfect."

"I know the timing isn't great, but I need to put in the time to get to know my daughter."

She straightens, crossing her arms and turning to me. "Can I come with you?"

I grip the railing harder, knowing my response won't make this easier. "I think we should wait until we tell her she's my daughter. Get her used to the idea first, then introduce you to her."

Her jaw clenches, and she curtly nods. "I'm going to call it a night. We can finish this conversation tomorrow."

I rear back that she's closed the door to the conversation. "I'm sorry I hurt you."

She doesn't spare me a glance as she heads into the house.

It isn't until she's closed the sliding glass door that I realize she didn't even ask what my daughter's name is.

"Her name is Monica," I say to the warm, salty air. "And she's amazing."

LILAH

So far, Jimmy has been true to his word. He hasn't mentioned anything about trying to win custody of Monica. My guard isn't completely down though. What if he and I argue over something and he uses her as a pawn? But I have to remind myself of who I'm dealing with.

Although he's still angry with me, it's clear that he's falling in love, if he's not already there, with his daughter. I have to believe that the Jimmy I've always known, the one who would never use a child to try to win an adult game, is still who he is.

Watching Monica become completely taken by Jimmy is surprisingly easy.

I pull the covers over Monica and I'm almost at the door when she calls out to me.

"Mommy?"

I turn with my hand on her doorknob. "Yeah, kiddo?"

"Will I get to see Jimmy again tomorrow?" Even in the dim room, lit only by her nightlight, her hopeful expression shines.

"Do you want to see him tomorrow?"

She nods.

I smile. "You'll be happy to know that he's going to watch you tomorrow instead of Eileen then."

"Yay!"

"All right, kiddo. Time to get to sleep." My hand rests on the doorknob.

"Okay, Mommy. Love you."

"Love you too, baby."

I leave the room and softly close the door before heading back out to the porch. I sit in the rocking chair beside Jimmy. Is he so deep in thought that he doesn't notice?

"That went well, I think." It's the only thing I can think of to say to him.

I hate how stilted and awkward our conversations are. After dinner, we did that stupid dance where all we want to do is pass the other but we kept going the same way. Never did I think this would be the two of us.

"Yeah, it did." He leans forward, his elbows on his knees, and pushes both hands into his hair until he's staring at the floor of my porch. He's still transparent when something's on his mind.

"Are you okay?" I ask.

"Fine."

I nod. I have to remember his thoughts aren't my business. "You staying at the motel in town again?"

Before he can answer, my phone rings inside the house and I rush to answer before it wakes Monica.

"Hello," I say breathlessly and step back out onto the porch.

"Hey, it's Parker. How are you, stranger?"

Shit. With everything going on, I never reached out to him. "Hey, Parker. I'm good. I'm sorry I didn't text you. Things have been a little crazy around here."

Parker and I went on a few dates before Jimmy popped back up. He's a nice guy who doesn't seem like he's in any rush to move things forward, which suits me fine. In fact, he's the first man I've dated since Monica was born.

"No need to explain. I get it. Though I was wondering if I could twist your arm and get you to come out with me tomorrow night?"

I hate to turn him down, because he is a nice man and there's the potential for us to be something down the road, but this weekend isn't the time. I need to deal with Jimmy first. "I can't this weekend, I'm afraid. But how about the weekend after next? Would that work?"

It's a ways away, but by then, Monica will probably be comfortable around Jimmy by herself. She already acts as if he hangs the moon and stars. Maybe Jimmy can watch her while I'm out, or I could always ask Eileen to do it. I'm sure he would welcome any extra time with his daughter though. And it would be a good show of my trust in him.

"We could do that," he says. "How about dinner and line dancing?"

There's a cute country bar one town over. I haven't been there, but some of the girls at work rave about it.

"Yeah, sure. That sounds good. Let's touch base before then and we can work out the details." I glance at Jimmy leaning against the railing.

"Perfect. I'll call you next week to confirm."

"Great. Thanks for calling." I hit the end button and shove my phone in the back pocket of my shorts.

"Who's that?" Jimmy asks without looking at me.

I walk over to stand beside him and mimic his position on the railing so I won't have to look at him. "You remember the guy who came over to our table at the diner?"

He turns his head to look at me, and I reluctantly meet his gaze. "Mmmhmm."

"We've been out on a few dates. He wanted to see if I'm free tomorrow night."

"You don't want to go?"

"It's not that..." I look at my foot pushed between the spindles of the railing. "We can get together in a couple of weeks. There's a lot going on right now."

I have no idea why I feel guilty talking about this with him, but I do. The man is engaged to be married to one of Hollywood's biggest stars. He doesn't care what I do with my love life, except how it affects Monica.

He's silent for a while, and the only sound are the crickets chirping away in the heat of the night.

"Have you dated much since Monica was born?" he asks.

I school my reaction, hoping I come off casual. "Um... no. Parker is the first man I've been out with since..."

I don't have to finish the sentence. We both know the way things ended between us.

If he's surprised, he doesn't show it, remaining stone-faced and emotionless. He pushes off the porch railing and circles behind me to the porch steps. "What time should I be here tomorrow morning?"

"Eight thirty is good. I have to start at nine."

He pushes his hands into the front pockets of his shorts and nods, then walks down the stairs and heads to his rental car.

I can't help but watch him climb inside the vehicle, reverse down the driveway, and drive off. As his taillights creep farther out of my sight, I wonder if I'll ever not miss him when he's gone.

Chapter Fifty-seven

JIMMY

When I got back to the motel last night, I called Adelaide. She didn't pick up. The text I sent her hasn't been answered either.

Things between us haven't improved in the week since I dropped my bombshell on her. I'm not sure what she's more upset about—the fact that I sought Lilah out in the first place or what I found once I did.

Having her ice me out pisses me off, but I can't worry about her right now because today I'm spending the day with my daughter. Just her and me. Lilah's let us have our alone time, but she's always close by. Today, it's just us, and I can't wait to be one hundred percent responsible for Monica.

I pull into Lilah's driveway and park off to the side so she'll be able to get her vehicle out.

It isn't until I'm taking the porch steps two at a time that I remember my conversation with Lilah last night. The unwanted irritation that pierced me when another man called her and the satisfaction that eased that irritation when I learned that she's remained celibate since I saw her last.

Guilt swiftly kicked in last night, because we were sharing an intimate moment. I shouldn't know how many partners she's had since me, and I damn well shouldn't feel relief that there've been none. I don't want to share moments like that with Lilah anymore. Our conversations need to stay on Monica at all times.

My hand is raised to knock, but before I can, Monica barrels toward me. "Jimmy!"

Warmth invades my chest and spreads down my limbs. I smile and pull open the screen door. "Hey, Monica."

She runs into me, hugging my waist and looking up at me with wide eyes that match my own. "Mommy said we get to spend the whole day together!"

I nod and spot Lilah walking down the hallway.

"Hey," she says.

She's dressed in pink scrubs with her name embroidered above her left breast, and her hair is pulled into a messy bun on top of her head. I'm not sure why seeing her name on her scrubs pulls out that feeling of pride. Maybe because embroidered means permanent and the Lilah from six years ago rarely wanted anything permanent.

"I left my work number and the number of the next-door neighbor on the kitchen table. Eileen looks after her when I work on Saturdays, so if you have any problems, you can always ask her. But don't hesitate to call me if you need me."

What the hell? She looks as if she's on the verge of tears.

"Hey?" I pat Monica on the top of her head. "Why don't you go head down to your room and I'll meet you there in a few minutes? I need to talk to your mom for a second."

"Can we play Barbies again?" she asks, looking as though she's hanging on the edge, waiting for my answer.

"Sure thing."

"Yay!" She gives Lilah a hug, and her mom squeezes her tightly then bends at the waist to give her a kiss.

"You be good for Jimmy, okay?"

Monica nods and runs down the hall to her room before disappearing inside.

"Why do you look like you're going to burst out crying?" I ask.

"Am I that obvious?" She walks into the kitchen, and I follow her.

"You always were shit at hiding your emotions, at least to me."

Our gazes lock for a second before she opens one of the cupboard doors and pulls down a travel mug. "I'm afraid to leave Monica with you today."

"Why?" My voice is a little louder than I intend.

She turns to me and her eyes brim with tears, her teeth on her bottom lip. Is she doing that on purpose? She knows what that used to do to me. Is she trying to manipulate me?

"I'm afraid you're going to take her and leave."

Her statement feels as if Mike Trout just swung his bat into my chest. Before I can answer, she carries on.

"I know you're not that guy, or at least you didn't used to be. But you have the money and the resources to make it happen. And then I'd have to fight you with what little I have to get her back and I'd never win. I'm afraid if I walk out of here, I'll never see her again, yet I know I have to. I know this is a step forward that I need to take, it's just hard not to let the panic take hold and—"

Tears track down her face and she looks as though her entire world is falling apart. I pull her into my arms, and she buries her head into my chest, crying. A minute later, I realize what I've done, and I stiffen. This is definitely crossing the line.

Lilah must sense the change in my demeanor, because she steps away, her cheeks pink, her eyes anywhere but on mine.

"I wouldn't do that. It would destroy Monica."

She nods, wiping her cheeks with her free hand, and fills her travel mug from the coffee pot on the counter. "I know, I do. I've just lived with that fear for so long that it's hard to shake. And yes, I know that if I'd been honest from the start this wouldn't be happening." She says the last as if I was armed and ready to throw that at her.

Funny, but that retort wasn't even on the end of my tongue.

At the fridge, she pours some milk in her coffee then turns to face me. "Any questions before I go?"

I shake my head. "Nah, I think I'm good. I'll text you if anything comes up."

"Okay, see you later then."

I head down the hall to Monica's room, eager to spend my first real day with my daughter.

Does Lilah think that I don't worry that tomorrow morning, when I fly off to LA, she might take Monica? I have money and resources, but Lilah could make her and Monica disappear too.

I guess we're both stuck having to trust each other. Our biggest issue that was probably the root cause of that night.

* * *

MONICA DECIDED on grilled cheese for lunch, which she sweetly refers to as 'girl cheese' Freakin' adorable. I sit across from her, intently listening to a story about the dog next door while she nibbles on her sandwich.

That's okay though. I'm eager to soak up everything she wants to tell me. I'll sit here for hours.

"Mommy said you live far away."

"I do. I live in California."

Her small eyebrows crinkle for a second, her lips pursing. She's so cute when she's thinking.

"Do you live by the ocean? I've never seen the ocean. Mommy has." She bites her sandwich, her eyes wide as she waits for my answer.

I nod while chewing. "My backyard is the ocean. Right behind my house."

The grilled cheese drops out of her hand onto her plate and her mouth hangs open. "Like that would be the ocean?" She points out the back door of the house, where Lilah has a small porch with a table and four chairs.

I chuckle. "Yeah."

"Whoa. You swim with dolphins whenever you want?" She shakes her head as though it's the best thing ever.

I laugh again. "Well, no. The dolphins don't come that close to shore and technically..." I let my words trail off because she doesn't need me to teach her about where dolphins migrate. "Maybe you can come see it some time?"

"Yah, yah. I wanna see it!" Her eyes bulge into two saucers.

My heart warms knowing that someday she'll get to see my house. If I have my way, it will become her second home.

Silence falls over the table for about thirty seconds. "Mommy said you're in movies."

"That's right." I'm cursing my fame because of how difficult it'll make Monica's life in the long run.

"How come I haven't seen you in a movie then?" She eats a big bite of her lunch.

"Well, the movies I'm in aren't for kids. They're adult movies, so maybe when you get older, you'll watch one." I wink.

She smiles. She grips her plastic cup with both hands and brings it to her mouth to take a sip. She sets it down, almost tipping it over, and looks at me, the corners of her lips falling. "If you're Mommy's friend, how come she's sad when she sees pictures of you?"

My chest squeezes. Never do I want to put Monica in a position to ask that question ever again. What Lilah did is unforgivable, but I have to find a way to forgive her. My daughter will not know the pain and anguish I felt growing up. She won't have to worry about an abusive parent or why she's so hungry all the time, but I'll be damned if I'm going to put her in the middle of parental bullshit. The two of us need to get everything out into the open once and for all then leave the past behind for good.

"Have you ever asked her that?"

Monica shakes her head and her bottom lip pushes out. "No. I try to make her smile then."

I take her hand in mine and squeeze. She doesn't pull away, and it's like a small victory.

"I can't speak for your mom, but if I had to guess, I would say that it was probably because we hadn't seen each other for so long. We used to be really good friends, then we had an argument and we didn't talk for a long time. But just because you don't talk to someone doesn't mean you don't miss them."

Just because you hate them doesn't mean you don't love them. I keep that part to myself, thinking of the mix of emotions that suffocated me after Lilah left my life.

Her little forehead creases. "Why were you mad at each other?"

"Adult stuff. The point is that we're not anymore."

Not exactly the truth, on my end at least, but what else can I say? "I'm pissed off at your mom because you're my little girl. She failed to tell me, so I have to pretend to be a friend."

"My teacher says cows have more than one stomach. Do you think so?"

I press my fist to my mouth, trying to contain my laughter. One thing I've learned about five-year-olds is they change topics faster than a politician changes their mind.

Chapter Fifty-eight

LILAH

My workday hasn't felt so much like time stood still since the first week I had to leave Monica. I must've checked my phone every five minutes to see if Jimmy had texted me with any problems. He didn't though.

While flossing and making small talk with my clients, my mind remained on the two of them. I couldn't stop wondering what they were doing, what they were talking about, how Monica was handling it being just the two of them.

I speed through town and pull into my driveway a few minutes earlier than I normally get home. Jimmy's rental car is parked in the driveway. After snatching my purse from the passenger seat, I hurry out of the car, up the front steps, and into the house.

"Hello?" I call and place my purse on the front table, waiting impatiently for noise to follow. The house is silent. "Hello?"

With no response, panic wraps around me like a vise.

Where could they be? Why aren't they here?

Jimmy didn't take her, did he? No, his car is there.

"Monica?" I yell, checking every room in the house. "Monica!"

My heart races and my breathing grows shallow when I reach the back of the house with no sign of either Jimmy or Monica. I run down the hall to her bedroom for a second time. Maybe they're playing a game to hide and surprise me.

"Monica!"

Then something catches my eye out the window, and I rush to see what it is. My whooshing breath tumbles out of me, and my hand covers my chest. They're playing leapfrog in the backyard. Eventually the coiled tension loosens and the panic attack that almost came fades.

After I change my clothes, I walk out of my bedroom right as Monica, on Jimmy's back, comes inside the house. I smile, and a weird sensation of déjà vu hits me. I know for sure this has never happened before.

Then it clicks. It's a scene so similar to the one I used to think of after rehab. My 'why' to getting clean. When Jimmy told me to picture myself ten years in the future. The difference is now, it will never be how I dreamed it. We're not a happy family unit. Jimmy isn't coming here to be with us. He's coming for Monica.

Jimmy gives me an odd look. "Hey, I didn't know you were home. How was work?"

"Mommy!" Monica yells and Jimmy crouches, sliding her down his back.

She runs and gives me a big hug. I squeeze her tightly. The warmth of her small arms around my neck is the best feeling in the world.

"Hey, kiddo." I kiss the top of her head. "Did you have a fun day with Jimmy?"

She pulls away and nods a bunch of times. "We did so much fun stuff!"

"That's great, sweetie."

"Well, I better be going. Thanks for letting me hang out with you today, Monica." Jimmy lowers himself to one knee, and Monica rushes over to give him a hug goodbye.

He closes his eyes, nuzzling his head into her neck as though he feels the same way I did moments ago. The warmth of love for his daughter. She backs up, and he ruffles her hair.

"Kiddo, why don't you go wash your hands and I'll say goodbye to Jimmy, okay? We're going to have dinner soon."

"Okay, Mommy."

I smile and wait until she's down the hall and I hear the water running before I nod at Jimmy to follow me onto the front porch. "Everything went okay today?"

"No problems at all. She's such a sweet girl. And she's so smart." His voice holds a hint of awe.

"She is. I'm glad things went smoothly."

He looks at me for a moment. Even though we haven't been close in years, I know he has something else he wants to say.

"What? Just say it." I brace myself.

"I was wondering if I could come by tonight after Monica is in bed? We need to talk." He shoves his hands into his pockets.

The phrase is ominous, but he's right. We need to figure out how to handle this situation going forward. Not knowing a schedule is wearing a hole in my stomach, and there are only so many meetings I'm able to attend.

"Okay sure. Why don't you come around eight thirty or so?"

"I'll see you then." He heads down the porch steps without a goodbye.

I'm reminded again of the long road we have in front of us, but just like those years ago when I pictured where I hoped to be, I close my eyes and think about my future. It might not be everything I want, but for Jimmy and me to be cordial friends would be nice.

There's nothing more awkward than no longer knowing the person you loved most at one time.

* * *

LATER THAT NIGHT, I sit on the front porch with a glass of iced tea when Jimmy's car pulls up the driveway. I squint and block his headlights with my hand.

My stomach tightens with knots from the thought of sharing Monica with Jimmy. Christmas morning without her. Not being able to tuck her in every night. Me watching through pictures as Jimmy shows her the ocean or takes her on exotic vacations. I want her to know her father. He's a good man, but the world he lives in isn't good. It's evil. And my stomach sours with the thought of her on the cover of a magazine, paps following her and Jimmy to snap a picture to pay their rent.

I'd be lying if I said I wasn't worried that I'll fall into old habits with her away from me—idle hands are never good. But I'll do whatever it takes for that not to happen. My daughter will never see me high and incoherent. Even if it means going to two meetings a day and picking up extra shifts at work.

"Hey." Jimmy walks up the porch steps and sits in the rocking chair next to me.

He's changed his clothes from earlier. With the cooling temperature, he's dressed in a pair of faded jeans and a long-sleeved Henley. I divert my eyes before he notices me checking out the way the cotton hugs his shoulders and arms. The growth on his face is more like a beard than stubble now, and his dark hair is curling up at the ends. He must be growing it out for a role since he's yet to cut it.

"Do you want something to drink?" I ask, wanting to disburse the awkwardness.

He shakes his head.

"So..."

"Sorry, this is... this is just harder than I thought it would be." He runs his hands along his thighs and concentrates down between his legs.

"I thought I was the one who should be nervous."

A small chuckle escapes him and he looks at me with a half grin. "You asked me what I was doing here the other day, and I never answered. The truth is that I was here to find closure. I wanted to understand what happened between us before I... before I marry Adelaide."

"Oh." I'm not able to hide my surprise. Of all the reasons he wanted to talk tonight, this isn't what I expected.

I'm about as uncomfortable hearing about his impending marriage as he seems to be with bringing up the topic. But I owe him enough to not make this awkward. Jimmy deserves to be happy, and if Adelaide is her, then I need to suck it up and support him.

The night everything went to shit feels like a million years ago, but in some moments, moments like this, when all the pain and confusion from that night flares up, it feels like yesterday.

He pushes a hand through his hair. "Walking in on what I did destroyed me. I never understood how you could do that. I pushed it away, locked it away for years. But as the wedding gets closer and closer, it's been on my mind more and more. I owe it to Adelaide to deal with my feelings about what happened so that we can start our marriage with no distractions from the past."

Listening to him speak of Adelaide and putting her needs first urges me to keel over in pain. That was supposed to be his and my story.

But this isn't about me. This is about giving Jimmy what he needs to get on with his life.

I clasp my hands in my lap. "What do you want to know?"

"Why you did it? It's not like you were attracted to Bernie. I didn't care about your reason why back then. Not even a little. The fact was that whatever your reason was, you didn't trust me enough, trust in *us* enough, to confide in me. Nothing you could have said would have made a difference. But as time passed, I wanted to know why you threw away what we had."

I look at my hands, unable to meet his gaze. Unsure whether it will make things better or worse between us, I inhale a steadying breath. "Bernie told me he wanted to meet me.

When I got there, he told me that your mom had been calling him, feeding him information about you that wouldn't play well in the press. Bernie hired a PI to dig into your past. He knew you sold drugs as a teen. He kept alluding he knew more or would find out more... I couldn't let that happen."

Jimmy's gripping his knees, and his knuckles turn white. "This was all because of my mother?"

"She started the ball rolling, but I was the one who went along with what Bernie demanded. At least at first."

Unshed tears burn in my eyes as the feeling inside me that day surfaces—like the one my father made me feel. No power to change the situation.

"He said if I... messed around with him... he'd drop looking and make it go away. I'm not making excuses, but I swear, I only did it to protect you. He had the coke. That wasn't mine, nor did I take any. Right before you walked in, I told him I couldn't do it. I was going to call you and tell you what had happened, but then you were there like he'd set up the entire thing."

I swipe the tears from my face, looking at Jimmy. "I'm sorry... sorry for ever putting myself in that position. I thought..." I shake my head. "I have no idea how I could have been so naïve. But you were so stressed about the upcoming role and I might have ruined my career, but yours was thriving."

Our eyes catch and his arm extends to my face, but he stops himself.

"I know I should have stormed out of his office the second he proposed what he did. But the things he said... they were so vile. They reminded me of who I was before rehab. Who I'd been my entire life. And I couldn't let him dig any further into our pasts. All I was thinking was that you'd protected me my whole life and how it was my turn to protect you because if he found out that you'd..."

"Killed your father," he whispers.

My eyes close. The words are finally out between us.

I crumple in on myself, leaning forward in my chair, my arms around my waist as quiet sobs surge out of my throat. That day is burned into my mind for eternity.

My father's angry eyes are right in front of me. Soon, I'm not on the porch with Jimmy, I'm back in that shack of a house...

The front door slams and my pen freezes over the page of my diary.

Was I that enthralled in my own mind that I didn't hear his beater of an old pick-up truck pull up to our makeshift home? Scrambling off my bed, I shove my diary and pen underneath my mattress. The hair on the back of my neck stands on end. I don't have to see to know that my father is standing in the doorway.

Turning slowly, my eyes close and my stomach clenches.

He leans against the doorframe, his eyes half shut and glossed over, his clothes wrinkled and half untucked. His drinking grows more out of control with every day. "Whatcha got there girl?"

He eyeballs my mattress. Shit. If I have any chance of getting out of here unscathed before he inevitably passes out, I have to walk the delicate line of not angering him and not gaining his interest.

"Nothing."

"Don't lie to me."

His heavy footfalls stomp into the room and he pushes me aside before lifting my mattress off the bed. The sheets slide off, and a picture on the wall crashes to the floor from the mattress landing across the room. He wobbles when he bends over. I send up a little prayer that he'll pass out before he finds what he's looking for.

But as usual, God doesn't answer my prayers.

"What's this? Don't look like nuthin." He holds my diary in his dirt-caked hands.

I stand as still as the thinnest tree branch before a big storm, waiting, hoping for a miracle.

He thumbs through the book to the last entry—the one where I wrote about Jimmy and me slipping down to the creek yesterday to fool around. How much I like the way I disappear inside myself when we're together.

His entire body tenses, and without warning, his hand snaps out and backhands me across the face. I fall to the floor, tears stinging my eyes but they don't sting nearly as badly as my cheek. I blink several times, waiting for my vision to clear.

"You fuckin' that boy?" he roars.

"No, Daddy. It's all just made up." I wobble to stand, but he swats me on the side of the head and I tumble back down, blood coating my mouth.

"Bullshit! You little slut. Just like yer mama." He throws the diary against the wall and it slides down to the floor, sprawled open.

A sense of profound loss hits me when I look at it open for anyone to read. I wanted one thing for myself. Just one thing that was mine alone and wasn't tarnished by all the terrible and lacking things in my life. I only ever wrote my happy moments between those pages, but now that's gone and ruined too.

"How long you been lettin' him take a dip in-between yer thighs?"

I look away from my diary and up at my dad. His fists are clenched at his sides. When I don't answer, he grabs me by the front of the shirt, yanking me up.

"Ow, that hurts!"

"You little bitch. Opening up what's mine for everyone on the mountain." He pushes me down onto the mattress that now lies on the floor and rips open the front of my shirt, revealing my bra.

I bat his hands away. "No, stop!"

"That's enough! I'm gunna teach you a lesson." He smacks me across the face and everything goes black.

Coming to, I blink. My dad's dirty beard is right in front of my face. I'm sprawled out on the mattress, and my pants and underwear are down around my ankles.

"You stupid slut! After I'm done with you, you're gunna know who owns you, Candy."

His hands wrap around my neck, and the words that I'm not my mother die in my throat.

I can't breathe.

I can't breathe!

I claw at his hands, trying in vain to get him to loosen his grip.

My father has long been sexually abusive, but he's never been like Jimmy's dad. He's never hit me.

My nails dig into his skin, trying once again to gain leverage, but his eyes have an evil glint. He's hyper-focused on where his hands are squeezing the life out of me.

My lungs burn, and blackness forms around the edges of my vision. My muscles lose their strength as the fight slowly leaves my body. One hand drops to the mattress, the other one following. I succumb to the fact that I'm dying. He's going to kill me.

Then his head falls forward, and he slumps down on the other side of the mattress, half straddling me.

I suck in huge gasps of air. Coughing uncontrollably, I think that whoever saved me was too late. I'm too far gone. Jimmy pushes my dad the rest of the way off of me.

His hands are on my cheeks, his beautiful eyes silently encouraging me to fight. "Oh my God, Lilah! Are you okay?"

My entire body shakes as he picks me up off the bed. "Ji... Jim... Jimmy."

"Shhh. You're in shock." He wraps me in his arms, arms that feel like a shelter in the midst of a hurricane.

He carries me out of the room and into our small living room, forcing me to sit on the couch. He grabs the old brown-and-orange afghan my mother knitted before she died off the back of the couch and wraps it around me.

"Oh my God, your face. Look what he did to you," he whispers. His hand rises to touch my face, but it stills in the air. Instead, he wraps an arm around me and rubs my arms.

"You saved my life." My voice is hoarse and my throat is sore, but I manage to get out the words.

"I told you that I'd always protect you."

I nod numbly and touch my face. My hand comes away with blood.

I remember now. When Jimmy hit him with whatever he did, blood sprayed down on me. I glance at myself. My ripped shirt hangs open, displaying my white bra and stomach. All covered in blood.

I should feel remorse, but I only feel free.

"LILAH. It's okay. You're here. You're safe. Everything's okay." Jimmy's hand rubbing my back catapults me back to the present.

I'd love for him to hold me close like he did that night, but I can't get used to him. He's not mine anymore.

"I'm sorry, I'm sorry," he whispers, his face so close.

I straighten up, and his hand drops. Wiping my face with my hands, I look at him. He always did wear his emotions for all to see, and right now he's worried about me—even though he probably feels nothing more than disdain for me. That's what makes him such a great man.

"You have nothing to apologize for. You saved my life that day. It's just a lot…"

He shakes his head. "No, things changed after that night. You were different and I closed up. You wanted to talk about it and I shut you down every time. If I'd sat with you and listened, maybe things would be different. If we'd gone to the cops. You had the marks on your neck. You never would have been forced into that position with Bernie."

"Stop." I take his hand, squeezing. "I made my own decisions that night. I was messed up long before it. I'll be forever grateful for you saving my life. It took a huge toll on you too. And you know with your past and the way that town went by their own rules, things would have been different."

His chin drops and he looks at his hand in mine on his lap. I slide mine from his.

After I cleaned up and got myself together that night, we wrapped my dad's body in a blanket and took it up to his aunt's place in the middle of the night, where we dumped it into the hog pen. By morning when we went back to check, there was no sign left of my father.

When people started asking, I said that he'd gone to check on his moonshine one day and never returned. That wasn't completely uncommon, and after a lackluster search effort, our small community figured he'd probably had a heart attack or fell off drunk somewhere in the woods and breathed his final breath alone.

Living up in the mountains wasn't like living in town. We didn't report our dead, and we buried our people on their plots of land the way it was done hundreds of years ago.

Once I finished high school, Jimmy had earned enough money to get us to Los Angeles and we never looked back.

"Still, I shouldn't have stopped you from talking about it. That was selfish."

"I don't regret what you did. I hope you don't."

His head whips in my direction. "I'd do it again in a heartbeat to save you from that monster. The things he did to you…"

"Enough." I wave him off, standing. "I only brought up the past to answer your question."

"Thank you. At least now I understand. I don't agree with what you did. You could have come to me right away. I wish you would have believed I'd figure something out. But thank you for your honesty. I feel like I can finally move forward."

Right. I nod. Move forward with marrying Adelaide. I swallow down my sorrow and inhale a cleansing breath.

"What happened between you and Bernie after I left?" I was always curious, since I never saw it play out in the press.

He shrugs. "Nothing. I wouldn't give that piece of shit the satisfaction of confronting him about it. I fulfilled my contractual obligations for the film, and I haven't spoken to him since. I'll never work for his studio again."

I nod. "He must have taken care of your mom then, I guess."

"I guess. She hasn't reached out to me since. Thank God." He stands from the rocking chair and joins me against the railing. "I realized something today."

"Oh?" I raise an eyebrow.

"As angry as I am at you for keeping Monica from me, I have to put it aside for her sake. I don't want her growing up with two parents at each other's throats."

I nod. It's not exactly forgiveness, but I'll take it. We look out at my front yard, shoulder to shoulder.

"Let's agree to put everything that's happened in the past behind us and start fresh. For our daughter's sake."

I sigh. "That's a lot of stuff to try to forget."

"It is. But we have a little girl in there who deserves all our energy to do so."

Sorrow and regret spread through me like creeping vines. Winding and winding, growing tighter around every inch. If I hadn't messed everything up, this man would be mine and we'd be a real family. I screwed up the chances of my daughter having her parents in love and living as a family. There's no way to undo the damage I've already caused, but I'll do everything in my power to give her the best life I can.

"I agree. We need to discuss how we're moving forward." Anticipation of his answer coils every muscle in my body.

"I think we continue on with what we're doing right now. I don't have any projects on the horizon. I'll spend the week in Malibu with Adelaide, getting ready for the wedding, and the weekends here with Monica, getting to know her better. We can see when it feels right to tell her I'm her dad."

"And after that?" I whisper. Where Jimmy can take things with ease at a steady path, I need to know what the future looks like. Where does he see us in a year?

He swivels to face me and grips my shoulders. "I'm not going to take her from you. You don't have to worry about that. We'll figure out whatever is best for her, okay?" He dips his head so we're eye level, waiting until I nod. "The press is something we have to discuss though."

I step back and wrap my arms around my chest. "I'm worried."

He pushes a hand through his hair. "The vultures will be camped outside of your house the second they catch wind of Monica."

"I can't let that happen. She would freak out." My mama bear roars to life when I picture the paparazzi hounding my little girl.

"Don't you worry about that. I'll talk to my team. Maybe we'll hide you out in a gated community far from here until the madness lessens."

"Jimmy, I have a job. A life here. Monica has school." Sure, it's not much of a life. I don't really have any girlfriends since they usually come with questions about Monica's dad and my own past. But I'm not ripping Monica away from the only town and home she's ever known. The introduction of Jimmy being her father is enough.

"I realize it's not ideal, but my first concern is protecting the two of you. It will require some sacrifices on all our parts."

The fact that he included me in his quest for protection doesn't sneak past me, and it very well could be he doesn't realize he did it. I've stolen enough time with Monica from him, so I'll compromise.

"We'll sort it out," I say.

"Good."

The question I've wanted to ask all night long is on the tip of my tongue, but I'm not sure how to approach the subject. Since we're laying everything out there tonight, I decide it's speak now or forever hold my peace.

"How did Adelaide take the news about Monica?"

His gaze catches mine, the moonlight shining on the side of his face. He holds it for a minute before looking away and resting his forearms on the porch railing. "I'll deal with Adelaide."

"That well, huh?"

"She needs time to adjust. I hit her with it out of nowhere and only a few months before the wedding."

I nod. "Fair enough." I yawn. The emotional night, on top of me not sleeping lately, means I've hit the end of the line.

"I should go," he says and straightens.

"Thanks for the talk. I can't apologize enough for all the pain I've caused you."

"Water under the bridge, remember?"

I give him a small smile and my hand extends, but I retract it. "I'm sorry for any trouble this is causing between you and Adelaide." And I am. I've hurt him enough for three lifetimes.

"Speaking of, I'd better go call her and fill her in on my day. The more I include her, the easier this will be for her."

A sad smile creeps across my face. "You'll make a great husband. I always knew you would."

I drop his hand and enter my house, closing the inside door and locking it before he sees my tears.

Chapter Fifty-nine

JIMMY

"**Y**ou know I have to go." I rein in my irritation, but I'm pretty sure it shows on my face.

"Am I finalizing all the details of the wedding on my own now then?" She tosses her purse on the kitchen island.

"You know I don't care about any of that stuff. I told you in the beginning that I just wanted to marry you. I don't give two shits about all the crap that goes with it. Whatever you decide on will be fine."

As she walks around the large slab of marble, her chin falls to her chest. I take her hand and tilt her chin up to meet my gaze.

"I've already lost five years with her."

"That's not my fault," she grumbles.

I give her hand a shake to grab her attention. "C'mon. I get this is a shock and not something you signed up for, but is this something you can deal with?"

Her head shoots up and her eyes widen. "And if it isn't?"

Fuck. "I don't know," I answer honestly.

"Good to know." She yanks her hand from mine and walks over to the cupboard, where she pulls out a glass. "I'll be fine. It's hard knowing you spend the entire weekend with *her*." She fills her cup with ice and water from the fridge.

I'm not touching that grenade she placed between us. It's been a stressful week. Both of us had meetings. Adelaide just signed on to star in a romantic comedy that starts filming right after our honeymoon. I promised myself to keep her in the loop, but our schedules and the fact she hasn't asked one question about my time in Kansas since I returned Sunday make it hard.

"We need to talk."

She spins around to face me, the glass still in her hand. "What? You're buying the house next door to her?"

I ignore her tantrum and pat the seat next to mine at the breakfast bar. "Come have a seat. I just want to fill you in on where things stand with Monica and Lilah."

Her lips form a thin line, but she sits down, placing her glass on the counter in front of her.

"I spoke with Lilah about what happened with Bernie all those years ago."

"Great. I'm sure it wasn't her fault."

I know this is hard for Adelaide, but her attitude is like a thirteen-year-old who just got told she can't date. Not to sound like a martyr, but I'm doing the best I can, given the circumstances, to include her and make her see that we'll get past this, but she's not making it easy.

I explain everything Lilah said to me, as well as our plan to keep things as they are until we figure out a more permanent solution and Monica knows I'm her father.

"You'll still be permitted to go on our honeymoon, right?"

I inhale a calming breath. "Of course I'm going on our honeymoon." I tuck a piece of her dark hair behind her ear, and she meets my gaze. The fear in her eyes reminds me how hard this is on her. The bond Lilah and I share—shared—was public news six years ago. "Everything is going to work out, okay? We're going to have the wedding of your dreams and our life together will be amazing. You just wait."

She relaxes, her shoulders dropping. "Okay." She places a chaste kiss on my lips, but her wedding phone rings. "I'd better get that."

She slips off the stool, and I watch as she answers her second cell phone, the one strictly for wedding stuff so the contacts won't be able to reach her after, as though her life is perfect. She gushes about the table linens and the center pieces for the wedding as I sit back in the chair. Will she really be able to hop on board with the new direction my life has veered?

* * *

A COUPLE OF WEEKS PASS. Monica has grown accustomed to me coming and going. Lilah's anxiety about me taking her away dramatically decreases with every Saturday night she returns from work. We're on a good track, and my anger toward Lilah has diminished a small bit.

I head back into the kitchen to clean up our dinner dishes after tucking Monica in. She suckered me into two extra books, but I would have done ten, so I feel as though I still won. I finish drying the dishes and putting them away and settle on the couch to watch TV until Lilah gets home.

She worked all day but asked if I could watch Monica tonight while she went out on a date. Of course, I agreed—I'll say yes to anything that means I get more time with Monica. At first, I was irked that she was going on a date, but then I calmed down because I'm engaged to marry another woman and Lilah has been nothing but supportive about that.

My phone vibrates in my pocket while I'm flicking through the channels. I pull it out and see Keane's name on the screen.

"Hey, what's up? I don't usually hear from you on a Saturday night."

"Turn on CNN," he says, foregoing any pleasantries.

Nausea wells up in my throat. I haven't told my team about Monica yet, wanting to enjoy this small window where I don't have to think about protecting my daughter from flashing cameras.

"Give me a sec." I pick up the remote from the couch cushion, envisioning my name splashed across the screen amid reports of a secret love child. Once I locate CNN on the guide, I click the channel and hold my breath.

But instead of me, there's a picture of Bernie Butler.

"What the hell?" I sit up straighter, my arms resting on my legs.

"Exactly," Keane says. "This just broke. Apparently, there's a report coming out on Monday in the *LA Times*. One of the journalists has been working on an investigative piece about how Bernie's been using his power and influence for years to sexually assault women in the business."

"Holy shit."

I watch the rundown in silence—how three women have come forward, detailing similar experiences where Bernie forced them into sexual situations, using various roles and jobs as negotiation points and telling them he'd ruin their careers if they didn't cooperate.

My mind travels to Lilah's experience with Bernie all those years ago. She wasn't alone. She was one of many.

Of course she wasn't. I was an idiot to think she was or to not give any thought as to how many women like her would've had the same thing happen to them.

"Have they named the women who have come forward?" I ask.

"Not as far as I can tell. Guess we'll see on Monday, if not sooner."

Plastic creaks and I set the remote control back on the couch before I break it.

"This is unbelievable," I say, though in hindsight I guess it's not. Pieces of the puzzle all click together—the rumors that surfaced from time to time, the actresses who would be at the height of their career and suddenly wouldn't be able to land another role, the way Bernie always spoke about women as though they were objects.

"Guess you were right not to sign on to that movie I was pushing you about weeks ago," Keane says, breaking into my thoughts.

"Yeah, guess so."

We watch the report for another minute before I decide it's time to get a plan in place. The shitstorm that's going to erupt over the next few months with the revelations about Bernie might actually work in my favor.

"Listen, there's something else important that I need to discuss with you. Any chance you have time to get together on Monday? I can drop by your office."

"Sounds serious. Should I be worried?" He chuckles, but the nervousness in his tone says he's already worried.

"In the end, it's a good thing. But we'll need Kyra and Liz there too."

I want my PR representative and my manager there so that I only have to fill in everyone once. Of the three of them, Keane and I are the closest and I trust him the most, but I'll need everyone's help to handle this situation in a way that's best for Monica.

"You didn't accidentally marry some stripper in Vegas, did you?" he asks.

I laugh. "Nah, man. I'll fill you in on Monday."

"All right. I'll get my assistant to contact Kyra and Liz and figure out a time that works for everyone."

"Just have her text me."

"Will do. All right, man, I've got a bunch of other people I have to call. This thing is gonna fill my every waking moment for the next week. I'll see you in a couple days."

"Thanks for calling, Keane."

"Don't mention it."

The line dies, and I set my phone on the coffee table.

Adelaide is at an industry event, so I don't bother texting her. I'll be back in LA tomorrow morning and we can catch up then. Besides, I'm sure this is the only thing they're talking about in the city tonight.

A half hour later, I'm still seated on the couch and watching the coverage when I hear a car pull up into the driveway. I walk over to the window. It's Lilah returning home from her date. I glance at my watch. Not too late. I push back the small part of me that's happy she's home early.

Heading back over to the couch, I hear her heels click on the wood floor of the porch then come through the door. My heart beats faster when I see her like this—wavy hair hanging down past her shoulders, a form-fitting V-neck dress, strappy heels showcasing the muscles in her legs. Her makeup is a little darker and her bee-stung lips are covered in red lipstick. Her natural beauty shines too, like in the last few weeks when she wears little to no makeup and her hair is pulled back or in a messy bun on top of her head.

There's no denying she's beautiful either way, but this is the first time I've seen her make an effort since I've been back in her life, and I'm a heterosexual male who used to be in love with her, so of course I notice.

"Hey, how was your date?" I pretend like I don't have a care in the world as I mute the TV.

She slips off her heels and sets them aside. "It was okay. Dinner was good. He took me to a new Greek place one town over."

I don't know if she's as uncomfortable talking to me about this as I am hearing it, but she sure looks ready to throw up. This is our life moving forward though, so we might as well practice.

"It's still pretty early?"

Her cheeks turn pink, and she sits on the other end of the couch. "I haven't really dated since Monica was born, so I'm taking it slow. Parker is a nice guy, but..." She shrugs, looking at her hands in her lap.

"But what?"

"I don't know." She finally meets my eyes. "It's just different..."

She doesn't need to explain. I know exactly what she means. I felt exactly the same way after I finished trying to mend my broken heart by banging anything with a pulse. Once I really started dating again, it felt pointless because I compared everyone to Lilah. I didn't have the depth of feelings or share the same kind of spark with anyone else. But I pushed forward and eventually realized that was just how it was gonna be. I'd share a different type of love.

"It'll get easier," I say.

"I'll take your word for it." Awkward silence envelops the room for a second. "Anyway, how was Monica tonight? Did she go down okay for you?"

My smile splits my face when I think of my daughter. "We had a great time. I let her stay up a little late, but she fell asleep almost as soon as her head hit the pillow."

"I can see she already has you wrapped around her finger." She smiles, her light eyes sparkling.

"You know it."

She leans back into the couch, making herself comfortable, but does a double-take when her eyes scan across the TV screen. I turn to look at the TV and see another picture of Bernie.

"What's going on?" she asks in a quiet voice.

"Keane called me about this a little while ago." I unmute the TV and worry for the first time how Lilah's going to take this news. She was one of his victims after all.

"Oh my God." She lifts her hand to her mouth, covering her astonished gasp.

Tears well in her eyes as she sits ramrod-straight, staring at the TV. The news anchors debate what will happen next and how these few brave women who have come forward might just be the tip of the iceberg. Her breathing slowly becomes more and more labored while pictures of Bernie flash across the screen. I slide down the couch until I'm beside her and take her hand. Will the sight of her in pain ever not feel like a knife jabbing me in my heart? I can't just leave her and return to my hotel room like nothing's happened.

I probably have to accept that a part of me will always care for Lilah, which I rationalize isn't a bad thing since she's the mother of my daughter. Anything that adversely affects Monica's mom affects her too.

Since she told me what went down with Bernie, I've only concentrated on how it affected me, the future I lost as a result. But in this moment, I understand what she lost too. I have even more newfound respect for her sobriety, knowing what her father did to her and witnessing firsthand the spiral it sent her on. The fact that she was able to stay sober after Bernie used his power and influence over her says how strong she is.

Guilt seeps into my pores as I watch her terrified gaze on the TV screen. Could I have done more to protect her? Everyone knew Bernie's reputation, and there'd always been murmurings of his casting couch escapades. Sure, I didn't know about her meeting with him, but was there something I could have done to prevent him from taking advantage of her?

"Are you okay?" I ask, squeezing her hand.

"It wasn't just me. I mean, I didn't really think it was, I suppose, but I never gave it much thought. There was so much going on in my life at the time and then Monica was born and…" Her eyes widen and she looks away from the screen and at me. "You don't think they're going to find out about me, do you? I cannot be in the press."

I shake my head, dropping her hand and giving her a reassuring squeeze on the shoulder. "No way. Unless you've told someone else who would sell your story?"

"No, no. I mean, I saw a counselor for a bit and I talked some about it in my meetings, but I never gave details that anyone could put two-and-two together." She heaves a big sigh and looks at her lap.

I place my finger under her chin and force her to meet my gaze. "Then it will be fine. I'm sure a lot more women will come forward, but it's entirely your decision whether you want to be one of them."

She shakes her head and a tear slips free. Before I can stop myself, I use my thumb to wipe the tear away. Realizing my mistake, I let my hand drop and inch back on the cushion a bit.

"I couldn't bear for Monica to find out." She wipes at another tear that falls, and my fingers twitch in response. "I know that someday I'll have to tell her about how it was growing up and my addiction issues, but she's too young to deal with that now. I just want to keep her in her bubble."

"Then what you told me stays between us." Then I realize I've told Adelaide what happened, and the guilt that was a seedling inside me grows to a creeping vine slithering through my body. "You should know that I told Adelaide though."

Lilah's forehead scrunches up and hurt flashes across her face for a second before she nods slowly. "That makes sense, I guess. You guys are getting married. She won't...?"

"No. No, she'd never share that with anyone. I trust her."

Her lips press together. "I'm glad you have someone you can trust in your life. I really am." A sad smile parts her lips.

"You'll find someone."

She shrugs. "Maybe, maybe not." She glances at the TV screen again then stands abruptly. "It's getting late. I should head to bed. Monica likes to be up at the crack of dawn."

"Okay, yeah. Listen, don't let this"—I gesture to the TV —"mess with your head. You've built a great life for you and Monica."

Wrapping her arms around her stomach, she says, "I won't. I'll go to a meeting tomorrow. I've been going more lately... with everything going on and the past coming back up. It helps."

"I'm glad. Who will watch Monica for you?" I ask, stepping toward the door.

"Eileen. She loves having her over there. Her own kids have long since grown and moved on, so I think she enjoys having the energy of a little one around."

I can tell by her smile that she thinks fondly of her neighbor.

I'm torn. I want to offer to stay, text the pilot and tell him to change our flight time, but Adelaide will pitch a fit. I've promised her that tomorrow afternoon, we'll finalize the invitations before they're sent out next month. In the end, I decide not to push my luck with Adelaide. This has been a big curveball for her too, and I need her onboard.

"All right. Well, if Monica needs anything this week, let me know. Otherwise I'll see you next Friday."

"Yep, okay." She gives me an awkward wave before I turn and grip the door handle. "Jimmy, wait."

I stop and turn to face her, halfway out the door. "What's up?"

"I was thinking that maybe next weekend we should tell Monica that you're her father. Maybe we can figure out what we want to say after she goes to bed Friday night and then Saturday you can stay for dinner after I get back from work and we can tell her together."

Excitement bubbles inside me as though I'm six years old and someone just said Christmas is coming early. Quickly, the excitement wars with nerves. How will Monica take the news? Will she be excited to know who her father is, and will she like the idea of it being me?

"I'm nervous. Are you nervous?"

A soft smile plays on her lips. "I am, but I think she'll be happy about it. Still, it will be a big change for her... having her dad in her life."

"I get it. It'll still take time to acclimate her to the new normal."

Lilah looks down for a second then back at me. "It's been a big change for all of us. Thanks for not pushing."

I step closer to her. "I only want what's best for her. I hope you know that."

She nods. "I'm starting to believe that. Anyway, I'll see you Friday. Have a good week."

I inhale, nod, then turn and leave.

This time next week, Monica will know I'm her father.

I didn't know about her until a month ago, but I can't help feeling that all the pieces in my life are clicking into place.

Chapter Sixty

JIMMY

Adelaide is in her pajamas, sipping coffee on the couch and watching the news, when I arrive home shortly before lunchtime. It strikes me as odd, because she's a get up, get dressed, get ready type of person. Not too much into lounging in your pajamas all day. Maybe she had too much to drink to last night.

I set down my bag at the entry of the room and hear from the TV that Bernie's story is once again making the rounds. Everyone's speculating as to what other skeletons might come out of the closet in the coming weeks.

"Can you believe all this shit?" I ask, making my way over. I give her a chaste kiss on the lips when she looks up at me.

"It's not entirely shocking, given his reputation in Hollywood."

I sit beside her. "I guess, but they're saying this is just the tip of the iceberg. We all knew the guy was a sleaze and had no respect for women, but this is something else entirely."

She shrugs, her attention still on the screen. "How's Lilah?"

The way she says her name with such venom takes me back, though maybe I should've expected it. She's threatened by her.

"Fine. Monica, however, is amazing. She's really taken to me. I can't believe how much she already knows for being only five years old."

"That's great." The words are positive, but her body language and tone are anything but.

Might as well get this over with.

"Lilah wants to tell Monica that I'm her father next weekend." My heart speeds up from saying the words out loud. Soon my daughter will know who I am to her.

"You must be happy about that." She shifts her body so that she's half facing me.

"Of course I am. I mean, I'm nervous about how she'll take the news, but this is what I've been waiting for."

"When do I get to meet her?" She crosses her arms and tilts her head, her lips pressed into a thin line as though my answer will dictate her mood for the rest of the day.

"I'm not sure." I squeeze her knee. "It's a lot for her to adjust to, and she should probably get used to the idea of me being her father before she meets her new stepmom."

She flinches at the word "stepmom," but it's so quick I can't be sure.

"I'll need to run it by Lilah, but maybe in a few weeks," I say.

"Oh, right because you need Lilah's stamp of approval. God knows she makes the best decisions."

I inhale what feels like my hundredth calming breath. She has to put her differences with Lilah aside.

"She really has cleaned up her act, though this whole thing with Bernie being on every news outlet shook her up. She's worried about someone digging up her past with him and bringing it all back to the surface."

"Not everyone would let it ruin their entire lives," she snipes.

"You say that like you're speaking from experience." I study her for a moment, and when she doesn't respond, my gut twists. Adelaide has a particular face when she's lying. It's the same one whether she's surprising me with dinner or a lie about flying to Vegas with her best friend on a whim. "Adelaide? What is it? Did Bernie do something to you too?"

She stands abruptly and walks toward the window looking out to the ocean.

My mind races to think of any interactions I had with both Bernie and Adelaide. All I can come up with is when we were filming *The Regulator* years ago and he summoned us to my trailer— she insisted that she'd wait for me to go meet him, barely spoke, and wouldn't make eye contact with him.

I walk up behind her and place my hands on her shoulders. "Honey, did something happen?"

She huffs out a breath and spins around. "Of course something did. Something probably happened with any female who's ever been cast in one of his pictures. That's just how it goes. But you move on. You don't let it ruin you, otherwise what's the point?"

My mouth hangs open, and after a moment of shock, my fists tighten at my sides and rage, like a hot, burning coal, pulses inside my chest.

"What did he do?" I ask between gritted teeth.

"It doesn't matter." She steps by me, but I gently grip her wrist, forcing her to stop.

"Tell me," I whisper. How long has she been carrying this around? Has she ever told anyone?

"It's no big deal. He forced himself on me, I succumbed to get the part on *The Regulator*. I knew a role like that could change the trajectory of my career and I was right. A few minutes on the couch was worth it."

I'm shocked by how callous she's being, and I can't tell if it's a protection mechanism or if she really can justify what he did to her.

"I'm so sorry." I reach out, but she swats away my hand.

"I don't need your coddling or sympathy, James. I'm not Lilah."

Her words punch me in the gut.

"I'm only trying to console my fiancée. For fuck's sake, what you went through is traumatic. It's not something you can just forget about."

"Well, I did, and I moved on. I won't be joining any pitchfork parade with all the other women he did this to." She walks to the dining table and sits down in front of the invitations.

I'm at a loss for words. I've never seen her act this way. Is it the stress of the wedding coming up? The fact that I have a daughter? I can't be sure.

When I don't speak, she fills the silence. "Now, let's move on. I need your opinion on the wedding invitations. They're being printed next week."

Pushing a hand through my hair, I walk over to the kitchen under the guise of getting a drink when really, I need space. Because I just realized from her confession that she probably had an idea of what Bernie pulled on Lilah six years ago when I went to her as a friend and confided in her.

And she didn't say anything.

Even to this day. Even when I explained to her what Lilah told me a few weeks back, she played dumb.

But she's a victim too and obviously masking her feelings so she doesn't have to deal with what happened, so I don't know if I have a right to be angry with her.

Whether it's right or wrong though, it feels a hell of a lot like deception. Because if she had let on six years ago as to what might have happened with Lilah and Bernie, there's no doubt in my mind I'd be living a different life right now—a life without her.

* * *

I ARRIVE at Keane's office with Adelaide. This will affect her too, once the press finds out about Monica.

We haven't spoken about the Bernie thing again, and I haven't asked why she never let me know that she might have an idea why Lilah betrayed me. At this point, my mind is a complete clusterfuck. Unless it's some minute detail about our wedding, she's unfazed.

"You can both go right in," Keane's assistant says.

"Thanks."

We walk into his office. Keane is at his desk, and Kyra and Liz are already sitting on the sofa set in the corner.

"Hey, everyone. Thanks for meeting us on such short notice," I say, taking a seat on the sofa. Adelaide sits beside me.

"No problem. Though you have me curious over what this is all about." Keane raises a brow and leans back, smoothing his tie down his chest.

"Is this about the wedding?" Kyra asks.

"Definitely not," Adelaide answers, leaning back on the couch and crossing her legs as if I dragged her here kicking and screaming.

"Are you pregnant?" Liz says, and I cringe inside.

"Adelaide isn't pregnant." Let's stop the what-if game now. "Do you all remember Lilah Robbie?"

Liz scoffs. Obviously, she does. Kyra and Keane nod, though hesitantly. The happiness in Keane's eyes is slowly faltering.

"I recently came back into contact with her and found out I have a five-year-old daughter."

Adelaide's hand tightens on her Starbucks cup. The other three are silent, staring and looking as dumbfounded as I probably did when Monica opened that door.

"Congratulations?" Kyra poses it as a question.

"Are you sure she's yours?" Keane asks.

"That's what I said," Adelaide adds, but I ignore her quip.

"She's mine. Haven't done a DNA test yet, but I don't have to. If you saw her, you'd know too."

"Shit," Keane says, leaning forward with his elbows on his knees.

"What's your plan?" Liz asks.

"That's what I'm here to figure out. We need to come up with a plan to tell the press before they find out on their own, but not make a spectacle of it."

"So you're planning on being in the child's life?" Kyra asks.

"Of course I am." I'm insulted she'd even ask. "And her name is Monica."

She nods, but her focus is only half with me. The other half of her brain is already in PR mode, trying to figure out the best way to play this.

"How's Lilah these days?" Keane asks.

"Good. Been sober for six years. Lives and works in Kansas as a dental hygienist."

"And she kept this from you why?" Liz asks.

"She says she was scared I'd try to take the baby from her and use her past against her to do it."

"Makes sense," Kyra mumbles.

"Not really," Adelaide murmurs.

"Okay." Keane claps once. "Let's get down to business and figure this out."

* * *

IN THE END, we decide that we'll issue a statement to the press, acknowledging that I have a daughter but offering no further information. We know there will be all kinds of speculation and digging to try to find out whether I knew all along or if this was a recent development but there's no way to avoid that. I won't give them any answers—they don't deserve it and anything I said could be dug up by Monica when she's older.

I'm not willing to tarnish Lilah just to satisfy the press's unending appetite for dirt.

Kyra agreed to draft a statement that she'd send my way for approval, and after Monica knows I'm her father, we'll release the statement. I just have to keep Monica's existence a secret for now. Since I've been successful thus far, I feel pretty confident I can do it.

The only people who know about Monica are Adelaide, Tripp, Keane, Kyra, and Liz, and I trust them all.

I still have to run everything by Lilah and figure out a plan for after the announcement is made, but I feel more confident now that a plan is in place. Given that the wedding is so close, Adelaide has requested I issue my statement after the wedding and I've agreed so it remains our day. If I issue the statement before, my having a daughter with Lilah will overshadow our wedding. Adelaide is dealing with this newfound territory I find myself in and she deserves to have the perfect day she's been planning.

But first, I have to tell my daughter that I'm her daddy. The best part of the plan.

* * *

I ROCK BACK and forth in the chair on Lilah's porch, waiting for her to put Monica to bed. Seems odd to do that together.

I think about how drastically my life has changed in such a short time. For the better. Yeah, it was a shock at first and I was full of rage at Lilah in the beginning, and yes, it caused friction between Adelaide and myself, but I can't find any other reason not to think of having Monica in my life as anything less than the best thing that has ever happened to me. The more time I spend with her, the more amazed I am. She's a beautiful little girl, yeah, but her spirit is what draws you in.

The screen door creaks on its hinges, and I turn to see Lilah stepping out onto the porch. She passes me a glass of iced tea before sitting in the rocker beside me.

"Thanks." I take a sip, puckering my lips when the sourness of the lemon she's added hits my tongue.

"She was out like a light right away. Must've had a busy day at school."

"Or it could be the fifty rounds of leapfrog we played in the backyard." I set my glass on the table beside me.

Lilah laughs. "Better you than me."

We're silent for a couple minutes, and it's no longer uncomfortable. That could come to an end though when I ask her what I'm about to. I don't think Adelaide will be happy, but it's what's best.

"I was thinking... what are the chances I could crash here when I'm in town? I could take the guest room or even the couch in the living room. I'm concerned—"

"That someone will recognize you? Yeah, me too."

I've been lucky so far that no one has figured out who I am, but sunglasses and a hat will eventually not be enough to quell the small-town curiosity about the guy who comes into town every weekend. Still, Lilah's deer-in-the-headlights look says she's not entirely comfortable with the idea.

"Never mind. I've gone this long without anyone realizing. I'm sure—"

"No, it's fine. I was just wondering what Adelaide would think, that's all."

"She knows she can trust me." And she does. Or she should. If she doesn't, we shouldn't be getting married.

"Still. Don't think I would like it if I were your fiancée." Her voice cracks on that last word, and I pretend not to notice.

"It'll be fine."

"Okay, then. You can take the guest room."

"Thanks. I met with my team this week. We came up with what we think is a good plan." I fill her in on everything I agreed to with my team. "What do you think?"

She shrugs, and the corners of her mouth tip down. "Sounds like the best plan, I suppose. I don't think anything will hold off the press entirely though. I've been wanting to talk to you about that. What do I do if they show up and you're not here? At some point they're going to figure out who your daughter is. What then?"

Her tiny fists are clenched in her lap, and I resist the urge to take her hand to soothe that fear for her.

"What do you think of getting out of here for a while? I can set you guys up in a nice place where you can lay low until everything dies down."

She shakes her head before I've even finished speaking. "I told you, I have a life here. I can't just up and leave my job, Monica's school, my house."

"I'm not saying forever, just while the press is like a bunch of hungry sharks. After, you can come back here, though you might have to think about moving. There's nothing to stop the press from camping out at the bottom of your driveway. You need a gated community or something."

"There are no gated communities here." She tips her chin down and massages her temples with her fingers. "I can't think about this right now. One thing at a time. Let's figure out what we're going to say to Monica tomorrow night."

I know she doesn't want to have this conversation, but it needs to be had. But I guess she's right that it doesn't need to be discussed right now, so I let it go.

"How do you think we should handle it?" I ask.

She inhales deeply and turns her head to look at me. "I think we tell her a version of the truth. When she's older, we can get more into specifics, but for now, I think we just tell her that you're her daddy and that we used to know each other a long time ago and that I wasn't able to get ahold of you, but as soon as you could, you came to find us. She should know it wasn't your fault that you weren't in her life before."

Relief floods through me. I was afraid that whatever Lilah wanted to tell her wouldn't make it clear that if I *could* have been a part of her life, I would've been. I don't ever want Monica to think I want didn't her.

"Yeah, that sounds good." Tears build in Lilah's eyes, and I frown. "What is it? Do you think we shouldn't tell her? Is it too soon?"

"No, it's not that." She shakes her head. "It's just that someday, I'm going to have to admit to her that I kept her away from you. She'll hate me." A tear slips down her cheek, and she wipes it away.

"Hey, hey." I take her hand and give it a squeeze. "That's not going to happen for a long time, and by then, she'll have had two parents successfully co-parent for years. She'll know that we both love her, okay? Yes, she'll probably be upset, but she won't hate you. I'm sure of it."

I'm not sure of it. Not really. But I do believe that however we frame it is what's important. And if Monica sees that I was able to forgive her mother, that will go a long way to her forgiving Lilah too.

Sitting here and comforting her for something she did to me that I was so angry about feels odd, but I do believe that she thought it was what was best in the beginning. After that, I think she allowed fear to rule her decisions. And truth be told, I can't say that she isn't correct in thinking I would've tried to take Monica away.

"I hope you're right. It's just so hard to think of her hearing about that and my addiction issues, because the press will be sure to bring all that up once they realize I'm her mother. Right now, she sees me as Mommy, and the way she looks at me just fills up my heart. I don't want her to see me as the flawed person I really am."

"Monica loves you. That won't change. If anything, you'll be able to educate her from your own perspective on the importance of dealing with your problems and not letting them fester, explain to her why you have to be compassionate toward people who suffer from the disease of addiction, and show her what a strong person her mom is for overcoming so many obstacles."

She sniffs and nods. I'm not really sure I got through to her, but she pulls her hand from mine and wipes her face. "Don't mind me. I'm sure there'll be more tears down the line. This is just hard. I'm happy you're in her life now, I really am. I'm just not happy with everything that comes along with you."

I chuckle. "I get it. Trust me. If I could make it so no one in the world cared about who she is to me, I would. But that's not reality and so we just have to come up with the best plan we can to deal with it."

She presses her lips together and nods. "Well, I'm going to head to bed. It's been a long day and I'm sure tomorrow will be no different. Can you lock the front door after you come in?"

"Sure thing. I'm not going to stay up much longer though. See you in the morning."

She nods a little sheepishly and turns and disappears into the house.

I spend another hour on the porch, running over everything in my head, before I text Adelaide good night and make my way inside. It takes a while for me to get to sleep, because though I'm pretty comfortable in this house by now, it feels weird to be sleeping here as though I belong. That and my mind is racing, wondering how Monica will react when she learns the truth.

Chapter Sixty-one

JIMMY

I spend Saturday playing in the house and the backyard with Monica while Lilah is at work. We have a fun day together, though I'm a little on edge knowing what's coming this evening.

It's clear Lilah feels the same when she arrives home from work. All through dinner, she's nervous and jumpy. I think we're best to spit it out and deal with the aftermath, so as soon as we're done eating, and before dessert, I nod at her in the direction of the living room.

She gives me a small nod, obviously in agreement. "Kiddo, why don't we all head into the living room? Jimmy and I have something we want to talk to you about."

My daughter's lips turn down. "But I want my ice cream."

"You'll get your ice cream after. There's just something important that we have to tell you."

"Fine." She slips off her chair and stomps off to the living room with her arms crossed.

Great. What a way to start.

Lilah and I follow. Lilah sits beside Monica on the couch and pulls her into her lap. I decide to take the chair off to the side, thinking Monica might want some space after she hears the news.

"Do you remember when I told you that I used to know Jimmy a long time ago?"

She nods. "And then he found us."

"That's right. He did. For a long time, he didn't know where to find us." She looks in my direction, an apology filling her eyes. "Well, what you need to know is that Jimmy isn't just my friend. He's... he's actually your father. Jimmy is your dad."

Monica's head whips in my direction. "You're my daddy?"

I nod slowly. Any words lodge in my throat as I watch my daughter soak up the information. My heart is ready to burst out of my chest when her eyes widen and her smile grows.

"Yay! I have a daddy!"

She hops off Lilah's lap and runs over to give me a big hug, which I return with extra tightness.

With her small arms around my neck, she whispers, "Daddy."

Love pours through me and I squeeze her a little tighter, hoping she can feel how much I love her. "My baby girl."

When she pulls away, I hope to always find this big of a smile looking my way. "Can I have my ice cream now?"

I laugh. "Sure, sweetie."

I ruffle her hair, and she skips off my lap toward the kitchen. We both watch her then turn to each other, shock in both our eyes.

"I feel like we got off easy," Lilah says.

"Don't worry. She'll be a teenager in less than a decade." I wink and stand to go get my daughter her ice cream.

Lilah cringes.

I hold my hand out for Lilah. "Let's not think about that. Let's go have ice cream."

She smiles, her soft hand sliding into mine. It's a move we've done hundreds of times, but tonight it feels as though we're in this together. This parenting thing, even if we're not a couple is exhilarating.

Chapter Sixty-two

LILAH

"I don't want you to go, Jimmy."

Monica wraps herself around his leg, her arms squeezing so tightly, her eyes are closing too. Jimmy's already delayed his flight to spend breakfast and mid-morning snack with us. Truth is, I don't want him to leave either. If I was five, I might be attached to his other leg.

Now that we've been in each other's company again, I remember how much I love hanging out with him. Maybe it's just having another adult around though. Monica has been my every waking and breathing moment for so long. The girls at work used to invite me out, but after I turned them down so many times, they stopped asking. We're friendly at work, but we're not friends outside of it. And I told Parker that I couldn't see him anymore. He's nice, but I have too much in flux right now to introduce a new boyfriend into the mix.

So that leaves Jimmy. And as much as I know he's moved on, it's hard sometimes to stop myself from letting all those feelings lying under the surface show. It's like a scab itching to be picked, but if I do, all those feelings from the past will pour out and the bleeding will never stop.

My heart tugs at seeing her so upset though. I don't know if it's because she's grown used to having him around or the fact she found out he's her father.

"Kiddo, Jimmy has a plane to catch. He'll be back next weekend."

"That's too long!" She squeezes her eyes shut and grips his leg harder.

He pleads for help with his eyes. This is uncharted territory for him. So far, to him, Monica's been nothing but a joy to be around.

"I have an idea," I say. Monica's eyes pop open, and Jimmy eyebrows rise. "Why don't we all FaceTime this week? That way you'll get to see him before he comes back."

"That's a great idea," he says, easing her off his leg.

"What's FaceTime?" she asks, one hand still gripping his jeans in case we're lying.

"It's where you call someone on the phone, but it's a video so both of you can see one another," I say.

"I wanna do that!" She jumps up and down and claps.

"It's a deal then." Jimmy gives her a hug. "Be good for your mom while I'm gone, okay?"

She nods, and he ruffles her hair.

"Why don't you go pick out a bathing suit and we'll head to the rec center and go swimming?"

"Okay, Mommy." She spins and runs down the hall to her room.

"Good save," Jimmy says.

I chuckle. "Thanks. One thing I've learned is that when in doubt—bribe."

He laughs for a second, but it dies with a weird edge. "Listen, there's something I've been wanting to ask you about."

He pushes a hand through his hair. He's going to be bald when we reach the other side of these awkward conversations. The press will blame me for ruining James Crawford's thick dark hair.

"What's up?"

"I was wondering when you thought Adelaide might be able to visit with me?"

The air rushes from my lungs. That's not what I thought he was going to ask, but Jimmy, being Jimmy, doesn't always wait for one thing to absorb before introducing the next obstacle. It's not like I didn't know this moment was coming. But I don't want to see her. I don't want my daughter to see her. I can't help but feel a little like Adelaide stole what was mine, even though I basically handed it to her with my fuck-ups.

I swallow my ill feelings. "Um... when do you want her to come?"

"Not next weekend. I'd like to give Monica more time to get used to the idea of me being her dad. But maybe the weekend after, depending on how it goes?"

"Yeah, okay. Sure."

"Great, thanks. She'll be excited when I tell her."

I nod and smile tightly. "Have a safe flight. We'll see you next weekend. Text me and let me know when it's okay for us to FaceTime you."

"I don't have much this week. Meeting with Keane to go over a few scripts to see if I can move out of unemployment after the wedding."

Every time he mentions his wedding, it's as if someone jabbed me with a knife to the heart. I've seen pictures of the two of them on magazine covers for more than a year now, so I should be used to it. But rather than pushing the unwanted feeling away like I usually do, I allow myself to feel the weight of losing him completely and acknowledge the need to move on. No good comes of me pretending something isn't bothering me.

"Well, good luck with that."

He nods and heads out the door. I watch him make his way to the car and wave at him before he climbs inside.

Two weeks. I have two weeks until I face Adelaide. Not nearly enough time to stop hating her.

* * *

Two weeks fly by, and before I can fully grasp what's about to happen, it's Friday night and Jimmy and Adelaide are due to arrive. I decide to make tacos for dinner. It'll keep me in the kitchen on meal prep, which means less time around *her*.

A knock on the door sounds, and Monica's footsteps barreling down the hallway comes next.

"Jimmy!" she says right before I step out of the kitchen.

I turn the corner and watch Jimmy pick up Monica. Adelaide's behind him with a strained smile.

"Hey, sweetie. How are you?"

"Good. Who are you?"

"Manners, Monica," I say as I walk down the short hallway.

"Sorry, Mommy," she says, her eyes still on Adelaide.

"Hello, Adelaide," I say, hoping there's pleasure in my tone. The two of us need to get off on the right foot for Monica.

"Lilah." She nods once and returns her attention to Monica, staring at her as though she's inspecting every feature down to her freckles.

I ignore the urge to tear Monica out of Jimmy's arms, shut and lock the door.

Adelaide's still as beautiful as ever, though her hair is shorter than when I last saw her. But it's easy to see why Jimmy would be attracted to her. She's a Hollywood starlet.

"This is my fiancée, Adelaide," he says, setting Monica down and stepping to the side to place his hand behind Adelaide.

"What's a fiancée?" she asks with her nose scrunched up in the adorable way she does when she doesn't understand something.

"A fiancée is the person you're going to marry."

Monica's expression slackens, and she draws back. "Why would you marry her? Why wouldn't you marry Mommy?" She turns to look at me, and my stomach sinks. "Mommies and daddies get married."

Oh no. We really should have prepped her for this.

"Kiddo, Jimmy and I aren't getting married. He's marrying Adelaide." Heat flares in my cheeks at having to say that as if it's the best thing ever and we should both be over the moon about it. In front of Adelaide no less.

"No!" She stomps her foot. "I want you and Mommy to get married!"

He glances at me, looking bewildered.

"Monica, that's rude. Now say hello to Adelaide."

"No!" Before I can stop her, she races down the hallway, tears streaming down her small cheeks.

"I'm sorry," I say. "I had no idea she felt that way. She's never said anything."

Adelaide's lips are pinched tight and her eyes narrowed as if she's a witch who's casting a spell for me to disappear.

"She's never let on that she thought we were going to get married. I fucked this up." Jimmy pushes a hand through his hair.

I hold up my hand. "No, you didn't. Give me a minute. I'll go talk to her."

"Let me." He steps forward, silently asking permission.

Technically this is his rodeo, so I step out of the way and nod. Forgetting that leaves me and Adelaide alone in the awkwardness.

I clear my throat. "Can I get you something to drink?"

"I'm good," she says and steps farther into the house, eyeing every inch.

"I was just going to start dinner. You can join me if you want."

If I'm going to teach my daughter how to be polite, I have to set the example, when I'd really like to ask her how being second-best feels. If this woman is so important to Jimmy's life, she'll be my daughter's stepmom and spend time alone with her. I don't want her taking any of her issues with me out on Monica.

She follows me into the kitchen and sits at the kitchen table.

"Hope you like tacos," I say, sliding the ground beef into the waiting pan. I turn the burner on medium.

When she doesn't respond, I turn to look at her and see that she's typing on her phone, paying me no attention. Great. The awkward silence continues while I chop up the lettuce and tomatoes until I can't stand it any longer.

"How are the wedding plans coming along?" I ask, figuring any bride is probably happy to discuss her wedding.

She slides her phone into her purse and grants me her attention. "Everything is pretty much done now, but it's been a lot of work by myself, what with Jimmy spending all his weekends here."

My chest tightens, and I look over my shoulder. "I'm sorry about that. I imagine this is hard position for you."

"Oh, I wasn't saying that to make you feel bad. You just asked and well... honesty is always the best policy, don't you agree?"

I might as well hand her a shovel right now if she's planning to take digs at me all night. "Right, of course. I know Monica really appreciates having him here, so thank you for understanding. And I'm sorry about how she reacted earlier. I should have prepared her better to meet you."

I'd told her Jimmy was bringing someone along this weekend, but not who. I thought he should explain the situation to her, and I had no idea that she had it in her head that Jimmy and I were meant to be together.

"It's fine, Lilah. You're worrying too much. I knew coming here I was the villain."

The knife hits the cutting board harder. "No. You're not." Even I hear my tone doesn't match my words.

"You guys are the blood relatives and I'm the outsider. I do wonder, I mean, Jimmy was talking about the paternity test. I'm assuming there's a hospital around here, and all it takes is a cotton swab."

I drop the knife next to the chopped lettuce and go to the stove to restrict her visual of my face. "Yes. Jimmy didn't say anything, but if that's what he wants, I'm more than okay with it."

The kitchen chair slides along the floor before her voice grows closer. "It must be nice to have all this control over him?"

I turn to find her leaning against the counter, her arms crossed. She's perfection, right out of a magazine. I don't envy those days when you never knew when your picture would be snapped. "I have no control over him."

A hollow laugh falls out of her mouth. "No? You tell him when he can come. When he can tell her he's her father. When I can be introduced. Is this how our life is going to be?"

I bite my tongue before I kick her out of my house. "I'm sorry you feel that way, and maybe when you have kids of your own you'll understand how delicate you have to be with changing their lives."

I want to pat myself on the back for being so nice.

"I didn't plan on having kids. I've never wanted them in my life."

Any hope I had for her being a great stepmom, being there when I can't, just disintegrated.

"Oh. I didn't know. Jimmy—"

"Didn't say anything? I'm not surprised. It's been all about him lately. He probably thinks your daughter will change my mind."

I want to blink to make sure she's the same Adelaide I knew six years ago. The last time I was around her, she was rude to me, but she was always respectful of Jimmy.

"Well, she is adorable, and I think you'll get along well with her. After all, you both love Jimmy." I stir the meat, my gaze falling on Monica's door down the hall. *Speed it up, Jimmy.*

"It's like his fan club here, right?" She laughs, although it's tight.

I drop the spoon next to the meat and walk over to her. "Listen, I can't imagine being in your shoes. I know you hate me, and that's your choice. I'm not sure what I ever did especially to you, but I hurt Jimmy and you love Jimmy, so I get you hating me. But I'm not here on the weekends trying to lure him to me. If anything, I'm not around when he's here because I try to give them time alone. But you're marrying Jimmy and Monica is his daughter, which the paternity test will prove, so we need to learn to tolerate one another."

She might as well put her hand in front of her mouth and yawn she looks so bored. "It's just awfully convenient."

"What? The fact he came to me? Remember that, Adelaide, I didn't go looking for him."

Hurt flickers in her eyes and she strips them away from me, but not before I see the fear. I can't say I wouldn't feel the same.

"All Jimmy's ever done is say how much he's looking forward to marrying you. I'm not a threat to you." The meat sizzles, and I rush over to stir it, putting in the seasoning and water. "The only think I ask of you is don't bad talk me or my daughter to the press. I'm scared of being swallowed up by their incessant interruptions."

"You know there are no promises what the paps will report, but I don't want my name attached to those kinds of stories either."

I glance over my shoulder. She seems contrite, so I have no choice but to trust her until she loses it.

Thankfully, before we can discuss any more topics, Monica's door opens and she and Jimmy step out.

"Everything okay?" I ask, studying Monica. She looks resigned instead of upset.

"Yep, we're good. Had a little chat, didn't we, sweetie?" Jimmy squeezes Monica to the side of his leg.

She nods.

"Great, well, dinner isn't that far off. Monica, why don't you show Adelaide all the Barbies you have in your room?" I throw her a bone she doesn't deserve.

"Okay, Mommy." She turns and heads to her room without waiting for Adelaide, who gives Jimmy an awkward smile and leaves the room.

"I'd better join them," he says.

"Before you go, fill me in on what she said."

He meets my gaze. "She said she thought that now that I was her daddy, you and I would be getting married because that's what mommies and daddies do."

My heart constricts. Her first disappointment in all this new territory. My poor little girl.

"I'm sorry, I had no idea she felt that way." I lean back against the counter. "I should have though. I should have had a talk with her about how it doesn't change anything."

"Hey." He steps forward and he's about to take my hand but stuffs his in his pockets. "This is on both of us. We did our best, but we're figuring this out ourselves. Give yourself a break."

I nod even though I don't agree with him. "Did she seem like she understood?"

"She did. I think she'll be fine. It was more a surprise than anything. As long as you and I continue to put her first and co-exist in front of her, we're good."

"Right."

We hold one another's gaze for a moment.

I blink and glance at the pan. "You should probably go join them so I can finish dinner."

Jimmy presses his lips together, nods, and leaves.

I remind myself that he's not mine and he'll never be mine again.

* * *

THANKFULLY, the evening continues without any more outbursts from Monica. She isn't her usual cheery self, staying quiet through dinner and even after when she plays leapfrog with Jimmy and chalks the sidewalk. Adelaide has been observant, with almost distain in her eyes when Jimmy interacts with me.

"Are you staying at the motel in town?" I ask as they stand to leave. At least the awkwardness will be gone.

No way is Adelaide staying in my house.

"No, we're driving a couple towns over to stay at the Hampton Inn."

I nod.

"How come?" Monica peers her head from behind my leg.

Jimmy crouches so he's at her level. "I just thought we'd be more comfortable there."

He's not saying the specific reason, but I'm fairly sure the motel in town isn't up to Adelaide's standards. I don't remember Adelaide being stuck-up, but her star power has increased tenfold since I knew her. Maybe she's gotten used to the finer things in life.

"Say goodbye to Jimmy and Adelaide, kiddo, then it's off to bed for you." I pat her back.

She walks out from behind my leg and wraps her little arms around Jimmy to give him a hug. "Bye," she says with sadness in her tone.

"Bye, sweetie. I'll see you tomorrow morning." He kisses the top of her head.

"Now say bye to Adelaide," I prompt her.

Monica comes to stand behind my leg again. "Bye."

"Bye," Adelaide says and gives a little wave. Her fake smile doesn't fool anyone.

"We'll talk," Jimmy says to me before they turn and leave.

I close the door behind them and lock it. The one thing I hated today was seeing Jimmy dote on Adelaide. The way his hand would guide her on the small of her back. His arm stretched along the back of her chair. Although I'm not happy to see Jimmy go, I was happier not bearing witness to them as a couple in real life right at my kitchen table. Maybe that's why it didn't bother me much before—they were a couple in a land I never wanted to return to. But now they're invading my space with their lovey-dovey eyes.

"All right, kiddo, let's get you to bed."

Monica changes into her pajamas and slides into her bed.

I tuck the covers over her and kiss her cheek. "Night, kiddo. I love you."

"Love you, Mommy," she softly says.

I walk across her room, turn off the light, and my hand is on the doorknob to close the door slightly.

"Why can't you and Jimmy get married?" she asks with the innocence that only a child has. Innocence because her world is black and white. She's too young to understand the layers of history between Jimmy and me—both good and bad.

"That's complicated, sweetie, but Jimmy and I aren't going to get married. We're just friends, but we'll always be your mommy and daddy."

"Well, I don't like it and I don't like her," she huffs, rolling over so her back is to me.

Neither do I. I sit down on the bed, rubbing her back with my hand. "I know, but you need to give Adelaide a chance. Get to know her. It's not okay for you to be rude to her. You need to be respectful. How I've taught you to be to adults, okay?" I run my fingers through her hair again, and she rolls over and yawns. "Plus, Jimmy cares for Adelaide. You wouldn't like it if he was rude to Eileen, would you?"

"No." She looks at the ceiling.

"Because you like Eileen, right? And you see all the good things there are to like about her?"

She thinks for a moment and nods.

"Jimmy sees good things in Adelaide, so you need give her a chance to show you those same things." I smooth her errant hairs off her forehead.

"Okay. I'll try." Her expression doesn't convince me.

I kiss her forehead, inhaling the scent that is unequivocally *her*.

After a few minutes, her breathing slows into a steady rhythm and I creep out of her room.

As if seeing them together wasn't torture enough, I dissect their interactions while I lie in bed. There was tension between them. Adelaide was clearly uncomfortable, and Jimmy needed to make everyone and everything perfect. The whole night was horrendous.

I roll onto my side, squeeze my eyes shut, and a tear rolls down onto my pillowcase. I allow myself one good cry over what I've lost, then the pity party ends. I have to move on and do what's best for my daughter.

Chapter Sixty-three

JIMMY

"So, what did you think of Monica?" I'm eager for Adelaide's thoughts as she buckles her seatbelt on the plane.

Normally I fly out on Sunday morning, but Adelaide insisted we leave tonight.

"She's cute," she says before popping an Advil with a sip of water from the bottle next to her.

I didn't ask her much on Friday night because things between us were tense and I was worried we'd end up fighting. I didn't want that to happen when we were going to watch her all day today. Friday dinner was awkward, especially after Monica's outburst. I'm not sure if I have Lilah to thank or not, but Monica was more receptive to Adelaide today. By the end of the day, she even invited her to play leapfrog with us.

"Did you like her?" I wave the flight attendant away because we're going to hash this out.

"I think the better question is does she like me?" She pulls her phone from her purse and buries her head in it. Who does she really have to talk to about the wedding at this time on a Saturday night?

"Could you put the phone down so we can discuss this?"

She sighs and sets it on the seat beside her, giving me an impatient look. "Sorry, time doesn't stand still while we're in Kansas. There are things that have to be done, and since I'm the only one who seems to care—"

"That's not fair. You know what I've been dealing with. What am I supposed to do—put everything on hold until after the wedding?"

I'm cryptic since the crew is moving around the plane, preparing for takeoff. The last thing I need is for the press to catch wind of Monica because of my flight attendants.

"It's all you care about lately. What about me? You think this isn't hard on me?"

I unclip my belt and cross the aisle to sit beside her. I pick up her phone and tilt her chin around to face me. "I know, and I'm sorry. I understand that the timing of all this sucks. But we have to be a team to get through these next couple months. There's so much going on, and it's going to be an adjustment for all of us."

She shifts in her seat to face me. "Can I ask you something?"

"Of course."

She hesitates, and I know whatever she's going to say, I'm probably not going to like it.

"How do you see this whole thing playing out?"

My forehead wrinkles. "What do you mean?"

"After the wedding and after Monica is used to me... how do you see this working?"

She's not asking something I haven't wondered a million times. At this point though, I'm trying to take it one day at a time.

"I'm not sure exactly, but it will."

"Are they going to move out to California? We're certainly not moving to Kansas." She must see something in my face because she doesn't allow me to respond. "You've got to be kidding me. I'm not moving to the middle of nowhere, James."

"I'm not saying you should. But if it means that I have to get a place out here for when I visit, I will."

"So what? You're going to spend every weekend here until she's eighteen?"

I push a hand through my hair. "I don't know!"

The flight attendant pops out of the cockpit to make sure everything is okay. I reassure her it is, and she tells me we'll be ready for takeoff in a few minutes. I turn my attention back to Adelaide once she disappears.

I lower my voice. "I don't know what's going to happen. But I do know that Lilah and I will work it out, all right? We both want what's best for her. Now, I don't know if that means uprooting her from everything she's ever known or not. But we'll figure it out, okay?"

"And I have no say?" At least she's keeping her voice low so no one hears.

"No, you do, but you're an adult. She's five."

"Whatever you say." She plucks her phone out of my hand and types away again, not missing a beat.

With an exasperated sigh, I cross the aisle and buckle back into my seat, staring out the window.

The pilot announces we're cleared for takeoff. I stare out the window as the plane speeds down the runway, my heart pricking as the fields of Kansas disappear while we ascend. I'm torn between the life I'm getting ready to live with Adelaide and the new role of father thrown into my lap.

And though I completely understand why Adelaide is struggling to see where she fits, my daughter's needs come first.

When the pilot comes on the overhead speaker to let us know we're free to roam about the cabin, Adelaide undoes her seatbelt and sits down beside me.

"I'm sorry. It's just... I don't want to see her hurt you again. This whole thing has sent me for a loop, but it's you I'm worried about."

"What do you mean?" I undo my belt and shift so I face her.

Her hand falls to my thigh. "You haven't even had a DNA test yet, honey. I'll admit the girl does resemble you, especially her eyes, but you don't know with certainty that she's yours, yet you're already so invested."

I stare blankly. "Adelaide, she's my daughter. Anyone can see that."

"Maybe so, but shouldn't you be one hundred percent sure? Lilah isn't exactly known for her honesty. She's pulled a lot of shit on you, you've said so yourself."

An exasperated breath leaves my lips. "She's not like that anymore."

"Well…" She brings her hand to the side of my face and runs her fingers through my hair above my ear. "Get the test done so you can be sure, but also to protect your rights in the event that Lilah won't let you see her."

Once again, she doesn't refer to Monica by her name, as though saying her name makes her real. Adelaide does have a point though. I don't believe Lilah would try anything like that, but a little insurance can't hurt.

"I'll talk to her about it this week," I say.

"Wonderful." Adelaide kisses me, her tongue snaking through the seam of my lips.

My hand winds to the back of her head, holding her to me. Our kiss lasts until the flight attendant interrupts to see if we'd like any drinks or a snack. Adelaide stays seated next to me and I link our hands, waiting for our drinks. I have to figure out how to bring up the DNA test without upsetting Lilah. I mistakenly trusted her completely before. This time, I'll cover my ass.

* * *

LATER IN THE WEEK, Tripp and I are relaxing with a few beers on my patio. Adelaide is off doing press interviews purposely scheduled before the wedding.

Tripp entertains me with tales from the tour, but my phone rings on the table and I glance down to see it's a FaceTime call from Lilah. I love the fact we no longer schedule our FaceTime calls. Lilah lets Monica decide when she wants to talk and makes it happen. Our conversations don't always last long—

she is five. Sometimes it's a good night, or a good morning, or guess what happened at school call, but they aren't forced.

"Want to say hello to my daughter?" I ask.

"No shit?" Tripp's eyebrows rise and he sets his beer on the table.

"No cursing." I hit the screen to accept the call and hold the phone away from me. Monica's face comes into view. Lilah must be holding the phone for her because whenever Monica holds it, I get a great visual of her nose. "Hey, sweetie. How are you?"

"Hi, Jimmy! I'm good. I want to tell you what happened at school today. Mommy said you would think it was funny."

I chuckle. "Okay, let's hear it."

"There's this boy in my class named Sidney, and when we were all sitting down so the teacher could read to us, he kept moving around, and when the teacher asked if he had ants in his pants, he said no and then he pulled a frog out of his pocket!"

"He did not!"

She nods frantically. "He did! He did! And then it jumped off his hand and the teacher screamed, and all the kids screamed! Mr. Craig had to come in and find the frog."

I laugh, picturing the scene. "What an exciting day."

"Okay I have to go now. My princess Barbie needs a new dress to wear. Bye. Here's Mommy."

Before I can say goodbye or introduce her to Tripp, she's gone and the image on the screen is moving around Lilah's kitchen. Her face fills the screen.

"Hey, sorry about that. We're still working on phone etiquette," she says, humor in her tone.

"Don't worry about it. Listen, there's something I need to talk to you about though. Is Monica in earshot?"

She turns her gaze from the camera, and I see she's walking down the hallway and out to the front porch. "What's up?"

I push a hand through my hair.

With the scrape of his chair, Tripp stands from the table. "I'm gonna grab us a couple more beers," he whispers.

I nod my thanks. He must sense the change in my demeanor.

"Who's that?" Lilah asks.

"Tripp. He's back from tour and filling me in on all the trouble he got into."

"Oh," she says and looks away from the screen. "What did you want to discuss?"

"There's something we should take care of. Probably should have by now and I want you to know that I'm not bringing it up because I don't believe you or anything like that... but I think we should get a DNA test done."

Hurt flashes in her eyes, but she schools her expression quickly.

"Lilah, please don't take this the wrong way—"

"No, I get it. It's fine. You have to cover your bases. Adelaide said as much."

"Adelaide? What di—"

We're interrupted by Monica yelling for her mom.

"Listen, you just let me know what you need me to do and I'll take care of it on my end. No worries. I have to go see what's up with Monica. See you in a few days."

"Yeah, okay."

The screen goes black before the words are barely out of my mouth.

Why do I feel so guilty for asking for the test?

I set my phone on the table as Tripp sets another beer in front of me.

"Everything all right?" He sits down across from me with a raised brow.

"Yeah. I just feel like a bastard asking her for a DNA test."

"Pfft. Don't. Anyone else? It would've been the first thing they asked for." He tips back his beer.

I pull up a picture of Monica and slide the phone across the table. "Have a look for yourself."

He studies it for a second. "She's beautiful, man. And yeah, no doubt she's yours with those eyes."

"See?" I say, taking back my phone and looking at her picture again. "I don't doubt it. I just want my ass covered."

"You're really enjoying this new daddy role." Amusement coats his tone.

"Honestly, it feels like nothing in my life meant anything before her. Doing right by her is the only thing that matters."

He raises a brow. "How's Adelaide feel about that?"

I take a pull from my beer. "She's struggling to adjust, but she's coming around. She met Monica for the first-time last weekend. It went as well as can be expected."

"I'm sure she'll come around."

"Yeah, me too. She has a lot on her plate. Pretty stressed out with the wedding. It's been a lot for her." Saying the words makes me realize that I need to make more of an effort to show her she's still a priority in my life. We need a romantic night together. "Anyway, any idea where I can get a DNA test done on the down low?"

He smirks. "Of course I do. You know how many women come out of the woodwork every year claiming I'm their baby daddy? My team has that shit on speed dial."

"Great, send it my way." I take another pull off my beer.

"Will do. But first, let's figure out what we're going to do for your bachelor party." He rubs his hands in front of himself like an evil genius, and I roll my eyes.

I have more important things to worry about than a bachelor party. We're going to be releasing a statement to the press in a few weeks, and I need to get things in place and have a conversation with Lilah about what that means for her and Monica.

Chapter Sixty-four

LILAH

I wasn't shocked when Jimmy brought up the DNA test, but it hurt. He stood in my kitchen, telling me we had to trust one another. But I have no way to take him wanting one other than a sign that he doesn't fully trust me. I get that it takes a second to break trust and a lifetime to rebuild it, but we've been on our way. At least I thought so, but maybe I was alone in that thinking.

He found a type of service that celebrities use, where things are kept very hush hush, and I mailed in Monica's sample last week via priority courier. I'm not scared of the results, but it still feels like a clicking countdown in the back of my mind.

Neither Jimmy nor I brought it up when he came to visit that weekend. It was the proverbial elephant in the room the entire time, but we put it aside for Monica's sake. It shifted us back to that awkward state though, so many emotions running under our conversations.

Before he left Sunday, he told me that next weekend, we need to solidify our plans for after the press release goes out. I know we want to be in control, but I've tried to avoid thinking about it, since it means a disruption to Monica's life. But it can't be avoided any longer. I need to work out what I want to happen so I have a say in this too.

I yawn as I click the button on the coffee machine and stand there waiting while the blessed aroma fills the kitchen. Reaching forward to pull a coffee mug from the cupboard, I still when I hear something outside. It sounded like a bump. My mind goes to the garbage tins at the side of the house and the raccoons who dig and dump out everything and drag it across the yard.

"Ugh. Seriously? So much for that guy at the hardware store and his miracle system to keep them out," I murmur.

I'm gonna need a jolt of caffeine for this, so I continue to pull the mug down and pour my coffee, adding milk. After a few gulps of the heavenly goodness, I set the mug on the counter and head to the front door to go around to the side. I open the inside door and have my hand on the screen door when I realize the sound wasn't raccoons.

My throat closes when I see camera crews and reporters lining the edge of my property. Vehicles are parked on both sides of the roads as people set up equipment. Panic squeezes my insides and all the air swoops out of my lungs, leaving me gasping through my tight throat.

In the few seconds it takes for me to make sense of what's happening someone spots me. The shouting of questions begins, only drowned out by the incessant clicking of shutters.

"Oh my God." I slam the door closed. "Oh my God."

A sick feeling swells in my chest and bile creeps up my throat. I swallow it back, closing my eyes and willing myself to take control of the situation right now and worry later. Racing throughout the house, I close all the blinds and curtains and ensure the doors and windows are locked. Monica is still asleep and her window and curtains are closed—since I check them every night before I put her to bed. When I'm done, I run back to the kitchen and pull my cell phone from the charger, hitting Jimmy's number.

He answers after a couple of rings, sounding groggy since it's earlier on the west coast. "What's wrong? Is Monica okay?"

"They're here. They're all here."

"Who's there? What are you talking about?"

"Reporters, paparazzi! My house is surrounded!" I pace the kitchen, my breaths shallow and short. I feel lightheaded.

"Fuck! You've got to be kidding me. How did they find out?" Rustling sounds in the background.

"You tell me! Did you release the statement? I thought we had another couple weeks?" Tears are welling and my nose is tickling. It's only a matter of time before I break down.

"We did. Someone must have tipped them off. Fuck!"

"Mommy?"

I freeze. Wiping the tears, I mask my emotional mess of a face and spin around. "Kiddo, what are you doing up?"

She yawns and rubs her eyes. "A noise woke me up."

Keep it together. Keep it together.

"Why don't you go play with your Barbies in your room, okay, hun? We're going to have a special day today. No school or work, how does that sound?" I plaster on a fake smile.

"Yay!" She wraps her arms around my waist.

I bend and kiss the top of her head. "Now you go play and I'll come get you for breakfast in a bit. But do not, do not open your curtains."

She screws her face up into a confused expression. "Why not?"

"Kiddo, you just have to do as I say, okay? Can you do that?"

She shrugs. "Okay."

"Promise? No opening curtains."

"Yeah." She spins on the ball of her foot and walks to her room, glancing back at me.

I smile like everything is peaceful in the world.

After she's gone, I whisper-shout into the phone, "What are we gonna do?"

"The first priority is getting you somewhere the press can't find you. I don't want them scaring Monica and hurling their bullshit her way."

"Agreed. But I'm cornered here. I can't leave without them seeing her."

"Leave that to me. I'm going to make some calls. You sit tight for now and do not go outside. Don't answer your phone either unless it's my number, got it?"

"Yeah, got it. Please hurry." I do a crap job of hiding my fear, because I know Jimmy's freaked out since he's not here, but I've never felt more trapped in my life.

"I'm on it." He hangs up.

I listen to dead air before I register our conversation is over. The phone shakes as I place it on the counter. I walk to Monica's bedroom and pull out her small suitcase I bought her before we went to Monument Rocks last year.

"Whatcha doing, Mommy?"

I grab some of her clothes and put them in the suitcase. "We're going to go on a short trip."

She jumps up. "*Yay*! Back to the big rocks? Don't forget my swimsuit." She runs over to her dresser and pulls out her striped one-piece swimsuit.

"You're so helpful. Can you get your underwear and socks too?"

She closes the drawer and opens up her top drawer, pulling out one pair of underwear and socks. She places them nicely in the suitcase. "There you go."

I smile. My amazing daughter is so helpful in this moment, although she has no idea how grateful I am that she is. "We'll need more."

"How many?" She stands by the open drawer.

"Just pack all of them."

"All?" Her eyes light up then dim. "That's a lot of nights."

"Always want to be prepared."

She puts her hands on her hips. "Last time you told me you never want to overpack."

She picks now to school me on the lessons of life I teach her?

"Difference circumstances. Come on. Bring them over."

She plops them in the suitcase. "What about Cecilia? She wants to go."

I hold up the small zipper section on the front. "I'd never dream of leaving her behind."

She grabs the Barbie doll and drops her in the suitcase.

I zip up her suitcase and put it on the floor.

"Are you packed too?" she asks.

I ruffle her hair. "Why don't you come into my room and help me?"

Instead of allowing her to walk, I carry her into my room. As I pack my clothes and everything for who knows how long, I realize the hard-won small-town life I've carved out through sheer will and determination is over.

I've been thrust back into the spotlight I never wanted to return to.

* * *

A COUPLE OF HOURS LATER, Jimmy calls. He's arranged for a private plane to take us to a residence he's secured in West Mercer Island, Washington. Body guards will be escorting us from the house to the airport.

I've spent my morning keeping Monica away from all the windows and doors without raising her suspicions. I've let her watch TV in my bedroom, since it's in the back of the house, and she thinks that we're going on some fun trip.

Jimmy says the bodyguards will be here in the next half hour, so now's the time to talk to Monica.

I sit down on the bed. "Kiddo, can we talk for a minute?" I click the off button on the remote and the screen goes black.

"Is it time to go?" she says, her eyes wide.

"Almost." I take her hands.

"Where are we going?" She bounces on her bum on the mattress.

"We get to take a plane." I muster up as much fake enthusiasm as I can under the circumstances. She's been begging to go on a plane, and the only good thing about this situation is I get to see her reaction.

Her eyes widen. "*Yay!*" She throws herself into my arms. "Thank you, Mommy."

"It's exciting, I know."

She nods a bunch of times. "Is Jimmy coming?"

Jimmy didn't mention anything about him coming, and I'm not willing to break any promises. Normally she'd see him on the weekend, but with this mess to deal with, plus his wedding only weeks away, I have no idea.

"I'm not sure, kiddo."

The corners of her lips tip down and the light in her eyes dims.

"He might join us later. I'll talk to him. But you and I can still have fun, right?"

"Yeah, I guess. I just like it better when he's with us." She sits down next to me.

I do too. "We're going to leave very soon, but before we do, there's something else I have to tell you."

She gives me her undivided attention.

"You know how sometimes you'll see Jimmy's picture on a magazine because he's in movies?"

She nods.

"Well, the reason you see those pictures is because a lot of people know who he is, even though he doesn't know them. And that makes them curious to know all about his life. Since you're his daughter, that means they also want to know a bunch about you."

Monica wrinkles her forehead. "Why?"

"That's just the way people are. Up until today, no one else knew that you were Jimmy's daughter. Now that they do, they want to know more about you." I inhale a deep breath, willing myself to keep my voice light. "When we leave for our trip, I'm going to carry you to the car and I'm going to put a blanket over you, just like I used to when you were a baby."

She nods. "But I'm not a baby anymore."

"I know you're not, but when we go out there, they're going to try to take your picture and they're going to scream things at us. Jimmy and I don't want them to get a picture of you. So, I want you to think of your favorite song and sing it in your head until I take the blanket off, okay?"

"Okay, Mommy." My heart squeezes when I see her wrinkled forehead and sad frown. "Will they hurt me?"

I shake my head. "No. You just hold on to me and we'll be fine, I promise?"

She nods slowly, biting her bottom lip. "Can I watch cartoons now?"

A genuine smile, the first one I've had today, splits my face. "Of course you can." I click on the remote and turn on the TV.

As I set the last bag by the front door, a knock startles me. I pull the curtain to the side just a bit and see a large man with dark hair and bronzed skin. He's wearing black cargo pants and a tight black T-shirt and must stand a foot or more taller than me.

My phone rings in my back pocket. I pull it out, seeing Jimmy's name. "Hey."

"They just arrived. They should be at your door." His voice sounds as upset as mine.

"Lilah Robbie?" the guys says through the door when he spots me.

I nod.

"We're here to escort you to the airport."

"Okay," I say to Jimmy.

"I'm sorry I'm not there to help you with Monica. She must be freaked out," Jimmy says.

I back away from the door and open it, keeping myself behind the shield of the door so the reporters can't see me. The large man steps in and eyes the bags to his left.

"Is this everything?" he asks.

"Yes. I just have to get my purse and my daughter."

"I'll take this to the vehicle and come right back to escort you both." He steps out with all of our bags.

"Okay, thanks," I say in a small voice, shutting the door. "This man is intense to say the least."

I rush back to my bedroom.

"They're supposed to be. They'll keep you both safe."

"Okay, I have to get Monica ready. Talk to you soon." I'm about to remove the phone from my ear.

"Lilah?"

I stop before entering my bedroom. "Yeah."

"I'm so sorry. I'm sorry I'm not there. I'm sorry my career is uprooting your life."

My back falls to the wall. "Jimmy, you being a part of Monica's life and having to deal with the press is better than you not being in her life. Don't worry about her, I'll make sure she's fine."

Silence echoes back to me. "I know you will. Let me know as soon as you're on the plane."

"Yeah."

I hang up, wrapping my way around the fact he trusts me with his daughter, and even though she's new to his world, she's his whole world in this moment.

I put on my happy face and enter my bedroom. "Okay, kiddo, it's time to go. Are you ready for an adventure?"

"Yeah!" She slides off the bed until her feet hit the hardwood.

"Okay, you remember everything I told you?"

She nods, her mouth a thin line.

"Okay, jump up into my arms and I'm going to wrap you in a blanket. Ready?"

"Ready, Mommy."

She leaps in my arms and I pull her up against me, squeezing tightly, and place a kiss onto her blonde hair. Tears well in my eyes as I cover her with her mermaid comforter.

True to what I told Jimmy, this will be worth it for Monica to have an amazing father in her life. But what those vultures will be surprised about is I have a mama bear side and I'm not afraid to show it.

Chapter Sixty-five

JIMMY

"**I** don't care what you have to do, but figure out who the fuck leaked the info, Keane. I want someone's head on a fucking platter. Do you hear me?"

One hand clenches at my side and the other grips my phone so hard the case squeaks in protest. Adelaide snakes her arms around my waist, but I shrug her off. I'm too pissed off to accept comfort. Hot rage poisons my blood when I think of what my daughter is going through unprepared because of someone's betrayal.

"You need to calm down, James," Adelaide says.

Through the phone, Keane says something similar. "I'll get to the bottom of it. Right now, sit tight and don't do anything stupid out of anger."

I heave ragged breaths in an attempt to calm my racing heart. "I'll do what I can. Just find out who it is." I hit End and shove my phone into my pocket. "Fuck!"

"Honey, calm down. You're going to give yourself a coronary." Adelaide rubs my arm, and this time I allow her to ease my distress.

"All I can picture is Monica trying to get out of the driveway and those leeches screaming at her and trying to take her picture. She's probably terrified."

"I'm sure she's fine. Her mother is with her."

"Someone talked, that's the only way they could have found out."

"It was probably that pilot or the flight attendant. Maybe the motel guy really did recognize you." She keeps on rubbing my arm. "What did Lilah say when you spoke with her?"

Her concern for Lilah, for a change, is nice. "She was freaking out. I could tell she was almost losing it. Didn't know how to handle it or what to do."

"Well, they're on their way to a safe place now. You've done what you can. You just have to wait for the dust to settle and see what happens."

I step away from her and pace the living room. "What kind of life is this for a child? The press trying to document your every move, never having any privacy and having stories written about you or your loved ones?"

Adelaide shrugs and sits on a breakfast bar stool. "That's the reality of this business. You have to give them what they want, otherwise they'll turn on you."

"Yeah well, I'm not giving those cocksuckers my daughter. You can be sure of that. I'll pay the price through my career if that's what it takes to keep her out of magazines."

"Don't be so rash. Whatever happens, you'll figure it out. I mean maybe..." She lets her words trail as though she's baiting me.

"Maybe what?"

She slides her finger over the breakfast bar. "Maybe you let them take a picture of her and Lilah. Their interest will wane. The more you keep her hidden like some door prize, the greater lengths they'll go to."

I stop midstride and stare at her audacity to suggest that I'd put my kid in the public eye right this moment.

"Oh, stop looking at me like that. It was just a suggestion." She stands and heads back to the bedroom.

Jesus Christ, who the hell am I marrying?

* * *

My phone must've rung a hundred times today—friends and people I've worked with reaching out to see if what was reported is true, and a few members of the press whom I'm friendlier with than most. My response was the same to all of them—no comment. Anyone who needs to know about Monica already does, and for now, that's how it stays.

My phone rings later that night and I release a heavy breath when I see Lilah's number. Thank God.

"Lilah, where are you?" I stand from the couch where Adelaide and I are watching TV. Well, she is. I've been staring at the screen, running various scenarios through my head to try to figure out who told the press Monica is my daughter.

"Hey, we're at the house." Her voice is slow and languid. She must be exhausted—mentally and physically.

"How's Monica? What happened when you left your place?"

"Exactly what you think happened. They screamed questions at us, snapped a million pictures—but I had a blanket over her—blocked the driveway, and made it near impossible for us to get out."

There's a boulder in the pit of my stomach. "Is she okay?"

"She's okay. A little unsettled. She's exhausted. I put her to bed as soon as we got here."

I picture Monica curled up in a bed that's not her own after the day she's had. All because of me. Great father I am.

"I want to see her. I'll spend the week up there with you guys and we'll come up with a new plan."

"James." I turn toward Adelaide's voice behind me. "You can't be away next week. We have the interview with *People* magazine. They're doing the exclusive on our wedding, remember?"

Fuck no. I did not remember because no part of me wants any part of that. Adelaide is playing it off as a charitable act, since the money they're paying us will be given in full to charity, but it's really about the attention and the press it will get us.

"Hang on a second," I say into the phone then hit the mute button on my screen. "You're going to have to reschedule it. This is more important."

From the expression on her face, you'd think I'd slapped her. "I can't reschedule it. There's no time. The wedding is in a couple of weeks and they're not going to say, 'Oh, when you have a free day.'"

"Then you're going to have to do it by yourself. I'm sorry, but I need to be with Monica."

She huffs and stomps down the hall.

I blow out a breath. I hit the unmute button on the phone and bring it back to my ear. "Sorry about that."

"Everything okay?" There's a sad lilt to Lilah's voice.

"Yeah, fine. Let me wrap up a few things here and figure out how to get up there without the paps tracking me. I'll see you guys in a couple of days. Call me if you need anything in the meantime."

"All right." She stays on, and so do I. "Jimmy?"

"Yeah?"

"Thanks for your help today. I don't know what I would've done without you." It's hard to hear her, she's so quiet.

"We're in this together," I say, meaning every word. She got Monica out safely and I arranged to keep them safe. We've always worked well as a team.

I hang up with a heaviness weighing on my shoulders. What a shit day. I wish I could have been there to hold Monica. To whisper reassurances that her strong daddy won't let anything bad happen to her.

I'm about to go find Adelaide and try to make her see that this is something I need to do when Keane's name flashes on my phone screen. I just know my day is about to go from bad to worse.

Chapter Sixty-six

JIMMY

I step out onto the deck. Inhaling the fresh air after finding out that Lilah and Monica are safe relaxes me, as usual. "What were you able to find out?"

Keane sighs heavily. "I still don't know for sure. I've spent the day backtracking to figure out who was the first to know, and it looks like it was Kevin down at *HW Life*."

"Okay. what's the problem?" I look at the ocean, leaning on the railing.

"The problem is that he won't tell me who it is unless you agree that your first interview discussing how you knew you were the father is with him. He wants an exclusive, and he'll only tell me what he knows if you agree."

I step to the edge of the deck and soak in the orange and gold rays that paint the sky. All I can think of is Lilah might be staring at the same sunset. We're miles away from one another, but somehow it feels closer now that we're on the same side of the country.

How badly does knowing who leaked the info matter now that it's out?

I could not agree to his terms and just move on. After all, will it make any difference in the end whether or not I know?

Fuck. I *need* to know. The select few who knew about Monica are people I trust with everything. They're my team, and if one of them is spilling my business, I can't allow them to be part of my future. I'll have to discuss fatherhood at some point. Kevin might as well be the first.

"James, you still there?"

"Yeah, sorry. Just working it out in my head." I face away from the ocean and lean back against the glass railing, staring into the house. "Tell him I agree. But that it needs to be on my timeline. It could be a year from now, but yeah, he'll get the first interview I give that involves a discussion about being a father."

"You sure? I know how private you wanted to keep this."

I stare at my feet with my hand gripped around the back of my neck. "I'm sure. I need to know who I can trust."

"All right then. I'll call or text you as soon as I know something."

"Okay."

"Listen… are Lilah and Monica doing okay?" he asks.

"Thanks for asking. They're shaken up, but they're somewhere safe now."

"Glad to hear it. Talk soon."

I spend the next hour pacing the deck, and once I can't stand the silence any longer, I go to face Adelaide. I can't believe she'd think I wouldn't go be with my daughter in a time like this because of some stupid interview she's set up for us to discuss the color theme we chose for the wedding or what designer she's wearing.

Things between us have grown more and more strained in the past couple of months. I'd like to think it's because Monica entering our life means Lilah's back in my life. I'd like to think she's being this way because she's scared but thinking that feels like I'm lying to myself.

When I come in through the sliding doors, she's in the kitchen, pouring herself a glass of wine. She looks at me and sets the wine glass and bottle on the counter.

"I'm sorry," she says with sincerity. She walks over and steps into me, wrapping her arms around my waist and pressing her cheek to my chest. "This wedding has been such a big undertaking and I want everything to go perfectly for the start of our lives together. Sometimes I lose sight of what's most important. Of course you have to be with your daughter."

Slowly I bring my arms around her back and return the hug. "This is a big change for her. If I could be here with you, I would, but Monica has to come first."

She nods, her cheek rubbing up and down my chest. "I know. I get it. I really do. It's just been hard with you so absent right before our wedding."

I pull away so I can look into her eyes. "I'm sorry for that. If I could've been here helping you decide who sits where and how big to make the ice sculptures, I would have, even though all of that sounds like a form of slow torture."

She smiles. "I know. Do you forgive me?" The hope in her eyes pricks my chest.

"Of course." I place a chaste kiss on her lips. "Want to watch a movie or something until it's time to knock off?"

"Only if I can choose."

"Deal." I smile, and she heads back to the kitchen to finish pouring her glass of wine.

When we're on the couch, Adelaide leans her back into me, her feet tucked under a blanket and wine in her hand. As much as I hope Adelaide can get past her animosity with Lilah and welcome Monica into our lives with open arms, I have to remember this is new to all of us. It's uncharted territory, and I can't expect her to react like I would.

She peeks up at me, and when I bend to kiss her forehead, she smiles. I have to keep fighting. Eventually everything will even out with all of us.

* * *

I'M out on the deck, nursing a beer and staring at the stars, while I think about everything and nothing. How, in a matter of months, has everything constant in my life changed?

My phone buzzes in my hand. I unlock it and press Keane's text message.

Keane: He says the tip came in from the number 213-878-1023 via text. I'll get someone on trying to figure out whose number it is in the morning.

Shit. I'd hoped for something more solid than a vague number. I sold my soul in exchange for some magic beans.

Thanks. Talk to you in the morning.

I take another pull off my beer and stare into the darkness. I feel as though everything in my life is swirling around me and I'm in the center of the tornado, unable to grasp hold of anything as it spins me out of control.

A couple hours later, I look at the time. I should head to bed, but my head is pounding with a stress headache. I'll never be able to sleep, so I head into the main bathroom to hunt for some Advil.

Shit. There isn't any. All of the local stores are closed right now.

Then I remember Adelaide taking one on the plane the other day. Maybe there's some in her purse.

Not wanting to wake her, I trudge out to the kitchen and find her purse on the kitchen counter. I rustle through a few loose receipts and open a small bag, but it just has makeup. I take out her wallet and spot another small pouch, but to get to it, I have to take more stuff out of the purse. It's like a bunch of small purses in one. No wonder it always weighs so much. Man, women carry around way too much shit.

Opening the pouch, I finally see the bottle of Advil in the bottom corner. As I shove everything back into her purse, I find a receipt from an alteration place. Staring at the total, I blow out an annoyed breath at how much this wedding is costing us. My eyes fall to the handwritten note on the receipt.

Call 213-878-1023 when ready.

That's not Adelaide's number, since her area code is 323, which I only remember because we had a whole conversation last year about area codes when she had to get a new phone number.

Sitting on the table, in the stack of everything I took out of her purse, is the phone she's been using for anything wedding-related.

I must be losing it. No way she'd do that.

I stare at the wedding phone in my palm, my breath ragged. There's no way.

Setting my phone on the counter, I pull up Keane's text message again.

> Keane: He says the tip came in from the number 213-878-1023 via text. I'll get someone on trying to figure out whose number it is in the morning.

I compare the number from the text to the alteration receipt.

I power up Adelaide's phone and dial my cell phone number. My phone screen lights up with the number matching the alteration receipt.

Unknown Number

213-878-1023

I reject the call.

Reality knocks the wind out of me, and I gasp for air. My chest hurts and my heart pounds out a rhythm my chest can barely contain.

Adelaide tipped off the press about Monica?

Betrayal slows the blood in my veins.

I shove my phone back into my pocket and squeeze hers while my feet pound down the hall. I flick the light on in the bedroom and stalk over to the bed.

"James?" She covers her eyes with her hand. "What the hell?"

"How could you?" Seething anger colors my voice.

Her forehead scrunches, looking confused, before her gaze dips to her phone in my hand. Her face pales. "What? I—"

I throw the phone across the room and it crashes against the wall before falling to the floor. "Don't even try to deny it. How could you betray me like this?"

She sits up in bed and brings her knees to her chest, her eyes filling with tears. "I'm sorry. But I did it for you, I swear. For us!"

I turn away from her, pushing my hands through my hair, unable to stomach looking at her. "How is putting my daughter in harm's way what's best for me?"

"When we went to see her, Lilah was going on about how she didn't want her to be exposed to the Hollywood lifestyle and everything that goes with it. Her reservations about going public... I wanted you to see now rather than later that it might be better if you're not so involved in your daughter's life. At least then you wouldn't get your heart as broken. Better to do it now before you get more attached."

I whip around to face her. "What does that have to do with betraying me by contacting the press and blindsiding Lilah and Monica when you know we had a plan in place?" My fists clench at my sides. The wall is tempting right now.

She throws her arms in the air and slams them down on the mattress. There's matching anger in her eyes. "Lilah, Lilah, Lilah! God, I'm so sick of hearing that woman's name! She's taking over our lives!"

"This had nothing to do with Lilah and everything to do with Monica!"

"Are you trying to tell me a part of you doesn't still feel a connection to her?"

"We share a daughter—we will *always* be connected now. That's no excuse for you to have done this," I seethe.

She springs from the bed and walks over to me. "I did this for you." She pokes me in the chest. "You can't tell me you haven't worried that she's going to screw you over. You just wait. Once the pressure of the limelight becomes too much for her, she's going to pull away and take your daughter with her. Or maybe you'll realize it too—that this town is no place for a child—and you'll willingly let her go. Either way, you're going to be broken from it. I was just thinking of you and trying to speed up the process!"

"You weren't thinking of anyone but yourself!" My voice is raw from yelling, but I can't contain my fury. The woman I was going to marry, the woman I love betrayed me for her own gain.

Adelaide brings a hand to my chest, but I step back before she can touch me. Her eyes water but no tears fall. "You'll see. One day you'll see that I did this for you."

I shake my head. "There will no longer be a one day, Adelaide."

She blanches. "What are you saying?"

"Exactly what you think I am. I can't marry someone I can't trust. If you knew anything about me, you'd know that."

"Oh, please. We're not breaking up over this," she scoffs. When I don't respond, tears set in her eyes. "James, we cannot cancel this wedding. The invites have gone out, *People* magazine is doing an exclusive... what will people say?"

"I don't give a fuck what people say."

Her eyes widen, and she clutches her chest. "Okay, maybe it was a mistake. I see that now, but you're really going to throw us away because of it?"

I step forward and stare down at her with my jaw clenched, inhaling a deep breath to calm myself. "*You* are the one who threw us away. In fact, right now, I feel like I never even knew you."

She shakes her head. "This isn't happening."

"I'm out of here." I turn to leave, but she grabs my arm, trying to pull me to a stop. I wrench my arm out of her grasp. "I'd suggest you stay out of my way."

"So, you can forgive *her* time and time again, but I make one little mistake and that's it?"

Whirling around, I bring myself face to face with her, our noses almost touching. "Lilah had her issues, but she never broke my trust. And when she finally did? She was out of my life too."

With those parting words, I storm out of the room, grab my keys off the counter, and slam the front door behind me.

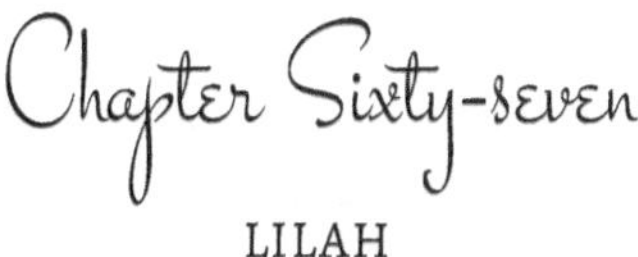

LILAH

Monica and I head upstairs to change into our swimsuits. The house Jimmy secured is large, with an indoor and outdoor pool. Monica keeps referring to it as a mansion. If she only saw the houses in Beverly Hills or Calabasas.

Part of me wonders if Jimmy intentionally got a house with two pools since he knows I still swim to relieve stress. Then I remind myself that Jimmy doesn't think of me anymore unless it has to do with our daughter.

A cool breeze comes off the lake as the end of the summer months approaches, so I've decided the outdoor pool is off-limits. Thankfully, Monica is excited to have the indoor pool all to herself.

The front doorbell rings and I freeze, one foot raised to step on the first stair.

I convince myself there's nothing to worry about. The press couldn't reach us even if they found out where we are. There's a coded gate to get on the property.

I look up at Monica, who's ahead of me on the stairs. "Kiddo, you go on and see if you can find your swimsuit in the drawers where I unpacked it. I'll be right up." I smile, hoping she doesn't notice how on edge a ringing doorbell made me.

"Okay, Mommy." She races up the stairs.

I walk over to the door, my stomach turning. I knew this would be what exposure would be like. How long will I be able to shelter her? You'd think we had GPS installed under our skin the way those photographers can find anybody they want.

I unlock the door and open it a crack, stilling before swinging the door wide open. "Jimmy, what are you doing here?"

"Sorry, I should've called. My phone is dead and I didn't have a charger."

"Are you okay?" I wave him in and shut the door before securing the locks.

"No. But I don't want to talk about it right now. I need to crash here for a bit though." His hair is going in a million directions, dark circles are visible under his eyes. Then I remember he might have been in LA, but how would I behave being hundreds of miles away knowing Monica might be in danger? I wouldn't be able to rest until she was in my arms.

"Of course, it's your place so..." I notice he has no bags with him.

He nods, his face pointed toward the floor, hand on the back of his neck. An awkward silence blankets us. I'm not sure whether he wants to be left alone or what.

"Um... Monica and I were just going to swim in the indoor pool. I don't know if you want to join us or..."

He tilts his face up and meets my concerned gaze. The spark normally present in his dark irises is missing. Clearly, something more than the worry about Monica has made him so upset. "Yeah, sure, I guess. I mean, I don't have anything with me, but I'll come watch."

I nod. "Okay, great." When we reach the bottom of the stairs, I turn and face him. "We just have to get changed. The fridge was fully stocked when we got here. I don't know if you're hungry or thirsty or anything?"

"I could use a drink. Flying always makes me thirsty."

"The kitchen is just through there." I point toward the back of the house. "Give us a few minutes."

He nods, his face a blank slate, and turns to walk away.

"Monica will be excited to see you," I call, hoping that pulls a smile.

He looks over his shoulder, a ghost of a smile on his lips, and nods.

I turn and walk up the stairs, deep in thought. Did something come out in the press that I don't know about? I've stayed away from the news and the Internet since we arrived, not interested in seeing how they're spinning this whole situation. I can only imagine the nasty headlines.

Oh God.

I stop, squeezing the bannister. There's no way they could have found out about my father... is there?

No. No way. Jimmy would have told me.

I change into my swimsuit and get Monica changed.

"Guess what?" I say after I've pulled up her straps.

"What?"

"There's a surprise for you downstairs." I fix her straps so her suit is straight.

"Really?" she says.

"Yep. Go and see."

She runs out of the room.

"Walk though, and careful on the stairs!" I call from behind her.

"Okay, Mommy!" But her feet are moving as fast as she can without technically running.

"Kitchen," I direct when she reaches the bottom of the stairs, holding her hands to her sides.

We enter the kitchen, but he's not there.

"Where, Mommy?"

"I guess we'll have to find it." I look around, wondering if he's hiding from her, but he didn't seem in the mood to play hide-and-seek. "Indoor pool."

When I heave open the door between the house and the pool, Jimmy's in one of the poolside chairs.

"Jimmy!"

He lights up as Monica pushes past me and runs toward him. "Hey, sweetie."

He scoops her up in his arms, giving her a big hug and kiss on the top of her head. When he sets her down, his eyes veer to me.

Suddenly the bikini I'm wearing feels entirely too small. It was an impulse purchase when I was feeling good about myself and the fact that I could still wear one after having a baby. But with Jimmy's gaze coasting over my bare skin, it now feels too risqué.

"Want to see what Mommy taught me?" Monica chirps, and he tips his head down to look at her.

I take a breath, no longer frozen by his attention, and walk over to a nearby table to deposit the towels I brought down with us.

"Of course," he says with affection in his voice and sits back down.

Monica runs over to me. "Mommy, do you have my goggles?"

"Sure do." I pluck them off the top of the towel and help her get them on properly, then I grab my own. "Let me get in and then you can jump in, okay?"

She nods excitedly.

Without looking at Jimmy, I dive into the deep end and swim over to where I can barely stand. "All right, kiddo."

Monica grins, slides her feet forward, and plunges into the pool. I help her get back up from under the water even though she can do it herself. She's an excellent swimmer, but I like to be careful, especially in a pool she's not familiar with.

"That was amazing!"

We both look at Jimmy, who's grinning with something like pride in his expression.

"No silly. That's not what I wanted to show you. Even babies can jump in the water," Monica scolds.

I push my lips together to keep from laughing. With her hands in mine, I pull her into the shallow end. She can't reach the bottom, so I continue to hold on to her until she nods to signal that she's ready. When I release her, she treads water then swims, tipping her head into the water as she kicks her legs behind her. A couple seconds later, she raises her head for air and repeats it all over again. When she comes up for air the next time, she reaches for me and I pull her into my arms.

"See, Jimmy? I can put my face in the water when I swim." Her dark eyes are alight with excitement and remind me so much of her father's.

"Are you sure you're only five?" Jimmy says teasingly. "You're not really eight or nine, are you?"

Monica giggles. "I'm five and a half, not five."

He chuckles and puts his hands up in a placating gesture. "My mistake."

We share a smile. I play with Monica and teach her to turn her head to take a breath rather than pulling her head right out of the water. We play around for another hour while Jimmy watches, a silent observer.

Eventually, he walks over to the edge of the pool. "Do you want to get some laps in? I can take Monica to get changed and hang out with her while you get your exercise in."

A small smile lifts the corners of my lips. He must know that I need my coping mechanism now that my entire life has been upended.

"That would great. Sure you don't mind?" I bring Monica over to the edge of the pool.

"Course not. Anything to spend some time with my girl." He smiles at Monica, who seems to preen at his attention. I lift her, and he bends down to pull her from the water.

"Yay! I don't have all my Barbies, but Mommy packed some so we can play with those."

"Super," Jimmy says with a chuckle and shares a look with me.

"Thanks," I say in a quiet voice.

He nods before leading Monica to the table and wrapping her in a large towel.

After swimming to the far edge, I pull my goggles down over my face and slip into autopilot, swimming back and forth across the length of the pool. My mind clears and a sense of calm washes over me as my muscles become fatigued.

Last night's fitful sleep doesn't allow me to swim as many laps as usual, but I feel good climbing out. I dry off and head upstairs to change. I'll shower later, so I throw my hair up in a wet messy bun and head to the kitchen.

When I enter the large open concept room, Jimmy's leaning against the kitchen island with both hands extended in front of him as though it's the only thing holding him up.

"She fell asleep five minutes ago when we were playing on the floor in her room. I wasn't sure what to do, so I just left her," he says, looking at me.

"I guess the pool tired her out. We can let her sleep for a bit. She must need it."

He nods and goes back to studying the pattern of the marble countertop.

I take a few tentative steps forward. "Jimmy, what's wrong?"

Slowly, he straightens out and faces me. "I don't even know where to start." He sucks in a breath, blows it out, his hard chest heaving with the effort. "I called off the wedding."

Shock knocks me over. I try not to show a reaction, but I know my eyes are wide and my mouth is hanging open. "Wha... what happened? Are you okay? I'm sorry."

I know I'm rambling like an idiot, but I'm processing the information that Jimmy is no longer getting married. I hate that a selfish part of me is relieved. Jimmy deserves happiness, whether it's with Adelaide or someone else.

"It was Adelaide who tipped off the press."

I stagger back and grip the countertop to steady myself. "What? Why? Why would she do that?"

The shock of the surprise doesn't last long before transforming to anger.

"She says she was doing it to show me that you wouldn't be able to handle being back in the public eye. And that I'd eventually agree it wasn't what was best for Monica. Claims she was trying to rip off the Band-Aid rather than letting it fester."

"Didn't she think of Monica?" I wish I could rein in my anger. "I can understand her wanting to fuck with me, but Monica is an innocent child!"

"I don't know what she was thinking. I feel like I never even really knew her at this point."

The devastation in his voice sets my anger aside. He doesn't deserve my ire. He had no control over her behavior.

"I can't believe she did that."

Silence falls over the room.

"So, you broke up with her?" I ask, trying to feel out whether it's just the wedding that's off—for now—or if this is a permanent thing.

"I can't be with someone I don't trust." He locks eyes with me, and my own guilt from my past makes me look away.

"I'm really sorry, Jimmy. I know you probably don't believe that, but it's true. I only ever wanted you to be happy." My hand itches to comfort him, but I can't. It'd be crossing a line I have no business crossing. So I stay where I am.

He frowns and, to my surprise, squeezes my hand. "I believe you." His voice cracks with the weight of his emotions, and he holds my hand for a second longer than comfortable.

I pull away first, unable to handle the electric current that still runs up my arm at his touch. "What are you going to do now?"

He shrugs. "Not sure. Thought I could hang out with you guys for a while if that's okay. Spend some time with Monica."

"She'd love it." Monica will love it, but for me, it's a form of slow torture—being around something I covet so badly but can never have.

"Were you able to handle things on your end?" he asks.

I nod. "I took a leave of absence from work. They were more understanding than I thought they'd be, but in all honesty, I think they're just hoping they'll get to rub elbows with you."

He chuckles.

"I'm serious. School is taken care of for Monica. I'm going to homeschool her a bit, and my neighbor will check on my house every few days."

"That's good. Listen, I'm sorry. If it weren't for me, none of this would have happened." He pushes a hand through his dark hair with a pained look.

"That's not true. If I had told you I was pregnant all those years ago, neither of us would be in this predicament. Let's just deal with the situation we're in now and do what's best for our daughter, okay?"

He glances away and nods. "Any chance I can use your phone to order some stuff to the house? I left without taking anything, and I'd rather have Amazon deliver it to the gate than go shopping."

"Yeah, I'll grab it for you. We need a few things too, if that's okay?"

"Sure thing, just let me know what you want."

I nod, then walk away to go check on Monica and grab my phone from my room.

While I know that this new arrangement is a blessing for my daughter, I'm not sure how I'll handle being around a now-single Jimmy all the time.

Chapter Sixty-eight

JIMMY

Most of the stuff I order arrives late the following day—thank you Amazon priority shipping. The first thing I do is plug my phone in to charge it. Lilah and Monica are swimming in the indoor pool before dinner, so I decide to wait to see if Monica wants to help me open the rest of the boxes.

I didn't want to watch their swimming lesson today. Not because I'm not interested in watching my daughter but because I'm too interested in watching her mother. My head is a mess, but I can still read my own attraction. When she appeared by the pool yesterday, the way the small scraps of fabric hugged her curves in all the right places didn't escape my notice and it should have. My life is complicated enough without adding anything like that to the mix.

Once my phone is charged enough, I power it on. It beeps and buzzes what seems like a million times, alerting me to a bunch of missed calls and texts about my surprise daughter. The majority of them are from Tripp and Keane. Ironically, the

DNA test came back, confirming what I already knew. Monica is my daughter.

I dial Keane first to fill him in. He thinks I'm playing a joke at first, but once he realizes I'm not fucking around, he assures me that he'll fill in everyone else on the team and advises me to stay put. He'll coordinate with Adelaide's team to figure out a joint statement to release. Amazing how we don't even have to answer questions regarding our breakup. Our people will handle it for us like it was a business venture instead of an engagement.

Once we're done, I call Tripp.

He picks up on the first ring. "Where the fuck have you been? I've been ringing you non-stop."

"Sorry, man. Shit's been crazy."

"I gather that. You and your 'love child'"—his voice is laced with sarcasm on those last two words—"are all anyone is talking about."

"Yeah well, there will be a lot more for them to talk about soon."

"What do you mean?"

I fill him in on everything that went down with Adelaide, the state of or wedding, and where I presently am.

"Didn't see that coming."

"You and me both."

"Fuck, man, that bites. I'm sorry."

"Thanks. So now I have no idea what I'm gonna do, but for the time being, I'm going to stay here with them and spend time with my daughter. She's the only bright spot in my life right now."

"Make sure you call me if you need anything."

"Will do, thanks."

"Oh, and James… you're probably going to be pissed at me for saying this, but I'm going to anyway. Be careful. I know how you are around Lilah and I get that you're hurting right now, but she's not your rebound girl."

"I appreciate your words, but the warning isn't necessary."

"If you say so." He hangs up. The man knows me way too well.

I slink back into a chair, steeple my hands, and think. My feelings about Adelaide's betrayal are so different from the what I felt after Lilah's. I don't feel a heavy loss when I think of Adelaide, only anger and betrayal. I'd like to think it's because Adelaide and I weren't meant to be. That doesn't mean that Lilah and I are though. We missed our chance at forever.

A FEW DAYS go by and I'm growing restless in this house. As nice as it is and with as many amenities as it has, a guy can only watch so many episodes of *Super Monsters* without his eyeballs bleeding.

It's a nice day out, so I join Lilah and Monica on the covered patio.

Awkward doesn't come close to describing how Lilah and I are around one another now. She's giving me a wide berth, which I appreciate, but at some point we have to bridge the gap and figure out a new normal.

"Do you guys want to go for a walk around the island? Walk down to the water and explore a bit?"

"Yah!" Monica jumps up, abandoning her coloring book.

"Are we okay to do that?" Lilah asks.

"I think as long we wear hats and sunglasses and keep to ourselves, we should be okay."

She nods, but if the way she's biting her bottom lip says anything, she's hesitant. I pretend I don't notice. "Okay."

The house sits at the top of a small hill on the island, looking down over the rooftops of a few other houses around Lake Washington. As soon as we step outside, the fresh air hits my nostrils and I inhale deeply. I can't wait to get some outdoor exercise. I've been making use of the home gym, but nothing beats the outdoors.

It's a sunny, late summer day, but since we're so close to the water, it's cooler than it would be on the mainland. Monica leads the way down our rural road with no sidewalks as if she knows where she's going.

Lilah and I awkwardly talk about the weather and the road, as though we'd rather do anything other than what we're doing. We reach the public pier and Monica sprints down the wooden planks.

"Hold up there, tiger." I scoop her up from behind, her giggles like music to my ears. "You can't get too close to the edge."

"But those kids are." She points at a couple of kids with fishing rods.

"They're fishing," I say as Lilah catches up and stands beside us.

"I wanna fish!"

Lilah chuckles, and I look from her over to Monica.

"Well, we don't have any fishing gear right now, but how about I order some and we can go one day while your mom is doing her laps in the pool?"

"Yah!"

I set her on her feet, and she walks a bit more slowly, her eyes soaking it all in.

"You know, your mom used to fish when she was little."

Lilah rolls her eyes, knowing what's coming.

"She did?" Monica looks at Lilah, her forehead wrinkled.

"She did." I nod. "We used to go to this river to fish when we were kids. But your mom was always too scared to put the worm on the hook, so I had to do it for her."

Monica's eyes widen, and I can tell she's listening intently, looking between her mom and me.

Lilah says, "Until one day Jimmy said he wouldn't help me anymore and I had to learn to do it myself."

I smile at Lilah. "So I showed her how to do it, and even though she put on a brave face and picked up the worm, when she went to put it on the hook, it squirmed, she yelped, and her hand jerked. She ended up stabbing herself with the hook."

Monica's face crumples and swings toward Lilah. "Were you okay, Mommy?"

Lilah chuckles. "Yeah. Look." She holds her thumb out to the five-year-old who is on the verge of tears. "All that's left is a little scar."

Monica pulls Lilah's hand forward and examines the thumb closely. "Did it hurt?"

Lilah nods. "It did, but not too much. Sometimes when bad things happen, all you have left to remember them is a scar. Nothing wrong with that. If you remember your mistakes, you can learn from them." She ruffles Monica's hair then turns in my direction.

Her sunglasses cover her eyes, and I wish I knew what she was feeling right now, what she could be hiding behind those sunglasses.

"Can we go fishing tomorrow?" Monica bounces on her heels, clapping.

"Maybe the day after. We'll order all the supplies and we can go later this week, sound good?"

"Yah! Can we go back home now? I'm hungry and Mommy said I could watch a movie after dinner."

"We can. Wanna ride on my shoulders on the way?"

Excitement lights her face. Totally worth the backache I'll have when we get to the house. There's no doubt I'll do anything for this girl.

Chapter Sixty-nine

LILAH

After we clean up dinner, I'm on the couch searching through Netflix for a movie appropriate for Monica. Jimmy emerges from upstairs in a pair of dark grey sweats and a fitted white T-shirt. I swallow down my arousal, noticing the way the shirt clings to his muscles and how the seams pull around his biceps.

I avert my gaze for fear of him seeing me check him out. If he knew the way I'm still drawn to him, he'd be uncomfortable.

During the past weeks, when we walk down to the pier with Monica or make dinner together, it's hard to remember that this isn't the Lilah and Jimmy show. He's here for Monica.

"You guys find anything to watch?" he asks, sitting on the far side of the couch from Monica and me.

"I think we've settled on this one," I say, pointing at the screen.

He nods and leans back into the couch, his arms extended.

I hit Play on the movie and wrap my right arm around Monica, who's cuddled into my side as she usually is when we watch a movie.

We're about five minutes into it when Monica looks up at me. "Can Jimmy sit down here with us?"

I meet his gaze over her head. "Sure, if he wants to." I keep my voice light, as if having him close won't affect me in the slightest. It shouldn't. I know that. But I might as well be put in a straitjacket with the last piece of food to keep me alive in front of me.

He smiles at Monica and slides down the couch so he's sitting in the middle. "Better?"

"Closer." Monica pats the space right beside her.

His eyes flick to mine for a second before he slides down more. Once he's where she wants him, the back of my hand is pressed against the side of his arm.

The heat from his body seeps into mine and my heartbeat picks up speed as if I'm running for my life. I'm completely rigid as I sit there pretending to watch the movie. In reality, I'm completely tuned to every muscle twitch, shift in weight, and breath that Jimmy takes.

It's maddening. My fingers itch to glide over him. I want to turn and look at him. Look in those honest eyes to see if he's struggling as much as I am. When it's enough that I want to crawl out of my skin, I shift Monica off of me.

"I have to use the bathroom." I stand.

"Want us to pause it?" Jimmy asks, sounding cool, calm, and collected—or simply completely unaffected.

"No, I'll just be a minute."

I end up taking five. Staring into the bathroom mirror, I gather the energy to be unfazed by our chemistry. *He's coming off a broken engagement. You're just his daughter's mother, you're no longer the love of his life.*

Repeating that mantra to myself, it's clear I've once again fallen for the only man who's ever held my heart.

* * *

LATER THAT NIGHT, a few hours after we've put Monica to bed and I'm in my room reading, I hear her cry out. I toss the book onto the mattress, throw off the covers, and rush across the hall.

From the glare of the nightlight, I see she's sitting up in bed.

"You okay, kiddo?" I ask, crossing the room.

She sniffles. "I had a bad dream."

I sit down on the bed and pull her into my arms. "Do you remember what it was about?" I rub her back.

She shakes her head into my chest.

"Think you can get back to sleep?" I pull away and look down at her.

She yawns, already halfway to sleepland again. Gently, I lay her back and pull the covers up to her shoulders. She snuggles into the pillow, and in under ten seconds, her breathing is deep and even.

I stand from the bed, careful not to disturb her, and tiptoe out of the room. Turning around, I admire her one more time before I close the door, backstepping into a rock-hard body.

Jimmy grips my upper arms. "It's just me," he whispers in a gravelly voice.

I whirl around, but the minute his scent hits, my nostrils I relax. The little light coming in from the window at the end of the hall reflects off his eyes. He's staring at me, and his hands have yet to leave my body. Heat from his fingertips trails a path directly to between my thighs.

I hold his gaze, my chest heaving as I suck in a breath from being in such close proximity to him.

The air between us charges, and the smallest move from either of us could ignite a flame.

Slowly his head bends down, our eyes locked, and I can't help the way my chin tips up. My chest is drawn to his, and his breathing is heavily audible in the quiet of the hallway. Our lips are inches apart, and my mouth salivates at the thought of tasting him again. Jimmy sucks in a breath as my teeth press down on my bottom lip in an attempt to keep my desire at bay.

His eyes slowly close as he inhales deeply and lets me go. I want to weep at the loss, but instead I slide down the wall a couple of feet and scoot past him into my room. I shut the door and lean back against it, trying to gather myself.

What the hell was that?

Chapter Seventy

JIMMY

Days turn into weeks, and soon my loss of Adelaide doesn't hurt. She called me a handful of times, but I think by the time it ended, we both knew there was no coming back from what she did. I realize that the truth is I only lost what I thought I had with Adelaide. The fact that she was willing to sell me out means she isn't worth my continued emotional turmoil.

A joint statement released last week declared the mutual end of our relationship and proclaimed our continued love and respect for one another. I have no respect nor love for Adelaide anymore. And I'm sick of moping around with this weight on my shoulders. So I promise myself that I'm no longer looking back, only forward.

This time with Monica has been a blessing, but it's bound to come to an end sooner or later.

"You two ready for the show?" Lilah asks as she steps onto the covered porch. She passes Monica and me our own bowls of popcorn and positions Monica between us.

According to the weather report, a storm is coming, a big one, and we'll be able to see it roll in over Lake Washington. We've parked ourselves out here, hoping for a light show. It's twilight, but dark clouds are rolling in west of us.

Monica tries to stump me with riddles while we wait, with the aid of Lilah and her cell phone.

"Wow!" Monica says in an awed whisper at the first flash of lightning in the distance.

The deep roll of thunder sounds soon after.

"Pretty cool, right?" I say to her.

"Will it do it again?" she asks, eyes wide with excitement.

"Yep. Wanna know a trick?"

She nods enthusiastically.

"If you count the seconds between the lightning strike and when you hear the thunder, that tells you how many miles away the lightning is," I say.

"Really?"

"Yep. Wanna try it on the next one?"

She smiles and nods.

Soon after, another bolt of lightning forks toward the ground.

"One, two, three, four, five, six," she rhymes off in quick fashion, her fingers also keeping count.

Lilah chuckles and kisses the top of her head. "That's a little fast, sweetie. Next time, let's try it like this... one Mississippi, two Mississippi, three Mississippi. I'll do it with you."

"Why Mississippi? That's silly." A light giggle leaves her lips.

I can't fight the smile that overtakes my face. I've grown addicted to that sound.

"Because it takes you a whole second to say the word, so it's a good way to count. You ready?" I arch a brow.

She nods, and the three of us look off in the distance and wait. Lightning flashes, then we all count out loud. "One Mississippi, two Mississippi, three Mississippi, four Mississippi, five Mississippi, six Mississippi, seven Mississippi, eight Mississippi, nine Mississippi, ten Mississippi, eleven Mississippi, twelve Mississippi, thirteen Mississippi, fourteen Mississippi, fifteen Mississippi."

A rumble of thunder sounds off in the distance and we stop counting.

"How far is it?" Monica's big, dark eyes look up at me as though I hold all the answers.

"About three miles. Every five seconds is a mile."

She shrugs and turns to look back out at the storm, her hand moving from the popcorn to her mouth without looking.

I meet Lilah's amused gaze over Monica's head, and the tension that worms its way in whenever we look at each other, ever since that night I almost kissed her in the hallway, creeps in.

We watch for another twenty minutes or so, and when I glance at Monica to count again, she's fallen asleep in her chair. I smile and reach over my daughter to grip Lilah's shoulder with a light squeeze.

She startles and turns to me with wide eyes.

I nod in Monica's direction.

Lilah smiles and meets my gaze. "Good thing I made her put on her pajamas before we came out here. I'd better get her into bed. That storm looks like it's rolling in fast now anyway."

"I'll take her up." I stand and gingerly lift Monica, careful not to wake her.

"Thanks," Lilah says. "I'll clean up out here."

I nod and carry Monica into her room and gently lay her in bed. I wiggle the covers out from under her and pull them up to her shoulders, gazing at the tiny blonde angel who owns my heart just as much as her mommy did when she was a little older than her.

Her eyes open. "Is it time to get up?" She yawns.

"Not yet. Why don't you lie back down?" I gently ease her head onto the pillow and pull the blankets up to her shoulders.

"Will you lay with me?" she asks in a sleepy voice.

"Sure thing," I whisper, lying beside her on top of the blankets.

"Do you think we can visit that place you said you and Mommy used to go to a lot?"

"Shhh, go back to sleep." I smile at her and make a mental note to speak with Lilah about having them come stay with me for a bit in Malibu so that Monica can see where I call home.

She's quiet for a minute, then her eyes open wide. "Am I allowed to call you Daddy?"

My heart stutters, tripping over a beat before picking up its regular rhythm. An indescribable elation fills me—part pride, part joy, part peace—as I gaze at my little girl with her mess of knotted blonde curls spread out across the pillow, staring up at me with big brown eyes that match my own and are filled with so much hope.

"Sweetie, I would love for you to call me Daddy." I kiss her forehead.

"Okay, thanks." A big yawn stretches her mouth so far it brings water to her eyes.

I can't help but smile at her innocence. She has no idea she's just rocked my world and given me the most precious gift.

"You'd better get to sleep. You mom will be upset if I keep you up much longer." I wink at her. It's our little joke that I'm always keeping her up past her bedtime when I tuck her in.

When I get back downstairs, Lilah is tucked into the corner of the couch in the family room, a book in her hand. She was right about the storm. Rain pelts the window, bolts of lightning illuminating the sky with thunder rumbling immediately after. She sets the book down when I sit in the chair besides the couch.

"Did she wake up?"

I sit in the chair. "Yeah. She asked me if she could call me Daddy."

Lilah's hands fly to her mouth. "She did?"

I nod, still a little dazed. "I feel like I can fucking fly right now. I can't describe it."

She raises up and hugs me. She squeezes me for a long time before she pulls away.

"What's wrong?" I brush a tear away with my thumb, cupping her cheek.

"I'm so sorry I ever kept her from you. It was the wrong thing to do. You're a good man, the best. I should've trusted all along that you would do the right thing for her and not take her away from me."

I don't know what to say to ease her guilt. I'm not going to sit here and tell her that what she did was okay and that I don't also wish she hadn't done it. "What's done is done. We can only move forward. I've forgiven you."

Another tear slips down her cheek as she sits back down on the couch. "But if I didn't, you could've had these moments with her years ago."

I don't know what to say to will her to believe that I only want to move forward and that this isn't something I want hanging over us, or even just over her regardless of what happens between us. "If we're going to move forward, we both have to forgive one another."

She nods. The way she's staring at me, fidgeting with her hands in her lap, it's easy to see that she wants to talk.

"What's up?" I ask.

"I need to talk to you about something."

My muscles tense. "Okay..."

"I can't stay here much longer. I appreciate everything you've done for us in setting us up here, but I have a job. They're understanding to a point, but I need to get back to my life."

It's not like I didn't know this was coming. I just hoped it wasn't coming so soon. Truth is, I've enjoyed the time here—

and it's not just because of Monica. It's Lilah too. As much as I hate to admit that, even if it's only to myself.

"The press will probably still be skulking around your place. There's nothing they want more than a picture of Monica."

She nods, her lips pressed into a thin line. "I know. But we can't hide out forever. At some point, we're going to have to deal with the reality of who her dad is in this world."

I push a hand through my hair. I hate that my daughter has to deal with this shit. Why can't I just do my job while the world leaves my offspring out of it? But Lilah is right. There's only so long we can hide from reality. At some point, they're going to get their shot and it'll be plastered all over every magazine.

"We're going to need to come up with some kind of plan. I'm not comfortable with the two of you being sitting ducks in your house. There's no telling how far they'll go, and I need to know you're both safe."

She opens her mouth, but a big flash lights up the room, followed by a large crackle. The house is plunged into darkness.

"Shit, that sounded like a transformer." I pull my phone from my pocket and turn on the flashlight.

"I think I saw some matches in one of the drawers," Lilah says. "We can light some candles."

I keep the light aimed at the floor so it's not in her face and see her rise up off the couch.

"Can you light my way? I left my phone upstairs."

"Sure thing." I follow her into the kitchen and shine the light on the drawer she's digging through. When she pulls something out, I bring the flashlight up to see what it is but shine the light in her face by accident.

"Ack!" She brings her hand up to shield her eyes and laughs.

"Oh my God, I'm sorry." I laugh. "Are you okay?"

"Yeah, but all I'm seeing are spots now."

"Here, let me help you." I take her free hand and gently clasp my hand around hers.

I exhale a deep breath. The feeling of her hand in mine is so familiar and comforting in a way that Adelaide's never was. Our hands fit so perfectly, as if they were made for one another. Her small hand twitches in mine and I squeeze, wondering if she may be thinking the same thing as I am.

"Come on," I say, my voice raspy, and lead her back to the couch.

She follows me, and though I'm trying to play off the fact, I'm hyperaware of her proximity. That weird vibe between us for the past couple of weeks seems to be concentrated in the spot where we're touching.

"Here you go." I align her with the spot on the couch. "Can you see enough now?"

"Yeah, a little better. I have that annoying line in my vision, but it's fading a bit."

"Okay good."

I use my flashlight to find all the candles in the room and light them. There are three, and though it's a good-sized room, it's enough light to cast a yellow glow over everything. I sit down in the chair again, close enough that our feet almost touch.

"So, where were we?" I ask, not wanting to have this conversation but knowing it's inevitable.

"You were talking about security."

"Right. I want to make sure you're both safe, so as much as I know you'll hate the idea, I'm hiring someone to take you to and from work and school and to keep an eye on the house to make sure no one tries to harass you. At least for the time being until we can figure out something more permanent."

"You keep saying the two of us." Her voice is low and unsure.

"What?"

"You only have to worry about Monica." She must be able to see properly again, because her eyes flick up and hold my attention.

"You're her mother. Of course I want to make sure you're safe." I'm trying to lie, but I taste the dishonesty on my tongue.

She's quiet for a minute, holding my gaze. "Is that the only reason?"

Lightning lights up the room for a second, but in that second, fear and uncertainty cloud her eyes.

I'm quiet for a beat as my head wars with my heart. I should say yes. The smart thing to do here is say yes, but in this moment, it also feels like the hardest thing in the world to do.

"No, it's not."

Her chest lifts, diverting my eyes for a moment. Slowly, I take her hand, pulling her off the couch until she's standing in front of me.

"Jimmy, what are you doing?" she whispers.

My hands grip her sides and I gently pull her forward, giving her plenty of time to push me away if she chooses. But she doesn't. Thank God. Instead she follows my lead and rests her knees on either side of my lap in the center of the chair, letting her weight fall forward.

I lean in and inhale her scent. I'm not sure I realized until this moment how much I've missed her. She trembles and sucks in another breath.

She always uses the best-smelling shampoo. All those years ago, when her scent finally died off my bedding, I remember being so conflicted—one part of me was happy to no longer be tortured with her scent, and the other was devastated I'd never smell it again.

After a minute, I lean back into the chair and take her in. The way the candlelight kisses her face reminds me of the Lilah after rehab. She's beautiful—inside and out—healthy and gazing down at me as though I'm her everything.

She's silent, sitting back and allowing me the pleasure. She's not fidgeting like she has been lately. She knows I'm hers. She feels what I do.

But it wasn't until I put a voice to my emotions that I realized how much I need to keep her safe. Why her safety is as important as Monica's. The pressure inside me releases, and I finally admit to myself that my concern isn't just because she's Monica's mother.

It's because she's Lilah.

My Lilah.

No matter the time and distance and circumstances that kept us apart, some things never change. And what we mean to one another is one of those things.

I wind my hand around her neck, drawing her face toward mine. Her plump lips part ever so slightly, and my dick hardens at the anticipation of having her lips again.

I rest my forehead to hers and we breathe and exist together for a minute. No words are needed, they never were. We speak to one another on a soul-deep level. Even if I were blind, I'd know she wants me as badly as I want her.

Our past is as tightly wound as our future is now.

To outsiders, this isn't the smartest decision we could make. Our entire life, we've had a turbulent relationship, but as I did years ago, I'm not listening to anything other than my heart. A newfound love, with respect and trust, is growing out of our control. We have no choice but to explore it because this time, we could really have a future.

"If we do this, if we cross this line, we leave the past behind. We start over," I murmur against her lips.

Her chest heaves with her heavy breaths, and she leans in an inch more and her lips press to mine.

My reaction is fierce and immediate. I growl into her mouth and slide my tongue along the seam of her lips. She parts them for me, and the taste of her rushes in on an ocean of conflicting emotions. Ever so slowly, we find that rhythm and the sting of betrayal fades and all I taste is her want and need that matches my own.

I grind my hips up. She gasps as my hard length pushes against the center of her thin yoga pants. Our kiss is deep and languid, and I slide one hand into her hair while the other glides along her thigh, up the side of her waist until my thumb rests under her breast. My mouth trails a path from her lips down her neck to her collarbone.

She pants, looking down at me with half-lidded eyes. Using the seam of her T-shirt, I pull it up and over her head, then I slide my hands around to undo the clasp on her bra. Lilah lets the straps slide down her arms, and the delicate fabric falls to the floor, exposing her to me.

If I were a dog, my tongue would be hanging out, dripping with saliva.

I admire the beauty before me and grasp her breasts, squeezing and tugging on her nipples until a harsh moan escapes her throat. Leaning forward, I suck one of her rigid peaks into my mouth and twirl my tongue around the other. Her hand flies into my hair and yanks at my strands. The sharp stab of pain only arouses me further. I growl and pull her nipple between my teeth.

She gasps and I sooth the pain with my tongue. Her hands loosen, and her head falls back with a moan. The need to taste and lick and devour her escalates.

I forgot how addictive she is, and it's too late. I've sampled the fruit and the sweet nectar runs through my veins. I'm finished.

"Jimmy..."

"Shh, I'm taking you upstairs."

She doesn't protest when I stand, lifting her weight with me. She wraps her legs around my waist, and I head for the staircase. Our eyes lock when I reach the top hallway, and somehow, I manage to make it to the doorway of my bedroom without hitting any walls.

"Last chance to back out."

She doesn't hesitate, taking my mouth. I step into the room and softly close the door, fumbling until I find the lock and click it into place. Lilah eases her legs from around my waist, and she slides down my body until her feet hit the floor.

In the middle of complete darkness, with the absence of candles, I only catch the mixture of vulnerability and need in her big blue eyes when lightning flashes outside the window. Thunder sounds and rain whips against the house while we breathe each other in.

The storm outside echoes the one brewing inside me. Emotions swirl like a tornado in my gut, grinding against one another and mixing with the desire this woman provokes. Has always provoked.

"Go get on the bed. I'm going to grab some candles from downstairs." She reaches for me, but I gently take her wrists and place her arms at her side. "I have to see you." I lean in and kiss her.

When I return with the candles, she's nowhere to be found. I place the candles across the room from one another and lock the door.

"Lilah?"

She steps out of the bathroom wearing light-colored lace panties, looking like my wet dream. Her wavy blonde hair hangs down her chest, playing peek-a-boo with her full breasts.

"You're even more gorgeous than I remember."

Motherhood did wonderful things for her body. She's still slender, but her curves are amplified, and I fight the urge to tie her up to explore all of her.

I step up to her and lightly run my hands from her hips up her sides until my thumbs rest under her breasts. She shivers, and her nipples harden further.

She brings her hands up under my T-shirt, running her palms over my hard chest. I reach back with one hand and tug my shirt off over my head. Lilah licks her lips before sprinkling chaste kisses on my chest. My hands push into her hair, and I bend my head to place a kiss on top of her head.

My balls throb with the need to claim her, but no matter if I'm barely hanging on after, I have to see her pleasure first. Tugging lightly on her hair, I pull her away from my chest and lead her to the bed. She crawls on, giving me a view that will star in my jerk-off sessions for the next month, then turns around and lies on her back. I crawl up over her, licking and kissing and biting my way up her inner thigh, trailing my tongue over the lace at her center.

She moans, and I glance up to see her eyes closed and she's palming her breasts. I add more pressure with my tongue. Though I know she's enjoying it, it's not enough to get her where she needs to be.

Hooking my fingers on either side of her underwear, I drag them down her legs and toss the panties aside. When I use my hands to part her thighs, she lets me, gazing down with hooded eyes that beg me to give her what she needs.

I'll give her everything I've got.

With the first swipe of my tongue up her center, her hips bolt off the bed and she releases a small cry. Grinning, I use my hands to keep her hips planted on the mattress. She tastes like heaven. Like home.

I tease her opening with my tongue, and her hand flies down to grip my hair. I suck on her clit. and she pulls harder on my hair until I increase my pace. My finger skims her entrance, teasing her until she takes matters in her own hands and grinds against my face. I ease my finger inside her and groan from how tight she is.

Fuck, she's going to squeeze my cock like a fist.

Her breathing becomes labored and she's biting on her lip, wriggling around the bed, voicing her pleasure in soft moans and strangled screams. Her insides pulse against my finger with her climax and her hand falls from my head to the sheets, fisting them instead. I continue to flick my tongue against her sensitive nub and her legs fall open, her toes curling.

Eventually, her orgasm wanes, and I slow the friction with my tongue until she lies flat on the mattress, panting and sated. My finger falls out, and I spread her wetness over her nipples before I lap it up with my tongue.

She moans as though she can't take anymore, but I know her. She can.

"Oh my God," she finds her voice. "That was... otherworldly."

I chuckle and lie on my side, looking down at her. My erection strains the confines of my pants and pokes into her side.

"Jimmy..." She rolls onto her side, her hand falling to my cheek.

"Shhh. Not now." I don't want to talk about where this is going or anything else. I just want to be with her.

I kiss her, and her tongue seeks mine, her hand sliding into the back of my hair until I roll onto my back. She rises over me and works her way down my chest, kissing and licking the dips and ridges of my muscles until she reaches the waistband of my athletic pants. Wasting no time, she grabs both sides and slides them, along with my boxer briefs, down and off my legs. My hard length springs free and arches toward my belly button.

She crawls back up, her knees on either side of my waist, licking her lips. My dick twitches, and she shoots me a devilish smile.

Her hand grips the base of my cock, and a growl rips out of my throat. She slowly brings her head down, eyes locked with mine, and slides her tongue from base to tip. If this wasn't our first time in years, I'd grip her head and push her down onto my cock. Instead, I resist the urge, lying back and letting her take the control.

Her warm, wet mouth engulfs the head and sucks, her tongue swirling. She alternates the actions until I'm bucking into her mouth and a minute from coming.

"I need to be inside you." I pull her up by under her arms, sliding her along the length of my body.

Lilah yelps and settles her hands on my chest. I lean my head up to lick the underside of her breast, and her eyes close.

"I'm clean, you?" I ask in a gruff voice.

The only way I know I am is because Adelaide insisted we continue to use condoms even though she was on birth control. She didn't want any accidents ruining all our plans. So though I'm fully stocked in condoms at home in Malibu, I didn't bring any here.

Lilah nods, biting her bottom lip and looking sheepish. But that's not what I'm focused on, because she knows what it does to me when she bites her bottom lip. I grip her hips to adjust her into the right spot over me.

"Wait... it's been a long time though."

It's then I realize she's not biting her lip to get the reaction out of me. She's biting her lip because she's nervous.

"Like, a really long time. Not since we..."

Then I grasp the meaning of her words. If she thought her confession that she hasn't been with anyone since me all those years ago would put me off, she's wrong. It has the exact opposite effect.

"Fuck, baby. I almost blew my load right there." I roughly grip the back of her head and pull her down to meet my lips.

Our tongues tangle desperately. I bite her full bottom lip and she does the same before she positions me at her entrance.

"Don't worry, I'm on the pill to regulate my periods."

I groan when she runs the head of my cock through her slippery folds. Then slowly, inch by inch, she sinks down until I'm fully seated inside her.

Our gazes lock as she lifts her hips slowly then pushes down again. I can't help the groan that leaves my lips at the feeling of her squeezing me. She keeps the same pace and her tits sway with the movement, begging to be sucked.

I pull her toward me and suck on a nipple, pounding into her from below. Her neck arches back and I run my tongue along it, squeezing her nipple between my thumb and forefinger.

My balls tighten up, and the tingling sensation ignites at the base of my spine. I'm not going to be able to hold off much longer.

I unwrap my arm from around her waist and let her sit back up so I can bring my thumb to her clit while she grinds her pelvis into me. Lilah's eyes roll back in her head and her back arches while she futilely tries to keep her moans of satisfaction in check.

She cries out as her orgasm squeezes my cock, her movements jerky, and I fall over the edge with her. She milks my cock until I have nothing left to give and she collapses on my chest.

Our sweaty chests stick together while we lie there, both trying to catch our breath. Eventually she rolls off of me and onto her back in an exhausted heap. I roll to my side and kiss her temple, then I position us so my chest meets her back.

The last thing I remember thinking as my eyes flutter shut is I feel more like myself in this moment than I have in years.

That has to mean something.

Chapter Seventy-one

LILAH

I'm so stupid. It's like I'm destined to make poor decisions when it comes to Jimmy.

I shake my head, arranging the last few items in my suitcase. Monica is downstairs watching TV, so she'll probably be distracted for another twenty minutes.

"What are you doing?"

I gasp and spin around to the doorway, my hand over my heart. "Oh my God, you scared me." I'm gasping for breath and my heart rate is through the roof.

Jimmy eyes the suitcase and meets my gaze. "Going somewhere?"

"I told you yesterday that I have to get back to my real life. I'm going to lose my job if I don't."

Hurt flashes in his eyes before he steps into the room. "You're taking Monica back to Kansas?"

I turn around and shuffle things around in my suitcase so that they'll fit. "She needs to get back to her regular routine. It's not good for her to be out of it for this long."

He steps beside me and crosses his arms. "Were you trying to sneak out without saying goodbye?"

I rear back and look at him. "Of course not. I'd never take Monica without letting her say goodbye to you."

"And what about you? Would you say goodbye?"

I turn from him and pull the top up over my suitcase to zip it closed.

How does he expect me to respond to that question? Last night was a mistake. Well, it's not like I regret it. I'll cherish the memory, like I do all the other times with Jimmy, but I'm not a free bird sailing through life to do whatever I want now.

I'm a mother.

And Jimmy is a father.

We're parents and have a responsibility to our daughter.

Which means things have the potential to get messy between us if we start blurring lines.

The fallout will only land on our daughter's shoulders, and that's unacceptable. After everything that's happened between us, I'm sure there's no way for Jimmy to ever really forgive me. Besides, he's just off a failed relationship. That's what people do—they rebound.

"Lilah, what happened last night—"

"Was a mistake," I finish for him.

"Is that how you really feel?" He brushes a piece of my hair behind my shoulder, and I shrink away from his touch.

Not because I don't want to feel his skin touch mine, but because I want his skin to touch mine too much.

"Look, you're just coming off a huge breakup and you're understandably confused and looking to push the pain away. I get it. But I shouldn't have taken advantage of your situation by jumping into bed with you. It only complicates things."

"I'm not some brokenhearted teenage boy. You hardly took advantage of me. I wanted you every bit as much as you did me. We've been circling around our sexual tension for weeks now. You're lying to yourself if you think otherwise."

I zip the suitcase and drag it off the bed. "We have a plane to catch."

"You already booked a flight?" His eyes narrow.

"Yes, and it leaves in a few hours, so you should go say goodbye to Monica."

He steps forward so that we're only a few inches apart and I'm forced to tilt my head back to see him.

"I'll book you a private flight. It will be a zoo if you go public."

I nod, another tally to what I owe this man.

"When will I see you guys again?" he asks.

The "you guys" in that statement doesn't escape my notice. "You can see Monica whenever you like. Just give me a heads-up."

His lips press into a thin line and he takes the suitcase from me. "I'll carry this down the stairs for you."

"Thanks." Tears well up in my eyes for some reason I can't pinpoint. This is what's best for all of us.

So why does him walking out the door feel so final?

* * *

"ARE you excited to see your dad tonight?"

It's been a week since we left Mercer Island. Jimmy's decided to visit. He'll watch Monica while I'm at work tomorrow since it's Saturday.

"He said that we can go to a movie tomorrow when you're at work!"

"That's great, kiddo. Keep eating your cereal. I'm going to go finish getting dressed."

I walk out of the kitchen, unable to keep from glancing out the front window before I head to my bedroom. Seth, the security guy Jimmy hired stands at the bottom of the stairs like he does every morning, making it known to the few lone reporters still hanging out at the end of my driveway that they're not welcome.

Seth even drives us around and stands post outside my work. My boss wasn't too happy about it, but overall, he's been pretty understanding about the whole thing. At least business has picked up. Everyone wants to get their teeth cleaned by James Crawford's baby mama. I've had more than a few awkward moments with patients in the chair since I returned. It's like people think I'm going to divulge my darkest secrets to them while I'm scraping their teeth.

The girls at work have been great though. Once they figured out that I used to model, they pulled up a million pictures of some of my old work. I've tried to assure them that my life was anything but glamorous back then, but they don't believe me.

I glance in the kitchen, and though Monica sits with her head propped on her hand, staring out the back window, she's chewing.

After getting dressed, I'm putting toothpaste on Monica's toothbrush for her when there's a knock at the front door. I startle, thinking it must be someone from the press, but Seth is out there, so there's no way.

"You brush your teeth, kiddo. I'm going to go see who that is."

"Okay, Mommy," she mumbles around the toothbrush she's already shoved into her mouth.

I walk up the hallway then peek out the side window to see Jimmy standing on the front porch, looking sexier than ever in a pair of worn jeans and a grey Henley that shows off his strong physique.

"What is he doing here?" I murmur, caught off guard.

I look down at myself, wishing I wasn't wearing scrubs and my hair thrown up in a ponytail. My cheeks heat instantly when I remember his mouth on my breasts only last week. Our entire night has been on repeat in my head like a teenager's first kiss.

Inhaling a deep breath, I swing the door open and plaster on my best I'm-not-remembering-how-we-rocked-each-other's-worlds-last-week smile. "Hey, what are you doing here?"

"Thought I'd surprise you guys."

There he goes with the "you guys" again.

He steps into the house, and I close the door against the few prying eyes.

"Well, Monica will be excited to see you."

"What about her mom?" He spears me with the full force of his dark gaze, and it's clear I'm not the only one who's been strolling down memory lane since we parted.

Before I can answer, Monica bounds down the hall. "Daddy!"

"Hey, sweetie." He lowers himself to one knee and scoops her up when she reaches him. "How's the best girl in the world?"

She giggles and gives him a kiss on the cheek. "You're silly."

"We were just about to leave in a few minutes," I say.

"I thought I'd drop you lovely ladies off at your destinations this morning. Seth can follow in his car."

"Yay!" Monica cheers.

Jimmy sets her down and looks at me, though I can't protest now.

"Okay, let me grab our stuff and we can leave."

I make myself busy gathering our lunches and my purse, double-checking that I have everything I need, then we all head out to Jimmy's car—a dark SUV not unlike the one Seth has been driving us around in. I'm quiet as we make our way to the school while Jimmy and Monica chat away.

When we reach the school, I hop out of the vehicle. "I'll take her. I'm not sure the rest of the moms are ready for the likes of you just yet."

Jimmy nods, says his goodbyes to Monica, and tells her he'll see her after school.

I guess we have plans I'm not aware of.

Before we slept together, I wouldn't have minded, but now I can't help but feel awkward around him, which is ironic because it's only due to the fact that I want him even *more*. Like I have permission to want him now with Adelaide out of the picture. So why do I want to see him *less*?

A minute later, I'm back in the SUV and the air hangs heavy with unspoken words.

"So, what are you going to do all day?" I ask as he pulls away from the curb.

He shrugs. "Probably get settled in my new place."

My back straightens. "What place?"

"I got a place nearby so that I could be around more."

While I don't have any issue with him wanting to be around Monica more, I can't deny that he's taken me by surprise. "Where is it?"

"It's in the next county over. It was the only gated place I could find so the press wouldn't be using zoom lenses to look in twenty-four seven."

"What about your life in LA?"

He turns onto the street where the dental office is located. "I told Keane I won't be taking on any jobs for at least another six months. My only job right now is to spend as much time as I can building a relationship with my daughter."

I shift in my seat. "Monica will be really excited to hear that you're going to be so close."

"And what about her mom?" He stops the car in front of my work.

With a sigh, I look at him. "Jimmy, we already talked about this."

He shakes his head. "No, you talked, and I listened."

"I thought we were on the same page?"

"I let you go last week because it was obvious you were freaking out and needed time to process. I didn't want to push. The last thing I want is to stress you out and have you…"

We both know he was going to say use.

"You don't have to treat me with kid gloves."

He removes his hands from the steering wheel and puts them up in a placating gesture. "Believe me, I needed the time to think too. You weren't the only one who needed to put things into perspective."

I glance at the dental office. "I have to get to work."

"Wait." Jimmy grabs my hand before I can open the door. A thousand watts of electricity races from my palm, up my arm, and straight to my heart. "There's still something between us. You know it as well as I do."

I press my lips together in an attempt not to agree with him.

He shakes his head and grins. "Always so stubborn."

I roll my eyes.

"Are you trying to say I'm wrong?" he asks.

"I'm saying I need to get into work."

"Do I need to prove it to you?" He leans in closer, and my gaze flicks to his lips. "I can if you want." His husky voice makes my thighs clench together.

"I have to go." But my voice has lost all its fight and we both know it.

"Whatever we used to have is still there, but... it's different now." He leans in a little more. "I want to explore what that might be."

And now my traitorous body leans in too.

"In secret. We don't have to let anyone, including our daughter, know until we feel the time is right." He moves closer until our lips are only an inch apart. "What do you say?"

I don't say anything though, because he bridges the distance and his lips are on mine. His tongue runs against the seam of my lips. And what do I do? I open for him. Then our tongues are coasting over one another's and his hand is in my hair and I'm lost—oblivious to the outside world and all the reasons why this is a bad idea.

He pulls away with a grin. "Think about it."

He winks, and anger replaces my desire. Anger at him. At myself for being so weak and giving in so fast.

I huff, grab my purse and my lunch from my feet, and hop out of the vehicle, slamming the door.

"Is that James Crawford?" Mindy asks outside the dental office doors.

"In all his glory," I grumble and open the door before heading to the back to erase him from my thoughts.

Which proves impossible since I'm hard-pressed to find any reason why I should say no to his proposal of giving us a try in secret.

Chapter Seventy-two

JIMMY

On Saturday night, I decide to flip the regular routine and have Lilah come over to the place I'm renting to pick up Monica. She reluctantly agrees. She's been skittish since I dropped her off at work yesterday, making sure to never be alone with me.

I'm not trying to pressure her into starting something—I won't do that to her. But we'd both be liars if we said there was nothing between us. Even before we slept together, there was *something* there. I think it's lived inside me since the day I met her. I tried to convince myself over the past six years that she was addicted to drugs and I was addicted to fixing her. Hell, a psychologist I saw right after, due to Tripp's urging, suggested it's common for a kid from an abusive family to be the fixer in a relationship.

Maybe that was part of it back when Lilah couldn't stay sober for even one day, when she made bad decision after bad decision. But the Lilah then and the Lilah now are worlds apart. She's independent, her head's on straight. She doesn't need me, but I do think I make her happy. If we could finally get our shit together, what a life we could live.

I get a notification they've let Lilah through the gate, and a minute later, there's a knock on the door.

"Mommy!" Monica races from the playroom to the front door and whips it open. Before Lilah can step inside, Monica's arms are wrapped around her mom's middle.

"Hey, kiddo." Lilah kisses the top of her blonde mop of hair. "Did you have fun today?"

Monica steps back and bounces up and down. "Yeah! There's a playroom here and it has all my favorite things! And there's this other room that's like a movie theatre with a big screen and these comfy chairs that come out and you put your feet up."

"Wow, sounds like this place has everything." She steps in and glances at me with a strained smile.

For the first time since I've been in Monica's life, I wonder if I went overboard. I'm not trying to show up Lilah, and I hope she doesn't see it that way.

"Dinner's almost ready," I say to her. "I'm just waiting for the baked potatoes to finish cooking on the barbecue."

"Great." She sets her purse on the circular table in the center of the foyer.

I lean down to eye level with Monica. "Do you want to show your mom around the place?"

"Yah! C'mom, Mommy!" Monica grabs Lilah's hand and drags her through the foyer.

I head back to the kitchen to put the finishing touches on dinner. I overhear Monica giving her the tour before they head upstairs.

Fifteen minutes later, I walk over to the intercom and press the button that will broadcast through the entire house. "Dinner's ready, ladies."

When I finish setting the condiments on the table, they stroll in hand in hand, and I love how natural this feels. It reminds me of when Lilah came out of rehab and we spent a lot of time at my place in Malibu, just doing regular people stuff—no red carpets, no sets, no interviews. Just quality time with the person I cared about. And that's what it feels like now. Only now there are two people I care about.

"I hope steak is okay?"

Lilah helps Monica get seated and sits beside her. I sit down directly across from Lilah.

"Looks great, Jimmy. I see you haven't lost your culinary skills." Lilah smiles at me and cuts a small piece of steak off the one on her plate for Monica, then she cuts Monica's into smaller pieces.

"Some things never change." I meet her gaze, and it's clear she understands I'm referring to more than just my cooking abilities.

She clears her throat and diverts her attention to Monica, asking what she did with her day. The rest of dinner is spent joking around with Monica and sharing a few stories from our youth—the ones we can tell anyway.

Earlier in the day, I promised Monica that we could watch a movie, so I get everything set up in the home theatre. Once Monica is settled into her seat, I stand.

"I'm going to go pop some popcorn," I say.

"I'll help you," Lilah says. "Kiddo, we'll be back in a few minutes, okay?"

She nods, transfixed by the screen filled with colorful characters singing and dancing.

The air changes when we reach the kitchen.

"When Monica was showing me around, she showed me *her* bedroom. Mentioned it was where she'd sleep when she slept over."

I look at her over my shoulder, tossing the popcorn into the microwave. "I meant to talk to you first. I was excited and it slipped out. I'm sorry." I punch the numbers on the microwave's keypad, hit Start, and lean against the counter, facing her.

She's leaning against the island with her arms crossed. She looks so much like the woman I fell in love with all those years ago—before Hollywood beat everything that was special out of her. She's fresh-faced and healthy-looking and her light pink lounge wear sets off the rosy tone in her cheeks. I'm trying my best not to notice how those clothes hug her curves, even though my hands are tingling with the desire to run my palms over them.

"It's okay. I figured as much. I guess... I didn't really think of the fact that you'd be spending time with her on your own and I'd be back at my place... alone." Her voice takes on a sad note.

It's now or never. I'm putting my cards on the table with no regrets. I step forward and run my thumb over her cheek. "Who said anything about you being alone? If you want to be here too, you can be. I thought I made that clear when I dropped you off at work yesterday?"

She holds my gaze for a minute and her pupils dilate, her breaths choppier. "I don't want to intrude."

A small chuckle escapes. "You are not intruding."

"How long are you planning on staying in Kansas?" she asks, her voice soft.

"As long as it takes."

Her eyes widen. "As long as what takes?"

Without responding, I lean in slowly until our lips are a breath apart.

The microwave beeps, breaking the spell.

She blinks a couple of times and steps back. With a sigh, I turn and head back to the microwave.

"We need to talk about... all this when Monica's not around."

Opening a cupboard door, I pull down a bowl and place it on the counter. "I look forward to that conversation."

She doesn't say anything, heading back to the theatre room to join our daughter.

ONCE AGAIN, Monica falls asleep during the movie and I convince Lilah to let her spend the night, so I carry Monica up to the bedroom then join Lilah in the family room. She's sitting on the couch, fiddling with her hands in her lap. Clearly, she's nervous about the conversation she knows is coming, and though I don't want to push her into anything she's not comfortable with, I get the feeling I need to apply a little pressure to get her to open up.

I sit on the coffee table to be across from her.

She glances up, and a deep line lies between her eyebrows. "Jimmy, what are we doing?"

I sigh and take her hands, my elbows on my knees. "I think the better question is what do we want to do."

She swallows and tries to slip her hands from mine, but I squeeze them and don't let her retreat. Sooner or later, this conversation has to happen.

"Look, Lilah, I think we can both agree that there's still something between us. If there wasn't, last week never would've happened."

She looks at her lap, refusing to meet my gaze. "But you were just engaged not that long ago. I can't..." She swallows hard, and her eyes shimmer. "I can't be a rebound for you."

A mixture of anger and hurt whirl inside me. How could she ever think she's my rebound? "In what universe do you think you could ever be a rebound to me? Rebounds are supposed to be easy and uncomplicated, and nothing about us has ever been either of those things. Now that we share a daughter, that's even more true. You would literally be the worst person for me to rebound with—if that's what I was looking for."

"What are you looking for?" she whispers.

"I can't make any promises. Neither of us can. I just want to explore whatever this is between us."

"What exactly does that mean? You want to sleep together again?"

I chuckle even if it's bad timing. "I'd be a liar if I said that's not on my top five list of things I'd like to do with you, but there's a list of more."

A small smile tilts the corners of her mouth. Finally. "Ditto." She blushes and looks back down at her hands.

I bend my head down so that she's forced to look me in the eye. "Did you just admit that you want to sleep with me again?" I ask with a grin.

She chuckles and pushes me in the shoulder. "Stop."

I laugh and take one of her hands, stroking the underside with my thumb. "Listen, I agree that we shouldn't let Monica think we're together at this point. I don't want to confuse her if we decide we're better as friends. But the way I see it, there's really no option. There's still something between us, and it's going to be there regardless of whether we decide to ignore it and date other people or not. So let's explore what it is, what it means, and at least then we'll know. And if we decide we're better off just as friends and co-parents, it won't be hanging over our heads as some unsettled issue."

She's quiet for a minute, but I resist the urge to try to convince her further. It's her time to come to me now.

"I'm not sure I can go through losing you again," she whispers, and the pained look on her face nearly guts me.

I squeeze her hand. "I'm hoping you won't have to."

She inhales a shaky breath and closes her eyes before she nods.

"Was that a yes?" I ask, trying not to be too hopeful in case I'm wrong.

"That's a yes. Let's try, let's see what this is that's still between us."

I smile so wide it hurts my cheeks and it makes her smile, then I embrace her, soaking in the feeling of her in my arms as truly mine. I'm elated that we're going to try again. She returns the hug, clinging to my T-shirt as if I might disappear.

When we pull apart, her eyes still hold a small amount of trepidation, but I vow to make her see that she's made the right decision. She never did trust herself enough.

Chapter Seventy-three

LILAH

Tonight is the first night I'll be staying at Jimmy's house. For the past two weeks, we've spent nights talking on the back porch after Monica has gone to bed.

Was I so naïve to not realize I was missing a piece of myself these past six years? Having him back in my life, I feel more whole. That's even with the fear of getting comfortable in something new because just as I was devastated six years ago, this time will be worse. Especially since he'll always have a starring role in Monica's life.

Monica is excited to stay at her dad's, carrying on and on about my room being right by hers just like in Lake Washington.

The truth is, neither Jimmy nor I have brought up the sleeping arrangements for tonight, so I'm just going to go with the flow. The most we've done in the past couple of weeks is kiss, so it's not a foregone conclusion that we'll be sharing a bed.

But even the kissing turns me into a giddy, stars-in-her-eyes high school girl.

My gut twists as the night progresses. With each minute, it ramps up a notch. We finish teaching Monica Go Fish, and from the way her head is laying on the table, we've exhausted her.

"Kiddo, I think it's time for you to get to bed," I say.

"No! Dance party first."

Jimmy looks across the table a little sheepishly. "I promised her we could have a dance party with you when you got home."

I shake my head and chuckle. "Oh, you did, did you?"

"Can we, Mommy?" Monica's practically vibrating off her seat, her sleepiness invisible now.

"Tell you what? How about we each get to pick a song, then it's bedtime?"

"Yay!" She slides off the chair and runs into the adjoining family room. "We can dance here."

I groan and push out my chair, following her. Jimmy's close behind.

"Ladies first, Mommy. What will it be?" Jimmy's holding his phone and clicks the on button of a Bose Bluetooth speaker.

I rack my brain and of course can't think of anything on the spot, so I name the first song that comes to mind that Monica might enjoy dancing to. "'Despacito.'"

He shakes his head at me. "Bieber? Really?"

I chuckle. "Monica likes this song, don't you, kiddo?"

"Yah! Beaver, beaver!"

Jimmy laughs at her pronunciation and cues up the song. By the end, we're all dancing around and singing at the top of our lungs, mumbling unintelligible Spanish words. When the last note sounds, we collapse in a heap on the couch, laughing at ourselves.

"Okay, sweetie. What song do you want?" he asks Monica.

"'Baby Shark'!"

Inwardly I groan because, oh my God, if I have to listen to this song one more time... but outwardly I smile and share a look with Jimmy. He's obviously been introduced to the repetitive nature of the song already.

"'Baby Shark' it is."

The song starts and we all sing along. Since Jimmy isn't yet familiar with all the actions, Monica and I teach him those as we go along. What feels like forever later, the song ends.

"What do you pick?" Monica asks her dad.

"Hmm." Jimmy makes a dramatic show of putting his finger to his lips as though he's really thinking hard about it. "It's a secret, but it's one your mom will recognize." He sends a warm smile my way that gives me a fuzzy feeling inside.

Jimmy fiddles with his phone and the song starts. Only a few beats in, I recognize Bruce Springsteen's "Dancing in the Dark."

"Oh my God, yay!" I dance to the beat the same way he does in the music video.

Monica does her best to mimic me, and Jimmy joins in.

"Your mom loved this song when we were growing up," he yells to Monica over the music.

It's true, I did. It was before my time, but something about this song always lifted me up when I was having a hard time. One of the only good things my dad gave me was my love of this song.

We sing and dance along as a group, Jimmy and I singing loudly like a pair of goofballs, and Monica falls to the couch, laughing and pointing at us.

When he takes my hand, drawing me into him, we dance chest to chest, laughing and singing. It's the closest and most intimate we've ever been in front of Monica, and it's one of those moments when I feel as though I'm above the scene. Though I'm present in the moment, I'm also somehow aware that it's burned in my memory forever.

The last notes of the song sound, and the three of us laugh, panting to catch our breaths.

That was the kind of moment I used to dream about sharing when I was pregnant with Monica. It's a moment I wasn't sure I'd ever get.

"What'd you think of that song?" he asks Monica.

"It's good. Who is it?"

"Bruce Springsteen," I say. "Every song on that album is pure gold."

"Oh yes, your mom loved Bruce."

I lightly smack Jimmy across the chest. "How can you not love the Boss?"

"Oh, I don't know, how about this?" He mimics Bruce's dancing in the video.

I laugh. "It was the eighties. That's what they did back then."

"Doesn't make it right."

I roll my eyes and look down at Monica, who's quietly taking in our banter. "All right, kiddo. Bedtime."

"I wanna stay up." The corners of her lips tilt down.

"Sorry, the time has come. Say good night to your dad and I'll tuck you in."

She stomps over to Jimmy with a huff and a frown. He picks her up and gives her a kiss on the cheek then whispers something in her ear. I don't know what he says, but whatever it is makes her giggle and turns her mood around. He sets her down and ruffles her hair.

"Good night, Daddy."

"Night, sweetie."

I lead Monica to her bed, where it takes only a couple minutes for her to drift off. After leaving one last kiss on her forehead, I quietly walk out of her room. I shut her door and turn around to find Jimmy waiting for me in the hallway.

Our eyes catch, and he holds out his hand with eyes filled with anticipation.

I meet him halfway. Without a word, he leads me to the master bedroom and closes the door.

If I wanted time to second-guess this decision, I don't have it, but all the trepidation that occupied my brain today disappears the minute Jimmy's hands are on me.

His fingers grab the zipper on my shirt, sliding it down and over the valley of my breasts. When he brushes my sweatshirt over my shoulders, it falls to the floor. He steps closer, his fingers digging into my sides before pulling my pants down my legs. I step out of them. Leaving me in my tank top and underwear, he guides to the bed and I crawl under the already drawn sheets, watching while he undresses down to his boxers and climbs in behind me.

With an arm around my waist, he drags me so that my back meets his chest. He slides one leg between mine and leaves his arm around my waist. He places a kiss just below my ear. "Good night, Lilah."

I lie there and soak in the feel of him around me and realize that I haven't felt this safe and supported since the last time we did this, all those years ago.

It's then that I'm able to admit to myself how much I missed this… how much I missed him.

* * *

I DON'T KNOW what time it is when I wake, but it's still dark outside. I jerk for a second when I don't recognize my surroundings, then I slowly relax.

We've barely moved since we fell asleep, and though his leg has moved, Jimmy's arm is still wrapped around me from behind. He groans, and his hand plays with the edge of my tank top. It slowly slides up my stomach until he grasps one of my breasts, squeezing and playing with the nipple until it's a taut peak.

His nose nuzzles into my neck, his tongue snaking out to taste my earlobe. Shivers rack my body while he continues to knead my breast and roll my nipple between his thumb and forefinger.

A breathy moan escapes me, and I circle my ass over his growing erection.

He sucks on my neck and his hand leaves my breast, coasting down my stomach until his fingers dip under the edge of my underwear and in through my folds. I whimper as his fingers skim over my clit, and I part my legs. Jimmy teases my entrance, pulling the wetness up to coat my clit with the pressure I need. His fingers rotate in the laziest circular motion, building pressure as he reads my moan. I push back into his rigid length, my hands grabbing my breasts.

His teeth bite my earlobe before his tongue coasts over the skin, featherlight.

With darkness around us, and only our pleasure-induced reactions to go off of, I feel as if the two of us are alone in the universe, in a bubble we've created.

The tension builds and builds between my legs until my climax is fast approaching, but Jimmy's magical fingers leave me and tug my underwear down my legs with the help of his feet. I moan when his fingers return to my clit and he pulls my leg to rest on the back of his, opening me further. At some point he must have either pulled down his boxer briefs or removed them entirely, because his bare cock slides through my folds from behind, teasing my entrance.

His fingers switch directions and increase pace, and it's enough to get me right back to where I was. I'm strung so tight I'm afraid I might burst apart, but as my climax hits me like a tidal wave, Jimmy thrusts into me and I cry out. His free hand comes around and covers my mouth to stop me from waking our daughter, and I dissolve into a million particles of light as my orgasm grips Jimmy's cock and his fingers draw out my bliss.

Jimmy removes his fingers, his other hand falling from my mouth. He grips my waist and slowly pumps in and out of me.

It's leisurely and unhurried, and somehow in this moment, that feels hotter than if he were pushing me into the mattress from behind and having his way with me.

His steel length drags in and out until I'm once again building toward another climax. Without a word, he rolls from his side onto his back while he's still inside me. My back is still to his front, but now I can move my hips, controlling the pace. One of his hands cups my mound and the other pinches my nipple and oh God, the way his cock hits inside me at this angle has me panting and moaning as our sweat-slicked skin slides together.

My rhythm increases and I'm almost there. His fingers leave my nipple and travel up between my breasts until his hand is around my throat.

He must sense how close I am because the next time I lower my hips and he hits that perfect spot inside me, his hand covering my mound comes up and smacks my bundle of nerves. I fall apart as if he has a magic power to detonate me.

I cry out and his hand tightens around my neck as he thrusts into me from below. His groan mixes with mine as he spills himself inside me.

We lie there catching our breath, his heart thundering against my back. Still silent, as if words might take something away from this moment, he wraps his arms around me and nuzzles into my neck. Eventually the sweat cools and he rolls me to my side and pulls out of me.

I want to moan at the loss of him, but instead, I say softly, "I'm going to clean up."

I head into the master bath, do my business, then sit on the edge of the mattress, glancing at the clock. "It's four thirty. I'd better go sleep in my room before Monica wakes up."

He's on his back, one arm at his side, the other behind his head, and the comforter pulled up to his waist. He looks sinful. No part of me wants to leave this bed right now, but I have to do what's best for all of us.

He takes my hand. "I don't want you to go."

I squeeze his hand. "Neither do I, but I should."

He presses his lips together and nods. I let his hand go and slide on my panties, then I gather up my clothes from the floor at the end of the bed.

"I'll see you in a few hours," I say. "Hopefully Monica will sleep in."

He smiles at me in a way that has me wanting to break down and cry because he hasn't looked at me like that in six years— like I hang the moon and the stars—and I realize how much I need it.

I turn and go before I lose the strength to fight the urge to stay. In the room we've deemed mine, I lie down in bed and bask in the afterglow of what happened. It's too late, my worst fear has come true—I've already grown attached to him.

Chapter Seventy-four

JIMMY

I lie awake for twenty minutes after Lilah leaves my bed. I'm completely sated physically, but my mind is a whirling contradiction of emotions. After what we shared, I'm more convinced than ever that what Lilah and I had before isn't only still there, it's better. More mature, more seasoned, aged to perfection.

Sleep not coming, I slip out of bed and pull on some pajama bottoms to head downstairs for a drink of water. When I make my way back upstairs and pass by Monica's room, I hear her sheets rustling and bed creaking, so I open the door to check on her.

She's sitting up in bed, rubbing her eyes.

"Can't sleep?" I ask. "Everything okay."

"Yeah. Will you lay with me?" she asks.

"Of course." I get comfortable next to her and she turns my way, her hand running along my face.

"Do you love Mommy?"

I still, not expecting that line of questioning from her. I'm not sure what to tell her. I don't want to confuse her and have her think that Lilah and I are going to be a couple, because we haven't had that conversation yet.

I opt for a slice of the truth. "I do love your mom, sweetie, because she gave me you. I'll always feel that way about her."

"I thought so." She yawns again.

"Okay, this time I'm really leaving. You have a good sleep."

"Thanks, Daddy."

Her eyes are closed, so she can't see my smile or the tears in my eyes. I brush a stray curl from her cheek and kiss the top of her head. Not wanting to leave the space of this moment, I stand at the door for a few minutes and watch her drift off before I pull the door closed and head down to Lilah's room. I have to share this with her.

I knock softly before pushing the door open. She's under the covers and her back is to me, but she rolls over to face me. I can tell that she hasn't been able to sleep yet either.

"I just put Monica back to bed, and guess what she asked me when I was in there?"

"What?"

"She asked me if I loved you."

Lilah's eyes widen, and she bites her bottom lip. That damn bottom lip. Despite the seriousness of this moment, my dick twitches in my pants.

"What did you tell her?" she whispers.

"The truth."

"Which is?"

"With every part of me. Now and forever."

Her breath hitches and her face crumples. "I love you too. I never stopped. Not for a minute."

She brings her hands up to cover her face, but I pull them back so I can see her. I tilt her chin so that she meets my gaze. "That's a happy thing, sweetheart. Stop apologizing, and let's spend our energy on the here and now, okay?"

She nods, wipes her tears, and leans into me. Our lips meet in a chaste but fierce kiss.

"Swear you'll try to move on and stop worrying about the past?" I ask.

She nods, and I hold my pinkie finger out between us. Her gaze flicks up to meet mine, hope shining bright. Lilah wraps her pinkie around mine, and we begin this next chapter in the story of us on a pinkie swear.

Chapter Seventy-five

LILAH

It's true what they say—time flies when you're having fun. Another few weeks pass in the blink of an eye. We spend most of our time at Jimmy's rental now. It's more private and secure, and the size of the house makes it easier when he and I want to get our own playtime in.

It's Sunday, and Monica is coloring quietly in the play area while I'm sitting at the breakfast bar, looking on my laptop for a recipe to make for dessert tonight, when Jimmy comes in. He takes the seat beside me and waits patiently for me to finish reading.

Moments like this feel surreal. Sometimes I find myself questioning if this is really happening, if after everything that went down, am I really here with this man again, feeling as though no time has passed at all.

"Do you have a minute to talk?" he asks when I face him.

"Sure, what's up?"

"I wanted to talk to you about the possibility of having you and Monica out to my place in Malibu. The Kids' Pick Honors are in a couple of weeks, and I thought that maybe we could take her. She'd get to meet a lot of the people she sees on TV. I thought she might get a kick out of it."

Anxiety tightens my chest and I struggle to breathe. I close my laptop. "I'm sure she would."

"But...?"

I sigh. "I don't want her exposed to that lifestyle. The last thing I want is for her to be paraded around the red carpet and photographed. It's one thing for the press to try to get a picture of her, and yes, I know that will happen at some point. We've been lucky to avoid it so far. But it's another entirely to invite them to do it."

"I should've been clearer." He takes my hand. "I have no intentions of the three of us hitting the red carpet. We can go in the back way, watch the show, and leave the same way. I'm sure they'll get some shots of the three of us in the audience, but it might be a good way to let the press get a look at us and most importantly, Monica. It would allow us to control what they see, and they wouldn't have the opportunity to ask questions or scare her."

I inhale past the constriction in my chest and bite my bottom lip but stop when I see the way Jimmy's attention goes there. "Are you saying you want to come out to the press as a couple? I'm not ready for that. Monica doesn't even know there's anything more between us."

"Screw the press. We don't have to give a statement to them either way. They'll speculate for sure, but if you want, I can always send out a statement through my people that says we're just friends and co-parents."

That eases some of my worry. I'm torn. We'll have to be in front of the press at some point, but I love this little universe we've created for ourselves. But it's not destined to last. At some point, Jimmy will want to go back to work and Monica will be old enough to understand what her dad does for a living. She'll want to tag along with him to events.

"You're not usually this quiet about your opinions. What are you worried about?" He looks at me with concern, and I know out of anyone in this world, I can confide in him.

"Let me check on Monica first, then we can talk."

He nods, and I use the distance to clear my thoughts. Once I make sure that Monica is still content with coloring and doesn't need anything, I return to find Jimmy sitting on the couch in the family room.

"Sit." He pats the space beside him. "Tell me what's on your mind."

I sit down. "I haven't exactly lived a saintly life, and most of it's been documented in the press. I'm scared to expose myself to that lifestyle again because it's going to bring all that up, even though I'm a different person now. And the worst part isn't just how it'll make me feel, but that my daughter will be exposed to all my wrongdoings."

Sympathy shines in his dark eyes, and he tucks a stray piece of hair behind my ear. "We're not going to put either of you in a position where the press will be yelling questions at you, okay?"

I nod. "I know that, but it's just bringing it all up. At some point, Monica is going to find out who I used to be. I'm just so ashamed. What if she looks at me differently? What if she doesn't love me anymore?"

I put voice to my biggest fear—the one thing that would be my complete undoing.

"Sweetheart, before that would ever happen, we'll have spoken to her ourselves, set the context and the narrative. She'll know her mom for the strong survivor that she is. Not perfect, no, but none of us are. Hell, I have my own secrets—"

"And she'll *never* know about that. Ever."

He smiles at my fierce tone. "I know, but my point is that I'm not perfect either. Monica won't expect you to be. Let's just take it one day at a time. Remember when you pinkie swore to leave the past behind us?"

"I'm trying. I really am. Sometimes it feels impossible to start over. The weight of the past and all the reminders of everything we've been through are constantly lurking around the perimeter."

"Hey, you got this, okay?"

I nod, though I still don't feel entirely confident. But encountering the media will happen one way or another at some point soon. Might as well do it on our terms rather than someone else's.

"Okay, why don't you go tell her? I'm sure she'll be excited."

He places a chaste kiss on my lips. "Thank you. I can't wait to see her face."

I smile as he takes off to go surprise our daughter. I push my uneasiness aside and decide to see if Monica wants to go for a swim at the rec center this afternoon. I need to get out of my head for a while.

* * *

A FEW WEEKS LATER, we land at a private airport in the Los Angeles area. With the rumble of the tires on the runway, my stomach churns with sourness from being in Los Angeles again. Add on the fact that I'm staying at the home he shared with Adelaide. At the home where we loved and hated each other, sometimes in equal weight. I've promised Jimmy a week, and I hope I can stay without running away.

Jimmy's given Monica a lot of firsts. I think he loves watching her reactions. I caught him smiling at her while she stared at the clouds the entire flight and asked a bunch of questions like where the birds were and are clouds cotton balls.

Monica buzzes with excitement when our driver pulls up in front of Jimmy's place. Another first—she's never seen the ocean.

A rush of memories floods my mind as we step through the door—some good, some bad—but I push them all back because in the end, they don't matter. We're starting anew. What matters most is where we are in the present.

Once Monica's run down every hallway inspecting the place and we've gone for a long walk along the beach, we have dinner and go through her bedtime routine. She'll be sleeping in the extra bedroom since the room I used to occupy is a gym.

Not much has changed about the room. The walls are now a pale blue and the comforter coordinates—Adelaide's influence, I assume—but the furniture is the same. I tuck her into bed and ease out of the room once I hear her breathing become deep and even.

I need to burn off some anxiety, so I go to my bag in his office where I'll be sleeping on the pull-out sofa and find my swimsuit. Once I'm changed, I head down the hall.

"I'm going to go for a swim," I say.

He looks up from his phone at the breakfast bar. "I'll come watch."

I chuckle, moving across the room toward the sliding glass doors. "You'll watch?"

He shrugs. "Yeah. I've always loved watching you swim. It's sexy as hell. Especially when you finish and come up out of the pool. You're like a Bond girl."

I laugh and step out onto the deck. "Whatever floats your boat."

And watch he does. At first, I'm very aware of him watching my every move but at some point, I disappear into myself as I always do, leaving my worries behind.

When I'm done, I step up the stairs with a little extra flair to my hips. His eyes hood and he licks his lips. I grab the robe he thoughtfully brought out off the edge of the sectional and wrap it around me before I get a chill. Summer is disappearing even here in California. I sit down beside him.

He trails his tongue up my neck until he reaches my ear. "Just as good as I remember."

His hand slips under the collar of my robe and he cups my breast, running his thumb over my nipple. It feels good, better than good, but I can't relax. Being here is raising questions, ones that have come to mind in passing before but now are at the forefront of my mind.

He must sense something is off because he pulls away. "What's going on in that head of yours?"

He always did know me too well.

I have to remind myself that there's no use hiding what feels like silly, girly emotions. If anything is going to come of us, I have to be upfront about everything.

"I feel awkward. This is where you lived with Adelaide."

He frowns. "This is also where I lived with you."

"I know, but that was a long time ago and not nearly as long as you were with her."

"For the record, Adelaide still had her own place. I'm not saying she wasn't here a lot, but we couldn't agree on where we were going to live full-time."

"Really?"

He nods. "Let's get this out of your system... we've never talked too much about Adelaide and me except for what went down at the end. Ask me whatever you want, then we can move on past this."

He's given me the green light to have all my curiosities answered and now I feel nervous to hear the answers. God, I need to get a grip.

"Okay, how did you guys start dating? I mean, I know what the press says and when you guys started showing up there, but you can't ever believe that garbage."

"We were still friends and talked quite a bit after everything went down with us. Over time, we kind of lost touch. Then I saw her again at an industry event. We caught up with each other, made plans to grab something to eat, and that was our first date."

I nod slowly. It hurts to hear, but I appreciate him being so open. "What about before that. Was there anyone special before her?"

He shakes his head. "I was desperate to do anything to push the pain away and stop thinking of you. I drank too much for a while, went on tour with Tripp and slept with a bunch of groupies, but none of it made a damn bit of difference. You were still there, lurking at the back of my mind, waiting to push into my thoughts the second I sat still." He's so calm, I'm envious.

"How are you not uncomfortable talking to me about this?"

"I'm not uncomfortable because I have nothing to hide. All I want is for the past to be in the past and us to move into the future—as a family." He places a chaste kiss on my lips.

I close my eyes briefly and take in the feel of him.

"Okay, what else?" he says.

I swallow hard and ask the most difficult question. "Does any part of you still love her?"

I hold my breath when he considers his answer to this question longer than the others. He drags me to him so that I'm straddling him and we're face to face.

"The answer to your question is no. But there's something else you should know." He brushes his knuckles over my cheek. "I never loved Adelaide like I loved you. Ever. Even when I proposed, I knew it was different, and I thought long and hard about whether I should even propose because of that. In the end, I decided that a person probably only ever gets to experience the kind of love we had once in their lives and that I'd have to settle for something that wasn't as all-consuming as what we shared. I think there are different kinds of love and what we have trumps them all."

My eyes well with tears, not just because his words are so poetic but because they match my own feelings for him.

"Jimmy, you've always been my person. That never changed. I wish there was another word for love because sometimes I feel like it doesn't sum up what we have."

His lips meet mine in a soul-consuming kiss, and we both pour our love into it. His hands snake into my wet hair, and I almost cry from how precious and loved he makes me feel.

He pulls back, and our gazes lock. "Just so you know... if Adelaide had asked me the same question about you, I wouldn't have been able to say that I didn't still love you. A part of me always carried you with me."

I smile and run my hands over his face, over his stubble, just to feel him.

"Is there anything you want to ask me about our time apart?" I figure we should do this now and check that box.

He grimaces. "Fuck no. I don't want to know anything about you with anyone else."

"Well, that would be a pretty boring story anyway, as you know. There basically has been no one else since you."

"I'm not gonna lie, that makes me happy." He gives me a chaste kiss.

"There is one more thing I was wondering..."

"What is it?" he asks, adjusting me on his lap as his cock grows underneath me.

"What happened to your mom? Did you ever hear from her again?"

A sigh leaves his lips. "She died a couple of years ago."

My hand flies up to my mouth. "I'm sorry. I had no idea."

Jimmy shrugs. "I had someone keep an eye on her after I paid her to go away. That's the only way I know. I mean, she was basically already dead to me after everything she did. Still, I paid to have her buried in Virginia and have a gravestone mark her spot. Figured it's the least I could do, seeing that she gave me life, even if she made it difficult in a lot of ways."

"How did she die?" I ask.

"Lung cancer. Apparently, she was still smoking up a storm until the end, if you can believe it."

I don't know what to say, so I'm silent.

"Anything else?"

I shake my head. I feel lighter now without the lingering doubts plaguing my mind. "Nope. That's it."

"Good, because now I think it's time for us to christen this deck." His hand slips around my neck, and he undoes the strings of my bathing suit. "What do you say?"

With a smile, I shed the robe and we end up making love under the stars like we did years before, although we're two different people now. Better people.

Chapter Seventy-six

JIMMY

"Are you excited?" I look down at Monica, who's between Lilah and me as we head toward the Santa Monica Pier.

She nods a few times, her blonde waves bouncing. "Can I go on the big circle?"

Lilah and I smile at one another over her.

"You don't think you'll be scared?" I tease.

She frowns and looks at me over her shoulder, pulling us both forward. "I'm not a baby."

I chuckle, and we keep walking toward our destination. Lilah and I are incognito—her with large sunglasses, her hair up under a large sun hat, and me with my own set of shades and my ball cap pulled down low so all you can really see are my nose and mouth. We won't be able to stay for hours, but I'm hopeful we'll be able to enjoy a couple hours together as a family.

Monica ends up loving the Ferris wheel and forces us to go on it three times. Lilah's getting as much joy from seeing Monica laugh uncontrollably in our special spot as I am. Once we've had our fun on the pier, we grab fries and burgers from one of the vendors and walk down the beach until we find a nice spot to sit in the sand and eat.

"Did you know that I named you after this place?" Lilah says, wiping the ketchup off Monica's face.

"You did?"

Lilah nods. "This is where your dad and I first came when we moved here."

"And it's where we'd come whenever we wanted time to ourselves," I add.

"What's it called again?" she asks, her head tilted as though she's trying really hard to remember.

"Santa Monica Pier." I ruffle her hair because she's just so damn cute.

Her face lights up when she registers her name, and she looks back at the rides in the distance.

"Can I go play near the water?" she asks, changing tracks without warning like she always does.

I don't have a lot of experience with kids, so I don't know if that's something they all do or whether it's just my daughter, but I'd be lying if I said I don't get a kick out of it.

"Sure, kiddo. But just put your feet in the water. No deeper than your ankles, okay?" Lilah says.

Monica nods. "Okay, Mommy."

She discards her shoes and runs up to the edge of the water. Lilah and I watch, and I slowly glide my hand over in the sand until it's on top of hers. She looks at me and smiles.

"It's great seeing her here, isn't it?" I ask.

"Yeah, I wasn't sure I ever would." There's a note of melancholy in her voice, but it doesn't stay. "She sure liked the rides."

"I know. I wasn't sure she would at first."

We sit in a comfortable silence, watching as Monica splashes around and chases the odd seagull that lands anywhere in her vicinity.

I hate to break the spell we're both under, but there's something we need to discuss. "I got a call from Keane a couple of days ago, reminding me that I owe Kevin of *HW Life* an interview about becoming a father."

Lilah's entire body stiffens. "Right... I forgot about that."

"I'm thinking that maybe early next week, after the awards, I'll do the interview, so we'll have to nail down what I plan to say."

"Okay, what are you thinking?" She stays focused on Monica.

"I have to run it by my manager and PR, but I think it's best if we say that the two of us didn't communicate for a long time and it wasn't until recently that we reconnected. When they press me and ask whether I knew about Monica or not, I'll refuse to answer."

Her head snaps in my direction. "You can't do that."

"Can and will."

She shakes her head. "It's not your burden to bear. They're going to call you a deadbeat dad."

"Listen, it's none of their business. I'm happy to talk about the arrangement we have now and discuss how much joy I'm getting out of being a father but everything else is none of their business."

"I'm not comfortable with you coming out looking like the bad guy."

Monica squeals, and we both look over to see that the last wave moved farther up the shore than she was expecting. She laughs and waves to us. We both wave back.

"Sweetheart, I know your concerns about the press. This is me doing what I have to in order to protect you."

She gives me a small smile. "I don't know..."

"Let me do this, okay?" I squeeze her hand.

She doesn't say anything but looks back at Monica.

"There's one more thing," I say.

Lilah lets her head fall back, looking at the sky, and her hat falls off and onto the sand. "God, what now?"

I chuckle. "Tripp texted me. He'll be back from Europe in a couple weeks. Wondered if he could meet Monica."

She rights her head and picks up her hat, dusting the sand off the top. "I never asked how he felt about this whole thing."

I shrug. "He was surprised at first obviously, but I think he can tell how happy I am."

"He's a good friend to you."

I nod. "He is."

"Sure, if he wants to meet her, he's more than welcome to." She faces me and points. "No women or other shenanigans though. I remember what he was like."

"As if I'd let him do that. He's mellowed a bit anyway."

She raises a brow.

"I said a bit, not totally."

We both laugh, and I feel better now that we've discussed the things that had been on my mind. One thing I need to learn is not to be afraid to tell Lilah everything. Years ago, I purposely hid info that I thought might trigger her to use. It feels nice to have an adult conversation where we both communicate our feelings. Now we just have to get through the Kids' Pick Honors tomorrow and Lilah will see that she still fits into my life.

Chapter Seventy-seven

LILAH

"I'm going to run and get my nails done down the road."

I noticed that the place I used to go to a long time ago is still there. Today is the Kids' Pick Honors and rather than sit around the house and continue to let this nauseated feeling grow worse, I'd prefer to do something—anything. And it's been ages since I had a manicure.

"Want us to join you?" Jimmy asks.

I shake my head. "I'll only be an hour. Mind if I take your car?"

"Of course not." He grabs the keys off the counter and tosses them to me.

"Monica, you be good for your dad, and when I get home, we'll get you ready, okay?"

She looks up from the puzzle she's working on at the kitchen table. "Okay, Mommy."

I wave bye to Jimmy, who blows me a kiss since Monica isn't looking. I return it with one of my own. God, we're so cheesy, I think with a grin. I wouldn't change it for anything. I remember how unpredictable our old relationship was.

I grab a hat off the hook as I leave out the front door and pull my sunglasses from my bag. It's not as if I'm some hotshot celebrity like Jimmy is, but I'd rather not take my chances.

I arrive at the nail salon and remove my sunglasses but leave my hat on. The man at the desk assures me I'll only have to wait a few minutes before someone can help me. While sitting at an empty station, I do some breathing exercises to calm my nerves and remind myself that we're not walking the red carpet. There's no reason I'll have to interact with the press.

I'm brought back to the present when a woman sits down across from me, smiling, and asks what color I'd like today.

"Do you have something in pale pink?" I ask, thinking that will coordinate nicely with the dress I plan to wear tonight.

She opens the drawer and pulls out the perfect shade, as if she can read my mind.

"Perfect, thank you."

We make small talk while she works on my nails. I don't offer much in the way of details about myself or my life, but I do what I can to be polite. By the time I'm pulling cash from my wallet to pay her, I'm feeling much more relaxed than when I came in.

I grab my purse from the floor beside me, thank her, and walk to the door to leave. I open the door and freeze.

Paparazzi are gathered on the sidewalk, and when they spot me, they snap pictures. The flashes from the cameras momentarily blind me, and I stand there, unable to move. The questions startle me into action though. I push my way through, moving toward where I parked on the side of the road.

"Lilah, are you still abusing drugs?"

"Lilah, why were you out of James's life for so long?"

"Lilah, are you the reason James and Adelaide broke up?"

"Lilah, are you using James because you want to try to get back in the business?"

"Lilah, is James really the father of your daughter?"

"Lilah, are you fit to be a mother? Were you using when you were pregnant?"

"That's James's car!"

I hit the button to unlock the vehicle and can barely open the door with the group of them pressing in on my back. My chest constricts and I struggle to breathe from the claustrophobia they've created. My heart beats so loud, it drowns out their voices.

I slide in, lock the door, and take a minute to gather myself before I have an anxiety attack. I try to slow my breathing and gain control over my body, but it feels impossible with them bearing down on me, still screaming amid the steady clicking of shutters.

I start the car, slam it into drive, and slowly inch out of my spot, making sure I don't run over anyone. Imagine the headlines then.

Once I'm clear and away from them, I try my best to breathe properly, but my body fights my attempts. I will myself to keep it together long enough for me to get back to Jimmy's.

Tears form when his iron gate comes into view. I hit the button, and it slides open at a snail's pace as a few press linger around. I smack my hand on the steering wheel a couple of times and scream, the tears having nowhere to go but out.

The car has barely stopped when I shove it into park, snag my purse from the passenger seat, and make my way up the steps to the house. When I push open the front door, I abandon my purse in the foyer and a sob escapes.

I slap my hand over my mouth because I don't want Monica to see me like this. Jimmy must have heard me though, because he makes his way to the foyer with a smile.

But when he takes me in, he races over and draws me up by the shoulders. "What happened?"

The urgency and fear in his eyes kills me. I wish, not for the first time, that I were stronger. "Where's Monica?"

"She's in the bathroom. Lilah, what happened?"

"I need to lie down."

Jimmy supports my body down the hallway until we reach the master bedroom. He helps me to lie down on the bed and sits on the edge, rubbing my back while I try once again to gather myself.

"Shhh, you're okay. You're here now." His soothing voice helps me to relax my body enough that I'm able to inhale a deep breath.

"The paparazzi was at the salon when I left. Someone must have called them. They ambushed me, asking all kinds of questions just like I knew they would!"

"Shhh," he says, glancing out the bedroom door, presumably to make sure Monica isn't nearby.

"I can't do this. I can't. You should've heard the things they were saying." I wipe the tears from my stinging eyes but it's useless because they're toppling over one another at this point.

"I'm sorry, sweetheart. I knew I should've gone with you."

"This isn't your fault."

"We have to leave in a couple hours. Are you going to be okay?"

I shake my head. "I can't go. You two go and enjoy it. Tell Monica I'm not feeling well."

He looks at me with a pained expression. "I don't want to leave you here on your own."

"I'll be fine. I just can't face the possibility of that happening again today. It'll be better if I'm not there."

"Fucking paps."

"It was bound to happen at some point," I say, getting control of my breathing again.

"Daddy?" Monica calls from another part of the house.

"Are you sure you don't want to come with us?" he asks.

"You guys go, have fun. I need to gather myself. I promise, I'll be okay tomorrow." I do my best to put on a smile, but I can tell he sees through it.

"*Daddy!*"

"Okay, I'll text you later."

He kisses my forehead before getting up off the bed to join our daughter. He closes the door, and I roll over, my head pounding as the adrenaline leaves my system.

I shouldn't be surprised. I predicted something like this would happen.

* * *

I WAKE to a hand rubbing my back. Slowly blinking awake, I see that it's dark outside. I must've drifted off during the adrenaline crash. I rub my eyes and roll over to see Jimmy there, still dressed and looking at me with concern.

"Hey, how was it?" My voice is hoarse from sleeping and crying.

"It was fine. She saw a few people she knew from TV, and we were able to get some pictures of her with them backstage. I'll show you tomorrow. How are you doing?"

I sit up and lean back against the headboard, blow out a breath, and run a hand through my messy hair. "I don't know."

He gives me a look like he doesn't believe me, like I'm holding back.

"I swear, Jimmy, I don't know. All I know is that I can't be here."

He rears back. "What the hell are you talking about?"

"I can't stay here. I can't be in this city, in this lifestyle, anymore. There are too many triggers for me, too much of my past to be dredged up and thrown in my face every time I step out the door. And the thought of them doing that to Monica?" I bite my knuckle to keep from crying again.

"Sweetheart..." He tucks my hair behind my ear and tilts my chin with his finger so that I'm forced to look at him. "It was a one-time thing. They caught you unprepared. It won't happen again. We'll make sure of it."

I throw up my hands. "By doing what? Hiding in the house all the time? Dressing in disguises so we can go out in public? Giving interviews where you lie so I can save face? Staying offline so I never have to see what they're saying about me? What kind of life is that? I can't do this. I left this life once because it wasn't good for me. I won't make the same mistake again. I can't. It's not just me I have to think of."

His dark eyes widen as he stares at me, and I can tell I've shocked him. "What exactly are you saying?"

I look down for a minute, gathering my courage to do what I know is right. "I'm saying that there's no place for me here. I don't fit in your life. I love you"—I brush my hand over his face—"but I'm going back to Kansas, back to my life."

He grabs the wrist of my hand on his face. "What does that mean for us?" His eyes search mine and reflect the same sadness and fear in mine.

"I honestly don't know. I wouldn't ever ask you to give up your career—I know the joy you get from acting. And you'll always be a part of Monica's life, no matter what. But this place, this town, this industry holds too many painful memories for me. I'm not trying to run from them—I know better than that now. I've accepted the things I've done, but I also know I can't exist in a space where they're pulled out as leverage or grenades to launch at me. I need my routine and my safe space." I blink, and the tears that have been building fall.

"But I need you," he whispers.

I lean into him, and our foreheads meet. I close my eyes and breathe in his scent. It is safety and home, but with him comes his lifestyle, and that's never worked for me. We're not the same people that way.

"I'm sorry." The words come out in a strangled whisper.

He doesn't fight me. I didn't think he would. He's such a good man. He'd never jeopardize my sobriety or mental health for himself.

"This isn't over between us," he says.

I don't know whether he's trying to convince me or him. He places a chaste kiss on my lips and leaves the room, wiping his own tears.

I settle back into bed and suck back the sobs leaving what feels like a giant crater in my chest.

Sometimes love isn't meant to last a lifetime. Sometimes it's a brief moment in time, but that doesn't make it any easier to walk away from.

Chapter Seventy-eight

LILAH

We've been home for a week and a half. Monica was upset that we didn't stay at her dad's for as long as we were supposed to, but she believed me when I said that one of the girls at work was sick and I had to return early.

It wasn't a total lie, because I did go back to work. I couldn't stand to sit around the house by myself all day. Every inch of the place now holds memories of Jimmy. Suddenly just the two of us at dinner feels weird. I'll catch both us staring at his chair. The corner of the couch we cuddle up in is lonely without him. I can't even sit out on the porch without staring at his chair motionless next to mine.

Each time an image of a moment we shared flashes in my mind, it's like the sharpest knife stabbing me in the heart.

And so I try to get back to my normal routine from before Jimmy reappeared in my life and made me believe that a future for us was possible.

He couldn't come out last weekend to visit, citing some meetings, but he and Monica FaceTime every night. I don't know if he really did have meetings or if he was avoiding me, but I'm thankful for the distance. Seeing him on my iPad is enough to set me on the verge of tears and leave me aching—I can't imagine what seeing him in person would do.

I haven't asked what he told the reporter from *HW Life* during his interview last week. He knew my feelings, and he'd do what he wanted anyway.

"Can we get Oreos, Mommy?"

I glance at Monica, who's ahead of me in the grocery aisle and push the thoughts from my head. "No Oreos, kiddo."

She crosses her arms and stomps her foot. "Why not?"

I sigh. Monica hasn't been her happy self since we left Malibu. I think she got used to having her dad with us every day and she's acting out because of it. "Excuse me, young lady, you do not speak to me that way, do you understand?"

She drops her arms and looks at her feet. "Sorry."

I want to scoop her up and squeeze her because I know she's hurting. I want to tell her that I'm hurting too. "I'll tell you what... we can get the Oreos, but you can only have one a day. And you have to promise not to hound Mommy for more after you've had your one for the day, okay?"

A big smile replaces her scowl. She grabs the package off the shelf but ends up knocking a bunch of them onto the floor. "Oh no!"

She drops to her knees to pick them up, but her little shoulders shake and they all fall to the floor again. I abandon my cart and rush over to her.

"It's okay, it was an accident." I draw her into a hug and rub her back. "Shhh, kiddo, it's okay." I place a kiss on her forehead and pull back to wipe her tears from her chubby cheeks. "Let's go pay for this stuff and go home. How about we watch a short movie before bed tonight?"

She nods into my neck. I manage to stand with her still in my arms and push the cart one-handed to the check-out line. Two shoppers are ahead of us, and the cashier asks for a price check. Perfect. I continue to rub her back while I wait, my eyes wandering, not wanting to give in to the temptation. Eventually, I look at the magazine rack to my right.

On a tabloid cover, Jimmy and a well-known actress are leaving a building side by side with the caption, "Has The Regulator found someone to heal his broken heart?"

My heart hammers and my mouth dries.

I don't believe the garbage they printed. I recognize the building as Jimmy's agent's, so I'm sure it's work related.

But one day it will be the truth.

One day he'll find someone who can handle the pressure of his career.

Before I can absorb one emotion, a pile of them topple onto me.

I'm so tired of feeling helpless.

I'm tired of reacting instead of taking control.

I'm tired of letting my wants slip through my fingers instead of fighting for them.

Am I really willing to let Jimmy, the man I love and the father of my child, go? He unselfishly let me leave because it was what was best for me. It's about time I do the same, because Jimmy Crawford is worth fighting for.

592

Chapter Seventy-nine

JIMMY

The driver pulls up to the airfield where the private plane awaits. This is my first trip to Kansas since Monica and Lilah left a couple of weeks ago.

It's been hell without them.

I've been able to talk to Monica every night, but my interactions with Lilah are nearly non-existent. The odd times I talk to her on her own, either over the phone or text, she shifts the conversation if it ventures to us.

I have no idea what's going on. Are we broken up? Were we officially together in the first place? I'd like to think so. We both want to be with each other, yet my career and geography stand in our way.

The most frustrating part is that I wish I could be pissed at her, but I understand her reasoning. Her being a good mother to Monica comes first, which means her sobriety comes before all of it. The press is not kind, nor are the trolls on social media. She knows her triggers and I love her, so I'd never willingly put her in the path of a runaway train. Anyone could predict the outcome.

But still... I love her.

Like I'll never love another. I've accepted that much. And so there has to be a way to make this work, not just for the two of us but for our daughter.

I thank the driver and take my bag, making my way over to the plane. The flight attendant lets me know we'll be ready to take off in a few minutes.

My phone buzzes in my pocket, and I pull it out to see Keane's name. I frown. I hope there's no issue with the contract. We've been in negotiations for me to sign onto a production, and I thought we'd ironed out all the details. I'm excited for this one. It better not go south.

"Hey, man, I'm just about to take off to Kansas. What's up? Everything okay with the contract?"

"Everything's fine with the contract. Check your email. I just forwarded you something from *HW Life*."

I blow out a puff of air and run my hands through my hair. "Giving that interview was bad enough, man, I don't want to read it and see how it was spun."

"You're gonna want to read this." He hangs up.

"What the hell?"

"Mr. Crawford, we're set for takeoff. If you could please put your seat belt on now."

"Sure thing." I set my phone aside and strap myself in before I pull up my email.

Keane simply sent a link. I click the link, wondering why I'm going to all this trouble to read something that will most likely piss me off. The name of the article appears, and I'm reminded why I hired Keane.

JAMES CRAWFORD'S BABY MAMA SPEAKS.

My blood slows.

What the hell is this about? Lilah sold me out?

As I read through the article, I realize that the interview I gave will probably never be published because Lilah did her own. Where I was polite but kept my answers short, she held nothing back. She talked about it all—her upbringing with an abusive father, her addiction issues, how Bernie tried to use his power against her, and how she kept any knowledge of Monica's existence from me.

The only part she left out was the death of her father, and I get the distinct sense reading this that it's more for my benefit than her own.

I can't believe she did this. She's basically given the press everything they need to crucify her—which has been her worst fear all along.

Halfway through the article, I have to take a minute to think of the ramifications for her after doing this. I still can't make sense of why she would.

Near the end of the article, I find my answer.

KEVIN: Some people might wonder why you've decided to talk with me today. Do you want to explain your reasons?

LILAH: I'm talking to you today because I've learned a very valuable lesson in life, though it's the one that's probably taken me the longest to learn. You cannot run from your past. I've been so afraid of what the press would say and what my daughter would think when she was old enough to look up all the things they'd say, but the fact is that the past is always going to be there. And I can't change it. So I'm talking to you today to take back my control. This is my story. This is what I've been through and I'm owning it. People can choose to believe it or not. That's not up to me. And when the time comes, I will explain my past to my daughter so that she knows the truth. I can't be afraid anymore. I have too much to live for.

I LEAN BACK in my seat and let my head fall back.

I'm in awe and more in love with her than ever.

I can't believe Lilah did it. I know how afraid she was for everything to come out and having to tell Monica one day, but she did it.

An overwhelming pride fills my chest. I'm proud of my girl. I love her, always will, but right now, I'm proud as hell of her.

I don't know what, if anything, this means for the two of us— whether this means she's willing to deal with the press on a permanent basis or not—but I can't help but think it bodes well. Maybe she'll give this a chance.

I glance at my phone and check the time. How fast can this jet get me to my girls?

"LILAH!" I yell, walking in through her front door. The few hours since I read the article have felt like days and I'm impatient to hold them both.

She walks out of the kitchen, eyes wide and uncertain. "You saw?"

"I saw." I head straight for her. I can't stop myself now that she's here in front of me. When I reach her, I cup her face and bring my lips to hers.

She doesn't try to stop me, and my tongue slips along the seam of her lips. When she opens to me, I push inside. I can't help the growl in my throat when our tongues meet. We devour one another, and her hands push into my hair while I tilt her head to just where I want it.

When we come up for air, our gazes are locked.

"When did you decide to talk to *HW Life*?" I ask.

"It was too painful being away from you, and I was tired of letting my past dictate my future."

I beam and run my gaze all over her face, committing the peaceful look on her face to memory. "You never fail to surprise me."

"I'm hoping you like surprises then."

"Does that mean..."

She bites her bottom lip, that damn bottom lip, and nods. "I don't want to be without you ever again. I want us to be a family."

"Really?" I ask.

"Really."

We both smile at each other.

I take a second to glance around the room. "Where's Monica?"

"At Eileen's. I wanted to talk to you in private about the article first."

"Does this mean we can tell her that her mommy and daddy are going to be a real family from now on?"

Her grin brings me more joy than I could have thought possible. "I think we should. But... we still have to figure out our living situation."

I take her hand and lead her over to the couch, where I position her right on my lap. "I was thinking about that on the plane... you know, in case things worked out how I wanted."

"Oh, you were, were you?" Her hands circle behind my neck.

"I think we should find somewhere to live full-time—somewhere not in Los Angeles. I'll keep my Malibu house for us to use when we want or if I need to be in town for a premiere or press junket or something, but otherwise, I'll live with you guys. I'm at the point in my career where I only want to take on passion projects anyway, and half the time I'm on location so I wouldn't be home even if we did live in Los Angeles. I want you and Monica to be removed from the press and the LA scene and only be as involved as you want. What do you say?"

Lilah brings her hand to my cheek, and I kiss her palm. "I think that sounds perfect. I'll have to figure out something to do though. It's become apparent that I won't be able to work a regular job."

I raise an eyebrow. "What happened?"

She shrugs. "Just the press calling the office or booking appointments and trying to pretend that they're patients so they can try to get information from my coworkers."

"I'm sorry, Lilah." I squeeze her hand.

"That's okay. You're worth it." She leans in to kiss me again, but I gently push her back by the shoulders. She frowns.

"I have one condition though."

Her frown gets bigger. "What's the condition?"

I can see the concern in her eyes. "This whole plan only works if you're my wife."

She gasps and her hands cover her mouth. I can already see tears forming in her eyes.

I draw her hands away from her mouth and kiss her knuckles. "I don't have a ring or anything with me since I was already on the plane when I read the article, but I'll get you the biggest, gaudiest rock there is."

She shakes her head. "I don't need a big ring, I just need you."

"Is that a yes?"

"That's a yes. Pinkie swear." She holds her pinkie out to me, and I wrap mine around hers.

"Pinkie swear."

I've wanted this for as long as I can remember. Even at our lowest points, I wanted us to be a committed couple. We sure as hell took the long way around, but in the end, we landed where we should be—together. And for the first time ever, I have no doubt it will stay that way.

MONICA

Twenty Years Later

I catch Mom and Dad in an embrace in the empty hall, and I'm not sure whether I should interrupt or not. They're always doing this—sneaking off to share a private moment together. Even if it's at a premiere for one of my dad's films, they always find time to share a private moment.

I wait until they pull apart before I clear my throat to gain their attention. Both their heads swivel in my direction.

"There's my girl." Dad smiles at me. I swear sometimes I still feel like a small child when he looks at me with this much pride.

"Everything all set?" Mom asks.

"Yep. The press is all here, and Zac and Noah are out there waiting too."

I don't bother to mention that I had to pull my teenage brothers away from hitting on the same girl. I love them, but those two are trouble. No wonder Dad has salt and pepper at his temples now.

"Okay, kiddo, we're coming." Mom walks over to me and pulls me into a hug.

I know this is an emotional day for her on many levels. When my mom first sat me down when I was younger to explain her past to me, I didn't know what to think. The person she described was nothing like the mom who doted on me and made sure everything in my world was right. I didn't ask many questions at first.

But as I grew older, I asked more and more. And my mom was always open and honest with me, no matter how much I could tell that it hurt her. I could tell it was difficult at times and she was worried about how I would react, but she trusted me with the truth. That, in turn, made me more forgiving of my own mistakes.

If my mom could own the things she'd done, then there was no reason for me to ever feel ashamed of who I was or for any mistakes I made.

My mom is the entire reason I ended up where I am right now.

Well, that, and my dad's money.

"You're going to be great." She pulls away and gives me a quick kiss on the cheek before giving my dad a chance to embrace me.

"You know how proud we both are of you, right?" he says.

"I know, Daddy."

I don't care how old I am, he's still my daddy. To the world he may be a movie star, but to me, he's always just been Dad.

He squeezes me one last time then pulls away, his hands still on my shoulders. "Should we go check that your brothers aren't getting into any trouble?"

I smirk. "Absolutely."

He wraps his arm around me, and as we head back down the hall toward the courtyard, I inhale deeply.

Jimmy

When we step out into the courtyard, I spot the twins goofing around behind the podium while they wait for the festivities to start. They spot us coming and I shake my head at them, hoping they'll take the hint.

I swear, those two will be the death of me. Monica never much cared about the Hollywood lifestyle, but my boys are more than happy to try to reap the rewards of having me as their father. They're not bad kids. They just take extra work to keep them on the right path.

I can't imagine what it would be like if we'd raised them in Los Angeles. They're bad enough when we visit. Even still, growing up in Northern California, they still had everything they could ever want and never hesitated to want more.

When we reach the podium, I address them. "Boys, keep it together, will you? This is a big day for your sister."

"Noah started it," Zac says.

"Bullshit, you—"

"That's enough you two," Lilah says, and they both shut their mouths.

I still haven't figured out how she does it, but when she talks, they always listen. Hell, I do the same, so I guess it's not that much of a mystery.

It's been twenty years since I proposed to Lilah on the couch of her small place in Kansas, and my love for her has only grown. Life hasn't been perfect, but I wouldn't change anything. She's as beautiful as she ever was and even more so inside. Motherhood and marriage have softened her in a way that I couldn't predict, but she still has the same steel spine.

"You ready to do this?" I ask her, taking her hand.

She smiles at me without reservation. "Of course."

Pushing up on her tiptoes, she gives me a chaste kiss that only leaves me wanting more. Twenty years and I still can't get enough of this woman.

"I don't say it enough, but thank you, my love. Without you, I wouldn't be here, able to do this." She runs her hand down my front, smoothing out my tie.

"That's not true. You always had it in you."

"Maybe, but without you as motivation, I may have never figured it out."

She kisses me again, and this time I wrap my arm around her and pull her forward.

"C'mon, that's so gross," Noah says behind us.

"Seriously," Zac says.

We pull away from each other, chuckling.

There's nothing we get more amusement from than grossing out our teenage sons.

Lilah

I step up to the podium with my notes in hand, but I don't need them. Not really. I plan to speak from the heart today.

"We're ready to begin," I say into the microphone and wait a minute while all the guests and press in attendance situate themselves.

The sun shines on the courtyard filled with flowers, vegetation, seating, and of course a pool. I look over everyone in attendance. Though I normally shy away from attention, I'm happy to be here, in this moment.

"Thank you all so much for joining us today. Today's opening has been a long time coming and has been a joint endeavor between my daughter Monica and me. While I'll be lending my support to everything that happens here, this is really my daughter's pride and joy. I'll let her talk more about what the philosophy of the Santa Monica Substance Abuse Center will be, but I'd like to say a few words first."

I take the opportunity to look at my family—my loving husband of almost twenty years and my rock, Jimmy; my intelligent and compassionate daughter, Monica; and the twins, Zac and Noah. They're still growing, still learning, but they're good boys.

I smile at them, tears gathering in my eyes. Not ones of sadness but tears of joy and gratitude for this life I was given. I already know my strength is inside me, but their encouraging smiles make it a little easier to pull it out.

"My addiction issues have been well-documented in the press over the years, as I'm sure you're all aware."

There're a few quiet chuckles in the crowd because we all know any time my husband has something going on in Holly-wood, the press loves to bring up the fact that his wife is a recovering addict.

"I was blessed to have someone in my corner who believed in me—always and unconditionally." I glance at Jimmy, and a soft smile tilts up his lips. "Not everyone is so lucky though. I've spent a good portion of my adult life volunteering in centers like this around the country, whether it be sitting with people in recovery and telling them my story, attending fundraisers to bring in money to support some of the programs they're running, or sitting with a distraught family member who is scared of what the future brings. Which is why when my daughter came to me years ago and said she wanted us to open a center of our own, I knew we had to do it." I swallow hard past the growing lump in my throat. "Some of us need two, three, four, or more chances to get it right. I was one of those people. My hope is that this building will be a safe place for people who are struggling. Where they won't feel judged or demeaned. Because the truth is that everyone matters to someone. Sometimes it just takes us a little longer to realize that. Sometimes when you don't love yourself, it's impossible to believe that someone else could ever love you. Our purpose is to be here until they believe it."

The crowd claps, and I can hear the photographers' shutters clicking.

"Now I'd like to turn the microphone over to my daughter Monica, who will talk about the different types of programs we'll be running here."

I step away as the crowd breaks out into applause, and Monica hugs me before walking to the podium. Jimmy draws me in so that my back is to his chest, and he wraps his arms around me.

I close my eyes and inhale. I still feel safest in his arms.

As I watch my oldest child talk about how the center will have both in-patient programs and a drop-in clinic for those who can't afford the cost of full-time care, I'm filled with a sense of joy and peace and contentment.

My childhood self would've never thought it was possible to be where I'm standing today—surrounded by a loving family and living a life of purpose. Still in love with the boy who grew up with me on the side of a mountain. I went from having nothing to having more than any heart or soul needs.

If I could tell that little girl anything, it would be to never stop believing. As long as you have hope, you have possibility, and sometimes life will surprise you with what's possible.

I know that much is true.

The End

Acknowledgments

That was a wild ride, wasn't it?

The impetus for this story began with Charlie Puth's song, Attention. It came on the radio while Piper was driving and she got to daydreaming (as she always does when she's listening to music) and thought of the dynamic between two people that this song describes—one who's desperately in love with the other, and the other who can't fully give themselves to the other person but doesn't want anyone else to have them either. And so, Jimmy and Lilah were born.

Life isn't always simple and uncomplicated. Sometimes it's messy. Sometimes decent people make bad decisions, one after the other until they find themselves in a place they could have never foreseen.

Neither Lilah nor Jimmy is perfect—far from it. Lilah is easy to dislike at times, there's no question. But at her core, she's not a terrible person. She was just lost and stuck in the past believing the mantra she was telling herself. Everyone has done things they wish they could take back, made decisions that weren't in their best interests or walked a path they knew would backfire on them. Some just do it more than others.

It's easy and justified to be angry with Lilah for lying to Jimmy. Absolutely. But it's also easy to understand her fear if she had come forward. Oftentimes, people tell themselves they'll get to something later and then a few days pass, a few weeks, maybe months. It gets easier and easier to keep pushing away that thing you're avoiding. Maybe it's sobriety, maybe it's a difficult conversation with a friend or a boss, or maybe it's leaving someone you're not happy with. Or if you're us it's diet and exercise. LOL

Once these two were back on the page again bonding over their daughter it was easy to see why they still had deep feelings for each other. Yes, Jimmy was engaged but we don't see him as a bad guy. He tried to make it work with Adelaide for all the right reasons, it just never would have. He was destined to be with Lilah.

We've been writing light-hearted romantic comedies together as Piper Rayne for years now, but we wanted to write a more complicated story about people fighting for their HEA. People you root for even knowing they won't come out the other side unscathed, but even still, it will be worth it in the end.

It takes a village, and we have a lot of people to thank for helping us get this book ready for readers...

Hang Le from Hang Le Designs – Your artistry is beyond compare! We couldn't be happier with what you've created to represent our story.

Cassie from Joy Editing for her insightful edits.

Shawna Gavas from Behind the Writer for her eagle-eye proofreading skills

Everyone at Valentine PR for making this first venture with our P. Rayne pen name a positive experience!

Bloggers – thank you so much for your support and for trusting that we're going to give you something worth spending your precious time reading.

And last but not least, to you, the reader. There's so many choices out there and we're humbled that you decided to spend your time reading our work. We hope you didn't think it was time wasted. <3

Next up we're dipping into a Mafia Academy series with Vow of Revenge. You're not going to want to miss it if you love a good anti-hero and strong heroine!

xo,

Piper & Rayne

About P. Rayne

P. Rayne is the pseudonym for the darker side of the USA Today Bestselling Author duo, Piper Rayne. Under P. Rayne you'll find dark forbidden and sexy romances.

9 798887 142166